T0369460

# The End Of Times Part 1

## Stacy A. Wright

authorHOUSE®

*AuthorHouse*™
*1663 Liberty Drive*
*Bloomington, IN 47403*
*www.authorhouse.com*
*Phone: 1-800-839-8640*

© *2011 Stacy A. Wright. All rights reserved.*

*No part of this book may be reproduced, stored in a retrieval system, or transmitted by any means without the written permission of the author.*

*First published by AuthorHouse 8/4/2011*

*ISBN: 978-1-4634-3881-4 (sc)*
*ISBN: 978-1-4634-3882-1 (e)*

*Library of Congress Control Number: 2011912746*

*Printed in the United States of America*

*Any people depicted in stock imagery provided by Thinkstock are models, and such images are being used for illustrative purposes only. Certain stock imagery © Thinkstock.*

*This book is printed on acid-free paper.*

*Because of the dynamic nature of the Internet, any web addresses or links contained in this book may have changed since publication and may no longer be valid. The views expressed in this work are solely those of the author and do not necessarily reflect the views of the publisher, and the publisher hereby disclaims any responsibility for them.*

"It was written a long time ago, that the Devastator shall never be allowed to walk the face of this Earth. If the darkest of Lords is given reign over this domain, the lands of this world will forever be shadowed in darkness. The time will come, centuries from now, when another band of heroes will be called upon to make the ultimate sacrifice to save the world. This will be the end of times."

Queen Bonna Min

Seven years ago...

On a small knoll in the everglades, shrouded from view by a fencing of tall saw grasses, two destined warriors meet as they have many times before; one the student, and one the teacher. "My student, you have truly mastered the ways of the ancients. With a long sword in your hands, you are as deadly as a dragon's fang." This ancient Japanese man bows to his protégé as a sign of respect and recognition. Withered and worn, this Master wears his skin like thin leather, aged by the winds of time. But do not be deceived by his appearance. There is more to this teacher than meets the eye.

Nickolas Landry, a tall chiseled man of American birth bows to his Master, as the sun starts to sink into the western everglades. He looks to his mentor with a smile, as his long black hair blows about his face on the breeze. "Master Masamoto, don't you think you could have come up with a better analogy than a dragon's tooth? I, well, nobody, believes in dragons any more."

The frail looking teacher known as Hiro Masamoto, smiles back at his student, recognizing Nick's skepticism.

"Just because you do not believe in something, does not mean it is nonexistent. You did not believe I could best you in a fight, but it did happen. In your heart, you believed that there was no more to learn, and yet I have opened your eyes to your true potential. You must open your mind and broaden your outlook, Nickolas, if you are to embrace the task I have for you." Masamoto bows to his student, and then vanishes from sight, only to reappear at his student's side. "Nickolas, most of all, you must learn to believe in the unbelievable, if you are to succeed."

Written by Stacy A. Wright
Edited by Paul Rabideau

In an old-fashioned little strip mall, on the west side of Miami, is a converted dance studio that now serves as a martial arts dojo. This quaint little studio may not be in the best of neighborhoods, but all the same, its doors are closed to no one. Belonging to Mr. Nickolas Landry; this is where he teaches children, and adults alike, the mystique of the martial arts. In the middle of the floor, on top of the red vinyl mats, sits this sensei surrounded by his students. They all sit perfectly still, and quiet, waiting for their teacher to dismiss the class. When he opens his eyes and springs to his feet, the class comes to life following his motions, with the exception of them jumping around sparring with one another. Nick stands still, legs together with his arms straight down by his side. He doesn't say anything to get their attention. He just simply counts silently in his head timing how long it takes for the class to come to order. When the last of the students fall in line, Nick starts to count again for just as long as they made him wait. At seventeen, he bows to his students and they show Nick the respect by bowing to him. "Alright class, that's it for this week. Practice your forms and techniques. We're testing for rank in class next week. The children make their way out of the studio as Nick motions for the door. He focuses on one student in particular, watching his course of direction across the dojo. This star pupil walks over to the corner and grabs his back pack, before joining his classmates at the door heading outside. This young man is held in high esteem by this teacher. In all the years that Nick has served as an instructor, never has he met such an intriguing soul. JD is like a sponge, craving to absorb everything Nick has to teach, and then excels for the simple purpose to honor his teacher. He doesn't believe in the words quit, or give up. From years of verbal abuse from his father, JD developed an attitude that there is nothing he can't do to perfection. It is these same qualities in Nick that have strengthened and broadened their friendship over the past few years. "Hey JD, hold on a second. I need to hit you with a couple of things before you go. I've got something I wanted to give you before you leave for college. Now I know you're not leaving for a couple of more weeks, but I didn't want to forget to give it to you, or leave it laying around for someone else to find." Nick produces a small wrapped package from behind his back. The gift is small, quaint, and wrapped in some kind of plain tissue with some Japanese writing embellished on the simple wrapping.

The ebony skinned youth stands at attention, waiting for his best friend to give him the gift. "Cool, what is it?" Almost eighteen, Jefferson David Johnson will soon be leaving his surrogate home in Miami to begin the next chapter in his life at college. JD, as he prefers to be called, has known Nick for almost three years and has become Sensei's top student. Six foot three, lean and trim, JD is a fine specimen of a young man and athlete, and yet he tends to prefer the more simplistic, laid back, approach to life by staying out of the limelight. His athleticism stems from a childhood of being the bully's target. If you can't fight, run, and run he did. When that wasn't good enough, he learned how to free climb, mostly out of necessity. It is these attributes that Nick has focused on as of late, honing JD's talents, other than his martial arts, to complete his training. "Hey, what does this symbol mean?"

"It's a journal of mine. There's a lot of information in there that will help you further your training. But, don't go reading it yet. Save it for after you get to school, so that it reminds you to keep practicing. The symbol means harmony; a reminder that you are part of something much bigger. When you are in harmony with the life around you, you will be as one with the world." Nick looks at the clock, remembering his evening appointment. "Listen, I know this is kind of late notice, but I need to know if you can do me a favor. Can you close up for me tonight? I need to take Sonny down to see her parole officer before seven o'clock." This isn't an unusual request, by no means. Nick trusts JD with his own life, and this dojo is part of that life.

"Yeah, no problem, Teach, I'll stack the mats and shut off all the lights, take out the trash, and do the dishes. You go do whatever it is that you have to do. I can take care of the studio for ya. Do you need some laundry folded too?" He's just joking around, and Nick knows that too, but it doesn't keep the teacher from giving the student a menacing look. "Just kidding, Teach, you know I'm just clowning around." JD is happy to oblige his friend, as usual. He gratefully accepts the package from his teacher with a bow, and shoves it into his back pack. With nothing to do after dinner, he sees an opportunity to find out more about his friend. There is a lot about Nick that JD already knows, but there is maybe a hundred times as much more that he doesn't know. "Don't read it yet." He thinks to himself, as he begins to stack the floor mats. "Wait until you're hundreds of miles away. Yeah, right Nick! I'm diving right into this one as soon as possible."

# Chapter 1

June 3rd, 2003

Megan gave me this journal for a Christmas gift, last year. I've never been one to keep a journal, unless you count my mission logs, during my six years in the Navy. Being twenty six, I felt that I was a little too old to start a diary, but I kept it any way, even though I thought I'd never have a use for it. You know; one of those things that you can't get rid of, but is always lying around. I find myself admitting that the events of this evening have proved me wrong. If ever something needed to be written down, it would be this.

Me, and Meg, were out for our date night, like every other Friday night, since I moved back to Miami. A phone call earlier from Sonny tried to put a damper on the planned festivities, but I was quick to put a stop to it, real quick. A lot has happened in my life since she was court-martialed, but I'm still her anchor to reality while she finishes out her sentence. The one thing I wish she could accomplish in prison is moving on with her life, without me. She says that she has, and wishes me and Meg the best. Any way, her call was to tell me that the courts were reducing her sentence, and that she would be out in time for the wedding. Of course, her adding the part about standing up and protesting the marriage is what sent me over the edge. She swears that she was joking, but knowing Sonny, as soon as the preacher asks why these two should not be joined in holy matrimony, Sonny would be the one to jump up, waving her arms.

Lucky for me, I was able to blow the whole thing off and return my focus to my night out with Megan. The dinner was good, but only because of the company. God, I swear I could enjoy ketchup covered cardboard, as long as I could stare into her deep blue eyes.

The movie afterwards was terrible, but Megan loves those romantic comedies. She tried her best to convince me that I was wrong as we walked down the street, which actually turned out to be more comical than the movie. Finally, after declaring the debate a draw, we stopped in an ice cream parlor for desert. It was there that we witnessed something that would change my life, forever. Meg thought that the parlor's old time flair was too cute to pass up. Knowing when not to dispute her call, I bought us both ice creams while she picked out a table. I did my best to enjoy sitting at the uncomfortable wrought iron chairs around the matching table on the parlor's front patio, but I don't think she would have noticed if I stood up and protested the accommodations. Her attention was focused on an old man standing in front of the alley across the street, who she thought was staring at us. I told her to finish her ice cream and pay him no mind. Now days, there are plenty of wackos out on the streets, staring at people. When she became concerned, I had to be concerned, or neither one of us was going to enjoy the rest of the night. Looking up, I saw the old man and quickly deduced that he was no threat to us, at all. What I did find disturbing was the group of hoodlums that were eyeing the old man as an easy mark. Most people wouldn't have seen it, but my training is what it is.

Before I could react, the gang was forcing the old man down into the alley across the street. Meg begged me not to get involved, but I wouldn't have been able to live with myself if I didn't. Six against one is bad odds for anybody, much less an ancient relic. I assured Meg that everything would be alright and took off across the street. I didn't hesitate charging right in and displayed my abilities, leaping over the gang to take a defensive stance between them and the old man.

One of the thugs had already taken a shot at the old guy, knocking his cane away before shoving him up against the wall. I took out that guy first, hitting him with a jab to the throat, expecting the rest to turn and run. I wasn't extremely surprised when they didn't, but I was ready for them all the same. Me, Charlie, and Sonny handled far worse opponents from all around the world, than these guys could ever hope to be. The fight was on and I quickly proved that the gang was no match. A few minutes later, I was helping the old man up and out of the alley, as Megan came running over.

His name is Hiro Masamoto, originally from Japan. According to him, he has traveled from afar, to seek me out. Of course, I had to ask the stupid question of how he knew I would be at the ice cream parlor at that specific time. His response was simply, "destiny." I guess most people would have walked right away from the situation, believing that the old man was off his rocker. Megan first believed that his comments and statements were just rantings of a lunatic, but something intrigued me about him. In fact, I was so curious that I offered him a room for the night.

Megan was apprehensive at first, but the old man quickly won her over with his eastern charm and humble personality. Personally, I think it was his reference to her as a perfect cherry blossom that made Megan swoon. After assuring me that he was good to walk, we set out for home as he kept us mesmerized by his fanciful tales of his past. Later on, me and Meg compared notes to see if we could determine what was fact, and what was fancy.

They are both asleep, right now. I set Masamoto up in the guest room, and Meg is passed out on the sofa. The crazy old man, I offer him a perfectly good bed, and he rolls out a bed mat in the middle of the bedroom floor. There is something about him that I cannot shake. I mean, during our walk home, he kept bringing up points of interest about me that not too many people know. It's not so much that I want to know how he knows these things about me. It's the why he knows that bothers me. I guess we'll find out tomorrow. According to Masamoto, my training begins at sunrise.

June 4th, 2003
Be careful what you wish for. I, I just don't know what to say. Megan left out early, claiming she was giving me a chance to acquaint myself with my new friend. Ha, Ha, she really did me a favor with that one. By the time I finally rolled out of bed, Masamoto was already out in the back yard. Where we found the ground level deck a good place for socializing, Masamoto found it suitable for his morning meditation.

With my cup of hot tea in hand, I stood at the back door and watched the old man as he performed some kind of Tai-Chi style of meditation ritual. His movements were smooth and graceful, and yet slow and precise, as if something else was controlling his actions, mind, body, and soul. I may not know his true age, but I am starting to think that this guy could've probably handled the gang, yesterday in the alley. If he wanted to, well, probably, okay maybe he would have made them think twice next time about targeting an old man.

I stood there in the doorway and watched him for at least thirty minutes, before he acknowledged my presence and motion for me to come over and stand before him. Honestly, I didn't think he really knew I was there. It was strange, to say the least, that he sounded insulted, when I presumed as much. Here I am, twenty six years old and a complete stranger was berating me like a lazy child. Apprehensively, I walked out into the yard to join him. He spoke out as I approached, never opening his eyes, and never pausing his exercise. "Your destiny is to safeguard the world from darkness. To do so, you must be of pure mind, pure body, and pure spirit." According to him, I had two out of the three. My mind, evidently, is the one out of sync with the other two, and the only way to get all three aligned was his form of meditation. "Peace must exist all around you. Strength can be drawn from that peace, and used to face the darkness."

I did learn something, even if it did take me all day to do it. Masamoto blindfolded me, forcing me to use my other senses as he instructed. If true focus is achieved, my mind's eye can rely on my other senses to see his actions. As I began my meditation exercise, he would circle me, tapping his cane lightly against the deck, in a very unbalanced repetition. Then, he would lash out at me, striking me on the leg or shoulder. On and on this continued with me trying to focus, and him doing all that he could to disrupt it. That is, until I reached a higher level of focus. I could feel the light vibrations of him moving about coming from the deck. I could hear the fabric of his loose clothing moving through the air, and the sound of his cane twirling around. It was like I could see an image of him moving, and visualize his proximity and actions. It was then, at that specific moment, Masamoto lashed out at me again to strike me across my chest. Even blindfolded, it was like I could see the attack and to my surprise, I blocked it. I've heard of stuff like this, but never thought of pursuing it. I mean, how often do you have to worry about someone attacking you while you meditate?

Masamoto didn't flinch, smile, or nothing. He just turned away like a pouting child. When I questioned him about it, his only reply to me was, "You have proved yourself worthy for the task at hand. That is all. I will return in two days. We will continue then."

There are few times in my life where I've been dumbfounded, with this being one of them. For one, I still can't believe that we spent the entire day in the back yard. It isn't often that I completely lose track of time like that. I have to be honest; I really thought the old man would have been more impressed with how quickly I picked up his little trick. Masamoto retired to his room and hasn't been seen since. Megan said that it was probably his way of saying goodbye. I'm putting my money on him being back in two days. The question is what will he have in store for me then? Megan is going out of town to visit her sister for a week or so. That will give me some good one on one time with the old man to try and figure out what he's all about. That is, of course, if I'm right, and he does come back.

June 9th, 2003
Okay, so this old man has me hooked on this destiny crap. There is something about him that seems almost supernatural. I don't know how to

explain it. The guy knows too much about me, that isn't common knowledge. I mean, he was rattling off stuff that he declared was pivotal in my growth for this destiny. The scary part is that some of that information died with people and family members a long time ago. Has he been stalking me for decades?

Upon his return, he hurried me out of the house with nothing but the clothes on my back, and we wandered through the everglades for two days where he explained his mission to me. According to him, this destiny isn't a world changing event. Instead, my duty is to keep that event from ever taking place. Should I fail; the world will become a living hell for all manner of creatures on Earth. When I pushed him for a little more information, he simply said that my focus must remain on the present that the rest will be revealed at the right moment in time. Tomorrow, he wishes to accompany me to my dojo. I'm starting up a new class designed to aid in the training of Navy recruits. If this works out, it could give me a long term contract between the base and my dojo. After all, who knows what a Navy SEAL needs to know most, than a former Navy SEAL?

June 10th, 2003

I declare that Hiro Masamoto is my idol. I say that because today I learned what true power really means. I took Masamoto to sit in on my classes like I planned. At first, I was a little disgruntled with the old man by the way he kept interrupting the class by critiquing my instructions. When I had finally had enough, I invited the old man to take over. That was mistake number one. Masamoto threw me around the mats like a dog playing with a rag doll. Then to quiet the recruits, he invited four of them up onto the mats. One of the guys makes a snide comment about hurting the old man. I'll never forget the look on the guy's face when Masamoto faced the opponent and told him, "You don't have what it takes to hurt me. Two minutes later, four Navy recruits were lying flat on their backs looking up at Masamoto. He then offered me the saving grace by pointing out that he was my Master, my teacher, and that everything I learn will be passed on to my students through how I teach. I am intrigued even more now that I have been accepted as his student. I'm curious about his fighting styles that seem to have no strong basis in any one of the Martial Arts. It's almost like an evolved combination of different techniques, but based on ancient forms. I truly believe that this could be the next level I've been searching for.

November 13th, 2003
Today was an exciting day for me. I was the lucky guy who got to play human pin cushion, as Masamoto used a blow gun to attack me. Sure, I had a shield about the size of a coffee can lid strapped to my left hand. Of course, it didn't do me any good being that I'm left handed, and usually block with my right. After a while I managed to doge a few off target darts and actually blocked a few more with my itty bitty shield. I should have a little time to come up with

a good excuse why I looked like I was attacked by hornets. Meg will be home tomorrow around lunch time. It'll be good to have her back. I never thought I would miss someone as much as I miss her. On the other hand, Masamoto insists that my relationship with Megan must come to an end. I don't know how he can expect me to do that. What's a guy supposed to say? Hi honey, I sure am glad you're home! How was your visit with your sister? Did you, and her, just sit around looking at wedding magazines? By the way, we need to talk. Yeah, sure, like that's going to happen. Somewhere down the line, me and Masamoto are gonna have to come to some kind of agreement on this matter. There's no way I'm going to give up everything just to protect something that might not even need protecting in the first place? I'm gonna need a little more convincing before we cross that road.

May 6th, 2004

Masamoto returned today, this being the third time he's disappeared in the middle of the night. Each time he's done this, he's given me some bullshit story about where he's been. The first time was about a six months ago, when I went to meet him at our spot in the 'glades, and sat there for seven hours wondering if he was going to show up. When I asked him about it, once he finally returned three weeks later, he told me that it wasn't my place to question him or his actions. At least the second time he pulled this little stunt, he gave me a line that the talisman was in jeopardy and he needed to lead the darkness away. This time, it was a long commune with the council, where he was able to learn more about my destiny, but wasn't at liberty to say what that was. I guess he's starting to break down a little though, because this time he did leave me a note telling me that he was going. It didn't say where or how long he would be gone, but I did know he was outta here. I'm glad he's back. To be honest, I'm looking forward to resuming my training.

August 28th, 2004
Everything has a reason and a purpose. Boy, that one was drilled into my head today. I think today was one of Master Masamoto's off days, as in off his rocker. Here I am, supposed to be this destined warrior who's gonna save the world, and Masamoto's focus is on how I should brew my tea. I keep telling him that he's wasting his time with the trivial stuff. I don't know what I was thinking, trying to argue with him about what to, and what not to teach. He went off on one of his little spills, comparing me to something else. This time it was the tea and the possible danger around me is the sugar. He said that like the hot tea, as long as I did not falter, the danger in my life will succumb to my will, as the sugar does to the hot liquid. Change my standards, and it will overpower me.

October 25th, 2004
I have begun a regiment of exercises that Master Masamoto says will benefit me with the next phase of my training. As I performed these

11

exercises, Master Masamoto would test me with his cane. If one move was out of sync, I would receive a bruise. Needless to say, I received a lot of bruises today. My meditation has improved and the training of my senses is coming along. I have now extended my reach, being able to map out Masamoto's movements from anywhere in the yard. I have to admit that I'm a little leery of Masamoto's skill of teaching. Nothing flows from day to day. He jumps around from in his sermons and demonstrations, and is really sketchy with his answers of half truths and misleading questions. I feel like, for whatever reason, he is holding back the whole truth as if trying not to dump it all on me at once, but keeps me asking why to see how committed I am to this. Man, I don't even know how committed I am to all of this. Like today, I asked him who these agents of darkness are, and how do I recognize them? He responds by saying, "There are agents and alliances on both sides of this war for Earth. You will be the one who must lead our forces against those agents of darkness." What the hell does that mean? I could be wrong, but I think I'm the one who got stuck with the short end of the stick. Still, all of this fuels my curiosity, wondering what he'll tell me tomorrow. Better yet, what he won't tell me.


November 1st, 2004

Each day my training increases a little more. Today, for example, we went out to the 'glades for my endurance run. My time the other day was a full fifteen minutes faster than the last time. Master Masamoto was so impressed that he decided to add fifteen more pounds of pack weight before I set out on my run. My time dropped down adding only four more minutes to my record. I thought it was impressive, but Master Masamoto scoffed at my remark and didn't speak to me the rest of the night. I still don't see what all of this running has to do with my defending the talisman. I've never been able to make a good defensive stance while I'm on the run. I'll worry about it tomorrow. I'm worn out and plan on turning in early.

The next few pages of the journal consist of drawings, sketches, and diagrams of movements and exercises that Nick has learned. This little tale of Nick's destiny has JD hooked. He stayed up late reading the journal, but mostly fantasizing about Nick's training for his destiny. Nick gave the journal to JD to help further his training after JD goes off to college, but the young man can't help but think that there is another reason as well.

Reading this has become first priority for JD's spare time, but first, he has to finish his semester finals for graduation, which he is about to be late for taking. JD grabs his back pack and heads out of his Aunt's house at a full sprint. He's got his last two tests today, and then school's out for the summer, or at least what's left of it. When JD moved to Florida to live with his aunt and uncle, he needed to make up several credits to qualify for graduation. This necessity is the reason he's spent the past two and a half months in summer school. That's not an easy task for a typical young man to accomplish, while living in Miami Florida. The reason JD lacks the necessary credits isn't because he as a learning disability. No, JD is very intelligent and devoted to his education. The reason he has had problems in school, is the same reason he's been living with his aunt for the past two years.

You see, JD's father is a preacher for an Atlanta suburb church, and has been all of JD's life. Violence was forbidden in the Johnston home, which made JD an easy target for the bullies in school. Four years ago, JD witnessed one of his best friends be beaten by a street gang, and was lucky enough that the police showed up before the attackers could get their hands on him. When word got out that JD would be testifying in the trial, he and his family began to receive death threats. His father had him pulled from the case as a witness and sent him to live with his mother's sister in Miami for safe keeping. Getting back to his missing credits, JD would skip school to avoid the bullies that harassed him constantly. His grades were good enough, tops in his classes, but it was his attendance that has caused him to suffer summer school.

Now all of that is behind him and he can start focusing on the future. Today consists of his last two tests, then his workout regiment at the beach, before heading to his Sensei's studio for his martial arts class. If it weren't for Nick, JD might not have survived the culture shock of his transplantation. For the passed two years, JD and Nick have developed a close friendship with the student becoming the teacher's protégé. The young man took to Nick's teachings like a fish to water. To Nick, JD is the son that Nick would never have, and he sees a lot of himself in JD's personality. First and foremost, the young man is honorable, loyal, and a Good Samaritan. It doesn't matter who they are or what their problem is, JD is right there to help if he can. You know the type, the kind of guy who can get along with anybody, and won't let race or nationality get in the way of a good time. But at the same time, he shows his naivety by wondering why everyone else just can't get along. JD's enthusiasm to learn the martial arts made him the perfect student, devoted, ambitious, and dedicated. All of these are positive attributes of Nickolas Landry as well, which is what drew JD into Nick's teachings. To JD, Nick was the perfect example of what a mentor should be. He was willing to talk to JD and more importantly listen, without ever passing judgment. Nick didn't know JD from the man in the moon, but he opened up his world to a stranger and welcomed him inside to see life from a different perspective. For all of this, and so much more, JD holds himself eternally indebted to Nick. Now, he has this journal to open his eyes up even more about the man he calls friend. It's amazing sometimes at how you never really know the people you call friends.

# Chapter II

The next day, Nickolas Landry walks up to the front door of his dojo, or martial arts studio, and fumbles with the keys to the lock. A warm Miami sun shines bright this afternoon, offering a welcome change to the recent weather. His neighbor bids him a good day while sweeping the sidewalk in front of the butcher's shop. Happy to acknowledge his friend, Nick returns the pleasantries and then directs his focus to the lock. His mind has been over occupied the past few days, with memories of a life long ago. It's been almost five years since his life was changed. Part of him can't believe that it's already been five years, and then in some aspects, it seems like it's been a life time since he was able to look into Megan's eyes.

To his surprise, the door suddenly swings open as JD appears on the inside. "It's open, Sensei. I thought the sign in the window would have given you the clue." JD points to the sign on the front door, poking fun at his friend. "Remember, I told you I was coming over here today earlier than usual?" JD steps aside to give Nick entry to the studio, while holding the door open.

"Thanks JD, to be honest, it slipped my mind. I take it

that you have everything ready for the afternoon's class?" Nick doesn't wait for a response. He knows that JD had accomplished everything, as Nick expected, without even being asked. Instead of wasted breath over an unnecessary topic, Nick crosses the mat covered dance floor installed by the previous tenant, and heads straight for the restroom with determination. A few minutes later, and he exits the small room with a look of relief on his face. "So, what have you been doing since the last time I saw you?"

"Reading your journal," JD replies, pulling the book from his back pack. "To say it's got me curious is an understatement. So, unless you have something for me to do, I figured I'd just hang out here and keep reading." JD freezes his actions standing there with the book half way out of the back pack, as if he was waiting for Nick to change his plan.

"No, you go ahead, and I'll take care of that stack of paperwork that has required my attention for the past week." Nick starts to head to his office in the back of the studio and then stops to look back at JD. "Hey, refresh my memory. Didn't I tell you to wait to read that after you went off to school?"

"Yeah, and if I'm not mistaken, I thought that your suggestion was like telling a pyromaniac to hold off on playing with the matches that you just gave him. I can't wait until some cold lonely night to read this. I wanna get it all now before I leave, so that you can't avoid my questions." Out of respect, JD bows to his sensei, and then leans back and slides down the wall, after Nick bows, returning the gesture of respect. The two part company with Nick heading on to his office as JD sits in the front room and begins to read. He opens the book to where he left off and starts to skim through the pages of the next few entries as if looking for more important information. Nick had given JD the journal for a better insight to further the young man's training, but

JD is more interested in Nick's teacher, and the old man's origins. He scans page after page, making mental notes of entries he will have to come back to later on. For now, he wants to stay focused on Masamoto's purpose and Nick's destiny.

March 27th, 2005

For the passed two weeks I have opened my mind to Master Masamoto's teachings, giving myself completely to his instruction. Never have I believed that someone could tap my potential the way he has. Today's teaching was more of a history lesson than martial arts training. Today is the day that Masamoto showed me what my destiny is.

According to Masamoto, I am connected to an event that happened over eight hundred years ago. This event I speak of was but the third uprising of Darkness to deliver this world to the Devastator. Three times these agents of darkness were defeated. This is where the story gets a little off balanced, but here it goes. The first attempt was defeated by; now get this, an Elf Princess named Teera Min. The second defeat came by the hands of her daughter, Lady Victorius, of Coventry Hall. For the third attempt, these agents of darkness spread out across the world to gather artifacts, idols, and talismans that were cast for the worship of evil. Then, they, the artifacts, were melted down and recast into pieces of a large key. This key was to be used to open the portal to the Devastator's realm.

Today, I saw a piece of that key, my charge and destiny. I have to admit that at first I thought the story was a load of fanciful BS, that is, until Master Masamoto reached out and touched my forehead with the tips of his fingers, while holding the talisman in his other hand. My body began to feel like it was electrified as I was shot back in time for a few seconds.

In front of me was a circular temple with what looked like, and it's the best way to describe it, a black hole stationed over it and its occupants. The grounds around the temple were soaked with blood and littered with dying bodies of both armies. The air was filled with the cries of agony and suffering, and yet I was compelled to move in closer. The plant life around the temple and beneath my feet was beginning to wither and turn grey. I slowed my pace and eventually stopped, but the dying plant life continued to spread out from around the temple, quickly working its way across the nearby countryside. It had to be the result of the portal being open, and the longer it was left open, the further the darkness would spread.

I pulled away from Masamoto refusing to see any more. The thought of there being someone out there, who would want to bring this to Earth, is revolting. I have served my country, and in doing so, I have opposed my share of wackos, who wanted to blow something up, but never have I encountered anyone who wanted to bring hell on Earth. This definitely changes things a little about this whole destiny gig. I don't know if I'm ready to take on the weight of the world right now. I guess the first thing I'll do in the morning is take a good long look in the mirror.

If for nothing else, just to see if I can see what
Masamoto's looking for in me?

JD skips a couple of more pages, uninterested in reading
any more redundant entries about how Masamoto pushed
Nick to his limits. Time was growing short with only thirty
minutes before their class begins. With no other students
arriving yet, JD flips through the next few pages until he finds
a passage of interest. He stops and goes back a few pages,
recognizing some of the illustrations as moves that Nick has
already taught him. A couple of students arrive and enter the
dojo, so JD dives right into the journal before someone wants
to strike up a conversation.

July 14th, 2005
Today was question and answer day, and I didn't
even have to ask. Master Masamoto saw it fit to
explain more to me about my destiny and duty.
I was allowed one question, and he would finish
the conversation from there. So, I asked him
the most obvious question; how did he get stuck
with the talisman?

His explanation goes back eight hundred
years, after the last event took place. Emissaries
spread out with the individual pieces of the key,
and took them to the ends of the earth. The
emissary that went to Japan spent the next ten
years searching for the most honorable man
in the country. His final decision was Master
Masamoto's ancestor. From then until now, it
has been passed down from father to son. But
in the end, it was Masamoto's father who broke
the family tradition. Evidently, the duty fell
to the eldest son, who would have been Hiro's

brother, Seko. According to Masamoto, his father became troubled with Seko, believing the young man was no longer pure of heart. Fearing the possible outcome, Masamoto's father had his metal smith split the talisman in two and gave one of the pieces to Hiro. He instructed his son to take the piece and hide it away from mankind. His father then placed a spell on the other half, hoping to forever keep the two halves separated.

Masamoto left his father's home as quickly as possible to carry out his father's command. When Seko found out about the treachery, against him, the eldest son confronted his father and revealed his true intentions, and the truth that Hiro's brother was no longer Seko Masamoto. One of the agents of darkness had possessed Seko's body with the intention of claiming the talisman. This Dark Lord was once known as Lord Doomsayer. His unclaimed soul was pulled from the afterlife eight hundred years ago to serve the Devastator. Since then, his spirit has been trapped here on Earth, searching for a host to serve his needs. Seko's weak mind and lust for carnal sin made him the perfect target for Lord Doomsayer's spirit, weak minded, sinful, and most importantly, heir to the talisman.

With the talisman in his possession, Doomsayer could seek out the other parts of the key. With the power contained in the key, the Dark Lord could resume his quest for power. Half of the talisman meant nothing to Doomsayer, and the spell placed on the other half by Hiro's father trapped Doomsayer, spellbound to the isles of Japan.

I asked him why this dark lord wanted the other parts to the key. Master Masamoto response was, "that is a question for another day." I guess for now, I'll have to go with what I know.

"Oh give me a break! I can't believe that he just left me hanging like that!" JD starts to rifle through the next few pages of the journal, when he hears Nick clearing his throat at the front of the class. JD looks up to see the students were all ready to begin their class with Nick patiently waiting for JD to join them. "Oh, Sensei, I'm Sorry." He looks up at the clock and realizes that the class was supposed to start five minutes ago. "Oh wow, I didn't even realize." Jumping to his feet, JD hooks his toes under one of the floor mats and falls face first in front of the whole class. Giggles and snickering from his classmates only intensifies his embarrassment, as he rushes to his position on the floor. He bows to Nick, and then shakes his head frustrated with his lack of composure.

"Don't worry about it, JD. I'm sure you can make it up to everyone by serving as their sparring dummy, dummy." Nick waits for the children to quiet down and bows to his class. With everyone in line, the class bows to their Sensei, and class begins. As they perform their different exercises, Nick walks through the ranks of his students, monitoring their movements. When necessary, he would demonstrate the proper technique to the student before moving on to the next. To his class, Nick is focused and in charge, but it is all a façade. His mind is troubled by a feeling that he has carried around for the last few days. Something is making him feel uneasy and he is unsure what it could be. That troubles Nick. For him, there is no telling what this feeling of his could mean. So, he has to bide his time until something else shows itself to give him more clarity. This is what Masamoto taught him, and it is the rule that he will follow.

JD picks up on Nick's slight distortion of personality, and should. He and Nick have become good friends through the martial arts classes. JD remembers back to when he first met Nick, and then to a time further back. One afternoon, JD found himself trapped in a circle of bullies who were wagering on which one would land the knock out punch. Several blows knock JD down, even drawing blood, but they didn't knock him out. It was the time in his life that JD had reached, where he wasn't going to take it any more. His father may have demanded that JD turned the other cheek, but JD wasn't going to be beat on any more. Somewhere, something was unlocked in the back of his mind that day. Later on, his therapist, Dr. Albert Greene, theorized that it was JD's strong desire for personal preservation that created this psychic barrier that his mind produced, and that JD's anger is what controlled its action. At first, the bullies' attack was simply halted, with their punches and kicks stopping a few inches from JD's body. Then, as his anger grew, the barrier expanded outward, sending the ring of bullies flying in all directions.

The good Dr. Greene was a friend to the church, and was contacted by JD's mother, after JD tried to explain the incident to her. His mother feared that JD was suffering psychologically from the constant attacks, causing him to create delusional exaggerations to hide his pain. Understanding her concerns, he agreed to see JD as a favor to the church. He met with JD on several occasions, but the young man never brought up the incident in question. Finally, Dr. Greene initiated the topic out of frustration, almost demanding that JD open up about it. Reluctantly, he did and received the same response that he got from his mother. Turning the tables, JD started a hypothetical conversation. He asked the therapist how a person could achieve this, if it was possible. After laying out all of the factors to the question and adlibbing with a little of his own knowledge, Dr. Greene came up with his theory. Still wanting to convince the therapist that JD wasn't crazy, he asked for a simple challenge. JD took the stapler from Dr. Greene's desk and opened it up. His challenge to the therapist was to see how many times he could hit JD with staples, standing four feet away. The first five staples hit JD in his chest and stomach, with one actually sticking in his skin. After that, his psychic barrier was produced, sending the remaining staples flying around the room. Disturbed by the incident, Dr. Greene told JD's mother simply that he didn't think she had anything to worry about, but was not interested in seeing JD again.

After moving in with his Aunt, JD played the role of recluse, weary of social interaction. After suffering months of taunting from his Uncle, JD finally ventured out to find that it really wasn't that bad out in public. That is, until the day he met Nick. Off course, and running late, JD decided to cut down on travel time by taking a few short cuts. Soon he was lost and turned around, not knowing where he was. As JD's luck usually plays out, it didn't take long before he found himself in a confrontation. With little fighting skills to speak of, JD does his best to fend off the muggers, and was successful for a little while. But, when one of the attackers produced a knife, JD found it in himself again to produce his psychic force field to repel the three men. This is where Nick came into the picture.

Walking from destination to destination as he usually does, Nick was passing the loading dock of the vacant building where JD was being accosted. He didn't witness how it started, but he did see the finale of it all. Intrigued, Nick approached the scene as the three muggers scrambled to flee. After introductions and assessing JD's cuts and bruises, Nick offered his dojo, a few blocks away, as a place where JD could clean up. They've been friends ever since. Nick taught JD how to train his mind to control his gift through martial arts. Seeing JD's potential, Nick took him under his wing and opened up a whole new life for JD, giving him the knowledge strength and confidence to never live in fear again.

Suddenly, JD finds himself lying on his back in the middle of the floor with Nick standing over him, smiling. "The book has you distracted, doesn't it? Focus on class for now, and we'll talk some afterwards, before you leave tonight." How did this happen to him. JD was staring at the full length mirror on the wall, but was oblivious to Nick's approach. Nick looks around to silence the snickering classmates, who found humor in JD's misfortune. He helps JD up and moves on to evaluate other students.

JD straightens his shirt and looks around to pick up the exercise, and falls in line with the rest of the class. Focus, how is he supposed to stay focused now, after reading the journal? Maybe this is why Nick said to wait to read it. Maybe JD just needs to find out more. When JD met Nick two years ago, he knew that there was something special about Nick. Could it have been this? Is the journal true, and Nick is some kind of designated savior of us all? Nick notices how JD was out of step and gives his start student a stern look. Okay, he'll try to focus for now, but somebody's gonna answer some questions after class.

He can't focus. JD may be going through the motions, but his mind is occupied with theories about how and why all of this is happening right now. Does Nick sense something wrong? Why did he give JD the journal? Sure, Nick said that there were exercises in it that could help JD, but he had to know that JD would've read the rest of it as well. Was Nick trying to send JD a message? Maybe he wants to team up with JD to tackle this together? "Get over yourself, Johnston. What does a former Navy SEAL and Martial Arts master need from a teenager?

JD's alarm goes off in the back of his head, warning him of impending doom. At the last second, he is able to block Nick's attack and counter with a move of his own. "Good," Nick replies. "Keep working on that, but remember not to bring your arm up too high." Nick motions for JD to recreate the move, and stops his arm from rising too far up his side. "Right there, then punch with your body coming around to follow through." JD bows to Nick and Nick returns the gesture. "Good job, kid. Now do me a favor and dismiss the class while I go take a leak." They bow to each other again before JD heads to the front of the class, as Nick makes his way to his office/restroom/janitor's closet. You get the picture; it's not a very big place, this converted dance studio. With the class dismissed, JD hurries over to return to his reading before Nick returns.

August 2, 2005
Again we set out to explore the Everglades. I have to admit how he amazes me with his philosophical views of life. He has this belief that every action is significant in life and how well you approach and succeed at the task, is determined by how well you prepare for that task. Now I'm beginning understand, and make sense of it all. I guess sometimes you need to hear a crazy man's view on the world, just to understand the craziness of the world. I've always considered myself an educated man, but I guess even the smartest man can become shortsighted.

When he started to talk about the

connections between life and death and beyond, that's when I thought the sun, was starting to get to him. Sure I have conceded to his philosophies about most stuff, but you can't expect me to just follow him blind right off the bat. Any way, according to Master Masamoto, there is a council that is gathered from beyond the grave. Evidently, "they" are the collective guiding conscience of the factions here on Earth that fights the forces of darkness. Masamoto said that one day; he would be my connection to the council's guidance.

I asked him why this council doesn't just step in and right the wrongs as needed. Better yet, why can't they just stop this Doomsayer guy, and keep him away from the key. Masamoto said, "free will cannot be controlled, and it is free will that is needed for success. Those who serve the council's bidding do so of their own free will. You have to choose to be a herald for mankind, and you must be willing to sacrifice and commit completely if you are to be victorious." I'm not sure what he meant by all of that, but I'm willing to bet that it will all be explained when he feels it's necessary.

JD closes the journal, seeing Nick exit his office. Finally, the time has come for JD to get some answers out of his teacher. JD has always been curious about Nick's calling. His teacher has let on a time or two, hints and examples about what he faces with this destiny, but JD never expected anything like what he's read in Nick's journal.

After shoving the book back into his back pack, JD hurries out to the middle of the floor where it is customary for him to meet with his teacher. Nick smiles at JD's enthusiasm and casually walks over to the store front windows of the dojo, and closes the long vertical blinds, shutting out the world. JD stands there patiently as Nick makes his way over to the front door, taking his time to secure the locks. Satisfied that his world is safe from jeopardy, Nick walks back to the center of the room where he greets his student with a bow. Then, both student and teacher cross their legs and squat into a seated position on the mat covered floor. Nick stares at JD for a second, gathering his thoughts before asking JD one simple question. "What do you want to know?"

JD just stares back at Nick, dumbfounded by his question. Nick wasn't supposed to just throw the doors open on the conversation like that. JD expected his sensei to give him just a taste of what he wanted, as usual, as if Nick wanted to keep the young man yearning for more. That's what Nick has always done with suggestive metaphors and half truths, just to keep JD's interest peaked, so why change tactics? Now, JD has to scramble to gather all of his questions from his mind and throw them out at Nick as quickly as possible, before the opportunity passes him by. "Is all of this for real? Can I finally see the talisman? What happened to Masamoto? Is he still around? Who was Megan? You've never mentioned her before. Do you know how long you have to safeguard the talisman, and is this big event suppose to take place during our lifetime? Why did you give me the journal? Is there something connected to me? If so, how can I help with all of…"

"Whoa, hold on there a second, Sport, you're gonna have to slow down a little if you want me to keep up with you." Nick closes his eyes for a second and focuses his thoughts on his answers. "As for if this is all real, I have to say more than you could possibly know." He pulls at a golden chain around his neck, retrieving the talisman from inside his tunic. "I have been in possession of this for five years, well almost any ways. The anniversary of Master Masamoto's death is coming up." He dangles the talisman in the air in front of JD, so that his student could see the full scope of the ancient artifact. The light of the room reflected off the golden talisman with a luster as if it was created just yesterday.

"What was he like? I mean, so far in your journal, you sounded as if the jury was still out on the old man's sanity. Did you ever change your stand on his senility?" JD asks, as beams of reflected light shine across his face.

"I could show you, if you'd like." Nick doesn't give JD time to answer. He reaches out and places his left hand on JD's shoulder, while holding on to the talisman with his right. "Now, don't go freakin' out, and don't move around. Do you trust me?"

"Yeah," JD answers, with the quick and nervous response. It isn't because he is fearful. No, it's more of a nervous anticipation of what's to come.

"Okay, everything you are about to see is real, but it happened a long time ago." Nick closes his eyes, leading JD to do the same. Suddenly, JD feels like his entire body was tingling from a low voltage electrocution. Unable to bridle his enthusiasm any more, JD opens his eyes to see what was happening. What he sees is not what he expected to see.

To JD's amazement, he finds himself standing somewhere in the everglades, miles away from Nick's dojo. There on a grassy knoll, surrounded by thickets of saw grass, a teacher and his student have come here today for a test instead of instruction. Here on this exaggerated sandbar, through the harshest of conditions, the teacher has handed down the teachings of the most ancient of arts. Today, the weather conditions favor the student as the sun begins to sink into the western edge of the everglades.

The teacher is Masamoto, an ancient little man who

sits cross legged on the highest point of the knoll, steadfast in his position with his eyes closed. The student is Nick, a younger Nick, performing exercises with a Japanese long sword, called a katana. He leaps and spins around his teacher, with the blade of his sword slicing the air around Masamoto. This test, or trial, is to prove Nick successful of this aspect of his Master's training. Like everything else in Nick's life, he aspires to be the very best.

Suddenly, the old man comes to life, showing that he isn't as feeble as one would believe. JD finds himself flinching at the old man's rise from the ground. The speed and agility displayed by Masamoto antagonizes a confrontation between student and teacher. Using only the staff that normally supported Masamoto's weight, the teacher attacks his student with the ferocity of a tiger. Nick is ready for his teacher, this time. He has trained well for this test, as he has for all of the tests in his life. Life, Nick's life has been one constant stream of tests, always pushing him on to better himself. To him, failure is not an option. When he served with the SEALs, Nick was always the guy who could find a way out of a "no win" situation.

Then, as quickly as it began, the conflict ends with both men at a standoff, admitting to one another that their confrontation concluded as a stalemate. Masamoto bows to his student, proud of Nick's accomplishment. "My student, you have truly mastered the ways of the ancients. With a katana in your hands, you are as deadly as a dragon's fang."

Nick bows to his Master and sheathes his sword as Masamoto resumes his seated position. "Master, don't you think you could've come up with a better analogy than a dragon's tooth?" Nick crosses his legs and squats to take a seated position in front of Masamoto. Resting the palms of his hands on his knees, Nick looks to his teacher with his blue eyes showing the still lingering skepticism in Nick's heart. "I, well, nobody believes in dragons."

The old man smiles at his student's remark. Reaching down, Masamoto gathers two little twigs about the size of matchsticks, from the ground. With one in each hand, held between his forefingers and thumbs, he begins to spin the ends of the twigs in the sandy soil. Faster and faster he works the pieces of wood between his fingers, back and forth, back and forth. "Just because you do not believe something exists, does not make it nonexistent." Never looking down, Masamoto lifts the two twigs from the ground and touches the two ends together. Without any warning to Nick, the two twigs erupt into flames. The old man pulls them apart and paints an image of a fiery dragon in the air between Nick and himself. The image flaps its wings twice before vanishing in a puff of smoke. "You must open your mind and broaden your outlook, if you are to embrace this destiny I have presented to you." Masamoto bows his head again, and vanishes from sight, only to reappear at Nick's side. "You must learn to believe in the unbelievable, or doubt will be your undoing."

Nick turns his head to face Masamoto and smiles at his teacher, still holding onto some measure of reservation about this destiny, even though he can't explain the old man's parlor tricks. "Let me ask you this, Master. What would have happened if I had failed your tests?"

"I would have been forced to kill you." Masamoto replies.

Okay, that wasn't the answer Nick wanted, or expected. With a somewhat puzzled look, Nick raises his finger to dispute Masamoto's statement. "But you said that I was destined to save the world. I'm the one who is supposed to take the mantle of guardian. If you killed me, wouldn't you be tampering with that destiny?"

Masamoto looks to the setting sun and stands up,

motioning for Nick to do the same. "You have proven yourself worthy of this destiny. That does not mean that you are the only one. It simply means that I was right about you being the best suited for the task. Should you have failed, another would have been sought out. The end of times is drawing near. Should you have not succeeded, there may not be enough time to train another. That is the weight of your success, and mine." Masamoto raises his hand to his brow and looks west one more time. "Always remember, Nickolas, there will be factions from both sides that will hamper your training and try to defeat your cause. You have passed your first series of trials, but be warned, you face a trial of three with each consisting of many tests and conflicts that you must overcome. Now, take me home so that I may consult with the council on your achievement."

Nick scrambles to his feet to join his Master who was walking towards their boat. "But Master, can't you tell me more?"

"No Nickolas; now is the time to go home, but do not fear for your education has only begun." The old man stops at the edge of the water and waits for Nick to board the boat. While standing there, the old man turns and faces JD's direction, and then bows, before Nick helps him onboard their small craft.

JD is shocked by the old man's action. Why did Masamoto bow to JD? How did he know JD was there experiencing an out of body event? The confused young man closes his eyes again, and then opens them to find he's returned to the present, sitting in the floor of Nick's dojo. He can't help but stare at Nick wondering what he should do next. "Dude, I think I know now how you felt when Master Masamoto showed you the past." JD stands up, a little disturbed by what had just happened. He looks around the room as if he was delaying the inevitable. "Nick, just before the two of you got on the boat, Masamoto turned and bowed in my direction, like he knew I was there. Man, that really kinda' freaked me out. Come on Nick, how could he have known I was there, when I was never there, but really here the whole time?"

"It's funny that you mention it, JD." Nick sticks out his hand, looking for JD's assistance to get up off the floor. "After Master Masamoto got on the boat, asked him who he was bowing to, and he said that it was a future ally of mine. Back then, I was quick to dismiss a lot of what he said, whenever it came across as odd or out of place." Nick walks over to the front door of the dojo and unlocks it for JD to exit. "Listen, I need to get on home to make sure Sonny's okay. We can talk a little more tomorrow, before class."

He did it again. Just when JD thinks he is getting somewhere, Nick manages to turn it all around and leave his student wanting more. "Dude, Sonny can take care of herself. Honestly, I don't know what you see in her. Sure, she's fine and all, but she really knows how to give me the heebee jeebees, sometimes." JD clasps his hands together as if begging Nick to continue with their conversation. "Come on, Teach, let's keep it going for just a little longer."

"Go." Nick replies.

JD drops his shoulders as a sign of disappointment. "Okay, besides I was starting to feel like one of your younger students begging for another fairy tale. Ya know; you sure do have a way of taking the wind out of a guy's sails. What about all of the other questions I have? What about the ones I've already asked?"

Nick laughs at JD's pathetic pleas, and still motions for the young man to hit the road. "I know this much, Jefferson, it is fifteen 'til nine and your uncle will have your ass if you're not home before he goes off to work. Now, get outta here. Your Aunt needs you more, than you need the answers to your questions. We'll talk more tomorrow."

JD looks back over his shoulder to see the clock on the wall. "Oh shit, yep, you're right. I have to get my butt home." JD grabs his back pack and starts for the door again, but stops to turn and face his Sensei. "Why?"

"Because Master Masamoto said you are my ally."

"Is that why you took me in that day, when we first met?"

Nick gives JD a playful shove out the door. "Get outta her, ya duck! We'll talk more tomorrow. Read some more of the journal if you don't have anything else to do, but do it at home." Nick starts to close the door, when he gets the feeling like he was being watched. "Hurry home JD, and watch your back." He warns, watching his student run off down the street. He waits until JD is out of sight before Nick heads back inside. For whatever reason, he can't shake the feeling of being watched. The street is empty, with most of the curbside shops closed up hours ago. He checks the rooftops and windows across the street one more time, but sees no signs of life. Uncomfortable with the feeling, Nick moves back inside to get his things so that he can head on home as well. He hopes that tomorrow will bring a better day for him; as he watches the thunderstorm to the south, off in the distance.

Aug 22, 2005

Today was a very interesting day for me. Masamoto told me the story of how his family was killed. I have to admit that I was completely surprised with how it all came up. It was as if he felt this need to tell me. Any way, his story drifted back and forth through time, but I think I've got the basics of it. His story began by him telling me about how his brother became the vessel for Doomsayer's spirit.

The dark Lord had followed the trail of the talisman on its route to Japan. He of course had possessed several bodies along the way, and met against opposition that would dispatch his spirit by killing the hosts he possessed, thus the need for so many vessels to carry him on. When he reached the Isles of Japan, hundreds of years later, he was once again met by opposition that killed his host, setting Doomsayer's spirit free, to seek out the possessor of the talisman. Many years passed before he found Masamoto's brother and tempted him with power unmeasured.

Even though there was two years between the son's births, Hokiro Masamoto never gave his eldest the respect of first born. His father never considered Hiro his favorite, but where Hiro found praise for his efforts where Seko was chastised for his lack of effort. This sprouted a grudge to form between the two sons that would continue to grow well into adulthood.

Earlier in their lives, Hokiro told his sons bedtime stories, of a great duty that was handed down through the generations from father to son. Masamoto and his brother both believed that one day, that duty would fall to Seko. Because of this, Seko developed a sense of entitlement, believing his glorious duty was his by default, and he had nothing to earn. It was this belief that weakened Seko's character with vanity and arrogance. As the years went by, Hokiro's disapproval of Seko's self serving ways only pushed Seko further from the light.

Seko believed that he would rise in power, anointing himself as the savior and guardian to his people. He truly believed that this duty was more than it was, and that fame and fortune would be bestowed upon him as homage to the Guardian. His father disapproved completely, always warning Seko that his path will end in ruin. His teachings said nothing of fame and fortune, and that the duty of the Guardian was a selfless act that no one could know about. Finally, the day came when Hokiro could tolerate his son's standards, and discredited him by sending Seko away. Crushed that his false dreams of life were dashed upon the rocks, Seko let hatred into his heart, opening him up to Lord Doomsayer's visits.

One day, while wandering through the wilderness, half starved and exhausted, Seko saw a reflection of himself on a clear pool of rainwater. This is not unusual to him, but seeing the face of the Dark lord standing behind him is. Seko spun around, but there was no one to be seen. When he looks back at the water's surface, Doomsayer's image is still there, smiling. The mystery reflection asked Seko why he was so heavy hearted. Seko responded by telling the dark Lord everything about his life and the duty taken from him. Doomsayer had found his next host.

After explaining to Seko how he could give the young man unlimited power to avenge the wrongs against him, Seko willingly gives in to the dark Lord allowing Doomsayer's spirit to take possession of Seko's body. The last thing Seko ever saw was Doomsayer's spirit pulling Seko's from his body. What Doomsayer didn't know was Hokiro's plan for the talisman, so when he approached the Hokiro under the guise of Seko, he was outraged with what he found. Doomsayer lashed out at Hokiro, and took the half that the once father still possessed. What the dark Lord didn't know was Hokiro had placed a spell on the piece that Doomsayer possessed, forever land locking him and the half piece of the talisman to Japan. This Hokiro spat out with his last dying breath.

Even though Seko's spirit was cast out of his body, Doomsayer still had Seko's mind and memories at his disposal. Knowing that Seko would accuse his brother of being part of this treachery, Doomsayer sought out Hiro's family, believing he would return home with my half of the talisman. He was right, but Hiro hesitated with his decision to return home, which was a blessing and a curse. In doing so, the surviving Masamoto son was not home when his family was slaughtered, but he did have to watch it happen from a distance, and was unable to offer any assistance. The dark Lord could sense Hiro was nearby, drawn to his half of the talisman. He yelled threats and warnings into the dark night that Hiro would fail in his attempt, and the world would fall to darkness.

Master Masamoto ended the tragic dark tale with a warning, again telling me that Megan could suffer the same fate as his wife and family, if I didn't end the relationship. I told him to quit worrying about her, and her safety. There isn't anyone on earth, living, dead, or otherwise that could hurt her while I was alive.

September 2ⁿᵈ, 2005

Master Masamoto has become more and more forthright with his information, as of late. Today, he told me about the second attempt to cast the world into darkness, and something about an event called the witnessing. Again, this tale involved the infamous dark Lord Doomsayer and his armies of darkness. According to Masamoto, two star crossed lovers took on the fate of the world to defeat Doomsayer and his minions. I'm actually beginning to wonder who's more thickheaded. On one hand, you have these agents of good, fighting against this Doomsayer who can't be defeated. On the other hand, you have this Doomsayer guy who just can't seem to get the job done. I can't help but wonder how I would do against this Dark Lord if we ever cross paths. Of course, I don't ever plan to go to Japan any time soon, so I guess I'll never have to worry about finding out. If he stays on his side of the world, I will stay on mine.

One thing troubled me today. Master Masamoto said that in a vision, he saw his death and the death of Megan too. I swore to him that I will prove his vision wrong. He just gave me an understanding smile, as if he forgave me for being wrong about what's to come. Am I? I understand that Masamoto's family was all killed because of the talisman, and that his concern for Megan suffering the same fate is genuine, but I see the situation to be different. When his family was killed, Masamoto had no idea what he was involved in. That's where I think I hold the advantage. I know what lies

ahead and I prepare for it daily, as I will continue
to do, if nothing else for Megan.

JD looks at the clock on his nightstand and closes the
journal. His eyes feel like they are bleeding and his whole
body is exhausted. The sun will be up in a couple of hours. If
he is going to get any sleep at all, he better do it soon before
the construction crew starts work next door, at six in the
morning. More tired than he realizes, JD quickly falls asleep
still wearing his clothes of the day.

# Chapter III

Every morning starts the same way for Nickolas Landry. He awakes to the sun shining through his window, with the warm rays serving as a natural alarm clock. After a half hour of meditation, he exercises to get his body ready for the day. After dressing, he has a cup of tea with another work out in the back yard, before heading out to tackle the day's schedule. Yesterday was volunteer day where Nick takes in classes of inner city youths. It may seem conflicting, but he doesn't try to reach out to them by enticing them with the violence of martial arts. Most of the kids have known violence in one form or another, most of their lives. No, Nick's focus with these troubled teens is to offer the full physical, mental, and spiritual aspects of martial arts. By teaching them to respect themselves as well as others, mind, body, and spirit, his effort has paid off with several going on to college, and one serving on the City Council. He may not be able to reach them all, and they all may not have what it takes to turn themselves around, but the ones he does help makes it all worth while. Today, he will spend the good part of the morning at several retirement communities around the city where he teaches awareness and self defense training to the elderly. With his mind focused on the day's agenda, Nick exits his bedroom and heads for the kitchen for his morning cup of tea.

Sonya Richards, to most men, waking up to find this long legged, blonde beauty, passed out on the living room couch in her underwear, would be a welcome sight. For Nick, it is a common occurrence, and also something he could do without. He looks at her laying there, mapping every inch of her long bronzed legs, and thinks about it for a moment that at one time, she could have been his. He wants to wake her and send her to her room, but opts to forego the ordeal this morning and continues on to the kitchen in silence.

It's been a love/hate relationship between them, for the past five years. Nick still loves her, but hates himself for it. At one time, their relationship was more than just friends. It started as friends in the Navy when Sonny was assigned to Nick's SEAL team. She was one of the first women to qualify for the teams. Nick admired that about her, where others shunned the decision. Nick stood up for her opportunity, and this was the basis of their friendship. Strong, beautiful, and deadly, Sonny soon found herself the center of attention, in more ways than one.

Nick often found himself to be the focus of Sonny's attention, with her pushing the issue of her and Nick being more than just friends. Of course, Nick did his best to play it cool, knowing that his new rank would be compromised, should he be caught in a relationship with her. That is, until one time on mission when Sonny saved Nick's life. Their team was deployed in the Middle East, somewhere off the eastern coast of the Mediterranean Sea. One of the US's "friends" was double dealing arms to known terrorist organizations. The team's mission was to locate and erase the arms dealer and surplus.

Well, the mission turned out to be a wash, but not because

they couldn't locate the arms dealer. It was due to inaccurate intelligence gathered for the mission that sent Nick's team of twelve in against an armed force of two hundred. Their infiltration began with a firefight that lasted until their extraction. When Nick was a no show at the extraction point, Sonny grabbed two rifles and rushed back in for her commanding officer. With the helicopter being fired upon, the pilot had no alternative but to leave her behind. She found her man holed up in a small bunker, and for three days she fended off their opponents while tending to his wounds, before ground support arrived.

It was during his recovery that Nick gave in to desire and began a love affair that had to be as covert as their missions. But their relationship wasn't the only cover up that was taking place. The Navy Brass and Pentagon Intelligence clashed over the outcome of the mission. An international incident was on the rise and no one wanted to take the blame. Soon, words got twisted and reports were mysteriously lost, and fingers started to be pointed at Nick and his team for botching up their orders.

Sonny wasn't going to stand for this and took her complaints to their commanding officer, demanding to know why they haven't been allowed to testify on their behalf. Of course, he was a prejudice man who cared nothing for a woman serving in "this man's Navy", much less on his SEAL teams. With no witnesses around, Commander McClain took the opportunity to turn the tables, so to speak, believing that he could force Sonny into some kind of confession to be used against her. As Nick has said many times, "Be careful what you wish for."

Something snapped in Sonny's psyche, when his threats became physically violent. She took the first shot, kneeing McClain in the groin. Then, she took his first shot, being a punch to her stomach. After that, Sonny beat the man almost to death with her bare hands, before the Shore police showed up to pull her off. McClain spent the next three months in ICU. Sonny spent the next five years in New Leavenworth.

Nick found out the truth of it all and used his purple heart as an exit from the Navy, coincidentally the same day McClain returned to duty. After his discharge, Nick returned to Florida where he has lived ever since. That was ten years ago, and a lot has happened since then, but it's the reason why Nick and Sonny are still close friends. Most of all, it's the reason why Nick has stood behind her through all of her turbulent times.

Nick takes a sip of his tea and heads for the back door. He had hoped to slip outside into the back yard before she woke up. Today, he isn't hat lucky. "Good morning, handsome." Sonny struts her way through the dining room to enter the kitchen. Nick enjoys the early morning, with its calm soothing sounds of nature waking with the day. Sonny is brash and in your face energetic, ready to kick the world in its balls, as soon as her eyes open. If opposites do attract, then these two would be prime candidates for each other.

"Good morning, Sonya."

Sonny takes a drink of milk from the carton, and then shoves the empty container back into the fridge. Turning around, she faces Nick with a pout on her face. "Oh come on, Nicky, you're not still mad at me for messing up your new wood flooring, are you?" Her pout quickly becomes a devious smile, before raising her arms high into the air as if she was stretching, but Sonny had ulterior motives. In raising her arms, the hem of her shirt is raised as well, revealing her panties. On the front is a screen printed image of an angry tomcat giving the onlooker the middle finger.

"Watch it girl, or you'll…"

"Oh Nickels, you know I'm just messin' with ya." She walks over to him and gives him a quick kiss on the cheek.

"I'm pickin' up my check from that temp agency today. It should be at least a couple of hundred dollars. You can have it all, okay?" She drapes her arms over his shoulders hoping to coax the forgiveness out of him one more time.

"The bill was three hundred."

Sonny bats her eyes. "Then I'll pay half, and keep fifty for myself. That way, I don't have to hit you up for gas money." Sonny slips around Nick and gives him a swat to his right butt cheek, hard enough to almost spill his tea. "Thanks Nickels, I've gotta go. Ain't nothing worse than trying to go jog on the beach, while a bunch of tourists gawk at ya."

"Bullshit, that's why you wear that thong and a tank top, ya duck." Nick blows off the incident as he usually does and quickly heads outside to try to return some peace to his life. At least this time she offered to pay half. He walks out into the yard and sits down on the ground level deck, beside the koi pond that surrounds three quarters of the circular deck. Nick tries to clear his mind but can't shake this uneasiness he still feels. It's not about Sonny, or her petty eccentricities. He worries that it's a premonition, or a warning of something to come.

Grabbing a handful of fish pellets from the storage box on the deck, Nick casts the food out into the water and watches the fish gobble up the pellets. "You guys need me to keep the world safe, don't you?" The fish wait for a moment, and then swim off when no more food is offered. Nick laughs to himself remembering something Masamoto once said in reference to the fishes. "The human race will turn away from you the same way, when you have nothing else to give them."

Sonny appears at the back door wearing a tight fitting tank top and a pair of boy shorts two sizes too small. "Okay Nick, I'm outta here. I've got my keys so don't worry about locking me out."

Nick turns to face Sonny, feeling the need to keep a close

tab on her, knowing her as well as he does. "Cool, so what's on your agenda today?"

Sonny looks up as if she's reading her list of things to do, pretending that it was written on the ceiling. "Jogging, go to the gym for a workout, pea in a cup, check on a temp job down on South Beach, and pick up my check before coming home." Sonny gives Nick a sly smile. "Since we're on the topic, what charity are you crusading for, today?"

Dropping his head, Nick closes his eyes as a sign of disapproval for her condescending tones. His professional activities are not open for scrutiny. "The elderly just like every other Wednesday." Nick finishes off his tea and stands up. "Give me a call, if you need me."

"Oh Nickels, you know I'll always need you. See ya later, handsome." She slaps her hand against her hip twice, and then points her finger at Nick. "Love ya, Killer."

"You too, Sonny, I'll see ya later." Nick heads towards the house, but then stops and turns around to look at the tops of the trees of the neighborhood. His feeling of being watched is still inescapable.

September 19th, 2005

Today was history class, again. Masamoto seems like he's trying to push more and more information on me, as if preparing me for something yet to come. Any way, his story continued of how Doomsayer set out to destroy Masamoto's entire family, save two. Yukio and Yukia Masamoto were spared, conceding to serve him, rather than taking the alternative of death. They too were possessed by Doomsayer's demons, who he called on using the power of the talisman piece in his possession. Yukio quickly used his newfound power to build one of the

45

largest crime syndicates in Japan, all to serve Lord Doomsayer's purpose. Each new member to join also received a demonic possession to strengthen and enhance the soldier's abilities. These are the agents of darkness who I will someday face. The problem is, according to Masamoto, there are even more examples of opposition, who are scattered around the world, building their armies for the coming war.

One such group is referred to as Jezana's minions. These beastly creatures are the foot soldiers of her army, ready to feast on the innocence of mankind. Masamoto said that there are specific factions known as hives watched over by one of her black knights. History states that they await her return to lead them to the Promised Land. If I understand him right, Masamoto said that there are two breeds of these minions. Most importantly, there are the pure breeds, and the slayers. Basically, the first creates the other, and the second does the slaughtering for food. At first, I thought the description sounded like a vampire story, but these dark creatures aren't after your blood. Masamoto said that they feed on the innocent soul. In fact, an innocent soul can't be turned. That is why the pure breeds pass them over, searching for the tainted spirits to turn, and let the slayers take care of the dirty work with the rest.

It's our little conversations like this that fuel my drive to work harder every day. Megan thinks I'm becoming a fanatic about this new found teaching, but gives me space just the same.

Sadly, she can never know that I not only do it for her, but the rest of mankind as well. I must stay diligent if she is to have a peaceful existence free of the Devastator's reign. It's funny, but I keep catching myself asking the question, "Why?"

Why would anyone want to sink the entire world into darkness? I've seen the kind hell it could be on earth, and there is nothing to be gained from that for anybody. If you hold any stock in what Masamoto says, societies will crash, governments will lose control, and millions will die, and that's before the real suffering begins. Every life, every creature will be stricken by this plague of suffering and tortured grief. No one, or no thing, will be exempt. How could it possibly make sense? The world may be screwed up as it is, but at least we've managed to hold it together so far, to keep it from going over the edge. I guess I'm the lucky one who gets to stand at the edge of the cliff and hold it back from now on.

JD skips through page after page, searching for more information about Nick's destiny, and the talisman's past. The pages of the journal are loaded with drawings and sketches, with a lot of blank pages that were skipped over. He stops a time or two to go back and look a little closer at a couple of the drawings, but doesn't waste too much time with them. One day he'll have to go back through the journal again and try to make better sense of it all, but for now his focus is stuck on the meat of the story. "Here we go, this looks promising."

September 29th, 2005
Today, I experienced my first encounter with

one of Doomsayer's minions. I was at the dojo preparing for my afternoon classes when Masamoto suddenly became defensive with his actions. I knew right away that there was something seriously wrong, and that "something" was connected to the talisman. I asked him what was wrong, but found myself doing so as I grabbed a sword from the weapons wall.

He explained to me that Doomsayer had spies encircling the world searching for the location of the talisman. The spell cast on it keeps the dark Lord from being able to pinpoint its whereabouts, forcing him to send his minions out to physically hunt it down. He told me that we must find the minion that was nearby and destroy it, before it discovers Masamoto's location to report back to Doomsayer. I asked him where and how. He responded, "It's too late, they are already here." Within seconds, two men enter the dojo to see Masamoto and myself standing in the middle of the room. To my surprise, these two men suddenly began to growl and hiss at the sight of Master Masamoto, as their bodies started to mutate and transform into demonic creatures. At the time, I didn't have the opportunity to clarify which kind of minion these guys were. Whether they were possessed by a demonic spirit, or some kind of soul sucking vampire, it was obvious that they were the enemy. Without warning, they attack with the full intention of slaughtering us both.

Masamoto dropped the first by forcing the end of his cane through the frontrunner's chest. The demon's body fell to the floor and then burst into flames, burning up any evidence of its existence in less than two seconds. Good things come to those who wait, or at least that's what I thought. When I seen the guy's body burn up like that, I thought he had to be one of those possessed by a demon guys. After thinking about it for a minute I realized quickly that I had no idea how any of them would die, which just left me back where I was before. Masamoto then points his hand at the second dark warrior, causing it to halt its approach. The demon must have realized that an attack would be futile, so it chose to retreat. Masamoto ordered me to go and hunt it down, making sure it stayed away from the public eye.

The dark warrior saw otherwise, leaping right through the store front glass of the dojo like it was tissue paper. Once outside in the sun, the demon resumed its host's identity and took off up the street. Masamoto warned that if I took the guy down in the sunlight, his dark powers would be ineffective. Living in Miami, I thought that would be an easy thing to accomplish.

I take chase after the guy, a little unsure about the outcome of this confrontation. To my surprise, my target was already at the street corner, and was timing the traffic to make his crossing against the light. That hesitation gave me the time to close in on him, but he still managed to get to the other side of the street before I could reach him. To my advantage, his haste drove him right into an angry mob that was waiting in the hot sun for the bus. Needless to say, none of them appreciated being knocked to the ground and were happy to let him know about it. With the light in my favor, I was able to close in on him once more. Accosted by the transit riders, and his escape routes limited, the guy darts into an alley just as I was about to reach him. I ran right in after him, never slowing my pace while trying to keep him in my sights. By using Masamoto's teachings, I allowed my momentum to carry me up the wall and then back down while maintaining a full sprint. To say that I was surprised to find that the man had vanished is a major understatement. One second, he was right in front of me, not ten feet away. Then, in a blink of an eye, he was gone. I remembered Masamoto's warning about the sunlight and realized there was none in the dead end alley. I heard a noise above me and looked up to see the guy hanging onto the side of the building like a fly on the wall. Catching me off guard, he used the advantage and leaped down from his perch, raking my chest with a handful of talons.

The dark warrior broke and ran, knowing it had to survive to report back to the dark Lord, its Master. It was up to me to see that it doesn't happen. Taking chase once again, I exit the alley right on the guy's heels. Trying to slow me down, he grabbed a woman and threw her into my path, before rushing out into traffic. The first car swerved to miss him and plowed into another car that was blocked in behind the bus. The guy then climbed up onto the hood of the wrecked car and then off on the other side where he looked back to see where I was. So distracted by me, he doesn't see the next car that plows into the accident scene, crushing the man's body between two cars. The dark warrior's body caught fire and burned up in seconds, eliminating all evidence that would substantiate the witnesses' statements, later on. With the onlookers focused on the accident, and amazed by what they saw, I was able to slip out and get back to the dojo to check on Masamoto. Now that I have seen my enemies first hand, I know that they are capable of striking from any direction. I can only hope that incidents like this are few and far between. If I was attacked while I was with Megan, or anyone else for that matter, their lives could be put in danger. This has to be why Masamoto warned me about my involvement with Meg.

November 11th, 2005
Today, I write this with true sorrow in my heart. Yesterday, my worst fears came true, and I still can't believe it's all real. I should be at the church right now, waiting for Megan to walk up the isle. God, I can't do this right now. I'm gonna go walk on the beach.

November 13th, 2005
As hard as it may be for me, this is something I feel I must do. Life sure does play sick demented games on a guy, that's for sure. It's been two days now, and I still feel like there is a huge black hole inside of me, sucking all of the life out of my soul. How do you go from having everything,

to losing it all, and still be expected to carry on a normal life? Normal life; now that I'm the guardian of the talisman how will I ever have a normal life? Why Megan? I mean, I've pretty much got a handle on this good and evil thing, and I understand Masamoto's fall. I guess for some time now, I've suspected him of knowing the time was at hand, but, why Megan? Was his warning more of a premonition of things to come, instead of what was possible? God, I miss her. I though I had it all figured out and that I could protect her from anything. If I had taken Masamoto's warning to heart, she'd still be alive. She'd be alone and miserable, just like me, but she would be alive. If I had taken her advice to heart, in the beginning, I would have never crossed that street that day. Now, I'm the one who's all alone, unless you throw Sonny into the equation. She needs a place to stay until she gets back on her feet. Readjusting to life on the other side of bars will take her some time to settle in. Despite her shortcomings, she has always been there when I needed a friend. I think I could use a friend right about now.


November 15th, 2005

Okay, I think I can get through this, so here's what happened, or at least the best I can recall. We were at our rehearsal dinner and everything was going off without a hitch. Megan screwed up a couple of times during the rehearsal, giving the guests at the dinner plenty of fodder for conversation. God, I'm suddenly drawing a blank. I never knew it would be this hard for a guy to recall his bride's murder. Maybe I need to give it more time. Maybe I just need to say the hell with it and go have a shot of tequila. Maybe I'll just try again a little later.

I love you Megan.

Here we go again. I guess I'll keep giving this a go, until I'm done, or the tequila runs out. Here we are folks, two in the morning, and it doesn't look like I'll be getting any sleep again tonight. Any way, we were all seated at our assigned chairs around the banquet tables when Megan and Masamoto began to feel ill. Minutes later, both of them had lost all control as if paralyzed, unable to move any part of their bodies, but were still able to see, hear, and breathe. Then, the attack came with the strike force descending into the banquet hall through the skylight at the center of the room. The shattering glass and black garbed men dropping to the floor sent the guests into a panic. Before I was conscious of what I was doing, I found myself leaping over the table with Charlie and Jorge following close behind, with the full intent of taking the party crashers out. My only hesitation was when Sonny screamed my name. Turning around, I saw the most horrific sight. As the intruders descended into the banquet hall, they attacked their targets being Masamoto and Megan. I know full well that the attack was meant for me and my master. God, why not me instead of her? I mean, if this destiny crap is really true and the world could be lost to the darkness, I would've still traded places with her. It may have only given her a little time, alone to live her life, but it would be more than she has now. I know why. It was because of my own arrogance that cost Megan her life. This is something I am going to have to deal with for the rest of my life. You were right Master Masamoto. Thanks for pushing the issue.

Any way, I fell back to Sonny's side as she was laying Megan down on the floor. Meg tried as hard as she could to speak to me before she died. To my surprise and disappointment, I heard Masamoto's voice in the back of my mind, warning me to hurry and take possession of the talisman. I reached up to the old man and pulled him over to lay him down as well, giving me the opportunity to retrieve the talisman without anyone noticing. Sonny did, and she also saw the sorrow in my heart that had darkened my eyes. Like a wild animal, she jumped up and rushed to attack her prey. As soon as I took possession of the talisman, I took chase as well, but I felt different, and still feel that way. I can't really explain it yet, and who knows, I may never be able to. I'm tired. Maybe I'll pick this back up another time. Why? What's the sense of it all any way? I'm not sure if I even know, any more.

"That's it?" JD rifles through the next few pages, finding nothing but blank paper. "Boy, you really do know how to leave a guy hanging." He closes the journal and looks up to see Nick walking down the sidewalk. JD jumps to his feet to get out of the way of the front door, so Nick could unlock it. "Man, I sure am glad you're on time today, Teach. I forgot my keys this morning, and the tables are turned with me needing to pee something fierce, right about now."

Nick greets JD with a bow and a smile before fumbling in is pocket for his keys. How are you doing, other than that, Sport? You look like your dog just died, or something."

"Naw, I just finished the end of your journal. Dude, I wanna say that I'm sorry, if it means anything." JD waits for Nick to enter, and then enters himself as Nick holds open the door. He has a newfound respect for his friend, seeing Nick in a whole new light. "If you don't mind me asking, how do you deal with everything you've gone through?"

Nick hangs the open sign in the door window, and looks outside, checking the nearby buildings for anything unusual. "Actually, it does mean something, JD. You are a caring person and your sentiment comes across as genuine as you are. So, thanks, but as far as dealing with it, that's just a day by day process." Nick points to the back wall. "Ya wanna go hit the lights and turn on the heat. Let's see if we can get this place warmed up a little so that the students can function. I'll be back in a second." Nick heads off to his office to drop off his things, while JD sprints to the light switches, then the thermostat, before making a beeline to the restroom.

His first motion is to set the briefcase onto his desk. After that, Nick walks over to what looks like the janitor's closet and places his hand on a small glass panel beside the door. A locking mechanism disengages allowing the door to swing open slightly. Nick grabs it and swings it open with all his might. What looks like an ordinary door, is really twelve inches thick and solid wood and steel clad. Inside, is nothing more than a black onyx dragon statue, about twelve inches tall, sitting on a waste high pedestal in the middle of the floor. From his neck he retrieves the talisman and hangs it around the dragon's head. Then, staying on pace, Nick exits and locks the room, stopping at the picture of his Master to pay homage to the old man. With his afternoon ritual completed, Nick heads back out into the main room of the dojo to help JD finish laying out the floor mats.

Nick knows that JD is full of questions and isn't quite sure which ones he should answer. He gave him the journal, hoping that it might open the young man's eyes a little more. Not so much to the darker side of life, but maybe it would give JD a little more appreciation for the life he possesses. After all, Nick is the one who has pounded it into JD's head that he should always live every day like it's your last. "So, you've finished the whole journal already, huh? Now, correct me if I'm wrong, but I know I told you to wait until you're off to college. What possessed you to defy your sensei like that?" Nick tosses another stack of mats out to JD, to spread out in the center of the floor. "What did ya think?"

JD stops what he's doing and turns to face his friend. "Are you kidding me? Dude, I've got so much swimmin' around in my brain that I don't even know where to start." JD straightens out the last mat and stands up. "All of that darkness stuff is for real, right?"

Nick exhales a snort and chuckles at the question. "More than I hope you'll never have to know, JD." Nick walks over and puts his arm around his star student. "Do you remember what I said about your ability, the night we first met?"

"Yeah, you told me that it was proof that I could do great things." JD slumps his shoulders, thinking that his questions are about to be avoided once again.

"I told you that this mental or psychic force field that you are able to produce isn't just a gift, or some freak occurrence in nature. You Jefferson, in trying to honor your father's rules and beliefs put upon yourself the need for its existence. You were an easy mark for any and every bully around, because you would not fight back. It was this strong will and determination that created your ability. You would not fight back, but your mind and spirit would not let you suffer the consequences. The need was there and you evolved to fill that need. That is the reason why I took you in, seeing the potential for you to be able to accomplish so much more. Once again, you have proved me right." Nick takes a surprise swing at JD, testing his student's reflexes.

"Ungh-uh," JD responds, grabbing Nick's arm before he could make contact with JD's stomach. He passes the test. "I know this may sound like a stupid question, but how do you keep going after all you've been through? I mean, come on Nick, as long as I've known you, I can't ever recall you being down and out about anything." JD throws a knee up to Nick's ribs, and then back flips over to the center of the mat covered floor. "Spar with me a little?" He asks, bouncing in the air on the tips of his toes. "I'm not going to be able to make class tomorrow night, so why not give me a few extra minutes now while we talk.

Nick laughs off the challenge, and then charges his student to land the first blow. He stops short of running into JD, and then delivers a volley of punches, jabs and kicks that are blocked well by the student, as Nick expected. He steps back and takes a defensive stance, waving JD in. "Come on, Sport, let's see what you've got for me."

"Tell the truth Nick, would you believe all of that stuff in your journal?" JD lunges forward and offers Nick a barrage of kicks and punches of his own. Nick fends the attack off with ease, and then counters by grabbing JD and flipping him to the mats. JD growls out of frustration about Nick getting the upper hand so quickly, and leaps to his feet. Squaring off against Nick again, he readies for round two.

"Let's put it this way, I believe that if it is true, the suffering of mankind would be too much to endure. Because of that alone, I'm willing to follow this destiny to its end. Would you want to be the one who let the world down?" Nick takes the offensive and delivers several key shots that open JD up for another trip to the mats. Again, the teacher takes a step back and motions for JD to get up.

Frustration sets in even further, sending JD scrambling to his feet to face off against Nick one more time. "But what if it's not true? Wouldn't you feel cheated in some way?" JD attacks again and manages to score a take down of his own, sweeping Nick's feet out from under him.

Nick claps his hands a couple of times, applauding JD's move. "Cheated, I don't think so. The decisions and choices I've made for myself, and my life, were and still are of my own free will. I have lived a good life so far, even though I've lost a lot, never compromising who I am, and I plan to continue to do so." Nick leaps into the air and delivers a kick at JD, but his student is quicker, dropping to the floor to avoid the blow. Nick follows JD to the mats, but his student is already taking the opening he sees. The opportunity closes fast with Nick rolling clear and kicking JD's leg away, causing the young man to spin around on the floor. The two combatants rise up and stand off again, when the first group of students enters the dojo. Nick takes a quick glance to the door. "Oh good, the class is arriving." He seizes the opportunity while JD is distracted and sends him back down to the mats once more, where Nick ends the session by dropping down beside his student to deliver an elbow to his sternum. Then Nick jumps back to his feet, and bows to his young audience, who were cheering their teacher's victory. The victor reaches down offering JD a hand up from the floor. "We'll pick this up Friday, before class, okay?"

JD takes the offer and pulls himself up off the mats. "That's cool, Teach, it'll give me some time to sort out the questions I do have." JD checks the time on the clock. "I've gotta get outta here. I told my uncle that I would cover a shift for him at his mini mart tonight. I'll see you on Friday, Nick."

"Yeah, well spend a few minutes reading some of the more important stuff between now and then." Nick motions for his students to line up so that he can begin their class. JD bows to Nick, and waits for the gesture to be returned, before he heads off to earn his keep.

His uncle's mini mart is only a couple of minutes away, about six blocks, so that should give JD plenty of time to get there and maybe even have a chance to thumb through a few pages of the journal before his uncle leaves. As he rounds the corner, and the store comes into view, JD sees a peculiar sight. There at the corner of the building stands a lone man dressed in a black three piece suit. What he finds strange about this is that the neighborhood is a majority of Hispanic and African American heritage, and this guy is Asian dressed to the nines. As JD walks passed, the stranger pulls his toothpick from his mouth and asks with an arrogant tone, "How you doing, Sport?" His English is broken and his accent is thick, but what bothers JD is what the guy said. Turning around to see if the guy was for real, JD finds the mystery man has vanished from sight. He looks around the entire area one more time, before heading into the store. "Weird."

As soon as he enters the mini mart, JD's uncle is in his face. His name is Benji Saliff, Indian by birth who came to the States in his early twenties when his father's health began to fail. "Jefferson, I need to go to the bank with today's deposits. Bring your martial arts outside and walk me to my car." Benji motions to the afternoon clerk to hand him the bank bag. "Libby, you can leave as soon as I drive away. Jefferson will be filling in for Robert tonight. I will see you tomorrow, and your drawer better not be short on the lottery tickets."

The old black woman tosses Benji the bag and then flips him off as a reply to his warning. JD laughs to himself at her gesture. He loves to be around when Libby and his uncle get into one of there bickering sessions. She's about as cynical as she is stubborn and guaranteed to give JD something to laugh about, whenever they're in company. As soon as Benji exits the door, she is grabbing herself a couple of lottery tickets for the bus ride home.

Following his uncle out the door, JD laughs at the notion that he is suppose to be serving as some kind of bodyguard. It's not like Benji's beat up Reliant K Car is seen as a hot target. Besides, his uncle really doesn't expect JD to risk his life for a couple hundred dollars, does he? "Hey Uncle Benji, you studied mythology and folklore in college, right?"

"Oh Jefferson, I have a vast knowledge of mythology, and the occult religions, but now is not the time to discuss these things. I must go to the bank before it closes in thirty minutes. We can discuss your topic tomorrow about myths and legends." Benji quickly climbs into his car, paranoid that someone was waiting to steal his money. JD waits for Benji to start up the car and drive across the street to the bank, before heading back inside the mini mart to relieve Libby's shift.

"Okay Mrs. Samuels, you can head on home now if you want. I'll take care of closing out your drawer for ya. Don't forget to grab a couple cans of food for the cats. You're off for the next two days, remember?" He grabs his back pack beside the front doors and walks around the counter. The first thing he does is grabs a few bucks from his pocket and drops them in the register to cover Libby's tickets and cat food.

"Thank ya, Jefferson; you are such a good boy. Yo uncle doesn't deserve a nephew as good as you." She waves goodnight and grabs a copy of the Enquirer before waddling off to her bus stop. Finally, JD can get back to the journal hopefully without any interruptions. After all, tonight should be a dead night for business.

June 7th, 2003
I thought he was trying to throw me off track today. Out of the blue he started up a conversation

about how each life was connected. Masamoto
said that in some way or fashion, my life is
connected to every living creature on Earth. It
is that connection that gives us strength. By
drawing on the strengths of others, we make
ourselves stronger. Using that strength, we
defend the others who can not defend themselves.
It is this strength that I must achieve if I am to
defend the world. To do that, I must reach my
highest level of awareness through my training
and meditation.

I have to admit that I'm looking forward to
this challenge. If for nothing else, I will better
myself mind, body and spirit. How bad can that
be?"


JD laughs at the last comment. Obviously, in this earlier
passage, Nick was oblivious to the perils to come. Hearing
someone clear his throat, he looks up from the journal to
see a police officer standing in front of the counter holding a
steaming hot cup of coffee. "Hey Officer Gomez, the coffee's
on the house tonight."

"Thanks, JD, is everything quiet around here tonight?"
Gomez takes a sip of his coffee and burns his lip. "Madre de
Dios!"

"Yeah, it should be a slow night, so I came prepared." JD
holds up the journal and waves goodbye to Officer Gomez.
Diving back into the book, he flips through a couple of pages
he's already read, and finds an interesting passage that he
overlooked before. "Hold on, what's this about?"


January 12th, 2004
Today will be filed in the stranger than fiction
category. It started out with an extreme

negative feelings. You can not change the past, so you must learn from your mistakes that you make and create a path for the future to avoid the mistake happening again." I told him that it is easier said than done for a perfectionist like me. His response was, "It is not your actions that make you a perfectionist. It is your desire to be that makes you who you are. This does not mean that you will not make mistakes, and that it is your desire for perfection that gives you the ability to overcome the mistakes made. Learn to see yourself making the movements in your mind, and your body will follow as smoothly as your thoughts flow." After three hours of more meditation, we were right back on track.


June 16th, 2004
Well talk about the shit you don't see every day. That crazy old man threw one at me today that knocked me off my feet and made me want to reevaluate my whole stand on all of this. He said that the time had come for him to leave with me, my first charge. I thought he was going to hand over the talisman, but then remembered that I would be the one to take it from him, when the time came. So I had to wonder what it could be. I know one thing, if he had thrown this one at me a year ago, I probably would have sent him packing, and kicked his crazy ass right out of my life.

After our meditation, he brought out a small lidded basket woven out of bamboo. From inside this basket, he produced a grapefruit sized orb that he claimed to be, a dragon's egg. The thing looked ancient like some kind of fossilized artifact, and yet appeared to be viable at the same time. Of course, with it like everything else, it comes with a story.

Once again, Masamoto took me back in time with his tale, just before the last attempt at giving the Earth to the Devastator's reign. Mistress Jezana had been reborn to lead her armies against the nations of man. The problem was that these armies were decimated two decades earlier with her previous attempt. Her dark priests had a solution; rebuild the armies and make them stronger using dark magic. Jezana and her priests set out again to collect every dragon egg they could find. Her high Priest, Mandal Rayne, had uncovered an ancient eastern practice where the hexed dragon's egg could restore the life of a fallen warrior, making them invincible. With a hundred of these eggs, she could continue to revive her fallen warriors while the ranks were being replenished. The spell cast on the eggs served several purposes for Jezana's cause. First and foremost, the spell made it possible so that the mystical energy from the dragon inside could revive the fallen warrior. Secondly, it kept the egg sustainable for all times. He warned me that if this egg fell into the hands of darkness, it could be used against our cause. I asked him why not just destroy it? His answer was that the same spell also protects it from destruction. Burn it, and it will not scar. Hit it with a sword, and you will not scratch its surface. So, for now it sits in my gun safe in the back of my closet. I'd venture to say that it's much safer now than in some bamboo basket.

October 19th, 2005

I feel like I'm drifting away from my reality. More and more of my time is being consumed by my training, causing other aspects of my life to falter. My volunteer work has fallen off dramatically as of late. I even find that I've been second guessing what I should be teaching to my classes, wondering if I should be preparing them for what's to come.

Thank God I haven't lost focus on Meg. She's my true anchor to what's real any more and I fear it's getting harder and harder to see her. I don't deny that she is so proud of me for what I'm doing, even if she doesn't understand it fully. Above all else, she sees the change in what and who I am, and she believes it's for the better. If she knew Masamoto's true plan and agenda, I don't think she would be so approving. Again, he urged me to separate myself from her. I don't understand this. Even with all the progress I've made, he still doesn't believe I could save her. I say he's wrong. I don't have to save her. I just have to keep her safe. In my book, that's two different things. I am going to marry Megan and that's the way it is. I actually thought about telling her the truth, but this close to the wedding, she would think I was making stuff up because I got cold feet. What do I do? I have to follow through with all of this.

About five or six blocks away, Nick closes up the dojo

for the night, flipping the cheap open/closed sign around on the front door, before turning off the overhead lights. With his class over and his students gone, Nick's mind resumes its focus on the overshadowing feeling of uneasiness that has invaded his life. Using the darkness in the room as his ally, Nick walks back up to the front of the room and looks outside at the city street. What is it that is causing him to feel this way? Scratch that, he knows what it is. It's his so-called destiny and the damned talisman hanging around his neck. The question is why does he feel this way? Seeing nothing out of the ordinary, Nick turns and starts for his office, when he sees something out the corner of his eye. It was movement he saw somewhere across the street. Or, at least he thinks he did.

Nick spins around and stares at the buildings across the street. He just stands there in plain sight, and that is where he wants to be. He may not be able to see anything, but if anything, or anyone is looking at Nick, he wants them to know that he is on to them, and he's right there for them to make their move. Nothing, minutes pass and he sees nothing to explain the alarms going off in his head. A few minutes later Nick tires of his stand and decides to resume his nightly duties. Nick walks into his office and turns on his computer to let it start up as he changes out of his workout gi. But just because he has moved on to finish up the night at his dojo, doesn't mean he's dismissed the feeling, or the fact that he thought he saw something. As he gets dressed, his mind analyzes the visual image of the buildings across the street. Using his training, Nick had the entire block of shops and storefronts memorized in a matter of seconds. Now he can take the time to go over what he saw. Each building is well lit, leaving few places for someone to hide in the shadows. Plus, each building was built right next to each other, eliminating any alleyways for someone to duck down. The motion he saw, or thought he saw, was lateral, eliminating the possibility of anyone going up a building. If there was someone or something across the street, he would have been able to see them.

Ready to close the case and dismiss the whole ordeal as a result of fatigue, Nick tosses his gi into his locker and goes to his secure room to retrieve his talisman. Inside, he stops at the picture of Masamoto and straightens it. "I think I'm finally starting to lose my mind over all of this shit, Master." He walks across the small room and retrieves the talisman to hang around his neck from the dragon statue at the opposite wall of Masamoto's portrait. "Okay, all I have to do is enter a few notes about tonight's class into the computer, and I'm right the hell outta here."

Just then, Nick hears a sound coming from the main room that sounds like the blades of two swords being scraped against each other. When he hears the clatter of the blades being brought together in battle, Nick nearly kills himself getting out of the office to investigate the noises he has heard, by tripping over a stack of file boxes stacked against the wall. Clink, clink, clink, the sound echoes out from the main room, as Nick tries to collect himself from the floor. He is sure that there is someone out there, and he wants to know who they are and what they are doing. Wanting to have an advantage for the confrontation, he grabs a sword from his office wall and charges out onto the red mats on the floor.

Out his office door Nick charges with his sword held high above his head ready to strike. The only problem is that there is no one in the room. He scans the perimeter of the room, but there is nothing, no one anywhere in sight, and his dojo was purposely laid out so that he had clear sight around the room. Now he is feeling a little spooked, trying to figure out if he had actually heard what he thought he heard. No, he knows that he heard the sounds of two blades hitting against each other. Nick looks over at the door to see that it is shut, but did he lock it? He remembers turning the sign around but can't remember turning the deadbolt. If someone had run out the door, Nick would know because it would still be closing due to the slow action of the automatic door closer. Still, he had to be sure, if for nothing else but to put his mind and anxiety at ease.

Half way across the room, Nick's foot catches something lying on the floor. He doesn't fall, or anything, like that. It's actually more of a controlled stumble as he tries to avoid whatever it was that he kicked. Spinning around to investigate, Nick sees two Samurai long swords lying together on the red mats covering the floor, instead of hanging on the wall where they belong. Nick takes a defensive stance and begins to slowly turn around to check his surroundings. He knows that there is nowhere for anyone to hide in the room, but someone or something removed these swords from the wall, and they weren't on the floor when class ended tonight. After picking up one of the swords so that he has a weapon for both hands, Nick moves over to check the door and finds it locked.

"Okay, that's too much, too late, tonight." Nick doesn't go back to his office. He doesn't take the swords and replace them on the wall where they belong. Instead, he just unlocks the door and walks outside and looks around. Unsatisfied that everything is alright; he locks up the door and heads for his car parked in the empty lot on the side of the building. Nickolas Landry is in full alarm at the moment and is very uncomfortable with the feeling. Stopping at the corner of the building, he looks around for anything posing as a threat. To say he is startled would be an understatement when the neighborhood vagrant makes his presence known, popping up right in front of Nick. The seasoned martial arts instructor leaps back and brandishes both blades, before he realizes who it is. Nick's vast training that prevents him from gutting the old man as his first reaction to the encounter. "Damn it, John, what are you trying to do, get yourself killed?"

"Oh no, Mr. Landry, I didn't mean you no harm. I do apologize for spookin' ya like that." Haggard, undernourished, and dirty, your first thought would be that John had recently crawled out of a grave. To Nick, the old man hasn't changed a bit in all the years he's known John.

"Its okay, John, here, I want you to take this." Nick reaches into his pocket and pulls out a five dollar bill. "Go buy your self a bottle and find somewhere out of the neighborhood to hole up tonight. There's a bad moon shining in the sky."

"Well thank ya, Mr. Landry. I'll do just that, good night."

"Yeah, same to you, pal." Nick looks the empty lot over to make sure there aren't any more little surprises, and then walks over and unlocks the driver's door of his car. Once more he scans the area, feeling like he's being watched. With nothing ominous in sight, he climbs into the mustang wanting to go home.

He sits there in the seat and tries to justify writing all of this off, as coincidence to the fact that the five year anniversary of Megan and Masamoto's death is upon him. Nick tries, but he knows that all of this is somehow connected to his so-called destiny, including Megan's death. It only makes sense, and explains the paranoia he's been feeling, brought on by his duty as Guardian. More than anything, there is this growing feeling of being alone to handle all of this madness. At first, he thought that he could handle any situation. Now he just wonders how long before he really breaks down. Master Masamoto once told him that there would be others that fight and will fight in the war against darkness. Nick wishes they would finally show themselves, sooner or later, just so that he doesn't have to keep going this alone.

He knows his own saying, "be careful what you wish for."

The fact of the matter is that wishful thinking is irrelevant, because destinies do cross and the outcome is never what you expect. Hundreds of miles away, in the state of Georgia, there is another destined soul who travels a different path. Soon Nick will know the destiny of this other, as their paths and destinies cross on the great fabric of time. He sits there for a moment and ponders the idea of a break, or vacation, before starting the car and backing it out of the parking space. After checking the mirrors and taking a deep breath, Nick puts the mustang in gear and points it towards home.

# Chapter IV

A tlanta Georgia, the sprawling metropolis of the South. It's along way from Miami Florida, but the two are connected all the same. One might say, the one being Masamoto, that every event was woven into the fabric of time, when it was first stretched across the loom of the universe. Blah, blah, blah, Billy Ray McBride doesn't buy into any of that. "It's raining again. It always seems to be raining." The best way to describe Billy Ray McBride would be a character from a role playing game. His personality best fits the role of the "chaotic neutral" character. He isn't doing this for fame or glory. His actions seek vengeance instead of justice, and yet he considers those who are innocent, willing to save the chance for retribution, rather than risk the welfare of innocent bystanders. He hates that he loves, for his loved ones die. He does love however, that he hates the man he has targeted for vengeance. This hatred fills the emptiness inside him. It gives him purpose, and fuels him on, but also clouds his judgment, leading his decisions to be rash and questionable. His heart has fallen away from honor leading to lies deceit and betrayal consuming his life and actions. It is this chaotic turmoil in Billy's life that has brought him to this point in time. The rebel vigilante stands in an alley on a Thursday night, hoping to quench the dark desires in his heart and soul. A slow moving train blows its lonesome call out into the night as it passes the freight yard across the way. Each tanker car connected to the massive steel chain bears the same markings on the side, "**Clean interior with hot water only.**" Billy notices this, but he doesn't really care. He counts the rail cars to pass the time, but has no reason why. His thoughts are and should be on one thing, one person, Antonio Callistone. "Forty seven."

He looks down the alley both ways and then slips back into the shadows. It feels good to him, being back out in the city's embrace. Billy tried to walk away, but it kept pulling him back. He justifies this, by convincing himself that he is maintaining his own philosophy on life that is singular in nature. Don't cross Billy Ray McBride, and he won't cross you. Unfortunately, Billy has been crossed, by one man, a mobster named Antonio Callistone. The mob boss had Billy's father, Federal Agent Walter McBride, killed for getting too close to Antonio's organization. For that, Billy had dedicated his life to avenge his father, not long ago. A life that has now been consumed by his dark desire for vengeance; he's just too thick headed to realize it.

Four months ago, McBride convinced himself that his thirst for vengeance had been quenched, when Callistone's son Darien fell to his death. The aging mobster may have been the one who ordered the hit on Billy's father, but Billy being there when Darien took the fall seemed like a fair trade off, at the time. The Callistone syndicate had been planning to relocate in the southern metropolis, but Antonio left Atlanta after his son's death, and hasn't been back since. Billy is certain of this, because he's been back out in the streets of Atlanta searching for any sign of the mobster, for the passed three months. There is a monster inside Billy and it longs to be let loose again.

The first month back on his ranch, trying to start a new life, with his new love, Taylor, seemed to come easy. Their time together seemed to give Billy the healing he needed to put his desire for revenge to rest, and he was willing to never look back. In fact, Taylor was the one who actually pushed the issue with Billy at first, talking about what a good team they made, and how she missed running around in her costume, kicking ass with him. Billy was against any possibility of him and Taylor running the streets as costumed vigilantes any more. He promised her that it was over, and that was the end of it. His defense was simple; he loved her and wasn't willing to risk her safety any more by chasing ghosts. Barbara Cox died because of her desire to involve herself with Billy's hunt for vengeance. It was an unnecessary loss that he didn't take very well. Billy has since stood at her grave to pay his respects and ask for forgiveness too many times, only to walk away unsatisfied. This is something Billy doesn't want to go through again with Taylor.

And then, there is his dear mother, Sarah McBride. He was finally starting to rebuild his relationship with his mother, again, and promised her his that his quest for revenge had died. Because of all of this, he had truly convinced himself that settling down on the ranch was what he needed and wanted the most. That is, until the dreams returned. Every night, after agonizing night, would be the same with him happy and content to fall asleep with Taylor at his side. But as soon as his mind was at rest, the repetitious loop of his Father being gunned down would start to run through his mind again. Over, and over, Billy relived the scene of his father dying right in front of his eyes.

Day after day would pass with him trying to live a lie. The days were bright and happy, sharing each moment with his beautiful redhead, as they enjoyed the peace and serenity that the ranch had to offer. Night after night, the pain would return forcing him from Taylor's side. Sitting in the dark, sometimes at the foot of the bed, Billy would play the "what if" game, pondering scenarios about what he could have done different. He tried to convince himself that it really didn't matter to him, because he wanted to believe his quest for vengeance was over. Making theories and passing judgments was simply a means for him to pass the long dark hours while he was awake.

He fought it off, this need for vengeance, for at least two weeks, when the call came. Billy was offered his old job and a new contract with a professional wrestling organization in Atlanta. Evidently, Big Edgar, the main attraction, had moved on to pursue his career on the west coast, so Billy was asked to come out of retirement. The glitz and glamour of the limelight could give him an outlet, or at least a distraction. He could lie to himself all he wants, but deep down inside, Billy knew that this would give him the opportunity to be in Atlanta, legitimately, to somehow find some kind of peace. He had spent night after night sitting in bed beside Taylor as she slept, remembering everything that had happened. He remembered his first beating. He remembered Barbara being shot. He remembered discovering his father's partner's involvement with the mob, and how good it felt when Harrison fell to the bottom of the storage tank. He remembers the battle in Stone Mountain Park, and he remembers how good it felt to hear Darien Callistone screaming for mercy before he died. Deep down inside, there was this dark part of him that still wanted to hear that scream again. Darien may have hired the hit man who killed Billy's father, but it was Antonio who should shoulder the blame. Reestablishing his wrestling career would give him the excuse to be in Atlanta again.

Every night would bring the question, why had the

nightmares returned? His only answer that made any sense was that Callistone had returned to the South. It was the only explanation that made sense. The lack of sleep weakened his mind and spirit, slowly sending him back down the dark road of no return. His mind began to play tricks on him, creating delusional justifications for what he really wanted. Was his father trying to tell him, no warn him, of Antonio's return? It must be so! Billy vowed on his father's grave to never give up. Was he being punished for not finishing the job? Or, was it a second chance for him to complete his vow, so that his father could finally rest in peace? The craving inside had awakened once more. His mind wanted to blame Taylor for his hesitation to return to the streets. She was the one who seduced him into giving up his crusade. She was the one who enticed him with love and beauty to stay with her and love her, and give up on his vow. He was losing his grip on reality. These thoughts and accusations were the cause for Billy to start to drift away from her, but even that was too much for his heart to bear. His heart; isn't it love that is the root to this evil inside of him? He loved his father, and it was his father's career that denied him the love he wanted in return. It was the chance at a father's love that was taken away from him, when Walter was murdered. It was Barbara's love for Billy that made her choose to follow him, resulting in her death. It was his love for her that made him crave retribution for her murder. Love; there can't be any place in his heart for love. The question is, can he live that way without becoming some heartless, soulless, zombie?

Somehow he had to find the balance between what he needed with Taylor, and what he needs to ease his pain. He had built a façade around his personality to hide the pain and torment he was suffering, and the toll that it was taken on his mind and body. This would quickly evolve into the lies and deceit that was soon to follow. This is where his former career

75

becomes instrumental of finding that balance. Billy jumped at the chance using his resurgence back into wrestling, as an excuse to be back in Atlanta. He convinced himself that he had the whole thing worked out. Billy would go to Atlanta for his wrestling matches, and then hit the streets searching for information on the whereabouts of Antonio Callistone. If by chance he was to get roughed up, he could blame it on the wrestling match. Taylor didn't have to know anything different, and no one would be the wiser. She hated the thought of him being involved with Professional Wrestling and didn't want any part of it. He was sure that he had found the way to have his cake and eat it too.

His first few ventures back out into the Atlanta nightlife picked up a couple of new leads, but then every source of information began to dry up. Soon, all that is left are whispers and half truths about the Callistone syndicate. The next two months paid off squat for his efforts. The downside to his wrestling career was the shows he had to do on the road. While out of town for a gig in New Orleans, word on the street was that Callistone had come back to Atlanta, during Billy's absence, and cleaned out his offices. Another trip out of town cost Billy a shot at Callistone's right hand man, Carlton Smithers, when he came to town to handle some real estate business for the Cornerstone Corporation. Since then, there has been no activity bearing the Callistone name, until tonight.

Recently, over the past month and a half, Billy had changed his tactics a little, investigating his leads with a little more diplomacy and more covert actions. If he couldn't get any information by beating it out of people, then he would join the ranks of the night life to learn what he could through the pipelines of the homeless. He was surprised at how much he was able to learn about his nemesis' empire, from the derelicts and degenerates on the street. One such bit of information has brought him to this alleyway tonight.

The rain drops falling from the night sky slap at his face with a numbing cold. He steps out into the alleyway hoping to find a more comfortable position only to jump back into the shadows as a set of headlights turn up the narrow drive. Billy pulls the sleeve of his trench coat up his arm to see his watch. "Ten o'clock, right on time." He mutters, wiping the rain from his face. He takes a deep breath as his adrenaline begins to flow, opening receptors in his brain that crave what is about to take place, action. With another deep breath and no hesitation, he leaps out into the alley into the path of the oncoming delivery van. The two passengers inside the truck have no idea what's in store.

"Holy shit, Jimmy, that guy's outta his freakin' mind!" The passenger finds a little courage in the shape of a sawed off, double barrel, shotgun. When Billy charges his hands with energy, the driver knows who Billy is, even without seeing his signature costume and cape. The passenger of the out of state van has heard the legend of the Confederate Soldier as well, always wondering how one man could threaten to take down an entire mob syndicate. Learning more about his fascination with the vigilante was one of the main reasons why he volunteered for the delivery. Now, he is about to learn first hand what is real and what is legend, about the mythical Rebel Vigilante. Coming face to face with that legend so soon is making him Sam very uneasy at the moment. "Run that freak over, Jim!"

Jimmy takes his partner's advice and steps on the gas. When Billy starts to run towards the oncoming van, both men begin to panic. "Well don't just sit there, shoot that crazy sonofabitch, Sam!" To their surprise Billy leaps up onto the front hood of the truck as Sam takes aim. The problem is that Billy's actions are more fluid and faster than either one of the men in the van could ever have imagined. Sam follows Billy's path pulling the trigger of his shotgun along the way. This makes Jimmy the unfortunate recipient of birdshot to the side of his face as Billy continues his path to the top of the delivery van. Jimmy collapses against the driver's door, barely able to stay conscious. As his strength weakens, he loses control of the delivery van allowing it to careen off the buildings lining the alley. Billy continues across the top of the van's cargo box, doing a flip off the van to land on his feet as the delivery van rolls onto its side before sliding to a halt. He rushes over and pulls the back door open to find the interior of the vehicle resembling a bomb blast with Sammy trapped under several large barrels of chemical.

"Come on, man, help me outta here." Sam begs, spitting blood from his mouth as he speaks. "Ya can't just leave us here to die."

"You give me what I want, and I'll give you what you want." Billy replies.

"Anything!" Sam pushes on one of the barrels to try and free his legs, to no avail.

"What do you know about the whereabouts of Antonio Callistone?"

"Screw you, man." Jimmy mumbles from the front seat.

"Forget you, Jimmy!" Sam struggles with the chemical barrel again, seeing smoke starting to rise out from under the hood of the truck. His efforts are futile having no position for leverage, leaving him to Billy's mercy. His only hope for survival is to give the rebel vigilante what he wants. "Callistone is meeting with our boss this weekend in Miami, to lock us in as his new drug source for the southern states. Word is that you're the reason he's been shopping around for new suppliers." Suddenly, the delivery van erupts with several different explosions going off, sending Billy flying through the air, only to stop against the nearby building with a bone rattling thud. He falls and hits the ground just as hard, gasping for air already knocked out of him, when collided with the building. His costume is singed and his trench coat caught fire, a little, but that's lucky compared to the two men inside the delivery van. Tonight, they have been reduced from two bit thugs to statistics in the morgue. They weren't Callistone's men, yet, but Billy finds the way to justify the event as preventive maintenance. This shipment has been officially cancelled, which means the "accident" should take a big bite out of Callistone's revenue.

Up the alley, Billy could see doorways lighting up at what looked like a vacant building. He assumes the men exiting into the alley were the receiving crew, awaiting the arrival of this shipment. The group of men sees Billy standing in front of the burning truck, as if daring anyone to face him. To Callistone's men, they see the twelve against one odds in their favor, and begin to run towards his position. These men are no concern to Billy, so why should he stay and risk injury? His true target will be in Florida soon, more specifically Miami. That is where he will take his crusade. He memorizes the license plate of the truck and takes to the fire escape of the building across the alley, making his way to the roof tops of Atlanta. Bullets ricochet off the parapet wall, but offer no threat to Billy. The gunfire will however attract the local authorities, which is something that he would rather avoid. Billy knows that he has to get home as fast as possible to plan his trip to Florida. Once again he has been affected by the virus known as vengeance. He doesn't know how long Callistone will be in Florida, so he will have to move fast. The thug in the truck said "weekend", but that could mean Saturday morning to Saturday afternoon. Plus, you have to weigh the credibility of the slime ball who gave him the information. It doesn't matter though, because this is the first lead he's had. After all, Billy's entire crusade against

Callistone has been based on long shots. One thing was for certain; for him to face Callistone on unfamiliar turf means that Billy will have to have a solid plan of attack. He doesn't know the players, muscle, or terrain, which could make this quite the challenge. Billy's always been the one to welcome a challenge, but the first obstacle to overcome is a certain redheaded woman.

Speak of the devil, Billy's cell phone rings causing him to stop his flight and check to see who the caller is. He hesitates for a second to catch his breath, not to give himself away about his late night activities. "Hello? Oh, hey baby, listen I was about to call you." Billy takes a couple of deep breaths while listening to her sweet voice coming through the phone. To be honest, it's almost enough to make him reconsider his plans. "No, nobody beat me black and blue tonight, but I do have a match in Florida, tomorrow night, so I probably won't be home until Sunday night some time."

Taylor loves the news she has just heard, wanting to use the opportunity to try and close the gap between her and Billy. Since Billy gave up his vigilante ways, the two of them seem to be drifting apart lately. "Oh Billy, let me go with you. I know I said I didn't like the career you've chosen, but at least let me get out of the house for a while. I can hang out at the beach and do some shopping on South Beach while you do your thing."

This was definitely not what Billy wanted, but he feels like he's caught between a rock and a hard place, again. His little ventures out have kept him walking a tight rope with her, trying to keep the truth hidden from view. Having her with him in Florida would only complicate matters, but the last thing he wants right now is to raise her suspicions any more. "You don't really want to go down there right now, do ya? The weather is bound to be screwed up with that storm out in the Caribbean. Besides, I was planning on taking the Harley out."

"Please Billy, you don't want me thinking you're on some kind of manhunt again, do ya?" She doesn't want to push too much, knowing that it was a difficult balancing act to keep from pushing him away.

Whether she knew it or not, that was the perfect thing for her to say to him. Immediately, his paranoia causes him to second guess the hand he was playing. It is a mistake he could be making that'll have life long effects for him. "Okay baby, I don't see why not. In fact, if ya want, I can probably get you a ticket for the matches." He knows that's a total bluff. There is no match taking place. He was going all in with this gamble, counting on her distaste for Professional Wrestling to win the hand.

"That's okay, Billy boy, you know I can't watch that crap, I mean stuff, especially when it involves someone kicking the shit outta you. I'll be happy sunbathing on the beach and spending your money in the shops. Then, when you're all done, maybe we could catch a sunrise or two together, before we come home." Taylor is surprised and happy that Billy agrees to let her go with him for several reasons. First and foremost, it gives her the chance to spend a little time with the man she loves, and put her doubts and suspicions at ease about Billy's activities.

"Alright, well pack your bags and be ready to go in a couple of hours." He hangs up the phone and heads towards his truck. "Have you lost your mind? There is no way this is going to turn out any way but bad." He does his best to convince himself that he's wrong and this won't be so bad. He can keep this all straight and forward and Taylor will never know the difference. One thing was for sure; by picking Taylor up in the middle of the night, he won't have to deal with his best friend's incessant whining about going with him. For whatever reason, Scotty had developed a strong infatuation with Billy's wrestling career, wanting to tag along every chance he gets. He hates to turn him down, but Billy knows that Scotty would compromise his covert activities even more than Taylor.

Miami Florida...

Nick happily watches his class as his students perform their exercises without flaw. As they finish, the young children all come to a stop, each with their hands down by their sides, while facing their sensei. Nick needed this in the worst way tonight, for several reasons. Most importantly, he wanted something to feel positive about. After class, three young martial arts students gather around their sensei, dying to find out how the story ends. "But Sensei, you can't leave us hanging like that! You have to finish the story you started before class. At least tell us what happened to the brothers." His students clamber about him, always enjoying Nick's tales of legend and myth.

Nick laughs at their pathetic pleas. "Sorry guys, but not tonight." Nick gives a nod to the group of parents at the back of the class, as if saying he promised not to keep them late tonight. Your parents need to get you home before the storm sets in on us. I will tell you guys this much; the brothers carried their grudge to the grave, never reuniting the divided clan. Now get out of here, my dragon's waiting for me."

"Yeah right, ha-ha!"

"Good night, Sensei."

"Dragon, uh-huh, you can be such a square sometimes, Sensei."

The three boys exit the studio still saying their goodbyes to their teacher, before starting their own conversation and debate about the story Nick had told them. Their teacher walks over to the front door and says good night and thank you to the parents as they leave. He watches as they make their way down the street, bragging about what they had accomplished tonight. He locks the front door of his dojo, looks outside to check the weather, and then makes his way back into the main room to wrap up the evening. It would appear the storm clouds are moving in faster than the weatherman anticipated. While his mind compiles tonight's class and puts it to memory, Nick works quickly to wrap up his chores so he can get home before the rains set in. Finished with the front room, he turns off the lights and heads back into his office/sanctuary to wrap up the evening.

Nick walks over to his portrait of Master Masamoto. The face was stoic and serene almost regal in nature, as if he was some sort of Samurai ruler. Hiro was nothing more than a simple man of simple means, who somehow managed to carry the fate of the world upon his shoulders for decades. "Master, tonight marks the fifth anniversary of you and Meg's passing. Ya know, when I try to wrap my brain around all of this madness that you've dumped on me, I get nothing but a headache. I guess its nights like tonight when I wish you and your brother had resolved this along time ago. Is it you reaching out to me, trying to tell me something?" Nick looks at a photograph that the old man was posing in, with Nick, and his friends, Charlie, Sonny, and Jorge, on the day of Nick and Megan's wedding rehearsal. He shakes his head, remembering when the picture was taken, right after the old man bested three out of the four of the top Navy operatives, at the same time. Whenever Nick needs a laugh, he can always look at this picture and remember the surprised expressions on his friends' faces, after being put down by Masamoto. Charlie and Jorge gave up after a while, but it was Sonny who didn't know when to throw in the towel. With the talisman secured, Nick gathers his briefcase and turns out the lights.

His feelings of gloom and doom are starting to come over him again. As he reaches the front door of the dojo, a bolt of lightning crosses the sky, lighting up the street and casting eerie shadows all around. It is followed by a crack of thunder that actually makes Nick jump, as several raindrops hit the glass of the front door. The storm has arrived, signaling Nick to quickly lock up and get to his car before the clouds unleash their fury. He climbs into his vintage Mustang convertible parked in front, just in time as the rain starts falling by the buckets full. He says a quick thank you prayer for his roof being up, unlike last time, when he was caught unaware and the storm flooded the car. Again, the idea of a break comes to mind, giving him reason to believe that maybe it deserves serious consideration. For the past five years, Nickolas has loaded his life up with so many different projects and activities, so that he didn't have time to think about his losses. Perhaps his anxiety is a byproduct of being simply burnt out. Shouldn't the Guardian deserve a break every once in a while? He suspects that Sonny might be plotting something for tomorrow night. Saturday he can meet with JD and give him his final test ceremony, and that should clear up his calendar. A simple phone call or two can reschedule next week's classes. There is potential here in this line of thought that could be proactive in restoring his sanity.

His drive home is brief but the rains chase him all the way. By the time he pulls into the drive, the storm's full rage is taking place in Nick's front yard. This is the one time when he would love to park in the dry surroundings of his garage, but as usual, his roommate's car is parked in the driveway, right in front of the garage door. He shakes his head and gives a defiant look to the sky, before climbing out of the car into the deluge of water falling from the ominous cloud cover. Nick hurries, but his haste causes him to get his briefcase hung up in the seatbelt, delaying his flight to the dry conditions of his home. Free of the car, he rushes to the covered porch, but is soaking wet by the time he reaches the front door. There he is greeted by his roommate, Sonya Richards, who was about to close the front door in Nick's face. "Hey, hold on there, Sonny. I'm coming in right behind you."

Sonny jumps, being spooked by Nick's sudden appearance. "Hey Nickels, I didn't hear you comin' up." She gives him the once over and then shakes her head. "I was just about to hit the hot tub. I'd ask if you want to join me, but it looks like you've already been swimmin'." She turns away as if not caring about his reply and starts to strip down before heading out onto the covered patio in the back yard.

Nick follows her out to the back yard with him stopping at the back door, ready and willing to discuss the parking arrangements one more time. "Yeah, well if you hadn't parked in front of the garage, I could have parked the Mustang in there, and not have to worry about wringing out my clothes." He stands there for a moment as she walks up the steps of the hot tub. He knows that she has some kind of snappy remark that would remove the blame from her. He just wants to hear what it is this time."

"You never park that wannabe hotrod in the garage. Besides, it was starting to rain. Do you really think I wanted to park on the street so I could end up looking like you? Sometimes Nickels, it's hard for a lady to read your so-called code of chivalry. There's too much small print." Sonny grabs a towel from the stack on the side of the hot tub and throws one at Nick, standing in the doorway. "Dry yourself off, Nicky. You're dripping on that expensive hardwood floor you're always bitching at me about."

"Don't you think you should at least put on a swimsuit?"

Nick tosses the towel back at her, hoping a little modesty would hit her and stick.

"Naw, the water's warm enough for my taste. Besides, there ain't nobody worth a damn around here to worry about seeing anything, any way." Sonny slowly, seductively, climbs down into the churning waters and lies back against the side of the tub. She closes her eyes and takes a deep breath. "Truth be known, Nickels, I had to go down to the parole office and pee for Perkins, again. Somehow, my test cup from last week was misplaced. I swear, sometimes I think that guy is spying on me, watching me dribble into a cup, when I'm in there." Sonny turns her head to face Nick but never opens her eyes. "You really ought to think about using this thing every once in a while. It might loosen you up and keep you from acting like a tight ass all the time."

Nick smiles at her actions and laughs at her comment. He remembers back to a time when there was a chance for the two of them to be more than friends. That seems like it was a lifetime ago, before her discharge from the Navy, and imprisonment for assaulting her superior Officer. Nick stood beside her through the whole trial, but in the end, the courts found her guilty and carried out the sentencing. It was during Sonny's imprisonment when Megan returned to Nick's life, setting in motion a chain of events that would lead him to this day. When Sonny was released, there was only room in Nick's life for her as a friend, the best of friends. The thought of Megan brings sadness to his heart for a moment. He turns away from Sonny and heads back through the house to his private sanctum. Here in his own little world, Nick pulls the talisman from inside his shirt and hangs it around the neck of a dragon, identical to the one at his dojo, only this one sits atop a granite base about four feet tall. There are only three things that make the dragon statues significant. Nick was born under the sign of the dragon, according to the Chinese calendar. The second is the nickname his sensei had given him, upon Nick passing his last and most important test. The third is that the pair of statues was a wedding gift from his best friend, Charlie Steiner. Nick lays his hand against a small panel, causing the statue to lower down into the base to be concealed from view.

"Hey Nickels," Sonny taps at the open door. "I've got a couple of tickets to a benefit concert at some ritzy nightclub down on South Beach. You wanna go with me? It starts at seven o'clock, tomorrow night."

Nick spins around, surprised that his roommate had gotten the drop on him. "What is it?" There was Sonny, standing in his doorway, wrapped in her towel but still dripping water all over his expensive hardwood floor. "Yeah, sure, but on one condition; you go put some clothes on and dry up my floor." Wasn't she the one who was making a big deal about water on the flooring, just a little while ago? To pacify her roommate, and to be a little devious, Sonny lets her towel fall to the floor where she uses her foot to dry up the liquid on the expensive hardwood planks. Then, just to tick him off, she kicks it up with her foot, landing the damp towel on Nick's head.

Sonny laughs at Nick trying to pull it from around his head, before leaving to go to her room to do as he asked, but calls back down the hall, "one condition though, you have to go jogging in the morning with me. The wet sand from the storm tonight will really give us a good workout." She flirts with him even more by flexing her calves to show off her muscle tone.

Nick steps out into the hall as she reaches the doorway to her room. "Ya know, if you hadn't violated your parole by putting those bouncers in the hospital, you could go without needing a chaperone."

"Yeah, and if the one guy hadn't copped a feel, the other

guys wouldn't have jumped in, because I wouldn't have had a reason to kick the first guy's ass, in the first place!" Sonny takes to the defensive, not liking the course of this conversation. Nick had struck a nerve and it was showing on her face. "Remember Nickels, you were the one who stood up in court and said the bouncers were the ones who provoked the incident in the first place, so drop the holier than thou shit, okay?"

Nick just stares at her for a second wishing he could punch her in her hard head, if for nothing else to knock some sense into her." Ya know, defending yourself is one thing, but when you put five guys in the hospital, two of them in ICU, there isn't anyone in their right mind that wouldn't look at it as excessive."

"Cut to the chase, Nickels, are ya going jogging with me tomorrow, or am I going to be forced to hang around here all day while you bore my ass with another one of your pacifist philosophy lectures?" Sonny gives Nick a half cocked smile, as if she was challenging him to more verbal banter. It's not really her fault. Nick just makes it too easy for her to bust his chops every chance she gets. It isn't that she doesn't appreciate all that he has done for her, or is ungrateful for the friendship. This is just Sonny's way of showing her love for him.

"Whatever, ya freak. I'll see ya in the morning. I have to get all of this work done tonight, or I won't be doing anything tomorrow, until it is done." Nick waves good night to her and returns to his mountain of paperwork on his desk. It takes him a moment to gather his thoughts. He wishes that Sonny could turn her head around and face life head on. The thought of her playing the role of the poor victim of society never sits well with him. She's better than that and capable of a whole lot more, if she would just try once in a while. Still, he holds a love in his heart for her, and because of that he'll never turn his back on her. Nor could he ever give up on her. Nick's invested too much time now to turn the page on her. He stares at the stack of papers for a few more minutes before convincing himself that it could wait until Sunday. He turns off the light and opens the bedroom window. With the sound of the falling rain playing a lullaby, he lies down on his bed and closes his eyes. If his day is starting with Sonny and ending with Sonny, there's no telling what could happen in between. Whatever it is, Nick's going to need all the rest he can get.

# Chapter V

Billy could use a little rest right about now. After his little escapade last night in Atlanta, he drove for two hours to pick up Taylor, and then another ten hours to Miami while Taylor slept. It may sound like a hard task to do on the back of a Harley Davidson motorcycle, but the boredom always seemed to put Taylor to sleep. So, to avoid her falling off, Billy fastened a makeshift seat belt to the backrest. Of course, she was rested and ready to go sightseeing when they arrived, so she drug Billy all over South Beach. He had an opportunity to get a little sleep while Taylor was turning heads on the beach, but instead he used the time to plan and plot the night's activities. With his father's laptop computer and software he confiscated from Walter's apartment, Billy set out to find the owner of the delivery truck from last night. He was amazed at how quick he is able to hack into the Florida DMV's mainframe. Scoring a lead in the form of a business name and address, Billy actually had the chance to take a little time to relax before setting out tonight. That was earlier this afternoon. For the passed two hours, he has sat on his motorcycle wondering if this long shot lead is going to pay off. The place across the street is a dump, making Billy wonder if he was on the wrong trail. After all, this place doesn't look like a drug refinery. As far as he knows, the two mules back in Atlanta could have stolen the van to haul the chemicals out of Florida. Still, it's all that he's got, so he might as well follow it through.

Easing back against the back rest of his motorcycle Billy uses his trench coat to shed the rain, while he passes the time recounting the changes that have taken place in his life. He is now officially lost to his thirst for vengeance again. His mind convinces him that he is doing the right thing by coming to Florida, to hunt down his target. He himself is the one who woke this sleeping giant that controls his thoughts and actions. In the end, he will be forced to stand alone for what he has done.

"It sure seems to rain a lot, no matter where I go." Billy leans his head forward slightly to drain off the rain that has collected on the brim of his cowboy hat. Through the thin curtain of water he can see the headlights of three cars and a truck heading towards him. He isn't worried about being spotted, with his bike hidden off the side of the road amongst the sweet deals of a used car lot. The vehicles pull up to the business across the street and then park in the vacant lot next door. According to the identity sign in front, the business was some kind of gravel and landscaping Delivery Company, which seemed a little odd based on the social type of the men exiting the vehicles. Billy was certain of one thing; these guys weren't here to load up a truck, or anything else pertaining to this business.

He waits for them to enter the building through the side access before he makes his move. His actions are fluid and precise as he quickly retrieves a small case from his motorcycle saddlebags. Inside it is a set of antiquated technology from his father's early years with the bureau. It was useful enough for his father to tail Billy during his teenage years, and more than appropriate for Taylor to track Billy down in Atlanta, so it should be more than adequate for Billy's purposes. He collects the four tracking sensors from their foam restraints and heads on off across the street. Darting through the shadows, he makes his way around the cars and truck magnetically attaching a sensor to each. After checking his surroundings, Billy then makes his way over to the building and down the side until he comes to a window. Inside, he could see the gathering criminal element that seemed to be waiting for someone else to show up. Billy watches them for several seconds trying to identify what sort of threat they might impose. It doesn't take him long at all to come to a conclusion. "Geez, this is the group Callistone is supposed to be meeting? With clowns like this in his organization, my job will be easier than I thought."

"Ya think so?" The voice comes from behind Billy warning him that he had dropped his guard, but before the rebel vigilante can turn around, he is laid out by the destructive force of an ax handle hitting him across the back and shoulders. The attacker stands ready and watches as Billy crumbles to the ground in a heap. Not ready to declare victory just yet, the man pokes at Billy's lifeless body with the end of the ax handle just to be sure Billy was out. Satisfied that his prey was unconscious, the attacker grabs Billy by his arm and drags him into the building. "Look at this, ya bums! And to think you guys doubted me and my decisions." Calvin Brewster drops Billy at the feet of his associates to prove his point. "Already our reputation is growing with our association with Callistone's organization." Brewster nudges Billy with the toe of his boot, rolling Billy over to reveal his mask and costume concealed under his trench coat. "Does anybody recognize him? This is the guy who killed Callistone's son." Brewster smacks himself in the chest with his closed fist and then points at his men as if he was proud of his accomplishment. "I'm telling you boys, handing this guy over to Callistone tomorrow night will give us the clout we're looking for to rank us high in the new regime here in Florida!" The men begin to cheer, laugh, and high five each other as delusion of grandeur rush through their minds. "Alright, alright, let's settle down and get to business. Where's my little darling Trixie at? Mike, I thought I told you keep an eye on her."

Mike Stringer shakes his head at his boss. "Dude, she's passed out in the bathroom over there, hugging the toilet like it was the only thing keeping her alive. I still say you gave her too much smack last night."

Brewster stands up and walks over to Stringer as if he was unhappy with his lieutenant's response. "Is she still here?"

"Well yeah, I said she's in the bathroom passed out."

"So then, you're saying she's not dead?"

"Yeah boss, she's still alive."

Brewster smiles and pats Stringer on his chest. "Then I guess I gave her just enough, didn't I?" Brewster motions for his men to close in and pay attention. Alright you guys, if you're all in on this, I want one thing perfectly clear. You screw up on this job in the slightest; I will shoot you myself and leave you for the vultures. That little tart in there has filled me in on a very important event. It is the one that will make us all wealthy men beyond our wildest dreams." Brewster lights a cigarette and blows the smoke at Billy just because. "I was down at this club, right on the Biscayne Bay, when I met the little hottie serving drinks in the place. Come to find out, she had a taste for the candy, and knew all about the club's security system. Intrigued by her topic of conversation, the two of us hit it off and spent the rest of the night getting her 'high' as hell, while she spilled her guts to me about the club. Evidently, she and the manager/ owner of the night club had a falling out and she would love to see somebody give the guy what he deserves. We are her prayers answered, gentlemen. We are going to give the owner of the club his side of karma."

Stringer points at Billy. "What about this guy?"

"We tie him up and bag him for safe keeping, go do this job at the club, and then hand over Prince Charming to Callistone. We'll be set for life!" Brewster nods his head smiling at his men assuring them of their potential success.

"That's not as great, or easy as you make it sound, tough guy." Billy uses the moment of distraction to spring to his feet and take a strong defensive stance within the circle of criminal minds. Right about now, his rage is reaching its boiling point, due to his self directed anger for letting Brewster get the jump on Billy outside. "In fact, it's the next to last thing you really want to do." Billy was unsure how long he was out, but his mask was still in place and he wasn't bleeding profusely from any new holes in his body.

Brewster is almost nonchalant as he faces Billy. "Okay wise ass, what's the last thing then?" Brewster asks while drawing down on Billy with his pistol.

Billy offers a sinister smile for the question, "To be the recipient of this!" Billy fires an energy blast from his hand that melts the pistol in Brewster's hand. He turns to face two men who jump at the chance to take on Billy, but the true attack comes from behind him. Two others tackle Billy to the floor and with a few well placed blows, his attackers have Billy doubled over and gasping for air. With a few more blows aimed at his head, Billy suddenly finds it hard to stay focused. How has this happened? He had thought this through, over and over, making sure he had it all figured out. Has his arrogance and overconfidence brought him to this point. Billy always thought that if he ever lost the fight, it would've been done somewhere in Atlanta against one of Callistone's top men, not some street thugs in Miami.

"What's wrong Mr. Rebel? Did ya forget you're not in Atlanta anymore?" Brewster motions for his boys to inflict more pain on their uninvited guest. "This is Miami, man! Everything is bigger, better, and stronger here." He snaps his fingers, calling his boys off as he walks over to Billy, wrapping a wet towel around his injured hand. To avoid showing injury, Billy never looks up at his opponent. He tries hard not to show the extent of his pain, but some things are easier said than done. Brewster grabs Billy by the head and forces him to look up at his assailants, who had just given him the rapid pummeling. "You see these guys? They are some of those MMA fighters. Problem is they are such mean bad asses, that no one will give them a match to fight. So I hired them to be my muscle. Look at them; have you ever seen or faced anyone who looked that mean? Not to boast, but I think it's safe to say that you have never seen the likes of my boys anywhere on the streets of Atlanta."

Rocko, Chain, Moose and Tank, have to be four of the roughest, toughest, opponents Billy has ever faced, on the street, or in the ring. Tank, and Moose, both fit their nicknames, being massive in size and strength. Chain, is, well, known for the heavy gauge linked chain hanging around his neck, connected by a large padlock. Oh, his reputation stems from using the chain to beat his opponents down. Usually, it was after he had lost a match, and that is what got him kicked out of MMA. Rocko is nothing more than a New York street thug who tried to use the MMA as a way to vent his overwhelming desire for violence. He left New York to avoid imprisonment for beating his girlfriend, and has been on the run ever since. A motley foursome to say the least, but they serve Brewster's needs perfectly. Brewster motions for his hired muscle to pick Billy up and take him out back. Then, he and the rest of his entourage make their way outside to watch the upcoming brawl unfold.

Two of the fighters grab Billy by his arms and drag him through the building to the truck yard out back. They toss him from the loading dock onto the muddy ground below. Billy doesn't resist during any of this. Instead, he uses the time to assess his injuries. There may be a cracked rib or two, but he doesn't believe anything else is broken, except maybe his nose. For a split second, Taylor crosses his mind as he wonders how he would explain a broken nose. He had told her that he was just at the wrestling event for show, and that he wouldn't actually be participating in a match. It was all part of the script and he was going to get paid well, or so he told Taylor. A mental note is made by him not to be so extravagant with his lies from now on. Then, Taylor is gone from his mind as the four fighters join him on the ground below. Able to catch his breath, Billy's ready to face these guys on his own terms. He rolls over just in time to see the first fighter moving in on him. Billy simply draws on his energy stores and unloads a blast that sends the thug flying back over by his friends in a blaze of glory. There's no way Billy is going to wait for the next opponent to step up. Instead, he scrambles to his feet and does his best to make a stand against them. Two more are blasted from their stance by another of Billy's energy blasts, but the strength of the impact only knocks these two to the ground. After everything he's done, and all that he's gone through, he still hasn't learned to control and regulate his energy stores. If he doesn't end this soon, his energy stores will be depleted, leaving him defenseless against these odds. He turns to face the rest but, is surprised to see the gangster wannabes are running away from the fight, instead of towards Billy. It is then that he realizes what they're running from. "It's not me scaring them off. It's the fuel…" The opponent that Billy had blown across the yard had landed under a leaky fuel storage tank and had caught the residual fuel on the ground afire. The man fights for his life trying to extinguish the flames on his clothes, but all he does is spread the fire around more, knocking over barrels and spilling the flammable liquid. By the time the man had succeeded, he had already suffered severe burns on his hands and arms, but didn't seem to acknowledge the pain. What surprises Billy about the scene is the fighter's desire for retribution for what Billy had done to him, only to be forced into a retreat with the rest of his associates. Billy turns to run as well, but it's too late for him, when the main tank erupts with a ferocity that sends him flying through the air, with the explosion carries Billy over the fence of the truck yard and into a nearby canal. Billy's impact with the water does two things. One, it extinguishes the flames burning on his coat and costume. This is a good thing and is appreciated to say the least. The second however is something he could have done without, as two nearby gators are stirred by Billy thrashing about. Startled by the appearance of the two beasts, he charges the water with his energy to encourage them to look for their meals somewhere else.

Winded, Billy makes it to the water's edge and crawls up onto the muddy bank of the canal. The fire has spread to most of the truck yard, engulfing the vehicles and barrels stored in the back lot. Over towards the front of the business, Billy can see Brewster and his men, but has a hard time hearing what they were saying over the roar of the fire and exploding trucks.

Brewster shoves one of his men out of his way, as he tries to reach a safe distance from the inferno." I want all of you to clear out of here as fast as possible, and keep this quiet. I don't want anyone to spoil this meeting with Callistone. He doesn't have to know about any of this, got it?" Brewster looks back at the inferno and shakes his head.

"Sorry about the business, boss, but what about the girl?"

"Is she still in there?" Brewster asks, sounding as if he could care less about the answer.

Stringer looks at the building and nods. "I think so, boss. At least, I never saw her come out."

"Sucks to be her then, doesn't it? What about that crazy ass rebel vigilante? Did anybody see him come out of there?" Brewster's men all shake their heads no, while asking each other what they saw. He's angry, disappointed, and even a little nervous about tonight's turn of events. "Good, then consider this issue a dead subject. Let's blow this place before the law shows up." Brewster points up at the night sky at the approaching helicopter. "All of you get out of here, now! That chopper will be here in a few minutes.

Brewster starts for his car as Stringer hurries to catch up with his boss. "What do we do about this place, boss?" He asks, climbing into the back seat with Brewster. "How do we cover up what happened when the law comes nosing around."

"What, the building? Oh, don't sweat that. It belonged to my silent partner. I actually had no legal ties to it whatsoever." Brewster motions for the driver to take off.

"Boy I bet he's gonna be pissed when he finds out."

Calvin Brewster laughs and then slaps Stringer across his chest. "Don't go losing any sleep over it, friend. He's been dead for two weeks. That's what makes him a silent partner." Brewster taps the driver on the shoulder to signal him to pull over next to Brewster's hired muscle. "Keep these gorillas out of trouble, Rocko. Everybody has to be sharp for tomorrow's big haul. Now get your asses' outta here before the cops have you in a line up." Brewster's car pulls away from the scene as his hired muscle climb into their truck to flee.

Billy kneels at the edge of the canal as the fires from the building light up the night sky. He has no choice but to wait for them to leave before he makes his way over to his bike. If he is seen leaving the area, his targets will slip away or at least be made aware of his pursuit. So, Billy waits impatiently until all four vehicles disappear down the road before he heads for his bike. As he passes the front of the building, something catches his attention out of the corner of his eye causing Billy to look back at the building. There in the front of the interior is the young woman, who was passed out in the restroom. Awakening to find herself in the center of hell sends her off in a maniacal drug induced panic, begging and pleading for help. Billy shakes his head at his choice of action, knowing it will only delay him even more. He motions for the girl to back up and then charges both hands with energy to release it on the storefront glassworks. Before the girl can see what was happening, Billy has already charged in to scoop her up, and whisk her outside just as the roof collapses into the inferno. As he runs across the street, he can't help but see the red hair in his face, and the dragon tattoo on her neck. The dragon doesn't mean anything to him, but the girl's red hair, even though it's a different tone of color, and a lot shorter, it still reminds him of Taylor.

With the girl at a safe distance, Billy sets her down on the other side of the street and makes for his bike. "I have to assume that you don't want or need attention from the emergency crews. Those bastards left you to die in there. I'd cut my losses, and connections, with them if I were you, or next time, there might not be anyone around to pull your butt outta there. Above the fire, circles a news chopper that records the event unfolding below. Billy is either ignoring its presence or oblivious to the fact that it's above him, as he rushes over and disappears under the trees across the street. He grabs the receiver from the storage case and switches it on, hoping to get a pinpoint on the vehicles' locations. To his disappointment, only two signals are being picked up from the four tracking sensors, and one of those is lying across the street in a mud puddle. "Well, I guess one is better than none." He jumps on the motorcycle and brings the iron beast to life. With the motorcycle pointing in the direction of the signal coming in, Billy takes off hoping that he was on the trail of the leader's car. If nothing else, Billy felt that he still had a score to settle with that guy. At least he did learn that Callistone was either still in town or hasn't arrived yet. Either way Billy still has a chance to exact his revenge.

It only takes a few minutes before he catches up to the fleeing vehicles. He knows that his presence behind them could be spotted right away due to the fact that there was no other traffic for miles, so he holds back just keeping their taillights in view. One by one the vehicles split off leaving Billy following the one lone tracking signal that was coming through loud and clear. Now his tailing of the vehicle must be done from around the block, and parallel streets to avoid being detected. Unfortunately for Billy, it is well into the early morning hours before the vehicle being tailed finally stops for the night. Billy is exhausted and in need of some rest, but his mind is only focused on one thing, getting to Callistone. He hasn't heard his phone ring, or chose to ignore it. He doesn't think about his injuries or even the consequences of his recent actions. No, there is a monster inside of Billy that has been forced to lay dormant for the passed few months, and now it has awakened. Until it can be put down again, Billy is lost to rational thought and cares about nothing except making that happen. His reasoning, morality, and desires have all been consumed by this beast within, that has started this perpetual spiral downward into darkness where Billy truly deep down doesn't want to be.

The vehicle he was following was the truck that belonged to Brewster's hired muscle, the MMA fighters. Its final destination is a parking lot of a weekly apartment rental complex. It and its surroundings seemed to suit these four hoodlums and their low rent lifestyles. Part of him wants nothing more than to rush over there and take them apart, right now and end their possible threat once and for all. The intelligent mind of the beast knows that they are but the means to lead him to his true prey. For now, he will just monitor their actions and wait for them to make their next move, when they meet up with the rest of their group tomorrow. He was unfortunate to be unconscious during the planning of their heist, but Billy figures he will find out what they were going to do soon enough. He parks his motorcycle across the street in a grocery store parking lot, leaving his bike close to the store for security, while he makes his way over to the cover of the landscaping near the road. From there, he can watch for his pigeons and stay as dry as possible until they fly the coop. Within seconds, Billy concedes to the needs of his body, being rest and healing.

Unfortunately for Billy, this rest that he needs, will be short lived. His cell phone rings out from its hiding place breaking the silence of the night, but not loud enough to wake Billy up. Again it is Taylor trying to find out where he is and if he's alright. Again she won't receive an answer to put her mind at ease. His body is in full healing mode at the moment and he is oblivious to the entire world around him. He doesn't hear the phone ring again, as Taylor tries back a fourth time. He doesn't hear the footsteps of three men walking towards him. If Taylor hadn't called back, they would have walked on passed never knowing Billy was there.

"Hey Rocko, do you believe this shit? It's that guy who torched Moose!" Kyle Dantzer, better known as Chain grabs Billy by the collar of his coat and snatches him out from under the bushes. The act wakes Billy abruptly, sending his mind off swimming in confusion and chaos. The thugs were simply making their way to the all night super mart for a midnight snack, at three in the morning. All three commence to beating Billy senseless, before he could figure out what was going on. In a matter of minutes, he is broken up, bloodied and bruised. So much so that his facial features are now indistinguishable.

Rocko grabs Billy by his blood soaked hair and drives his fist into Billy's face one more time. "That was for burning Moose!" He exclaims as he gives Billy a final kick to the ribs. "That's for being stupid enough to come back for more. Pick him up guys and let's take him back to the apartment. I want to make sure that this guy stays put so we can personally deliver him to Mr. Callistone ourselves. We'll be able to sidestep Brewster and possibly earn a spot in Callistone's own organization."

Tank is surprised by Rocko's statement. "Hold on there a second, Rocko. Do you really think we should be plotting against our boss, before we have the chance to do this first job with him? Besides, this guy took what we gave him, blew up in the explosion, and still found us here. Maybe we should just do him now and hand over the body."

"Naw Tank, handing him over alive is all for extra credit. Word has it that this guy tossed Callistone's son off of a high rise in Atlanta. Think about the gold stars we can earn if Callistone has the opportunity to do this guy personally." It doesn't take long at all before greed has the three men in agreement. Chain and Tank drag Billy towards the street while Rocko walks ahead of the others to make sure their path is uncompromised. Rocko doesn't have a plan devised yet, until he walks passed a carpenter's truck. Lying in the truck bed was a hammer and a bag of long nails that are usually used for hanging rain gutters on the side of a house. He grabs the bag of nails and hammer and hurries up the stairs motioning for his two friends to move faster.

Once inside the apartment, Rocko kicks the coffee table out from under Moose's feet, sending it sliding across the floor. Moose wakes up, angered by Rocko's carelessness. "Dude, what the hell are you doing?" In his condition, Moose doesn't appreciate his buddy's rough treatment. Of course, his anger subsides when Moose sees Billy being carried in by Tank and Chain. In fact the large man begins to smile as he thinks of ways to exact his revenge. Rocko moves back over to the door once his cohorts enter the room, and checks the balcony walkway to make sure no one had seen anything. Then he quickly pops back inside the apartment and closes the door, motioning for his friends to lay Billy in the middle of the floor.

Tank grabs Billy's arm and stretches it out away from Billy's body, pinning it to the floor under the weight of his knee. The fighter known as Chain does the same with Billy's other arm and readies to stake Billy to the floor. Rocko just stands back with a sadistic grin on his face as he hands the hammer and nail to Chain. He too is a little sadistic, enjoying what he was about to do. He places the point of the large nail against the palm of Billy's hand and draws back the hammer to drive the nail home. With one hard swing, the nail pushes its way through Billy's hand embedding itself into the floor. "One shot did it. Let's see if you can top that, Tank." Blood starts to pool up around the head of the nail, but there is no acknowledgement from Billy.

Tank takes the hammer from Chain and a nail from Rocko, but just can't bring himself to do the deed. "One of you guys are gonna have to do this. I can't do it, that's for sure."

Rocko snatches the hammer and nail from Tank and waves him away. "Get out of here, ya big sissy. I'll show you how it supposed to be done." Rocko steps on Billy's wrist and shoves the point of the nail against Billy's other palm. He plans to administer a lot of pain with his actions, wanting to take all the time in the world to drive the nail home. His first swing of the hammer hits the nail, causing it to barely penetrate Billy's skin, but the rebel vigilante does flinch this time. Rocko hits the nail five or six more times before sinking it into the floor. It was as if he was aggravated that he didn't get any more of a rise out of Billy, but there is still no sign of Billy regaining consciousness, much less any signs of pain or agony.

"Dude, what are you going to do about his legs? These nails ain't long enough to stick to the floor."

Rocko looks at the situation and then looks around the room. Without any hesitation, he hurries over to the corner of what should be the dining area, and grabs to of the largest dumbbells beside the weight bench. "Tank, get over here and grab these two fifties. I've got the sixty fives." Rocko carries the weights back over to the unconscious Billy and drops a dumbbell across each of Billy's ankles. Tank walks over and does the same, pinning both of Billy's legs to the floor with over a hundred pounds for each. "There, now I would like to see him get out of that! Come on, boys and let's go clean up and really go get something to eat. We've got reason to celebrate, and I've worked up an appetite!"

Across the street, Billy's cell phone rings again in the bushes of the super mart. Again and again Taylor keeps trying, hoping that Billy would just answer the phone. She knows that something is wrong, but alone in a strange city; she has no idea what to do, or where to do it.

"Let's go sleepy head. It's five o'clock and time to rise and shine." Sonny pauses for a minute and thinks about what she just said. "Better yet, let's make that rise and run." She snatches the sheets and blankets off of Nick and is surprised with what she sees. "Jesus Nick, do you take that thing everywhere you go? Although, I guess you do look kinda cute holding it like it's your teddy bear."

Nick sits up, unwrapping the chain from around his wrist, and hangs the talisman around his neck. "Ya know Sonny, one of these days, I'm gonna…" He doesn't bother to finish his threat since Sonny just turns away and walks to the door. She stops and looks back to blow him a kiss before slapping her hand against her bare butt cheek, visible below the hem of her T-shirt. "I'll be ready in less than ten minutes, Nicky boy. Will you be ready, to get your ass handed to you again, Ha, Ha, Ha, Ha!"

Nick climbs out of bed and grabs a shirt and pair of shorts from the dresser drawer and sits back down on the edge of the bed. Despite his rude awakening, Nick was actually looking forward to spending the morning with Sonny, today. They haven't had much time together lately, and he is ready for a good workout. Sonny always had a way of pushing him to his limits, but in a good way most of the time. After dressing, he turns around to find Sonny standing right behind him. "Whoa, you know what? One day I'm gonna drop you like a bad habit, sneaking up on me like that!"

"Not on your best day, buddy ol' pal. Are you ready to go?" Sonny looks around the room for Nick's running shoes. "Oh, and I called my parole officer and told him we were going jogging this morning. Boy, he's sure pissed at you." Sonny looks at Nick's bare feet. "Where are your shoes?"

Nick's head spins around with a surprised look on his face. "And just why would he be pissed at me about, Sonya?"

"Because, I told him you were supposed to call him yesterday, instead of me at five o'clock on a Saturday morning. That's why he's pissed at you, ya puss." Sonny walks over and picks up Nick's shoes and hands them to him. "Don't you want these?"

"No, what I want to know is why you told him a line of bullshit like that?" Nick tosses the shoes back over against the wall and looks back to Sonny for her answer.

"Listen, it's no top secret that the guy respects you for your history and standing with the community." Sonny proceeds to imitate her parole officer giving Nick accolades for his good works.

"Oh knock it off. Listen to me, one day you are gonna cross that line with that kinda stuff, and there won't be anything my reputation can do to stop the inevitable."

"Yeah, whatever, are you ready, barefoot Bob?" Sonny doesn't wait for Nick to answer. Instead, she takes off jogging out of the house and down the street. It doesn't take Nick long to realize that this could wind up being a very long day. They reach the beach just in time to catch the sunrise on the horizon. "Keep up if you can." Sonny takes off running down the beach resembling a fugitive during a prison break, as if she was running for her life. Nick laughs at the thought and then takes off after her setting his own pace. Part of him feels sorry for her and her situation. The house arrest seems to be harder on her than being locked up behind bars. At least in prison she couldn't look out the window to see life taunting her as it passes by. During rare moments like this, she is able to feel the sensation of freedom on her face, like a wild mustang roaming the free range. Sonny's not a bad person, or somebody who looks for trouble. She's really just somebody who suffers from bad timing. Sometimes, he thinks that he is the only person in this world who would truly understand her.

Billy opens his eyes and gasps for air. The blood in his mouth and throat has now dried, blocking his airway causing him to cough and gag. Once he is able to take life giving oxygen into his lungs again, the pain of it all is almost too much to bear. Dazed and confused, he looks around at his surroundings hoping to figure out where he was, and what happened to put him here. It's at this time that the feeling was starting to return to his arms and legs, as the nail holes begin to throb and ache. His mind focuses on these two injuries alone, deducing that they were the cause of his limited movement. Billy looks at his left hand and grimaces seeing the nail head sticking up a half inch out of his palm. As if he didn't believe what he saw, Billy tries to move his hand but the instant he does, pain shoots up his arm and straight into the center of his brain. Feeling neglected, the rest of his wounds start revealing their measure of damage to his consciousness. The first thing he needs to do is control his breathing. That will reduce some of his agony so he can focus on escaping the spikes that hold him down. The slightest movement, and he can feel the entire length of metal reopen the wound in his hand, spilling his precious blood onto the floor again. Billy closes his eyes and starts to take a long deep breath. With his lungs holding all the air possible, he grits his teeth, holds his breath, and shoves his arm outward with the nail offering temporary resistance. The pain is agonizing taking Billy to his threshold, before he finally feels the nail give a little. After a few short breaths to calm him self down, he looks over at his hand and sees the nail is now tilted away from him. With clenched teeth, he quickly pulls his arm towards his body. The nail gives a little more leaning towards Billy, but he doesn't stop there. Letting out a blood curdling scream, he shoves his arm outward again until the head of the nail is pulling against his palm. Then, it concedes to his efforts and releases its hold in the in the concrete floor. Billy slowly moves his wounded limb back towards his body until it falls across his chest. Never in his life can he remember ever feeling such excruciating pain. He holds his hand up to examine the wound, but the thought of being able to see through it is enough to make him pass out again.

"So, what are we going to do for the rest of the day?"

Sonny asks, as she reaches the front door. Without any consideration of onlookers, she begins to strip down out of her sweaty clothes right there on the front porch while Nick unlocks the door.

"Oh, I don't know, maybe we could find you some modesty somewhere." Nick lets her enter the house first to avoid any further embarrassment with his neighbors. To repay his gesture, Sonny flips her shorts off of her ankle, hitting Nick in his chest with them as she enters the house. "Good luck with that one, Sport. I'm hitting the Jacuzzi to unwind. Are you coming in?" Sonny turns around just in time to see Nick throwing her shorts back at her.

"Naw, I need to get down to the dojo. There's a whole list of kids who are testing for rank today." Nick stops in his tracks and turns to head for his room. There was no need to follow her any further. If he did, it would just turn into another one of their verbal sparring sessions, and a waste of time. Unfortunately for him, this time the sparring session follows to seek him out.

"What are you talking about, Nickels? You know that you have plans with me this afternoon! Don't stand me up tonight, Nickels, for a bunch of snot noses who want to learn to break boards." Sonny turns away from the doorway, giving Nick her version of the cold shoulder. "Remember Nickels, you promised, and pals come first."

"Don't sweat it kid. You know that you'll always be my top priority." He watches her disappear down the hall. "Keeping you out of trouble, that is." He says to himself, knowing full well that she couldn't hear him. Still, if she was trying to give him a guilty conscience, it worked. It's that bleeding heart side of him that always caves in to her needs. He's always justified it to himself by the fact that she has saved his life too many times to count. When he agreed to go to the concert with her, he neglected to remember the class tests today. One thing is for certain, he wants to go to this concert for several reasons. He could use a night out to keep his mind off of the little anniversary that has come around again, to give him his yearly dose of pain and loss. Most importantly, by taking Sonny out this morning and tonight will get him off the hook for at least two or three weeks. There was still enough time left in the morning for him to get the testing over and get back to Sonny before her temper erupts. Nick just has to pay attention to the clock and monitor his time.

He walks to the bathroom and starts his shower. Standing in front of the vanity, Nick stares at his reflection in the mirror as the glass begins to fog up. There have been more twists and turns in this man's life, than a mile stretch of Mulholland Drive. He has always been a crusader for the needy. His biggest problem is that he never knows when to quit, or throw in the towel. Over the passed few years he has become more and more aware of the burdens he bears. His cell phone rings breaking his train of thought. Instead of answering it, Nick just lets it ring and continues to stare at the mirror. With the steam from the shower fogging up the glass, He gives his reflection a nod and opens the door to the shower stall. The warm waters attack his aching muscles and force them to relax. He's got two hours to kill before his students arrive at his studio, and Sonny hasn't used up all the hot water for her shower, which means Nick has a rare opportunity to enjoy this for a chance.

# Chapter VI

Billy awakens to the throbbing pain of his wounded hands. He takes a slow deep breath and examines his other wounds from the inside out, taking note to the severity of pain from each location on his body. It would appear that his broken ribs and internal injuries have healed at least enough to where he can breathe, without feeling like the act was going to kill him. His right hand aches from the puncture, but has healed enough to seal the wound. His left hand however still seeps blood from around the nail head that is still sticking out of his palm. With his mind clearing, Billy summons his energy and focuses it to his left hand. Immediately, the nail is disintegrated, freeing his wounded limb and sealing the wound at the same time. Anxious to be free from the floor, Billy tries to stand, only to quickly sit back down. His mind may be ready, but it's obvious that his body is not a willing participant yet.

How could he have been so stupid? Has his arrogance grown so much that he perceived himself to be invincible? The thoughts and questions racing through his mind start a fire burning under the simmering anger and rage inside of him. Barbara told him once that his arrogant, "I can do anything" attitude, was going to get him killed. The thought of her saying, "I told you so," fuels the fire inside. And to top it all off, there's Taylor to think about. What is he going to tell her? Last night wasn't supposed to happen. Part of him can't believe he lost total control the way he did. The other part chooses to deny the truth. The time has come for him to quit lying to himself. The whole reason he came to Florida was for Callistone. What part of his screwed up brain thought it was a good idea to bring Taylor along to begin with? "Oh yeah, bringing her with me could erase her doubts about my activities! How am I going to explain this?" All of the lies, all of the deceit and guilt, eat at his heart and soul. It is a rude awakening to truly see that he has only been lying to himself.

Billy tries to stand, and then makes his way to the front door. This has to end now. He can't go on in this condition. Home, that's what he needs right now. Go get Taylor, try to make amends and go home. Sometimes, it takes an event so powerful in a person's life, to open their eyes, so they can see the light. This near death experience is such an event for Billy. For now, he can only hope that this realization of his hasn't come too late.

Judging by the conditions outdoors, it had been raining earlier, with water puddles now littering the parking lot and street. Billy looks across to the parking lot of the super mart and sees his motorcycle parked safely and undisturbed by the front of the store. He looks up and says a quick thank you before slowly crossing the street. With his mind a little jumbled, Billy tries his best to recall the events that took place before his attackers found him. He remembers pulling up close to the store and leaving his bike there. To stay out of the weather, he found an area in the landscaping where he could stay somewhat dry. Then, it all comes back to him, with his memory leading him to where he needed to go.

Billy crosses the street and heads to where the three fighters found him; constantly checking over his shoulder to make sure the attackers weren't coming back for another round of beat on Billy. The signs of the attack and the blood stains from the wounds inflicted cover the ground and parking lot. The sight is enough to begin the blood boiling inside him, forcing him to suppress it again so that he can think with a clear head. He leans over and opens the landscaping irrigation box and retrieves his keys and his cell phone. The little red light flashing on his blackberry tells him he has messages. Dreading this part, he pushes a few buttons to speed dial his voice mail, only to have the battery die on him. Frustrated, Billy makes his way back over to his motorcycle, taking his time and moving slowly, trying to avoid aggravating any of the injuries inflicted on him last night. They were healing, but the soreness will linger for quite a while. Billy starts up the motorcycle, bringing the engine to life with a low rumble. On the side of the motorcycle, below the seat, Billy opens a compartment, pulls out a cord and plugs it into his cell phone. He gives it a second or two, and then turns the phone on to redial his number. It is no surprise that the first message belonged to Taylor.

"Hey Baby, I was just wondering when you were coming back to the hotel? Love ya."

The compassion in her voice for him is painful for his conscience. Billy erases the message and presses another button to hear the next call.

"Billy, please give me a call or at least text me to let me know you're alright. I love you, Baby. You're starting to scare me."

Billy again erases the message, this time with a little heavier heart. He checks the next message, not surprised that it's her again, only this one knocks him down.

> "Billy [sobbing], why didn't you just tell me what was going on? The last thing I wanted to see again is you on the late night or morning news without me at your side. You told me you were through. Who was the girl that you carried out of the building? Was she just a damsel in distress, or just another… [Sobbing] Listen, I've gotta go; there's someone at the door. I love you Billy Ray, but I can't handle all of this lying and deceit. You told me once that if I didn't like the way this train was going, I could get off. Maybe this is where that happens."

His heart begins to ache as he erases the message, to play the next.

> "Billy, I had to call you back to tell you that it's over. I'm going home Billy. I have to tell you to stay away. I think the time has come for me to straighten out my life."

The message ends with Billy staring off into space, as if he couldn't believe what he had just heard. "What have I done?" He has no one to blame but himself. He is the one who told the lies. He was the one who was sneaking out. He was the one who was so stupid to believe that he could bring Taylor to Florida, and everything would be alright. The anger begins to swell in him again, not at the situation but at himself for screwing up big time. His mind starts to run with the guilt, pain, and heartache for what he has done.

Billy pulls the collar of his coat up around his neck and sits down on the seat of his motorcycle, just to try and figure out what he should do next. He can't beat the hell out of himself, to vent this growing rage. His anger clouds his thoughts. This was a contingency that he never really believed would happen. Had he become so arrogant? Unanswered questions fuel his anger more. Reaching back for his helmet, Billy sees the lights flashing on the tracking receiver in the saddlebag of his bike.

Release; he recognizes the opportunity to expel the pain welling up inside him. He grabs the box and straps it to his handlebars before readying to pull out. His darker side has won out again, urging him to seek out his attackers from last night. Rational thought is quickly replaced by vengeance and rage. It is the brawlers who will pay for Billy's wrong doings. After all, it's already been established that he can't inflict the punishment on himself. This is all going to end today, but with Billy suffering from the feeling that he no longer has anything to lose; things could get really ugly, really fast. The most frightening thing of all is that Antonio hasn't even crossed Billy's mind, yet. When a man loses sight of his purpose, does he have anything left to lose? In Billy's case, he hasn't necessarily lost his purpose, it's just been redirected. For Billy, this could be detrimental as well. At least before, he had reason to consider personal safety. Now, that has gone out the window as well.

Nick stands proudly at the front of his class, smiling at his students lined up awaiting his next command. "My students, you have honored yourselves and your teacher with the displays of knowledge and ability that you have provided today. For that, I congratulate you on achieving your next ranks." Nick turns to his start pupil. "JD, would you lead them through the closing exercises while I go get their new ranks?"

JD bows to his teacher accepting the task as Nick bows to his class and walks back to his office. Nick's uneasiness has been with him all morning and his star student knows Nick well enough to notice that he can't shake this ominous feeling that weights him down. Nick actually feels as if he is being warned of something but isn't sure of what it could be. He finds himself caught in some kind of trance as he stares at the portrait of his Master, hanging on the wall of his office. Is this feeling somehow connected to the talisman, and Masamoto?

"Hey Nick, I dismissed the class for you, but they're all waiting around for their belts." JD enters Nick's office, only to find his sudden unexpected appearance catches his teacher off guard. Surprised, Nick spins around with lightning fast speed to take a defensive stance that causes JD to jump back a little. "Whoa Teach, sorry man, I didn't mean to spook you. Are you okay, Nick?"

Yeah, sorry JD, I've just got a lot on my mind right now. Here, will you take these out to the kids and hand them out. I'll be out there in a minute." Nick turns away from his star pupil, if for nothing else to hide his embarrassment of JD getting the drop on him. Nick rights it off as good teaching being the justification of JD's accomplishment. JD takes the belts and returns to the waiting students. Nick tries to laugh it all off so he can focus on having a good time with Sonny later on. He gathers his things and turns off the lights in his office.

As soon as his office door closes, the younger students rush to him and bow. "Hey teach, tell us a story!"

"Yeah, tell us one about ninjas and dragons."

Nick laughs at their enthusiasm. "Sorry guys, we don't have time for one today." The students all slump their shoulders to show their disappointment with his answer. "Ah, come on guys, I've got a dragon at home that will eat me alive if I keep her waiting. Catch me next time after class, okay?" He hustles the students from the studio and holds the door for the rest of the class to exit before he locks up. "Hey JD, refresh my memory and tell me when you're heading off to your new college life?"

The young man spins around to answer Nick with no hesitation. "In three weeks, but I won't be starting any serious classes until I get the rest of my prerecs out of the way. Hey, we're still gonna do that ceremony with the swords and stuff, right?"

"You can count on it. It's your right of passage, after all. Listen, I'm going out with Sonny tonight, so I probably won't be too active tomorrow morning. Give me a call around lunch time, okay?"

Wow, you're braver than I thought. I know you have to let the cats out of the cages every once in a while, but Sonny's one tiger I wouldn't want running loose if I was holding her chain." JD knows all too well about Sonny's situation, and Nick's involvement. He applauds his teacher's efforts, but still wouldn't want to be in his shoes. JD has had the luxury of seeing Sonny's "other" side once, and that was one time too many for him.

"Yeah, well consider yourself lucky then. Listen, I'll talk to you later on, okay?" Nick looks up and down the street, still unable to shake the eerie feelings that have haunted him as of late. It is as if he was being watched, but there was no one on the street to be seen. He waves goodbye to JD and heads for his car. Luck is with him this day. There is still plenty of time for him to get home and get ready without having to listen to Sonny's crap. With a couple of hours to kill, JD sits down at the bus stop in front of the dojo and pulls out his new favorite book to read. With three hours to kill, he's going to see what he can find that's interesting.

May 5th, 2004

Yesterday was a day straight from the Psycho Circus tour, for sure! But first, I have to back up a little. This insane event really began a week ago, when Masamoto made another profound declaration that he had to go away, again. I though, no big deal, he's done it several times before, right? Well, after the second day, I was beginning to worry; bad enough that Megan agreed to go to her sister's alone. I think she was happier that way, so that the girls could do their window shopping for the wedding without pressure from any men.

By the fourth day, I was really becoming concerned about the Master's welfare. When the morning of the fifth day rolled around, I was seriously considering going out to look for him. The one thing holding me back was the fact that I had no idea where he went. Then, when my anxiety had reached its peak, Master Masamoto showed up to assure me that everything was alright. I don't know why I became so uneasy about his absence. Any way, he explained to me that he had assembled a training ground for my next level of training. This intrigued me. The last time he did something like this, I almost drowned in the middle of the everglades.

Getting back to yesterday, we left out early in the old jeep and headed out north of alligator alley. Needless to say, by the time we reached the destination, I was seriously wondering how the old man walked all the way up there and back, in five days. Much less have time to assemble any kind of training ground. So, when we entered the clearing, I was astonished by what I saw. Somehow, Masamoto had constructed this training ground, all out of bamboo and vines complete with towers and obstacles, all working off a series of ropes strung overhead. If I didn't know any better, I'd swear that all of this stuff was shipped over from Feudal Japan or at least from the movie lot where they make those B-rated martial arts movies.

The first thought that came to mind, was trying out for one of the Cirque Du Soleil shows. You know the type, where men and women train to accomplish impossible feats? Me and Meg caught one of their shows a couple years ago when we were in Vegas. I know I'll never forget the name; KA.

Evidently, this first run was going to last five days. Oh, did I mention that he brought this little tidbit of information, after we got there, with no supplies?

JD's train of thought is interrupted by the voice of a very large woman. "Hey, are you going to get on this bus, or not?" JD looks up to see the bus driver staring back at him. To be polite he holds up the journal and says that he's just reading. The bus driver gives him a scorned look, and closes the door to drive off. "Kids always sitting around doing nothing, and this one expects me to believe he's reading!" As the bus pulls away, JD laughs at her comment and dives back into the book.

Master Masamoto said that all of this was to hone my body's ability. I looked at him wondering what it was supposed to hone my body to do. There was a specific path built into this bamboo menagerie, with a stated purpose in this chaotic clearing. According to Master, there are several levels to this training, and the first must be accomplished before I moved on to the next. Personally, I was beginning to think I'd be better off skipping the whole ordeal. It was like he was trying to explain what we're doing, without telling me what it is. Before I knew what was happening, the old man had led me into the trap and sprung it on me before I could protest. Evidently, the first stage was designed to put me into orbit. I looked down, taking notice to the fact that I was standing on a small platform, about two foot square. Connected to the middle of this platform was two groupings of vines that were braided together to make a strong rope. Curious to where these organic ropes oriented from, I followed their lengths until I realized that they were tied to the two towers located in the middle of the clearing. I looked back at Masamoto immediately, but it was already too late. He stepped on a trigger, and this oversized slingshot sent me flying up into the air, like somebody had taken a rag doll and flung it up into the air like a pinwheel.

JD erupts with laughter at the thought of Nick flying up into the air, and scares homeless John, who had sat down beside JD minutes ago. Of course, the old man jumping up

119

off the bus stop bench, startles JD. "Oh wow, Homeless John, You've got to be careful sneaking up on people like that."

After I picked myself up and brushed away the embarrassment, Master Masamoto finally offered me an explanation of what I was supposed to accomplish with this training. "You must learn to control your body in flight to reach the desired destination. Examine the bird in flight. Notice how they use the subtle movements of their bodies to maintain their glide and change direction on the air currents. The crane uses the muscles in her entire body in a graceful symphony as she soars on the winds. To reach your destination you must learn to control your body and go where you want to go, instead of being taken where you don't." To prove his point, Masamoto stepped up onto the platform himself, and showed me how it was done. To my surprise, the launch sends him through the entire training course, flying, bounding, flipping and turning his body through the air, avoiding the obstacles to reach the other side of the course without injury. Sometimes, all you need to do is see the possibility of an effort to understand what must be done. Seeing his success made me want to try again, and again, and again, until I finally landed wrong and sprained my wrist when I was slammed into one of the obstacles that were stationary, in the middle of the course. I guess I should have zigged when I should have zagged. Still, he was impressed with my drive and determination and said that we will attempt this again after my wrist recovers. Deep down inside, there's a part of me that wishes I had broke my wrist, just to give the rest of my body a chance to recover as well. I didn't realize how much of a beating I took, until a little while ago when the soreness started to set in. One thing is for certain; he's either going to succeed with his attempt to make me a great warrior for the cause, or kill me in the process.

"Here's the bus again, JD." Homeless John's statement causes JD to look up at the bus driver, who was waiting again for him to get on the bus.

Courteously, he waves the bus on and looks at his watch and realizes that he's going to be late again, getting to his uncle's store. "Hey John, have you eaten today?" Pulling a sandwich out of his backpack, JD hands the vagrant his dinner, and folds the page over to bookmark his spot and then back flips over the bench to land on his feet. "Take it easy, John, I've gotta go earn my keep." With that, the young man sprints off, leaving Homeless John more confused than usual.

"Nickels, will you get a move on? I don't wanna be one of those poor shmuks who has to stand out on the boat docks to listen to the concert! Sonya Jackson dances around in her roommate's doorway on one foot, while trying to put her shoe on the other foot. She hurries off to find her hand bag, while still nagging at Nick to pick up the pace. "I swear man; I think that martial arts crap has taken over your life."

"If you only knew," Nick replies, dropping the talisman down inside his shirt. "I don't know what you're complaining about, Sonny. I've been ready for fifteen minutes. You're the one heading out the door still getting dressed." He points out as he follows her out the house.

"You drive, Nickels That way I can put on my face on the way to the club." Sonny commands, as she unlocks the passenger side door of Nick's Mustang and climbs into the seat. Nick just stands beside the car with his outstretched hand waiting for her to hand him his keys.

"Thanks, now if you don't mind, I'm gonna go lock up the house. I'll be right back." Nick shakes his head as Sonny completely ignores his comment and starts to apply her makeup. He heads back to the front door and locks the dead bolt. Again he gets the feeling that he is being watched. In the reflection on the plate glass window in the door, Nick sees someone standing in his front yard, but by the time he turns around, there is no one there.

"Come on Nick; let's get a move on, Commander!" Sonny puckers up her lips and applies her lipstick before smacking her lips together. Just to antagonize her a little, he slaps his hand against the hood of the car, causing her to draw outside the lines with her lip liner. "Shit!"

With a push of a button, Nick activates the convertible top of the car, sending it back down into the rear of the car. "We're off to the ball, M' Lady." He jumps into the driver's seat and starts up the car.

"Geez Nick, you can be such a cornball, sometimes." She gives him a ration for his comment, but deep down inside she really does appreciate how he tries to keep everything light.

"Yeah, and you can bite me, Sonny." Nick throws the car into gear and speeds off down the street. He blows off her grumblings about how his driving hinders her application of makeup. Their banter back and forth is all in good fun, as a significant aspect of their relationship. Nick's problem is that he could never take it to the next level. Charlie, now there's a guy who could stand toe to toe with Sonny and never back down. Nick could sit, watch, and listen to the two of them go at each other for hours. Nick turns up the music and lets his thoughts run about the passing of his family and friends over the passed few years, especially Charlie and Nicole. They were two of the best people Nick has ever known. What happened to the two of them was a crime. One thing is for certain; the cast of characters in this play of life are constantly changing as fast as the plot. Now, the plot has thickened with Nick assuming his role as determined by his destiny. Destiny, the word weighs heavy on Nick's heart. The loss that has impacted him the most was his love, Megan. Of course, the death of his master ranks right up there as well. After all, if not for the death of Masamoto, Nick wouldn't be in the position he's in today. He can't help but wonder if these flashbacks of lost loves are connected to his 'bad feeling' he's been carrying around for the passed couple of days. Masamoto once told him that the world around him was connected to the afterlife by but a whisper. Was someone trying to reach out to him from beyond the grave?

"Come on Nick, snap out of your trance and pay attention!" Sonny slaps him on the shoulder to bring him back to reality. "Look at you, you're going to drive right passed the place!"

Nick hits the brakes and pulls into the night club parking lot. After debating the pros and cons of valet parking with Sonny, Nick parks the car in the spot that Sonny deemed to be the furthest from the establishment. His Mustang is a classic, and he isn't about to let anyone do anything to cause any damage to her. It's one of the few times he can actually claim victory over one of their debates. "Oh Sonny, quit your pouting and let's get moving. Weren't you the one who wanted to get a good seat?" Nick takes off for the front entrance just to antagonize her a little more, while she tries to make her way across the gravel parking lot in three inch heels.

"Screw you, Nickels! You could have at least parked on the pavement!" Sonny does her best not to break her ankles trying to make it to the smooth and solid surface of the legitimate parking lot. Hiding her embarrassment and humility for her situation, Sonny strolls up to the entrance where Nick waits for her with the door standing open. Just to make sure he doesn't forget Sonny gives him the finger before entering the establishment. The only thing separating this joint from any other tavern or bar is the high dollar drinks and the higher dollar amenities.

Following her training, Sonny scans the interior of the nightclub familiarizing herself with her surroundings. The club was designed to cater to the upper class of society with the interior décor accentuating the lifestyle of the rich and famous. Still, Sonny knows how to put on the ritz to blend in with the high dollar crowd. All it takes is good looks, a low cut dress, and legs all the way up to the short hem. Always dressing to make a statement, she thought, or at least hoped that she would stand out in the crowd. This however is not your ordinary crowd of nightclub patrons. The place is packed with money, and the women are here to be shown off by their men. She looks down at her own natural cleavage and concedes that the plastic surgeons of Miami have outclassed her tonight. "Wow Nickels, look at all of these chickies in here." Her voice is but a whisper as she tries to hide her gawking nature. "Where's Robin Leach when ya need someone to tell you who is who?" As she walks under the huge chandelier over the dance floor, the light reflecting off the crystals shine down on her like laser beams.

"I think it's pretty easy to see who is rich. As far as who's famous, who cares? Let's just get out to the patio and find us a table." Nick sticks out his thumb and points to a bulletin sign directing everyone through the nightclub to the rear veranda, overlooking Biscayne Bay. "You can continue your people watching from the comfort of your chair." Nick motions for Sonny to go first, gesturing with his hand for her to take the lead. She obliges, rudely pushing herself passed him, knocking Nick into the couple who had just entered behind him and Sonny. Nick politely apologizes to the couple and then follows them to pool deck entry doors. There, Sonny waits for him tapping the toe of her high heeled shoe as he makes his apologies again to the couple for his friend's rude behavior.

"Now this is what I'm talking about," she whispers to herself, staring at the upper class lifestyles. This is what she desired out of life, and felt she deserved. Busting Nick's balls is just her way of balancing the pain of her financial and social misfortune. "Ya know, you could always see about sitting at their table if ya want their company instead." Sonny hands the Maitre de' her tickets and grabs Nick by the arm, to lead him outside. It was a perfect night for a concert under the stars. The vast patio, or veranda, stretched out the entire length of the back of the building with a boat dock bordering the edge of the property. Just like the parking lot out front, every slip was occupied by a high dollar yacht with the owners boasting and bragging about their vessels, and the women in their lives. The tables are set up across the veranda floor, resembling a setting for a formal dinner instead of a concert. "What a perfect night for a concert," Sonny declares looking up into the sky. The sun was setting in the west, casting orange and purple hues across the sky, and Biscayne Bay. Sonny lets go of Nick's hand and bolts to a vacant table that was being eyed by her favorite couple from the front door. "Here we go Nick; these ought to be great seats."

"Sorry about that. She doesn't get out much." Nick mumbles as the couple storms off. Nick takes his seat across from Sonny and gives her an uncomfortable smile.

"No, no, no, you have to come over and sit closer to me. I don't want any of these middle aged men coming over here and hittin' on me." Sonny lets her paranoia get the best of her, causing her to look around to see several older men looking her up and down. "Please?"

Nick laughs off her comment. "That may suit you just fine, Miss Richards, but what if I do want some of these fine looking ladies to come over here and hit on me? You may not want to be, but I'm still available."

Sonny erupts with laughter. "You should forget about anything like that, Nickels. These women are way outta your league." Sonny looks around to see one of the hostesses coming their way. "Oh good, cocktails," Sonny waves the girl over with her finger to place her drink order.

"Whoa there, hot legs, you know as your chaperone, I'm held responsible for your actions. The last time you tested for alcohol, Perkins threatened to lock me up." Nick holds up his index finger and gives the young girl a smile to ask her to wait one second before she takes their order. Nick takes notice to the young lady's nervous appearance. She's cute, and definitely not out of his league. She may be a little young, but she's still in the ball park.

"Sonny snaps her fingers to draw Nick's attention away from the young red head. "Perkins threatens you because you're a puss, Nickels. Besides, he's cool with it. I told him it was your birthday and we wanted to celebrate." Sonny waves the girl on over. "I'll have a shot of tequila, a shot of bourbon, and a Guinness Black and Tan to chase 'em down with." Sonny takes notice of the girl's tattoo. "Hey your dragon is the same color green as your eyes. Ya know, your red hair really makes it pop off your shoulder." Sonny pulls her leg out from under the table. On her ankle is a tattoo of a sea lion holding an M-16 and smoking a cigar. "Me, and him, have this tattoo. We got them at the same time in Korea, right after we took out some gunrunners who were supplying arms to North Korean guerrilas." Sonny gives the girl a devious smile.

"Real cool," the hostess responds in an unsettled way. She looks at her watch in a nervous manner and then bows out of the conversation, without even taking Sonny's order, acting very much intimidated by Sonny. His roommate looks over at Nick who just hangs his head in shame. "Oh shut up and get closer to me. The excitement is about to start." There is something wrong with the little hostess. Nick might not have picked up on it, but Sonny sure did. For whatever reason, the girl seemed nervous, or jumpy, but there wasn't an apparent reason. Or, at least Sonny had no reason to feel guilty about pushing too hard.

Billy's day has been as frustrating, and painful, as last night. After two tanks of gas and driving most of the streets of Miami, he has finally caught up with his prey, seeing their van parked outside a run down hotel, on the upper west side, just out of town. He hasn't thought about the loss of Taylor from his life. He hasn't even pondered the possibility of confronting Callistone. No, all that Billy's mind sees is retribution, and how he will exact that towards the four men who changed his life. But just when he thinks that there couldn't be any more complications, his four targets exit the hotel room with eight other men. Billy remembers most of them from last night. There are a few more new faces but they can either stay out of the way or become statistics themselves. Whatever it is they're planning, it's going down soon. These guys are even more arrogant than Billy, the way they're flashing their guns around. "I hate guns," Billy states, as he waits for his pigeons to leave the hotel parking lot before he starts up his bike. He doesn't know what they are going to do, but he sure is going to enjoy screwing everything up for them.

"Okay you guys, we hit this gig hard and fast. Mr. Brewster expects us to pull down enough to finance our little side operations for the next couple of years, with all of us living large. So, if any of you guys screw this up, I swear to God I'll shoot you in the head myself, got it?" Rocko pulls the van into the parking lot and drives around the outside perimeter stalling for time. "Here's how this is going down. In Brewster's car is an electronics gizmo that will scramble all of the phone lines and any cell phones these rich bastards might be carrying.

Moose, riding shotgun, looks over at Rocko curious about the set up. "Yo Rocko man, what's so special about this club?"

"It's not the club, mummy man. It's tonight's clientele that makes this job so special. Somebody's throwing some kind of benefit concert to raise money to help clean up the beaches from the oil spill." Rocko pulls the van up to the side entrance of the back courtyard and parks. "You know, it's one of those ritzy charity gigs, where every high dollar sonofabitch in town has to be seen showing off his money and high maintenance bitches. We're going to relieve them of those riches and maybe a couple of bitches." One of the newcomers to the group becomes agitated by Rocko's remark. Everyone notices it because just a few seconds ago, the guy was as lifeless as a statue. "What's your problem, Sanchez?"

"Oh amigo, I didn't know we were going to be taking away from the fishes. My family hasn't worked in months because of the oil running the shrimps away." Sanchez looks around the van at his comrades to see if anyone else felt the same way.

Rocko gives the hulking thug a serious stare, and then breaks out in laughter. "Sanchez, after tonight your family won't have to worry about working any more."

The big Mexican smiles, "Okay, since you put it like that, let's get this started." Sanchez grabs a 12 gauge pump and loads a shell into the chamber.

Rocko spins around in his seat just in time to see the signal from Brewster's car. The other two cars begin to unload the passengers giving Rocko's boys the cue to do the same.

Billy sits on the seat of his motorcycle watching the gunmen enter the establishment. "Okay, blue sedan, red sedan are both from last night. The white van and brown sedan are new arrivals. And then there's my buddies' van, totaling eighteen to twenty guys all carrying guns. Why guns? I hate guns!" He climbs off the motorcycle and starts toward the nightclub. Suddenly, there is an explosion up the street as a car runs into a parked bus. Billy scans the surroundings seeing a truck broke down, blocking the other direction of the three way intersection, leaving only one way in or out and the traffic was already backing up. "These guys are good. Let's go on in and screw up there well thought out plans." Billy walks right up to the building and makes his way around to the side entrance like he belonged there. Someone had to have seen him crossing the parking lot. He has no doubt that he will be confronted any second.

"Hold it right there, pal." The burn victim of the group of modern day desperados steps out behind Billy from his hiding place Billy here's the slide being pulled back on an automatic weapon. Moose keys up his microphone. "Yeah, I got him. No problem, he's dead meat if he makes the wrong move." Moose turns off his microphone and taps Billy on his shoulder with the barrel of his rifle. "Now why don't you just turn around real slow and this won't get messy."

Billy is happy to oblige, but the sight of Billy's face catches Moose off guard. This was the last person he would have ever expected to see here, tonight. The energy glowing around Billy's eyes gives off an eerie, frightening effect, making Moose wish he had time to rethink his agenda. Seizing the opportunity, Billy grabs the barrel of Moose's weapon and melts it with his touch. "Need a little aloe for those burns?" Surprised by Billy's recovery, Moose finds himself being slung into the stucco wall of the nightclub before Billy hits him with two energy blasts. The pain and agony of this attack sends the wounded big man collapsing to the ground. If Moose was the only one guarding the side entrance, Billy now has a clear path into the activities.

The report of gunfire silences the audience and band, as the gunmen exit the building and scatter out amongst the concert area. The gunfire also sends Nick and Sonny to the floor due to their military training, where they assess the situation. This isn't an easy thing to do with frightened patrons trying to flee the scene. Another burst of gunfire sends the standing people falling to the deck of the large patio, either shot or fearing for their lives. "Good evening, may I have your attention, please? If anyone else tries to move, you will be shot. Tonight's proceeds are being diverted to a new benefit, namely ours." Brewster raises his pistol and shoots a man in the head for trying to dial out on his cellular phone. "Your phones won't work, so save your lives by leaving them in your pockets. Now, if you would be so kind and remove all jewelry, money and wallets from your purses and pockets and hand them over to my associates as they pass the collection plates. Cooperate, and no one else will be harmed. If you don't," Brewster shoots one of the night club's bouncers just because he looked like a threat. "You'll end up like him."

Nick grabs Sonny's arm to hold his friend back. The last thing he needs is for her to go off half cocked in a situation like this. So focused on Sonny, Nick doesn't sense the gunman's presence behind him. "You heard the man, hand over the cash and valuables." Nick slowly gets up from the floor as he slowly turns his head to see the man's face, while giving Sonny the hand sign to stand down. "What's the matter, pretty boy? You have some kind of problem with my request?" The gunman shoves the barrel of his automatic pistol up against Nick's temple, and uses it to push Nick's head to the side.

Nick fights back all of his instincts to keep from ripping the two bit thug apart. His training tells him that this is a bad time to make his move. Too many innocent lives have already been lost. He should wait for a better time to strike. Unfortunately, the gunman's action causes Nick's collar to stand open, revealing the chain of the talisman around his neck. "Oh, so you thought you would hold out on us, huh?" The thug draws back his weapon and hits Nick in the back of his head, driving his face down onto the table.

"You sonofabitch!" Sonny screams, lunging at the gunman as he pulls the chain from around Nick's neck. The leash is off and the wild cat is loose. Even unarmed, she is a lethal adversary, but the numbers standing against this former SEAL tonight are too much for her to overcome. Tank was moving over to assist his cohort with the confrontation when he saw Sonny leap at Chain. Tank's reaction is mostly out of shock at how brazen Sonny's attempt is. He squeezes the trigger of his gun, causing the hammer to rock back and forth sending bullets flying into Sonny's chest. The impact force drives her back over her chair and to the floor in a lifeless heap.

Immediately, Tank is blown from his stance as Billy crosses the patio to seek refuge by the stage. The next volley of energy blasts are intended for Chains, but the rest of the gunmen open fire on Billy's position driving him back behind a stack of loud speakers. More screams sound out from the audience as the gunmen start to move towards the door. With Billy pinned down Brewster calls for the rest of his men to retreat. He isn't sure why this guy has returned to haunt him again, but Brewster can't wait to ask his associates about it. Rocko stops beside Nick who was now huddled over

Sonny's body. "Sorry about the hottie pal. Tell her to stay in her seat next time." Rocko points his pistol at Nick as the former Navy SEAL stares defiantly up the barrel.

Billy ducks his head and looks to his right as bullets ricochet around him. He finally realizes who he was sharing this space of safety with. "The Black Eyed Peas? Hey, you guys are great! My girl really loves that one song, One Tribe." Then, Billy is reminded of the fact that Taylor is no longer his girl. He motions for the entertainers to stay down when a volley of bullets ricochet around them. "Y'all keep your heads down, okay?" The three men and gorgeous female stare at Billy with disbelief as he pushes the stack of loudspeakers over for a clear shot at Rocko. He hits four of the gunmen with energy blasts before they are able to reach the nightclub. Rocko is shocked at the sight of Billy standing there in all of his rugged glory. With lightning fast reflexes, Nick leaps up from the floor and produces a short blade from his sleeve and slices Rocko from his belly all the way up to his chin. The ex-MMA fighter simply falls over backwards, dead before he hits the concrete patio. Nick starts for the main entrance to take chase after the men leaving with his property.

Billy sees Nick make his move but has no idea about Nick's motive, or history. All he knows is that he sees a gun aimed at Nick and the gunman had a clear shot. All of this appeared to be unknown to the former SEAL, giving Billy reason to make his move. While tackling Nick to the ground, Billy rolls his body over and fires off another energy blast that hits the gunman square in the face, eliminating the threat immediately. "Are you insane? Listen pal, I don't know if you realize this or not, but these guys are playing for keeps! The best thing for you to do is go check on your friend, and let me handle this situation. This is what I do!" Billy jumps up and takes chase after the bad guys, fighting his way into the nightclub through the chaotic crowd of patrons who are fleeing the danger.

Nick jumps up to take chase, but is stopped when he hears Sonny's voice behind him. "N-Nickels, you better get those bastards s-so I don't have to be ashamed to call you roommate." Sonny coughs a couple of times before she collapses back to the concrete deck and passes out. Nick grabs the linen tablecloth and stuffs it down the front of her sundress to slow the bleeding.

Nick stands and looks around at what has happened. Behind him and Sonny are a couple more people who were hit by the gunfire. There are more gunshots coming from the front of the nightclub. Nick assumes that the mystery party crasher has them pinned down at the front door. This is his chance. If he can get to the one who has the talisman, then his participation in this madness could end swiftly, but lethally if necessary. "Hang tough, Lieutenant, I'll be back for you in a minute." Nick looks over at the stunned hostess and grabs the red head, pulling her down beside Sonny. Nick forces the girl's hand down on Sonny's chest. "I don't know why, but I have a strong suspicion that you're connected to this some how. If you want to save face, you better not move until help arrives."

He leaves her side, heading right for the firefight taking place inside the building. Whatever it is that's taking place between the gunman and the vigilante, is of no concern of Nick's, at the moment. With the talisman back in his possession, he can return his focus on his wounded friend. The thieves have no idea what they have in there possession, and Nick plans to keep it that way. As he enters the rear of the nightclub, Nick sees Billy pinned down behind an overturned table. As Nick expected, Billy had the gunmen at a stand off, and he was blocking their only exit. Nick reaches down and retrieves a handful of shurikens, or throwing stars, from a small pouch strapped to his ankle. With a flip of the wrist, Nick lets two of the stars fly, eliminating the two gunmen that had Billy locked down. He sends another flying that takes out one of the men moving over to get a bead on Billy. "You look like a guy who could use a little help."

"Hey man, this isn't a good idea." Billy releases another energy blast that destroys the area of booths and tables on the opposite side of the dance floor, sending the gunmen hiding there flying into the air. Billy then hits another man with an energy blast, who was trying to make a break for the door. He can't help but notice that his energy stores were beginning to weaken, but he doesn't have another option at the moment. "Don't you think you should be tending to your girlfriend out there?" He asks, as Nick squats beside him.

"The best way to help Sonny is to get these guys away from here so that the paramedics can get in to do their job. Otherwise, Sonny or anyone else wounded doesn't stand a chance." All of this has taken place in mere minutes, but Nick's anxiety makes it seem like hours. By all rights, he has failed at his duty by losing possession of the talisman. Now, the agents of darkness who seek it can focus on its location, and try to reclaim it. If that were to happen, he and the rest of the world would be doomed. And then there's Sonny, lying on the patio probably dying. How did all of this happen? He has failed in his duty, and has failed his friend as well. At least he can rectify one of these situations. Trying to stay focused on current events, Nick glances over at Billy, noticing the gunshot wound to Billy's shoulder. "He pal, you're bleeding."

"Naw, that's old news." Billy leaps at Nick, tackling him to the ground, as one of the drivers appears at the front entrance holding a compact rocket launcher. The projectile flashes over their heads and impacts with the back wall of the club, giving the guests out back something else to scream about. With Billy and Nick down, the rest of the men get the chance to flee the scene. Billy scrambles to his feet just in time to see Chain heading out the door with four of his associates. "There you are, you sonofabitch." Billy charges his hands and launches an energy blast right at the chandelier over the dance floor. Chain is able to clear its target just in time, but his four friends are not as lucky.

Nick jumps up and joins Billy in his pursuit towards the door. All around him is unnecessary death and destruction. So many innocent lives lost, and Nick feels responsible, due to his so-called destiny. He should have picked up on what was going on, along time before it took place. What he doesn't know is that his ally is feeling a similar guilt that the body count here could be a result for his interference. His quest for vengeance has lead to more people dying. Silently, both men make the same vow to stop these murderers and see justice served. At the same time, Nick has to find a way to regain the talisman, all the while worried about Sonny's condition. "Well that was a bit of a surprise." Nick admits, as the two would-be allies stop at the entrance. "The guy you targeted is the same one I want. What's your plan?"

"Buddy, I've fought thugs, hoodlums, armored goons and robot killing machines. Nothing surprises me any more. As for the man who has your trinket, we've got to stop them now!" Billy exits the nightclub and unloads an energy blast on one of the cars. The vehicle is lifted off the ground and dropped right in front of Rocko's van. The van slams on its brakes and quickly reverses its direction heading right for Billy Ray McBride. With his energy stores low, his only choice is to dive to safety as the van rushes by. Quick to react, Billy rolls up to his feet to take chase, just in time to see the van slam right into Billy's Harley Davidson. "My Bike!" Billy turns to Nick. "Dude, tell me you've got a car!"

# Chapter VII

Navy SEAL instincts tell Nick to cut his losses by delivering a thrust to Billy's throat. His martial arts philosophies, and intuition, tell him to trust the young upstart, and ally with him to regain possession of the talisman. "Follow me." Nick motions for Billy to follow as he takes off running across the parking lot. He stops at the trunk of the car and retrieves a duffle bag, all the while never losing sight of the fleeing van. "Here, you drive." Nick throws Billy the keys before climbing into the back seat. "Lose that chain and we're good to go."

"Not a problem." Billy charges his hand with energy and launches the blast at the parking lot barricade chain. The blast is weak, so weak that it only weakens the steal links, but this doesn't stop Billy. He starts the car and throws it into gear, stomping on the gas pedal to send the classic Mustang lunging forward. The chain snaps with ease allowing the chase to begin, starting with the crowded intersection ahead. The Mustang leaps over the sidewalk and curb and out into the busy street. Billy snatches the steering wheel left and right, cutting off traffic as he follows the van down the crowded street. Driving is Billy's expertise, and something he displays perfectly, as he cuts the car sideways as he turns the corner at the intersection, barely missing crashing cars and approaching emergency vehicles. "Man, the police sure mobilize quicker around here, than they do in Atlanta."

Why is he doing this? Billy should be asking himself this question, at the moment. It is human nature to have purpose for every move we make. Chaos from the unfolding events clouds his mind, blinding him of rational thought. Personal history shows that without it, morality and ethics, right and wrong are blurred and hard for him to recognize. When this happens, Billy has the advantage of following his instincts and acting accordingly. Like a predatorial machine, he will follow his last course of action until the situation is resolved. But none of this explains why he is still here participating in this madness. For this answer you will need to go deep into the heart and soul of Billy Ray McBride. This goes beyond his revenge against Callistone, and the attack against him by the thugs in the van in front of him are irrelevant by now. This has to do with who Billy is, whether he's blinded to it or not. He is the great Samaritan who is always there to help those in need. That's why he stood up for Scotty in high school. It's why he took on the rednecks when he first met Taylor, or the girl that he saved from the inferno last night. It's the reason he's here driving Nick's can, and whether he realizes it or not, or if he wants to admit it, Nick is the one in need and Billy is here to help. That is his role in life, like it or not. No matter what, there are some things about a person that cannot be changed. Who you are, is who you are.

The big truck that was supposedly broke down a couple of blocks away, suddenly starts up and pulls out of the way for Rocko's van. The driver starts to back up, by order of the attending police on the scene, just as Billy closes in. "Hold on back there. This might get a little bumpy!" Billy jerks the steering wheel to the side, sending the Mustang up onto the sidewalk where it barely slips passed the truck before the gap is closed. What Billy can't avoid is the bus stop structure that is stationed in the middle of their path. The Mustang hits the glass and aluminum enclosure and takes to the air through the exploding glass. An entire squad of police cars come screeching to a halt as the Mustang lands in the middle of the next intersection. Billy doesn't bat an eye. If the vehicle can handle his driving, he can handle the vehicle. Adjusting the rear view mirror, Billy sees Nick looking back at the pursuing police cars.

"Here, take these and throw them out the window in front of the police cars. Nick holds out his hand to give Billy the small objects from his duffle bag. "Be careful."

Billy reaches back over his seat to take the handful of small spiked spheres and smooth faced orbs. He doesn't ask any questions. Billy simply rolls down the window and tosses the objects back behind the car. Instantly, the roadway is filled with blinding clouds of smoke, sending several of the police cars careening parked vehicles on both sides of the street. The spiked spheres take out the tires of the three remaining cars that plow into each other before grinding to a stop. Billy checks the side view mirror to make certain that their pursuers were eliminated, and is impressed by the outcome. "Cool trick, but that one certainly brought the cops' attention down onto us, don't you think?" Billy looks up into the rear view mirror to make eye contact with his ally. It's then that he sees Nick's new attire. "Well I guess that explains the trinkets you handed me. Did you learn how to use the throwing stars at ninja school too?" The van takes the freeway onramp doing sixty with Billy right on the van's rear bumper. As they speed up, so does Billy, when the van slams on the brakes, Billy cuts the car over into the next lane, barely missing the van's rear quarter panel, and the front end of the big rig behind them.

Nick cringes as they clear the van with less than an inch to spare. "I am not a ninja, nor do I practice Ninjitsu." Nick pushes the front passenger seat forward, and then lifts up on it before laying it back flat. Now he is able to climb into the front. He has to admit that his choice of clothing would, and does, make him stand out in a crowd, but Nick wears the black with white and red garb of the Guardian with pride and honor, "The true ninja are assassins and spies, who do not follow the same code of honor as I do. If you feel the need to catalog me, list me as a samurai. The title best suits my purpose. It means…"

Sending the Mustang over into the express lane, Billy stomps on the gas to get around the two cars between him and the van. "Yeah, I know, to serve, right?" Billy finishes Nick's statement with a touch of arrogance, and a touch of doubt. "Who, or what in the hell do you serve?"

"It's a long story." Nick answers, with his own touch of self doubt. "Get up alongside the van," Nick suggests, as reaches over and unlatches the convertible top. The rushing wind over the car rips the canvas top off and sends it flipping back into the path of a Highway patrol car.

Billy waves at Nick to get his attention. "Let me ask you something, sport. Would you be so quick to react if those clowns didn't have what's yours?" Billy stomps on the gas to pull the car up beside the van.

"Mister, if I had what's mine, we wouldn't even be having this conversation." Nick unsheathes his short sword and steps up onto the seat and door while holding onto the framework of the windshield. Without any hesitation, he leaps from the Mustang to the side of the van where he buries the blade into the metal skin of the vehicle. With a shift of his weight, he then uses the sword as a step to climb up onto the top of the van.

Billy watches in awe as Nick boards the moving van. "And

people call me a crazy sonofabitch!" Looking over to his left, Billy spots a young boy in a car in the next lane video taping the pursuit and getting a close up of Billy's masked face. Knowing this was going to end up in a bad light, Billy gives the kid a disagreeable half smile and shakes his head. "Great, that's exactly what we need floating around on youtube!" He looks back at the kid to see the boy just staring back at him with a huge smile stretched across his face.

In the back of the van, Julio feels a harsh burning sensation in his chest. Looking down, he's surprised to see the tip of Nick's sword sticking out of his ribcage. He coughs once, spitting blood on his cohorts before slumping over dead. If not for Nick's blade, Julio would probably tumble on over to the floor, but instead he is held in place for Brewster and his men to see. The man called Chain leans over to check on his friend. "Hey Brewster, what's going on out there? Julio just got iced from the outside in!"

Brewster checks the rear view mirrors and sees Billy following them in Nick's Mustang. "Chain, get up here!" Brewster jerks the wheel sending the van swerving into Billy's lane, forcing Billy to drop back to avoid a car in the inside lane. "I need you to tell me something! If that guy from last night is nailed to the living room floor of your apartment, how is he driving a car behind us?"

"Uh, I don't know, Mr. Brewster. I told Rocko we shoulda' iced the guy when we found him." Chain tries to look out the window to verify Billy's presence.

Brewster shoves Chain out of his way. "I asked you at the club if that was the same guy, and you said no! You said that's impossible. There's no way. He's nailed to our living room floor. Well guess what? You were wrong!" Brewster pulls his pistol and shoots Chain in the head.

"Uh Boss, I think somebody's on the roof." Russell

Stringer looks up at the roof as if he could hear Nick's movements.

"Shut up Russell, and hand me that medallion hanging around Chain's neck." Brewster swerves into Billy's path again eliminating his opportunity to move alongside the van again. Billy has no idea what Nick planned to do on top of the van, but whatever it is, Nick was doing a good job. "You guys earn your keep back there, and get rid of this dead weight along with that maniac tailing us!"

Again the question tries to register in Billy's mind. Why is he doing this? Billy isn't even sure if Callistone is still in the picture. He could call off the chase and let Nick handle his own mess. What more could Billy gain from this? The rear doors on the van suddenly swing over as Brewster's men toss Chain's body out at the front end of Nick's car. Before Billy could react, Chain's head was shattering the windshield of the Mustang. He slams on the brakes and snatches the wheel sending the Mustang into the next lane. Most of the guys who beat the crap out of him are already out of the picture. This poor sap lying through the windshield might just be the last of the group. There's nothing else to gain from this, and yet he finds himself unable to let go. With no other option at hand, Billy pulls the Mustang in behind the van, with no other choice but to wait to see what happens next. That comes very quickly as the rear doors on the van suddenly swing open again, with the gunmen in the back firing their weapons at the pursuing car, while several others dump Julio's body out onto the pavement. A quick reaction time, and pure instinct, make Billy pull the car back into the other lane again, and avoid both the gunfire from the back of the van, along with Julio's body as it bounces down the freeway.

Finding an opening, Billy pulls the Mustang alongside the van to avoid the flying bullets, while frantically looking up at Nick, "Whatever it is you're going to do, you need to do it now!" Distracted by Nick, Billy doesn't realize that the van was coming back over into the Mustang's lane, until it's too late. The van collides with the Mustang, forcing it over, and wedging it between the van and a fuel transport truck. The next few seconds take place in silence, as Billy does everything he can to save his life. Bullet holes appear on the side of the van as the men inside shoot blindly at Billy's assumed location. Billy slams on the brakes sending the car shooting out from between the other two vehicles. The sudden change in momentum dislodges Chain's body from the windshield, allowing the dead man to roll freely off the fender of the car. This was fine with Billy; he was getting a little disturbed by the dead man staring at him any way. The van and tanker collide, beginning a grisly chain of events right in the middle of the freeway. The truck driver had barely recovered from the first contact with the Mustang, and somehow managed to keep the big rig upright. The much larger van hits the side of the fuel trailer with much more force, pulling the wheel out of the driver's hands. The random gunfire from the van's interior rupture the fuel tank, and hit the trailer's tires, taking away what little control the driver had left with the big rig. When all is lost, the tractor trailer rolls over onto its side and erupts in a blaze of fury, blocking all of the lanes just before the next overpass.

Billy stomps on the gas and cuts across three lanes of traffic, with cars spinning and sliding out of control all around him, trying to avoid him and the inferno in front of them. Barely missing cars as he tries to get to the side of the roadway, Billy sends the Mustang rocketing up the overpass 'off' ramp, where he blows through the intersection at the top. A three car pile up is created as he takes the 'on' ramp back down to the freeway. Smoke begins to rise up from under the hood, warning Billy that the Mustang didn't have much left to offer. He checks the gauges, and then the hood again.

It is then that he sees the police cars in the rear view mirror, falling in behind Nick's car. This is about to end one way or another, whether Billy likes it or not.

Stringer ejects an empty shell from his shotgun and loads another into the chamber. Without any warning, he blows a hole in the roof of the van, barely missing Nick on top. Brewster jerks the wheel, surprised by his driving companion's actions. The act sends Nick over the side, hanging onto the top edge of the van's roof for dear life. Billy sends the Mustang rocketing back down onto the freeway, falling in right beside the van. He looks over at Nick, wondering what in the hell was he planning to do on top of the van in the first place. Inside the vehicle in question, Brewster fights to gain control of the vehicle while questioning his right hand man's actions. "Are you out of your mind?"

"There's somebody on the roof!" Stringer looks out the driver's door to see Nick reflection in the side view mirror, dangling above the roadway. Stringer points the shotgun into the back of the van. "Move or I'll shoot you guys too!" He looks down the barrel of the gun sending the thugs in the back diving to the other side of the cargo box. He pulls the trigger, blowing a softball size hole in the wall of the van, as Nick scrambles back up on top of the vehicle.

"Man, this has to cinch it. To all of the people who have the nerve to call me a lunatic, this guy's for you!" Billy pushes the Mustang to its limits trying to avoid the cars swerving all over the freeway, while keeping his eye on Nick, and dodging the random gunshots from the rear of the van. Once he is able to get a good view at the back of the van, from a safe distance, Billy sees the occupants readying to take their shots at Nick on the roof. Nick, who's crouched down swinging a weighted chain around is about to make his move to disable the van, or driver, or both. It's more than obvious that he is unaware of the pending onslaught that's about to hit him. Who will get their shot off first, Nick, by taking out the steering of the van, or the gun toting thugs about to blow Nick off the vehicle? None of the above, Billy pulls in behind the van wasting no time sending an energy blast into the back of the van, eliminating the threat to Nick. The next thing Billy knows, Nick is diving off the disabled van, and onto the hood of the mustang. "Dude, are you out of your mind? You've got to tell me what you were planning to do! By the way, what were you planning to do? To tell ya the truth, that was about as ballsy a move that I've ever seen. And trust me; I've done some pretty wild stuff myself." Billy continues to jockey the car back and forth, and side to side, avoiding as many bullets as possible.

Nick climbs into the speeding car and into the passenger seat. He looks over at Billy to respond, when he sees Brewster's car that seemed to appear out of nowhere. He also sees the man hanging out the window pointing an automatic machine pistol at Billy. "Look out!" Nick grabs the wheel and jerks it to the right as the gunman opens fire. Bullets riddle the car, taking out the engine and driver's side tires, with one bullet catching Billy in his shoulder. The Mustang veers off the road and launches itself into the air, before landing in a canal along the freeway. The impact with the water sends a wave fifteen feet into the air, before raining down on Nick and Billy. This pretty much announces to everyone that they are out of the chase, and both Nick and Billy would like for everyone to think just that. Nick jumps from the car and helps Billy free himself as the Mustang goes under. They make their way up the embankment and see the wounded van rolling off to the side of the roadway. Brewster's car rolls up to save the day, as the survivors of the van begin to transfer the loot from the heist. A few seconds later, the men are in the car and speeding away. Nick takes a look in the opposite direction to see the fleet of emergency vehicles racing towards him. "You're wounded, friend. You should cut your losses before the Police arrive." He looks up and sees a squadron of Police and news helicopters in the night sky that are bearing down on them.

Billy is actually miffed at being dismissed by Nick. To prove he isn't a liability by being wounded, He reaches under his trench coat and uses his own energy to cauterize the gunshot wound. It is actually the first time he realizes what the effects of his energy blasts have on his opponents. "And what makes you think you can go it alone the rest of the way? After all, you needed me to drive the car while you played 'Frogger' on the freeway."

"In the video game 'Frogger', you jumped between the cars to avoid them, not on them." Nick doesn't have time for small talk. He searches the area for any signs of his target. If I'm not mistaken, they are heading for that marina over there. To answer your question a few minutes ago; my plan was to disable the van and learn what I could, if the first motive couldn't be accomplished. Since they were able to get away, I have to follow the information that I was able to gather. They're going to a meeting with their boss and some guy named Callistone." Nick declares, pointing towards Biscayne Bay. "The meeting is being held on a yacht called Azule Pescado." He slings a small bag over his shoulder, while watching the Cadillac take the next off ramp and head towards the marina in question.

"Okay, so we go find a boat called the Blue Fish, and get your thingy back." Billy takes off jumping back into the canal, using the hood of the submerged Mustang to get to the other side. Could his luck really be changing? Is it truly possible that after all that has taken place, Billy really could have a shot at his original target? With his focus reset, Billy soon loses track of Nick and makes his own way to the marina, using his energy to burn holes through the numerous chain link fences that block his path. Once inside the security fencing of the Marina, Billy skirts the perimeter of the main parking lot, to work his way out to the docks and boat slips, to find his "Blue Fish." He takes note of the two guards at the gate, one more stationed at the entrance to the marina's store and management office, with two more guards riding around the docks in a small golf cart. Billy may be unsure how many more there are roaming around, but judging by the price tags of some of the boats in here, there has to be a lot more of these under-classed, out of shape, security guards around. Final assessment; the security maybe high, but the workforce looks inadequate. Billy could probably take on all of these guards at once, if it was brought down to throwing punches. But all it takes is one of these old farts to ring the alarm and his chance at Callistone is lost again. That being the case, Billy stays with his covert approach, hurdling a handrail of a small bridge. He does this just in time to have himself driven to the bridge deck by Nick. "What the hell?"

"Stay down, friend, this is for your own good." Nick throws his cloak over Billy and himself, and uses his two swords to form a makeshift frame to resemble a crate under the tarp, as another golf cart carrying two more guards approaches the bridge. They are searching diligently for something or someone, checking under and around the bridge before they drive across it, never once taking notice to Billy and Nick hiding under the large black cloth. The security guards head off in the opposite direction, away from Billy and Nick's target, tied off just two slips away.

"Neat trick karate dude, do ya wanna explain the secret?" Billy asks, as he and Nick stand to cross the bridge. Working their way out onto the numerous docks, the two would-be allies begin their search for the mystery yacht. Nick taps Billy on the shoulder and points to the one dock furthest from the entrance. What makes it so special are the numerous security guards posted along the walkway beside a large blue yacht, bathed in a glow of light from the dock's lighting fixtures. To Billy's surprise, Nick suddenly slips off into the shadows, leaving Billy to plot his next move alone. "I hope you know what you're doing karate dude."

Ramon Cortez can't believe the hysterical babbling that is flowing from Brewster's mouth. Calvin Brewster has been with Cortez's organization ever since he came to this country, and killed Brewster's old boss. His history is in good standing with the Colombian drug lord, but what is being displayed at the moment, is completely out of character. "Now let me see if I have this straight, my friend. A maniac, for no apparent reason, shows up at one of your front companies and attacks you, and your men?" Cortez gives Brewster a concerned look while taking a draw off of his Cuban cigar. "Then, later on, you, and your men, ran into the same guy again. Your men kicked the shit out of him, but let him get away, only to have him foil your "activities"? Amigo, what have you gotten yourself into?"

Callistone knows what's going on. He has heard this kind of report before, or at least something similar from his own men, back in Atlanta. He remembers the confrontation with Billy at the airport and gets an eerie feeling. Why didn't he listen to his daughter and postpone his meeting? "Cortez, we need to leave here, immediately!" Callistone pulls a pistol from the inside pocket of his coat and shoots Brewster in his head. Suddenly, a standoff occurs as men from both criminal factions draw down on each other. "He got what he deserved, Ramon. If your pet moron hadn't brought that rebel sonofabitch, down here on us, he would still be alive. Call off YOUR men, before I have MY men eliminate all of you!" Callistone turns his pistol to Cortez, to emphasize the request. "Now, get me out of here, before that rebel maniac gets here to take us all out!" Then, all of the light poles throughout the marina suddenly shut off, making it very dark around the large blue yacht. "It's too late, he's already here." Antonio Callistone has visions running through his head of this vigilante laying the aging mobster to rest beside his dead son, and becomes very disturbed by the turn of events. Suddenly, Margaret's request for him to postpone this trip doesn't sound like such a bad idea.

"Not to worry, Mr. Callistone, everything is under control." Ramon Cortez picks up a phone that serves as a direct line to the yacht's bridge. "Amigo, get us out of here and under way, immediately. And, turn on all of the lights on board my blue fish, so that the ship can be swept for unwanted passengers. If you find anyone on board who is not supposed to be, I want him brought to me at once, comprende?" Cortez turns to face Callistone once again who doesn't seemed to be eased by Ramon's gesture. "Now, Mr. Callistone, I apologize for my man's actions that brought us to this point. It is a shame however, that you had to go and kill him the way you did. Now I will have to find someone to replace him." Ramon hits his cigar and picks up a glass and offers it to Callistone.

"Ya know what bothers me, Cortez? I tell you that there is a madman on the loose and you're acting as cool as a cucumber." Callistone gulps the alcohol down, hoping it will calm his nerves a little. It doesn't work.

"Mr. Callistone, as I have said, I have everything under control." The debonair Columbian reaches over and lays a porcelain statue over and presses a button that is concealed underneath. The action causes steel panels to slide down over the doors and windows of the main cabin, sealing them in from all outside interference. "Now then, we are in here safe and sound, while your madman is trapped outside with twenty of my men."

"You say he's trapped outside. I say we are the ones trapped, on the inside!" Callistone begins to look around nervously as Cortez hands him another drink. The mobster gulps this one down as well, before he begins to wonder whether his retirement will remain voluntary or willfully imposed. The liquor doesn't seem to be working, or at least not yet. He looks at the empty glass think the second shot didn't ease his nerves either.

From the safety of the third level sundeck, Billy watches three gunmen searching the bow of the yacht. The men are methodical with their efforts, searching every inch, before moving back towards the stern of the ship. So focused on the men below, Billy doesn't hear the thug who had spotted him and was moving in for the kill. That is, until Nick plants a throwing knife into the man's back, eliminating the threat without a sound. Billy turns around and catches the dead body to keep it from making too much noise by hitting the deck. "Glad you could make it. I hate to be the bearer of bad news, but it looks like we're going for a little cruise. I wonder which one of these guys gets to play the role of Gilligan, if we're shipwrecked?" Billy leans over and whispers after Nick moves over to his side, "I was beginning to get worried about you." He adds as Nick squats down beside him. They're working their way to the back of the boat."

Nick is beginning to wonder if he made the right choice in allying with Billy. For one thing, it's hard for Nick to get a bead on how serious Billy is, when he's constantly cracking jokes. "Then let's move down to the bow and fall in behind them where we will have the element of surprise. Come on and follow me." Nick leans over the edge of the sun deck, mapping the sloping front exterior of the forward level below. Being that the surface is all glass, anyone in the forward compartment would see them. He eases himself over the edge and takes a peak inside to find the compartment empty. "It's all clear below, so watch what I do and stay close." Nick goes back over the edge again and starts down the glass surface until his toes of his Tabi boots catch the edge of the sundeck above. With his arms outstretched he is able to let himself slide down a few inches, where he catches the trim separating the glass of the upper deck from the glass of the bridge. After changing his grip on the trim, Nick allows himself to slide down a little further, so that he can look in through the porthole slits in the metal plates that cover the bridge. The bridge crew was moving about frantically, due to the fact that they were trying to pilot a two hundred foot yacht with their bridge blindfolded. Nick waits for the right moment before flipping his legs over to perform a somersault to the deck below. He lands with the sound of a feather and looks around before signaling Billy to make his move.

Billy laughs to himself at Nick's actions. Seeing Nick make his way down to the main deck seemed easy enough, so Billy begins the maneuver. Lying on his stomach, Billy starts over the edge and down the first section of glass. He slides down to the steel plates covering the bridge and peers inside. To his surprise, Billy sees one of the crewmen looking back at him. The man begins to scream in Spanish about Billy's presence, making Billy more than a little nervous. "Oh shit!" Billy loses his grip and slides down the steel plates to the main deck below, head first. He tries to flip his legs over like Nick did, but it's already too late. His effort only causes him to land hard, with his arms and legs spread out like an outline at a crime scene.

Nick looks at Billy not knowing what to say. That was the most ungraceful display he has ever seen. Unfortunately, the commotion made by Billy's landing has pinpointed their location. Hearing the footsteps of the gunmen running back towards the bow, Nick draws his swords and readies for battle. "Well I guess any element of surprise is gone. You got any bright ideas on ya?"

Billy jumps to his feet and charges both hands with

energy. "Yeah, we fight until we can't fight any more!" Billy's first opponent appears from around the corner and is blown overboard by one of Billy's energy charged punches. Billy makes a mental note of the act and how it seemed to be beneficial, and productive, in the fact that the energy used was minimal and yet multiplied the force of Billy's punch off the charts. He hears gunfire ring out, causing him to look over at his unlikely ally. When he does, Billy sees Nick fling his short sword at the gunman, burying the blade in the man's chest. With a clear view of the gunman, Billy can see the gunman's accomplice hidden from Nick's view. Taking the advantage, Billy hits the man with an energy blast that removes the threat from the sundeck above. Nick gives Billy a nod of appreciation and takes off down the port side of the yacht. With his own number of aggressors running towards him, Billy takes off down the starboard side to meet his opposition head on.

Inside the main cabin, Antonio Callistone is having his first anxiety attack. He tries his best to maintain his composure but every time a body or bullets hits the steel plating, or when one of Billy's energy blasts cause the steel plating to glow red hot, Antonio slips a little more. His daughter warned him to postpone this trip, saying that it was too soon for Antonio to be conducting business such as this, believing Antonio hasn't had the proper time to grieve his son's murder. When the noise outside subsides, Antonio is unsure whether he should be happy, or worried about what comes next.

Billy meets Nick at the stern of the yacht. Neither is worse for wear, surviving the odds on both sides of the ship. Then more gunfire rings out between them sending Nick and Billy to opposite sides to seek shelter. Nick looks over at Billy and points towards the bow. "It's going to be a long swim back to shore if we get out past those breakers."

"Leave that to me. I'll draw their fire, while you take 'em out." Billy takes a deep breath and darts out into the open before heading back up to the bow of the yacht. He hears the two men hit the wooden planks of the deck, knowing that Nick's aim was true. Without batting an eye, Billy charges both hands with everything he's got, and blows a gaping hole into the front of the bridge with a massive energy blast. Nick races to the explosion to find Billy standing there wearing a smile. "There, that should keep us from sailing the Atlantic, and a doorway to get inside the ship." The smile on Billy's face tells him that the young man enjoyed this too much.

What's left of the bridge crew begin to open fire on Billy and Nick, frustrating Billy all that much more. "Did I ever tell you how much I hate guns?" Billy unloads two more blasts of energy that erase any signs of possible threats. "After you," Billy suggests, motioning for Nick to take the lead.

Antonio Callistone has had enough of the madness. The debris raining down the stairwell from the bridge tells him that Cortez's security precautions are no longer intact. With his pistol pointed at Cortez's head, Antonio tries to speak as clearly as possible. "Get me the hell outta here, or you'll die where you stand!"

"Calm down amigo, we are on the same team, you and me." Cortez starts to slowly move towards the bow while avoiding Antonio's pistol sights. "Follow me, Mr. Callistone, we will go down to the next level and access the launch from there. The only way for him to get to it, is to follow us.

Suddenly, Antonio's courage returns as he motions for everyone to move on ahead down the forward stairwell. Believing he was trapped clouded his thinking. He sees that there is a way out, and a possible chance to avenge his son's murderous demise at the same time. Antonio sits down on the steps, aiming his pistol through the access way where he can see the entire main cabin. Now, he just waits like a spider in the center of his web.

Billy pushes passed Nick and starts for the main stairwell that leads down to the main cabin. If Callistone is on this boat, and Billy has a shot at him, He isn't going to miss it. After everything that has happened on this trip, everything that Billy has lost, it's really hard for him to believe that he still has the opportunity to end this, once and for all. This is not an opportunity he can let slip away. The sudden appearance of another gunman doesn't slow Billy in the slightest. Instead he just blows the man back into the radio room with an energy blast before leaping down the stairs into the main cabin. From the moment his feet hit the floor, Billy is scanning the room like a predator searching for its prey. A small fire had started on one of the sofas, by a piece of hot debris. Papers that were scattered into the air by Billy's entrance to the room, slowly settle back down onto the furniture and floor. Billy assumes they are business dealings of Callistone's, but pays them no mind. There is no more need for clues or evidence, if this ends tonight. Slowly, he stands and turns, wondering how Callistone could have vanished. Then as he faces the bow of the yacht, he sees the gleam of Antonio's pistol barrel in the flickering firelight. Before Billy can react, Antonio sends a .45 caliber slug straight through Billy's chest.

Nick descends the stairway just in time to see Billy being driven to the floor by the force of the bullet. He leaps down beside Billy and looks around, but the stairwell behind them is now empty. Just a few feet away from them, is Brewster's dead body, with Nick's talisman still in his clutched hand. Nick pulls the chain free from the lifeless fingers and hangs the chain around his neck. The stairwell in Nick's view is the only way out of the cabin, so he takes chase. There is no rational explanation for his actions. Maybe Nick felt that he owed it to Billy. At the bottom of the stairs, he sees the entourage exiting the corridor at the other end. Callistone's bodyguard, Douglas Deadlocke, stops and uses his awesome strength to kick a hole in the corridor wall, and ruptures the fuel tank on the other side. He then tosses his lit cigar back up the corridor to seal the fate of their pursuers. It is then that he sees Nick standing at the bottom of the stairs. Deadlocke gives the would-be adversary a salute and then follows his employer into the launch. With the fuel flowing straight for the cigar, Nick has no time to lose if he is going to get off the yacht before she blows. He heads back upstairs, and to his surprise, he finds Billy sitting up. Nick rushes over to help his ally and warn him of the pending danger. "We've got to move, chum, if you've got anything left in you."

Pushing away from Nick, Billy begins to look around frantically for his prey. "Where is he?" He asks, struggling to breathe. His blood is soaking through his shirt with a strong burning sensation traveling through his chest. Without waiting for a response, Billy staggers towards the stairwell, when the corridor below erupts into flames. Falling back to avoid the heat, Billy bumps into Nick and almost collapses to the floor.

"Yeah, you don't want to go that way, pal." Nick tries to help Billy, only to have the upstart pull away from him. "Take it easy, you've taken a bad one to the chest, this time." Nick stares at Billy's wound, but can only see his roommate with her chest punctured by bullets in a similar way.

Billy ignores Nick's concern and shows his anger by letting his energy flash around his eyes to accentuate his mood. "Where's Callistone?" Even near death, Billy refuses to give up. He has thrown away his life to pursue this quest for vengeance. There is no way he is going to let it be in vain.

Nick steps aside to let Billy pass. "He's headed out the back of this boat, aboard a launch, but he's the least of our worries right now. This thing is on fire and heading out to sea."

Billy dismisses Nick's warning, as he struggles to exit the main cabin. Up the stairs he climbs, ignoring his pain, ignoring his erratic heartbeat, trying to accomplish his goal before collapsing at death's door. Billy reaches the rear of the bridge just in time to see Cortez's motor launch slipping out the stern, and into the wake of the yacht. Billy feels that his time is coming to an end. He gasps for air, finding it harder and harder to keep his vision focused and his body upright. Antonio was getting away and Billy's vow was about to end unfulfilled. Anger quickly turns to rage as the thought of failure taunts his mind and spirit. Callistone can see Billy standing on the yacht when the rebel vigilante's entire body begins to glow. Trying to keep his prey from escaping, Billy lets out a scream and releases all of the built up energy at once. The blast obliterates the stern of the yacht and sends Billy flying back into Nick's arms, who was the unfortunate one to be exiting the bridge.

Nick grabs Billy and takes him over the railing and into the black waters of Biscayne Bay, just as the fuel tanks aboard the wounded vessel erupt. This blows the rest of the stern deck off the yacht, further crippling the doomed ship. Nick can only do what he can to fight the currents and keep Billy above the briny surface at the same time. Somehow, the two of them have survived this ordeal, and reclaimed Nick's property. Watching the speed boat that carries Cortez and Callistone away from the scene, Nick can only wonder what lies in store for Billy. The young man is unconscious now, and Nick is having a hard time in the water, trying to determine if Billy is even breathing. To aid his efforts, Nick strips Billy of his waterlogged trench coat. Dead or alive, Nick knows that he has to get Billy to shore. After that, his unlikely ally is on his own.

Antonio Callistone punches the buttons on his cellular phone with his fingertip, franticly dialing a number. "Margaret, you told me that you were taking care of this matter in the South. That maniac almost had me tonight! I'm going to South Carolina to conclude a business dealing there, before I return home. I expect a full report on your progress when I get there! Do you hear me, girl?" Antonio holds the phone away from his face and stares at it. "Damned reception," he states, shoving the phone back into his pocket. He turns in his seat and stares back at the burning yacht as it runs aground on the breakers.

"Tell me something, boss man. What makes you think he survived all of that?" Douglas pulls a cigarette from the pack in his pocket and lights it for his employer.

"Survived, I'm sure he survived!" Antonio takes the cigarette and sucks hard on the filter, longing for the soothing tranquility of the nicotine. "This guy is my own personal demon, Douglas. He is of my creation. This I'm sure of, now. He's been beaten, shot, blown up, set on fire, and the guy keeps on coming back. The only way to get rid of your demons is to conquer and destroy. I am unable to do this personally, although relish the thought, but I have the means at my disposal to have the job done for me. If my daughter doesn't step up and honor her vow to me, I will be forced to take matters into my own hands, and handle the situation my way."

Douglas sits back and stares out at the night sky. "Well let's hope it doesn't come to that, boss man. Nobody needs a body count that big."

Billy suddenly regains consciousness, spitting the salty sea water from his mouth and fighting Nick's attempt at saving Billy's life. "Did I get him?"

"I don't think so, Sport, but now isn't the time to be worrying about that. We've got more pressing matters to deal with." Nick clutches the talisman with one hand while trying to keep Billy afloat with the other. For the first time since taking possession of the talisman, Nick uses its power to serve him. He and Billy suddenly become invisible, at least to the eyes of the approaching police and harbor patrol that was moving in on their location. Spotlights shine out over the waters as the boats pass their position, but none of the authorities see anything but black water. Once Nick is sure that the helicopters and boats are well on their way, he releases his grip on the talisman and continues on towards shore. The authorities' main concern at the moment seemed to be the burning yacht at the mouth of Biscayne Bay. The use of the talisman seems to have set wrong with Nick, making him uneasy about the event, in a weird sort of way. He isn't sure how Billy feels about the situation and doesn't plan on bringing the topic up any time soon. "Come on, friend, we've got a lot of swimming ahead of us if we're going to make it to shore.

# CHAPTER VIII

Nick helps Billy up to the front door of his house. The young man is still weak, but Nick is impressed at how Billy was able to hold his own after a while. He pulls a note from the door, left by a Police Detective wanting a word with Mr. Landry. For a split second, he had a vision of Sonny walking through the front room buck naked as Billy is walking in. After what has happened tonight, Nick would probably welcome such a scene from his wild roommate. "Make yourself comfortable. I'm just gonna check out the local scene for a second." Billy happily eases himself down onto the sofa and happily welcomes the opportunity to finally rest a little.

Allowing his investigative side to take control of his actions, Nick turns on the TV and switches the channel to the local news broadcast. Next he walks over to his answering machine and punches a couple of buttons to check his messages. He becomes a little melancholy performing the action, as he suddenly remembers how Sonny always gave him shit for hanging onto antique crap.

"Hello, Mr. Landry, this is Detective Rawson

with the Dade County Police Department. A Miss Sonya Richards, your roommate, was brutally shot this evening during a robbery attempt in South Miami. She was admitted to Miami General and was taken directly into emergency surgery. I'm afraid to say that the doctor's prognosis doesn't sound very promising. If you plan on stopping in to see her, there is a Detective Rodgers stationed at her room who would love to talk to you. If not, save us the hassles of hunting you down, and come pay us a visit down at the Precinct."

Nick dismisses the Detective's menacing tone and erases the message before starting the next. Once he's sure that his inner circle is intact, he will give the authorities their due time.

"Hey Nick, it's your number one student. Listen bro, I heard about what happened to Sonny. Give her my love, okay? You call me if there is anything I can do."

Nick presses the button again to start the next message, but it was a hang up. It's probably for the better, any way. Nick can't believe how much his life has been turned upside down, and inside out, in less than twenty four hours. He turns around to face the TV only to see the events of his activities tonight being broadcast on television. The news reports were laying it all on the line including Sonny being shot at the nightclub.

"It sounds like the cops are pretty interested in you." Billy sits up and gestures towards the TV. "Hey look, you're famous, like me, now." The video footage on the television caught Nick as he was riding on top of the van earlier, during the big chase scene on the freeway. "You've gotta admit, it is pretty cool to see yourself on TV and be the only one that knows it's you." Billy looks down at his clothes, taking notice to the fact that his shirt and pants were both reduced to tattered rags. "Hey man, you wouldn't happen to have something I can change into, do ya?"

Nick actually chuckles at Billy's pathetic portrayal of a raggedy man, and gives him a nod. "Sure man, but you have to tell me how you did this healing bit." Nick steps into the guest bedroom, just off the living room, and grabs Billy a jogging suit and a pair of running shoes. "I think these will fit you." He declares, handing the clothing to Billy. "We look like we're close to the same size. "By the way, we were never properly introduced. My name is Nick, Nickolas Landry. How are you doing? Because, I have to admit that I didn't think you were going to make it to shore, much less having this conversation."

"Thanks, yeah, I'm a quick healer, and have been as long as I can remember. My mom said it was a gift, but mostly she rode me all the time for using that as an excuse to do crazy stuff as a kid." Billy pulls the ripped up shirt over his head and drops it to the floor.

"No offense kid, but your still doing crazy shit all grown up." Nick points out as Billy pulls the fresh shirt over his head.

"Yeah, well after this weekend, I think the time has finally come to change that lifestyle. The name's Billy, Billy Ray McBride." Billy struggles to stand and then struggles even more to get out of his burnt torn and blood stained jeans and quickly slips into the sweat pants so that he can sit down before falling down.

"Glad to meet you, Billy." Nick reaches down offering Billy a handshake. The minute Billy takes Nick's hand, Nick senses the darkness that envelopes Billy's life. He doesn't see it as a threat to his duty as Guardian, but can see full well how it could be a threat to Billy. "So, what will you do about your pursuit?" Nick asks, stripping down out of his ceremonial garb of Guardian.

"You mean Callistone? To be honest with you Nick, after tonight, I'm not sure I have any chase left in me." Billy leans back and covers his face with his hands. "This little trip has cost me a lot. The first thing I need to do is go home and try to repair as much damage as possible." Billy moves his hands and looks at Nick. "If not for you, I would have died tonight. That sorta' thing can weigh heavy on a guy, so thanks. What are you gonna do?"

There is only one answer for this question to Nick; he has to face reality and the truth of it all, Starting with his roommate. "The first thing I need to do is go see Sonny before I sort all of this madness out. You're welcome to hang out as long as you'd like. I'm gonna go put on some sensible clothes before I head out, so make yourself at home." Nick starts down the hall and then stops to turn and face Billy once more. "Listen, I just wanted to let you know that I feel the same way. If not for you, I might still be chasing this thing around Miami." Nick shakes the chain of the talisman inside his shirt as reference to his statement. "Thanks, it means more than you could ever know."

"So, that chunk of gold is more valuable than it appears."

"More than you could ever know." Nick continues on down the hall to his room as Billy eases back on the sofa once more. Just because his wounds have healed; it doesn't mean that there isn't some amount of residual pain still raging inside him. Given time, his body will heal completely as it always does. There are some wounds from this venture that will surely take longer others. He's exhausted and needs sleep if he's ever going to regain his strength to make his way home. Nick comes walking back out to see Billy resting on the sofa without his shirt, letting the scars of his battles be seen. After seeing this, Nick is having a hard time believing Billy has survived this long. "Damn, that looks like a whole lot of pain." He sets his bag down and takes a closer look at the scars that riddle Billy's torso. Nick himself owns a scar from a gunshot wound from his service time, but this guy looks like he was the point man during an ambush. "Could you imagine how strong our military would be if we had an army of your clones?" Billy laughs hard, so much so that he aggravates his injuries. He knows that there is no way an army of Billy clones could do anything. They would all have too much fun bucking authority rather than doing their job. Nick just shakes his head. "Like I said, make your self at home. To be honest, I'm not sure when I'll be back, so…"

"Yeah, it was good to meet you too. Now go check on your friend, and good luck, because it sounds like you're gonna need it more than me." Billy leans back on the sofa one more time, closing his eyes to try and get some more rest before heading out himself.

Nick makes his exit and walks out into the front yard where he parks his street bike. He looks back at his house for a second, wondering if he was making the right decision, leaving Billy there alone. It's not that he doesn't trust the young man. At some time tonight, that became a moot point. No it's not Billy's trustworthiness, it's what if the cops show back up here and find Billy tending his wounds. There would be enough circumstantial evidence on display to lock the both of them up for life. After a few seconds more, he climbs onto his motorcycle and opts to leave Billy on his own, and go take care of his own problems.

Billy is already at the door by the time Nick pulls out onto the street. He watches the road for a few seconds expecting something to happen, and isn't surprised when it does. A dark colored sedan with its windows tinted black, starts up and pulls away from the curb on the other side of the street. In the fifteen or twenty seconds Billy had stood there, he never saw anyone get into the vehicle, which means they were bird dogging Nick's house. With a clear shot at the corner of the street, Billy sends them a parting gift in the form of a small energy blast that blows out their front tire. Nick deserved the chance to see his friend before the cops started sticking their heads up is ass, looking for clues. He stands there for a second, watching the driver of the car rant and rave about the blown tire. "Good luck, karate dude."

Billy walks back into the house and closes the door, before heading back to the comfort of the sofa. He knows what he has to do, but just hasn't found the right way to get going yet. Stopping to kick off his boots, he reaches down into the bottom of his left boot to see if his ID is still tucked under the insole. "Well, it's a start," he admits, pulling his driver's license out. If nothing else he can prove where the biggest dumbass in the world lives. How did this all go so wrong, so quick? He threw away everything that was good to him, to chase this fantasy of something that was never going to happen. He knows that in the sole of his other boot is a picture of him and Taylor. He just doesn't want to torture himself right now by pulling it out. Starting for the sofa again, Billy notices an envelope with his name written on it, lying on the dining table. Beneath Billy's name is a note that reads, "Go home." Inside the envelope are several one hundred dollar bills. With his next question answered, Billy heads over to the telephone and dials information. "Yeah, can you get me the number for Delta ticketing at Miami International? Thank ya, ma'am." He waits for a second for the call to be connected and then a little while longer listening to Bertie Higgins classics on the telephone. "Yeah, hi, I was wondering if you can tell me when you're next flight leaves for Atlanta."

Nick sits in the parking lot of Miami Dade General Hospital, contemplating his next move. What he plans to do is all based on the myths and legends he learned from his master, told to Nick years ago. He knows the power of the talisman and what it can do. Master Masamoto demonstrated that to Nick many times. Nick himself demonstrated the power earlier tonight, hiding his and Billy's presence from the Shore Patrol. This is a little different. This is a hospital, fully lit with at least a thousand people in and around it. According to the shift nurse, Sonny's condition is critical. Nick asked for more information, saying that he was Sonny's brother, but the only thing the nurse said was that he should talk to the doctor. This usually means that the patient isn't given long to live. Nick had a plan for that as well, but doesn't really know if he's working on faith, or just grasping at straws with this one. In his tote bag is the egg that Masamoto had entrusted Nick with, to safeguard along with the talisman. The old man told him that it would heal the fallen warriors of the past, and that if Masamoto's brother got his hands on it, he would use its power for his own purpose. If that's the case, the thing should still work for Nick, and save Sonny at the same time. That is, as long as it doesn't send her on over the edge, and kills her off.

The nurse's prognosis isn't good, and even the Detective's message made it sound like she isn't long for the world. So, anything at all would have to better her chances, right? After a good self convincing that he was doing the right thing, Nick slips off his motorcycle and starts towards the hospital. It's a busy night in the emergency room complete with uniformed officers dealing with the ongoing chaos of the Miami nightlife. With everyone rushing around dealing with numerous cases of critical care, Nick is able to slip in unnoticed and quickly makes his way to the nearest service elevator. This is where his Navy SEAL training comes in handy. Nick led his teams into many a building on foreign soil. If he can reach the top floor of the embassy in the middle of Bosnia, undetected, he should be able to find the ICU floor of the local hospital. As the elevator reaches the third floor, Nick takes the talisman in his hand and concentrates for a second. As the doors open, two police officers walking by look inside and are surprised to see the elevator car empty. Nick breathes a sigh of relief and then exits the elevator into the hallway. He starts up the corridor, quickly taking notice to how the hospital seems run down. The nurses and doctors moving about in the hallways seemed like they were overworked, and undernourished, with no sleep in weeks, and barely able to carry out their duties. Patients sit huddled in the rooms and halls, suffering from ghastly wounds and unbelievable pain. Then he starts to see shadows moving around the rooms. No, not shadows, these are dark spirits moving from one person to the next like vaporous clouds, offering a tortured existence to those residing in the hospital. As Nick steps around the corner of the hall, one such spirit looks Nick in the eyes and starts towards him. He steps back around the corner, hoping the apparition passes him by.

"What is going on?" Nick leans up against the wall and takes a deep breath. Is he hallucinating? Why is this hospital in such disarray? The handle on a wheel chair bumps his leg causing Nick to look down. Beside him is a middle aged man who appeared to be half dead. On the man's chest, neck and head are large grayish brown growths that ooze a thick black substance. Whatever it is was spreading with the fowl smelling secretion as it slowly flowed across his skin, devouring the man alive. To make it even worse, the man's head rolls around to the side, revealing the same black ooze squirting and drooling from the man's eye sockets, nose and mouth. The sight of the man pleading for death is more than Nick can bear. Losing focus, he rematerializes to see the Hospital was now in pristine condition. The lights are brighter, the rooms are cleaner, and the medical staff seems to be much more lively and energetic, willing to do their jobs. Oh, and he is now visible.

"Whoa, you've gotta be careful how you sneak up on people!" The man in the wheel chair exclaims, looking up at Nick. "Are you here for an MRI too? I can't believe the machine downstairs is on the fritz. They've been routing people up here all day, keeping patients double parked here in the hallway, instead of in our rooms where we'd be more comfortable." The man looks around as if he had a secret to share. "Listen, Mack, I've been sitting here for three hours, and even worse, trapped in this dump for four days. Can you help a brother out and wheel me outside. I'm dying for a cigarette."

Nick thinks about the request for a second, wondering how he should respectfully decline without sounding judgmental. Saved by the bell, and orderly appears out of the imaging room, and wheels the man in. "Good luck buddy," Nick offers. "You're going to need it," he thinks to himself. Nick doesn't need his investigative background to figure this one out. The growths Nick seen are probably cancerous, which is why the guy is here for an MRI. The question is what did he really see? It has to be the fatigue setting in on him. That's the only logical explanation he can come up with. Still uncertain, Nick hurries off, bothered by the feelings created by what he saw, or didn't see.

Hoping to avoid another unexpected confrontation, Nick crosses the hallway and makes his way down to the end seeking the seclusion behind the stairwell door. Nobody takes the stairs any more, right? He takes to the steel staircase without making a sound. In a few seconds he is standing in front of the fourth floor doorway. A few seconds more, and Nick is at the end of the corridor. He looks around the next corner and sees a uniformed officer and a Detective seated outside one of the ICU room doors. "There you are, girl." Nick grabs the talisman and concentrates on its power once more. As he fades from view again, the lights begin to dim as does the morale of the hospital staff. He stands there for a second watching the wall coverings peel away from the drywall. So shocked by the perversion of reality, he almost lets go of the talisman, and certainly seal his fate. He has to stay focused if he's going to pull this off. "Now how am I going to get into the room without alerting the cops to my presence?" Even though he's invisible, Nick is still solid in form. He can't open the door without alerting the Detective who is leaning against the doorjamb.

Unlimited power, He only has to figure out how to use it. It's not an easy thing to do when your reality is being turned upside down by macabre visions, that Nick is pretty sure aren't real. Walking over to the nurses' station, Nick focuses his attention on a young LPN going over a stack of files. To him, she looks like she hasn't eaten in days, and hasn't slept in weeks. Her work load seems overwhelming, and yet she continues to trudge through it like a mindless slave. In reality, for whatever reason, the young nurse looks up for a second, as if sensing someone standing in front of the counter. Seeing no one in front of her, she happily returns her attention to the doctor's medication notes on the file in front of her. "Here goes nothing," He thinks, reaching out and touching the young lady on her forehead with his fingertips. At first, she is startled, and then filled with an overwhelming desire to get up and check on Sonny's status. The young lady finds Sonny's file in the mountain of folders in front of her, and walks over to the door, giving the Detective reason to move. Entering, the nurse throws the door open wide, giving Nick his entry into the room. Once inside, the nurse closes the blinds as she would usually do, and proceeds to conduct her patient evaluation. A few seconds later, and the nurse is exiting the room to head back to her desk. When she sits down, the young lady is freed from Nick's trance. With no memory of going to Sonny's room, she looks around for a second, slightly confused about what just happened, and a little embarrassed about feeling that way. Dismissing it as fatigue, she returns to her files and continues her work, knowing she only has a few more hours left in her shift.

Nick stands there in the corner of the room with his eyes closed, when he releases his grip on the talisman. He's seen plenty of whacked out shit while under the cloak of the talisman's power. The last thing he needed right now is to see any of that happening around Sonny. Working fast, he retrieves the dragon's egg from his bag. To start with, he isn't sure how this is supposed to work, or if it will at all. All he knows is that the egg is supposed to be laid on the wound of the fallen warrior, and the power of the egg would do the rest, reviving the fallen warrior to fight again. This was the warning that Masamoto gave him years ago. If the egg was ever recovered by the agents of darkness, they could use it to revive their troops to fight against the forces of light. He looks at Sonny's face and finds himself overwhelmed by sorrow and compassion. She looks so peaceful lying there. His cynical side makes him laugh, remembering that the only time that Sonya Richards actually looks peaceful, is when she's asleep. His mind is made up that Sonny has to pull through this, no matter what the sacrifice he must make. She did the same for him in the Middle East. Now he can repay the debt to her by healing her wounds.

Closing his eyes, Nick takes a deep breath and says a short prayer to whoever was listening, asking that his actions help Sonny in her moment of need. The time has come and he has nothing else to offer, so he lays the egg on Sonny's chest and steps back. He looks at the clock and watches the second hand slowly tick around the clock face. He looks back at the egg, but nothing is happening. Nick looks back at the clock, at the monitoring equipment, her face and then back to the clock again. Time is running out and nothing is happening yet. He is becoming quite nervous with this turn of events. Fearing failure, Nick reaches down and takes Sonny's hand wanting to apologize. "I tried, kiddo, but I guess…" Then, it happens. The surface of the egg begins to quiver and shake as the tendrils that covered the egg shell begin to vibrate. All at once, they seem to withdraw back inside the egg, but leave no sign of any penetration to the shell. Then it is Sonny who begins to tremble and shake, as she goes into some kind of convulsion, from her body rejecting what was happening. "Come on Richards, you can do this."

Alarms sound out as the EKG monitor flat lines, warning the medical staff of Sonny's condition. Time is running out for Nick, but he can't pull himself away from her bed. He had to know that she was going to be alright before he moved on. His anxiety for the situation reaches his breaking point as the first to respond to the alarms bursts into the room. She is an elderly nurse content with finishing out the last few years of her career here at Miami General. Turning to face the bed, Rosa Gomez watches Nick vanish from sight in the blink of an eye. "Aiieeey!!!" She screams out, bringing the police detective and his collection of uniformed officers into the room. The only thing they see is the nurse huddled over in the corner. "I'm telling you, it was Muerta, Death walking among us! He has come for her soul and I have disturbed him. Surely he will now seek me out, for disturbing his work!" The nurse bolts from the room and heads straight for the hospital chapel, with Nick right on her heels. The doctors and police dismiss the entire incident, concluding that the nurse was a firm believer of her native religion. The hiccup with the equipment is unexplainable, so after tending to their patient who was sleeping peacefully, they exit the room curious about what had happened.

Staying focused is getting difficult for him, the further and deeper he travels into the hospital. All around him is nothing but agony and suffering, with no relief in sight for anyone, especially Nick. Agonizing cries echo through the hallway as patients crawl out of their rooms. They reach up to him from every doorway, each one suffering from a worse affliction than the one before, wanting an end to it all. All he needs is a few seconds where there isn't anyone around, so that he could drop this act of invisibility, to end these horrific visions once and for all. The problem is he's managed to travel away from the exits and stairwells, trying to avoid as many people as possible. The whole ordeal weighs heavy on his mind, almost as if it was taxing his sanity. Finding a vacant restroom, Nick slips inside and releases his grip on the talisman. Instantly, the tormented sounds and horrific visions disappear, returning the interior of the hospital to a brighter, more tranquil state. Even so, he slowly opens the door and looks back down the hall to see if the ghostly spirits were still in pursuit. The sooner he's out of here, the better. There's nothing left for Nick to do. Hell, he doesn't even know if what he did helped Sonny or not. Still, he has done all that he can do for her, and that puts his mind at ease for the moment. This should allow him to focus on straightening out his own life, so that he can put all of this behind him. He sets his bag on the gas tank of his motorcycle and reaches down to the right side of the motorcycle to grab his helmet. In the brief seconds that it takes for him to put the helmet on, Nick is vulnerable.

A portly man about five foot nine, runs his fingers

through his thinning hair and takes a deep breath. "Good evening, Mr. Landry, tonight has been a very busy night for all of us, hasn't it?" The Detective asks, appearing out of the shadows of the hospital. First impression would suggest that he is close to the end of his twenty years of service, wearing his clothes the same way he wears his badge, sloppy and worn. "My name is Detective Bill Rawson. I have to admit, you're a tough man to track down. It must be all of that Ninja training of yours, right?" Rawson pulls a cigarette from his shirt pocket and shoves the filter into his mouth. "What'cha say you and I have a little talk for a minute." Rawson suggests before lighting his cigarette.

"Okay, let's start with the fact that if I was a trained assassin practicing the art of Ninjitsu, you would have been dead, before you stepped out from behind those bushes." Nick is aggravated by the fact that he let the Detective get the drop on him, but the arrogance of the cop blowing second hand smoke into Nick's face sets Nick off. "As for this nasty habit of yours, I think you should keep it to yourself." With lightning fast reflexes, Nick reaches out and plucks the cigarette from Rawson's mouth and drops into the Detective's open shirt pocket.

Rawson fights to get the burning cigarette out of his pocket, breaking it in the process, and then glares at Nick wanting to punch the martial arts instructor in the nose. "No," he replies, drawing the word out nice and slow, as he makes sure that there aren't any burning embers in his pocket. "I was talking about you, so let's start with your past." Rawson looks around, and then faces Nick again. "Keep in mind that if you try any more of that Kung fu shit again, I'll have twenty cops crawling all over you, got it?" The Detective thinks about lighting another cigarette, but foregoes the act and retrieves a small notebook from his back pocket. After flipping through a few pages, he looks at his broken cigarette on the ground before looking back at Nick. "It says here that you're an ex-Navy SEAL, who was discharged in two thousand and two. Now you teach martial arts to under privileged kids and the elderly. That makes you a killer gone Good Samaritan, now don't it? What is it, are you trying to make amends for what you did in the Navy? I've heard about you SEAL boys and how ruthlessly aggressive you can be." Rawson props his foot up on the fender of the motorcycle's front tire, and turns the page in his notebook. "Here's what I find interesting. According to this, your roommate, an ex-felon, was shot tonight, multiple times, at a night club robbery attempt. At first that wasn't so strange, because there were several other people shot at the scene. What I discovered was that her Parole officer stated that you were the one who escorted Ms. Richards to the concert earlier this evening. Now, correct me if I'm wrong, but she was a member of your team, right? Tell me something, Landry. Where does a guy run off to, when one of his best friends gets shot? I mean, after all, I didn't think you guys would leave one of your own behind."

"What have you got on me, Detective Rawson? I haven't committed a crime, yet. As far as I'm concerned, you haven't got anything on me, and until you do, stay the hell away from me, and my friends!" The muscles in Nick's arms, chest and neck begin to tighten up like a cobra ready to strike. It would be the wrong move to make, but Nick isn't going to stand around and let some gum shoe try to strong arm him.

"Don't you threaten me, boy!" Pushed to his limits, Rawson grabs another cigarette and lights it to calm his nerves. "Let me tell you what I do have! There's a luxury yacht on the breakers of Biscayne Bay, two dead perps on board who are connected to the robbery, your car sitting in a canal, and you without a solid alibi for the passed five hours." Rawson throws his cigarette to the ground and stares at Nick. "Got anything to add?"

Nick steps forward, snuffing out the cigarette on the ground, and leaning in close to the Detective, while darkening his demeanor. "I chased several of the guys out of the nightclub, and watched someone driving off with my car. Since they were following the get away van, I can only assume that they were part of the robbery attempt. As for the yacht and the men on board, if they were connected with the robbery, then they got what they deserved. Now, get your foot off my paint and back the hell off of me, or I swear to god I'll file suit against you and your Department for harassment!"

Rawson is spooked by Nick's appearance, but tries not to let on. "Oh come on now, Landry. You mean to tell me that a tough guy like you is going to hide behind the law?" Rawson removes his shoe from motorcycle fender and then wipes the mud away from the paint. "You were an investigator for the Navy, right? From one detective to another, just hear me out." Rawson flips through a couple of pages of his notebook. "Tell me how close I am with this theory, okay? Your roommate, Sonya Richards, is shot, several times at close range. You were there, but vanished after chasing the perps into the nightclub. It's elementary, my dear Watson. You took it upon yourself to avenge Sonya, thus the dead perps and yacht on Biscayne Bay. Tell me; is that pretty much dead on, or what? Oh, and if so, can you give me the name of your accomplice as well? I have a buddy up in Atlanta that would love to talk to him for a while."

"Here's something for you, Detective. I live a clean life and run a legitimate dojo. I give to the community the way I see fit and expect nothing in return. I have a number of friends on the city council who applaud my efforts, and support whenever and however I need. I don't mess with anyone, and I don't let anyone mess with me, got it?"

Rawson stares at Nick with a determined, defensive nature. "Confessions of tonight's activities, or are you threatening a police officer?"

"That's not a threat, Detective Rawson. Besides, there isn't a witness anywhere around that can vouch for you." Nick lowers the visor of his helmet. "Consider it fair warning. Cross me on the wrong ground, and I will take you apart."

"I know who you are, Landry, and what you're about. So you better watch your step, because if I see you stumble or trip, I'll be all over you. We, on the police force, don't take kindly to vigilante justice. You left a big mess for us to clean up, and we have a team of forensic officers combing through the mountain of evidence that you left behind. We find anything linking you to what happened, I'll be the first one knocking at your door!" Rawson lights another cigarette, needing to calm his nerves and his anger. Nick starts up the motorcycle and puts the bike in gear. Rawson steps up onto the curb to let Nick drive away. Rawson isn't a stupid man and can sense the danger that resides in Nickolas Landry. This isn't the prototypical kind of guy that can be bullied by the badge. No, Rawson knows deep down in his gut that Landry was involved with the events of tonight, and he will have to play this by the book if he's going to prove his theories right. One thing is for certain, there is more to Mr. Nickolas Landry than meets the eye.

Nick drives off down the street, watching his rear view mirrors to see if anyone is following him. His mind is being consumed with chaos as the events of tonight begin to register. How could he have lost control with Rawson like that? Being a control freak, Nick is always on top of himself not to lose that control that governs his actions. He knows how quickly a person's life can spin out of control, when the person in question holds the fate of the world in his hands. He drives passed his house once to check the surroundings for any signs of more surprises, before driving back and pulling up into the driveway. Convinced that his front yard isn't littered with Police, FBI, or ninja garbed assassins hoping to get the jump on him, Nick shuts off the bike and climbs to head up onto the front porch to make his way inside the home. There, he finds a note from Billy taped to the glass, thanking Nick for his help and hospitality. He says a quick farewell to Billy's memory, before entering the house to seek some much needed rest. Finally, his night is over.

# Chapter IX

"Wake up!" Hiro Masamoto shakes a confused Nickolas Landry, until his student opens his eyes. "Get up, unless you are here to die!" Masamoto pulls Nick up from the ground and starts to run, pulling Nick along. Not understanding what is going on, Nick tries to keep pace, having no idea where he is, or where they're going. The ancient little Japanese man that taught Nick everything he knows about the talisman is now outrunning Nick at an unbelievable pace. Not an easy task to accomplish at his age, much less when he's supposed to be dead.

Nick is shocked at what is taking place. It seems like only a few minutes ago, he was lying down on his bed to get some sleep. Now, he is running for his life through some dreary, ominous, landscape without knowing why, or what, he is running from. This has to be some kind of morbid dream, brought on by fatigue and the residual effects of using the talisman, earlier. If that's the case, then Nick is just along for the ride, until he wakes up. After racing up a small hill, the two men stop at an ancient stone temple and seek shelter within its stone columns and walls. "Master, where are we, and aren't you dead? If you are dead, then does that mean

I've died too? If so, the outcome sucks," he declares, and then adds, "no offense."

"Ah, Nickolas, you still seek knowledge one dimensionally. As for where we are, this is the realm in which I now dwell with the rest of the council. As for why I have brought you here, is to warn you that danger now stalks your life." Hiro walks away and enters the center chamber of the temple and waves his hand through the air. Numerous candles around the room light up by his gesture, casting an eerie lighted glow about the room, as the old man moves toward a stone altar in the center. "Why Nickolas, why did you use the power of the talisman? In doing so, you have now set in motion a chain of events that cannot be stopped." Masamoto crosses his legs and sits down on the dirt covered floor and motions for his student to do the same.

Nick follows Masamoto's lead and sits down. "There were circumstances beyond my control. I had to do whatever I could to make things right. I didn't foresee the unexpected involvement and had to act accordingly." For whatever reason, Nick has the same feeling again that he had when he was using the talisman to cloak his presence. "Where are we, Master?"

"We are in the first realm that was conquered by the Devastator, over five thousand years ago. We are safe here, for Deronibus has claimed all that was viable and has discarded this realm." Masamoto closes his eyes and bows his head. "There will always be unexpected involvement as long as you interact with humanity. I warned you to give up your ties with your society, and that the protection of the talisman is the only duty of importance." Masamoto opens his eyes, "You must listen to me, Nickolas and heed my warning. By losing possession of the talisman, you have broken the spell that kept it hidden from others. The one who possesses the other half of the talisman now knows the location of the other half that you possess. His minions will be moving in to test you. It will be the first of three tests that you must face. The second will be a test of honor, and the third will be a test of love. Duty, honor, and love, are three keys to why you are destined to be the Guardian."

"Master, you are referring to your brother, right?" Nick looks around the room, sensing movement somewhere in the darkened corners of the room.

"Remember what I have told you, Nickolas, for it was spoken to you for a reason. My brother no longer exists. In his stead, is a dark creature of great power, determined to destroy the realm of Earth. He holds the secret to the talisman's power and it is he that will have you sought out for conflict. With the half that you possess, he will be unstoppable in finding the other pieces to the scepter. Once that is accomplished, Earth will fall to his crusade."

"Doomsayer, right, you called the spirit that took control of Seko's body, Lord Doomsayer?"

Masamoto looks around the room and ceiling of the temple, not focusing on one spot. "Go, Nickolas, your student is with you, and seeks your council." The old man reaches out and punches Nick in the chest.

The effect of his teacher's action is like being hit by lightning. Nick opens his eyes and finds himself lying on his bed with JD standing over him, displaying a concerned look on his face. "Damn, Teach, you really had me worried there, for a minute. I ain't never seen anybody sleep that deeply before." JD offers Nick a hand to sit up. "You were like off in some far away place, dreaming your ass off, weren't ya?"

"You have no idea." Nick takes JD's hand and sits up on the side of the bed. "What time is it, man?"

"5:30 am, bro, remember we were going to do our endurance run this morning? But, after everything that happened last night, I figured you weren't gonna be up for it, so I decided to stop in and check on you, before I went out on my own." JD walks over to the front window and peeks out the blinds. Looking back at Nick, he asks, "Any word on how Sonny's doing?" He looks back out the window again, trying to be as inconspicuous as possible.

Nick stands up and walks over beside JD. "What are you looking at?"

"I'm checking out those cops across the street. For some odd ball reason they think their cheesy cover hides their identity, but I had them pegged from a mile away." The student turns to face his teacher. "You okay, Nick? You don't look like yourself."

"I'll be alright, JD." Nick gives the young man a half assed smile, hoping to squash the next round of twenty questions. "Right now, you should be more focused on the next chapter of your life. Hey, aren't your parents supposed to be coming down for your big celebration and send off?" That should change the subject long enough for Nick's condition to be moved back to the back burner, so to speak.

"Yeah, they got in Thursday night, but they're leaving this afternoon, so dad can get home to prepare for his sermon. After all, his flock of sheep is more important to him than I am, and every other religious building in the world is full of sacrilege compared to his church. That's okay with me though. Aunt Shirley's house is huge, but it always seems crowded when he comes to visit." JD takes chase after Nick who starts through the house towards the kitchen. "Hold on there a second, Teach, I've gotta know something. Was that you on the news last night, doing all of that crazy shit on the highway? And who was the guy driving your car? I know one thing, judging by the footage I saw on the news and YouTube, that dude's got skills! I'd love to hang out with him for a while. I bet the guy would be a hoot at parties." JD knows that it's a long shot, but he hopes that he'll get a straight answer this time from the King of sidestepping.

So much has happened to Nick in the past twelve hours that he truly doesn't know where to start. Not to mention the fact that there were a couple of incidents, including the little dream sequence, that have Nick doubting his own sanity at the moment. "Careful what you wish for, JD. This world is so small; you might run into the guy. Personally, no offense to you or him, but I don't think he's your type."

"I don't want to date him! I just said that I wouldn't mind hanging out with him."

"Did you tell your father?" Nick finishes off his glass of water, and starts back to his room. Surprising JD, Nick continues on down the hall and stops at Sonny's bedroom door. Usually, at this time of morning, she would be moving about the room, before her forty minute shower that starts her day. Now the room is lifeless making the entire house seem empty. "Hang in there, Sonny," he says to himself, turning to face JD.

"No, I didn't get the chance to talk to him about it. I'll try to work up the nerve after lunch, maybe. I always seem to have more courage when my stomach's full." JD gives Nick a friendly punch to his shoulder. "You hang in there, Nick. You've got me worried about ya."

Walking back to the living room with JD following close behind, Nick picks up the TV remote. "I'm going to be alright, JD. You go for your run, and then go be with your family, and respect your father. We can meet up down at the dojo later on this afternoon. In fact, plan on dinner, because I still owe you a birthday meal. I'll go check on Sonny and then meet you around four o'clock, deal?" Turning the TV on, Nick sits down on the sofa, hoping the interrogation can be postponed until later. There ate some things he can't share with JD, like what he did at the hospital last night.

Alright Nick, I'll see you around four." JD heads for the front door but stops to look back at his mentor one more time. He can see that Sonny's brush with death is weighing heavy on Nick. "I think I'm gonna go mess with the cops. Do you want me to leave the door open?" JD waits for a response and then heads on out, walking straight across the street to the undercover cops posing as utility workers. Seconds later, the work crew packs up and leaves, as JD jogs on down the street.

Nick stares at the TV as the news footage shows what's left of Cortez's yacht being removed from the breakers. Sitting back, Nick closes his eyes, remembering the escapades of last night, and the dream he had of Masamoto. The old man warned Nick that in losing the talisman, his enemies now know where he is. Has he failed in his duty? No, because he reclaimed the talisman and it is still in his possession. He will do what he has to, in order to correct his shortcomings. If someone wishes to challenge him then step right up, Because Nick isn't going to let this happen again.

The news footage continues, showing clips from the nightclub's security system of Billy in his costume and trench coat, and spectator footage of their high speed chase on the freeway. Of course JD knows it was Nick, leaping from vehicle to vehicle. Nick's student has seen the ceremonial attire, and there was Nick in the footage wearing it to be seen by the world, with his only reason being it's purpose to conceal his identity. This is a matter to be addressed later on. For now, Nick's thoughts are of Sonny. He played his hand last night with Rawson, and learned where he stands with the authorities. This gives him a little breathing room, as for him going back today to check on Sonny's condition. Nick has given his statement about what happened and he's going to stick to it, unless they can find something to dispute it. As far as Nick can tell, there isn't anything out there that can

181

be used against him, so he can maintain his posture and not worry about Rawson's investigation.

If that's the case, Nick has to continue his life and not be distracted by last night. If he is to portray the role of innocent bystander, he must act accordingly and carry out his daily duties as if nothing happened. First, he will go down to the dojo for his morning classes, before heading down to the hospital to check on Sonny. Hopefully, his plans with JD for the evening will be uneventful. To get things started, he pulls himself up off the sofa and heads to his room. With a quick detour to the bathroom, Nick turns on the shower to get the hot water flowing before retrieving his clothes for the day.

Once in the shower, the hot water soothes his aching muscles and washes the worries from his mind. Even so, he thinks about the dream he had last night. He still hasn't ruled out that it was some kind of message from Masamoto, from beyond the grave. In fact, with everything that's connected to the talisman, Nick is willing to bet the farm on the fact that the two are connected. Now he has to figure out exactly what Masamoto meant. The first step is to forget about figuring out the how part of it all. Nick knows when and when not to question Masamoto's abilities, apparently even after his teacher's death. For now, he needs to stay focused on one thing at a time, until he can clear some space on his list of things to do. First, he'll go see Sonny. Once he is through at the hospital, He'll work on the next thing.

After turning the water off, Nick reaches out of the shower to retrieve his towel. It is at this moment in time, where one droplet of water runs down from his hair line, and finds the one spot where there was the smallest of amount of soap that didn't get washed away. With his body turned and leaning just the right way, gravity and the curves of his features sends that soapy water drop right into Nick's eye. For a second, he is blinded by the stinging pain of the soap in his eye. By blinking and squinting, Nick does all he can to bring the torture to an end, But it is during this time that his mind picks up on something out of place. His eyes open and close repeatedly, and during the split second that his eyes open once, there is a form of a man standing in front of him. It happens so fast that it doesn't register in his mind until the next time his eyes open, but the person is gone. Nick Quickly looks around doing all that he can to regain his visual focus. Was there someone there, or was it just his mind playing tricks on him? Being a creature of habit, He wraps a towel around his bare hips and proceeds to search the house as quickly as possible, without killing himself. Not being able to see, he ran into two tables and a chair before he could make his way through the entire house.

Returning to his bathroom to get dressed, Nick laughs the episode off as a case of his eyes playing tricks on him. He looks into the mirror and laughs at his antics. "What's wrong with you, Nickels? You're letting all of this stuff get to you," he says to his reflection. Then, something catches his eye again. In the reflection, he sees someone again, standing outside his window looking in. He spins around and looks out his bedroom window just in time to see the intruder dart away. Nick was right that there was someone in the house and isn't about to let them get away again. Taking to the hall, he heads for the front door and throws it open wide. Off the front porch he bounds out into the middle of the front yard, expecting to tackle the peeping tom to the ground, but there is no one there. Nick heads to the sidewalk then hoping to catch sight of the fleeing man, but runs right into the neighborhood mail delivery. To say that the middle aged woman is surprised would be an understatement. For anyone to think she is offended by the sight would be wrong. "Oh, uh, hello Delores," Nick stutters as he tries to pull his towel up around his waist. "Someone was looking in my window. Did you see anybody come by here?"

"No sugar, I didn't, but I can see why they were peeking." She looks Nick up and down one more time to remember his chiseled features and rippled muscles. She's a firm believer that thoughts like that can come in handy on some cold, lonely, night.

Nick looks around the neighborhood one more time, hoping to get a glimpse of anything that might be out of the ordinary. He scans the yards, and looks around at the nearby houses, but there is no sign of his mystery man dressed in black. Frustrated, and chilled, Nick heads back to the house and double checks every point of entry to make sure each window and door is locked. Now he has to wonder who it could have been. The Police, maybe, or it possibly could've been the FBI. If there was probable cause for the Federal boys, they could've been the ones snooping around. But as much as he doesn't want to admit it, it could've been someone or some thing connected to the talisman. In Nick's dream, Masamoto warned him that the agents of darkness could pinpoint Nick's location now that the spell has been broken. Could they have moved that quickly to his location? If so, it definitely changes his scope of work, not to mention explain how the intruder was able to get away so quickly. None of this makes Nick feel good about what is happening.

For now, he has to carry on with his daily duties. He was the one who believed he could carry on with his life and serve as Guardian. A picture of Megan reminds him of how he has already been proven wrong with that assumption. He shakes off the feelings the picture brings out in him, knowing he can't afford to go down that road right now. His confidence has to be high and his awareness at its peak, if something is coming his way. Dressed and ready to face the day, Nick takes off to teach his students his craft.

The entire drive to the dojo is spent by Nick scanning his surroundings and checking his rear view mirrors, watching for something, anything to show itself. This isn't a safe practice by any means, as proven when Nick almost runs into the back of a truck while studying a crowd at a bus stop. He apologizes to the driver for scaring her before she drives off. He's got to calm down before he loses his mind or kills himself. Pulling up in front of the dojo eases his tension somewhat. Now he wants to get inside and out of the public eye to ease his paranoia.

Nick looks around before getting off his motorcycle, and then looks around once more before he walks over to the front door of his studio. After unlocking the door, Nick looks around one more time before walking inside. He does make a mental note about something while turning on the lights. For the past few days, maybe a week or so, Nick has had this feeling that someone was watching him. But today, when there was an obvious intruder standing outside his window, Nick sensed nothing that was out of the ordinary. Was the earlier "feelings" a precursor of what's to come, or has he just gone off the deep end after everything that has happened. Maybe he just needs to take a little time to relax.

Sitting down in the middle of the floor, Nick closes his eyes and begins his form of meditation. Once his mind has cleared and his pulse slowed, he will slowly stand and begin the exercise taught to him by Master Masamoto. With his mind, body, and spirit, calmed and relaxed, Nick rises to begin the second part of the exercise. Seeing his students standing in front of him causes Nick to jump up and back, taking a defensive stance. This startles the students causing them to jump back as well. Nick looks around at the clock on the wall and is shocked that what seemed like minutes, an hour and a half had gone by. "Sorry guys, I didn't expect to see you there."

"You're sorry, man I peed my pants when you jumped up like that!" The students laugh at their classmate's misfortune, and then run to their spots on the floor, while the unfortunate one heads for the restroom.

"Sensei, are we going to test for rank today?"

Nick turns around and faces his class. This is a great idea and definitely something to take his mind off his problems. "Yeah, ya know what? That's a great idea! Everyone tests, and we'll have a good evaluation for what needs to be worked on." He lines his students up with a bow, and then waits for his lone student in the restroom to hurry out and join the class. For the next hour, his thoughts are miles away from the intruder, Sonny, Detective Rawson, and the rest of the madness that took place last night. Maybe today will turn out better than how it started.

After class, Nick walks into his office and changes clothes to ready himself for his visit with Sonny. It isn't until he is pulling up in front of the hospital that he realizes that he drove all the way there without worrying about looking over his shoulder. Pulling into the parking lot, the sight of a police squad car stirs Nick's negative emotions, making him second guess coming here. Is he pushing the limit by showing up here after his confrontation with Rawson last night? To hell with that! Nickolas Landry has never been the type to turn away from a friend in need. He's going to march right in there and find out what's going on with Sonny and if she's going to pull through. No one is going to get in his way and nothing is going to stop him.

"I'm sorry sir, but it is hospital policy. We do not give out patient information unless you are an immediate member of the family." The nurse looks back to her paperwork as if she expected Nick to just walk away. Obviously, she doesn't know Nickolas Landry. "Is there something else I can help you with, Sir?" Her tone is aggravated and short, as she looks up above her glasses.

"Listen, I'm the closest thing Sonny's got to family. In fact, I was named her guardian by the state when she was released on parole. Doesn't that make me close enough for family?" Nick looks around to make sure he isn't causing too much of a distraction.

"Well, her parole officer was in here this morning, and he didn't say anything about a Mr. Nickolas Landry being named as next of kin, or emergency contact. So, unless you can get me some kind of legal document that says as much, I can't let you in to see her, or give you any information." The nurse removes her glasses and stands up to face Nick. "Listen, Mr. Landry, I hope you can understand my position. It's not that I don't want to tell you, but my job would be on the line if I did. I'm really sorry, but policy is policy." Nick hangs his head in frustration. Out the corner of his eye, he sees a man dressed in black at the end of the hall. Nick doesn't move because he doesn't want to alert the man, if it's the same guy from this morning. Instead, Nick just stands there with his head low with his hands propped on the counter. "Mr. Landry, are you alright?" The nurse looks around real quick, and then whispers, "She's stable for now, but the doctors are carefully monitoring her."

"Yeah," Nick turns his head and stares the man down. The action lasts only a second, before the man breaks and runs, but it is enough for Nick to get a read on the guy. Long black coat, black boots, pants and shirt, with a black beanie and sunglasses finish off the suspicious man's attire. In the middle of the day in Miami Florida, this guy will be hard to lose. Nick sprints up the hospital corridor, knocking people to the side trying to get to his prey. He won't lose this guy again. Reaching the closing stairwell door, Nick lays a shoulder into the steel clad barrier, knocking the door from its hinges. His target leaps to the landing below to avoid the door sliding down the steps and to put a little distance between himself and Nick. Down the stairwell they race, both with a goal of their own, but every time Nick seems to close in, his prey is able to regain the distance between them. Nick knows he has to end this as soon as possible. His body is still depleted from last night's escapades and that could limit a long distance pursuit.

The mystery man leaps to the ground floor of the stairwell and rips the door free and uses it to shield himself from Nick leaping down onto his position. Once an object is placed in motion, it will remain in motion until outside forces impede its progress. Nick is reminded of this physics lesson as he crashes into the door, before being deflected down under the steel frame of the stairs. This doesn't stop Nick, but it does slow him down a little. Master Masamoto instructed Nick a long time ago the art of blocking out pain. Feudal soldiers and Samurai warriors used the practice long ago to sustain injuries and yet continue to fight for their cause. Nick uses this now as he takes chase once again. He doesn't have any broken bones or internal injuries, but bouncing around under a steel staircase can leave a mark or two.

Out the stairwell Nick runs, taking notice to the people who had moved or were moved out of the way by his target. Some pointed the way of his prey, while others stood around in shock, not believing what they have seen take place in a hospital. Nick sees his target disappear outside, as the man leaps through the glass doors of the main entrance. Nick doesn't slow down at all. He sprints right at the entrance and right through the shattered opening, where he is slowed down by the front end of a patrol car. Not to be stopped, he spins around the front of the car and continues his pursuit. To Nick's advantage, the man runs out into traffic, where he is rolled up onto the hood of a car, before being thrown to the ground. It doesn't stop him, but it slows him down allowing Nick to gain some ground. Once across the street, the man runs into a narrow alley just seconds before Nick does. Sometimes, seconds is all a man needs.

Into the alley Nick runs, and can't believe the luck of it all. There was no way the guy had already reached the other end of the alley. No one can run two hundred yards in less than three seconds. Remembering a similar chase from years ago, Nick looks up at the sides of the building just to make sure the guy wasn't hanging around above him. Out the other end of the alley Nick runs, right into the unsuspecting presence of several police officers who were attending the scene of an accident between a scooter and a van. Nick looks around and then breaks and runs up the street, thinking he saw a glimpse of his mystery man. Behind him, the cops call out for him to stop, and then call in for backup on the radio.

Nick hears none of this; being focused on the man he sees again, a block ahead of him. His legs are starting to burn as his muscles crave rest and oxygen. He blocks this out for the time being, but can't do anything about the internal clock that is ticking down. If he doesn't catch this guy soon, he will lose the chase. Pushing himself harder, Nick dodges oncoming pedestrian traffic and hurdles a mail carrier kneeling down in front of a public mailbox, before leaping over the hood of a passing car at the intersection. His path takes him right in front of a small truck that barely misses him, but Nick pays no mind to it. His focus is on one thing and one thing only, and he won't stop.

Nick makes the next intersection in record time and sees the police car pulling up to block his path. He sees the cops get out of the car with their guns drawn, but this doesn't slow him down. It is almost comical how they appeared to think he would lay down for them when they draw down on him and yell, "Freeze!" Nick doesn't hesitate. Before either officer could fire a shot, Nick is already in the air above them, landing a kick to one cop's chest, while knocking the gun free from the other officer's hand. Before the officers could regroup, Nick is well on his way on up the street. He watches as the man climbs the fence of the city bus depot yard, where Nick hopes to have him cornered. Up the fence he goes, using his talents to scale the fence and flip over to the other side without worry of hitting the razor wire along the top of the chain link. As he passes over, Nick is quick to notice that his target was not as lucky, leaving blood smeared on the blades of the razor wire. The man is wounded, which could benefit Nick by slowing the man down. There are workers moving about in the main yard. Nick will listen for them, should somebody spot his prey before he does. After all, both Nick and his target are trespassing on City property.

"Hey, you sonofabitch, are you the one who shoved me down in the mud!?!" Nick spins around to see a very large man, covered in mud from head to toe, walking towards Nick with raging determination. "I'm gonna kick your ass!" No, no, no, not now, Nick is so close to catching this guy! He doesn't have time or the energy for a confrontation like this. It's a last ditch effort, but Nick goes for it, running out from between the buses into the main service yard where he is seen by every worker on the property. "You guys stop that jerk, so I can bust his skull for what he did to me!"

It's over, and Nick has lost his chance at finding out who his target was, and why he was watching Nick. If things aren't bad enough for him, three police cars roll up to the main entrance, producing two armed police officers for every squad car. There is only one way for Nick to get out of here. He has to use the talisman. Back flipping towards the muddy worker, Nick plants both feet into the man's chest and drives him to the ground. With the immediate threat out of the picture, he runs back in between the parked buses and grabs the talisman hanging inside his shirt. When the man rolls over all he see is the grass growing in the gravel between the bus tires, but there is no sign of Nick anywhere.

He's tired, aggravated, frustrated and down right pissed off. Nick can't help but wonder who that was, and why the man was spying on Nick. There are a lot of possibilities and scenarios that can be put into play. Cops, FBI, agents of darkness, hell it could be someone from his past. His SEAL team made plenty of enemies during their missions. Nah, even Nick knows that would be a further reach, than demonic warriors flying around. Has he brought all of this onto himself? It is becoming more and more apparent that the turmoil entering Nick's life has to be connected to his so-called destiny. The words echo in his mind about how his destiny would destroy the life he knows. For the first times, nick realizes that the destruction brought on by the talisman didn't stop with the deaths of Masamoto and Megan. For now, he will let this one go, unless the man shows up again. It's like they always say, "Third time's the charm," and Nick is going to make sure the guy won't get a fourth shot at him.

# Chapter 8

Nick and JD make their way down the street from dinner, walking to Nick's dojo. For the time being, he has blocked his chase scene out of his mind, so that he can dedicate his time to his student. But, this doesn't mean that Nick has dropped his guard by no means. His mind and body are on high alert should the mystery man make his presence known again. This is something that JD has picked up on but hasn't pushed the issue, yet.

"...but Nick, tell me how I get him to understand that what you have taught me can exist, without defying his beliefs and wishes?" JD doesn't look at Nick as they walk down the street. He already knows what Nick is going to say. They have had this conversation time and time again, always with the same results. When Nick doesn't give his usual response right away, JD feels he has to confront Nick. "Are you alright, Teach? You seem like you've been miles away all evening."

"Yeah, I'm sorry, JD. Listen, the best way for you to handle a situation is head on, with the truth as your ally." Nick can't believe he just said that. It's more a matter of do as I say, not as I do. JD doesn't have to worry about standing up for the world. All he needs to do is stand up to his father and be recognized. As for Nick's distractions, he thought he had been successful in hiding his concerns for their welfare while at dinner. Obviously, their friendship gives JD the insight needed to see through his façade. Did he really think it would be that easy to hide the truth from JD? "Don't sweat it," he thinks to himself. "I may have brought about the end of the world but I think I can handle it." His self inflicted sarcasm has no effect on his present attitude. That feeling of being watched has returned again, but there has been no sign of his friend in black. All the while, his Master's words from the dream continue to run through Nick's head, over and over. They stop at the front door while Nick unlocks it. He looks around the neighborhood for a second, and then opens the door.

"Come on, man, let's get inside." JD pushes passed Nick and hurries over to turn on the lights. He turns around and faces his mentor, staring Nick down. "I've got two questions for you, Teach. Are you able to give me my final test tonight, and are you going to give me a straight answer about last night?"

"Yes, we can test for your last belt in a little while. First I would like to spend some time talking to you. I don't want to be doing anything to exert myself until my dinner settles." Nick walks over to the middle of the floor and takes a seat, motioning for JD to do the same. "As for a conclusion to our previous topic of conversation, just because you defend yourself when there is no other alternative, doesn't mean you are expressing an aggressive nature. It simply means you are expressing your right for survival. You, like every other creature on this planet has the right to survival. No one wants to lie down and die, or beaten, or mistreated in any way. If you want some ammunition, remember these little shots. Your father's god said that your body is the temple of your soul, where the lord resides. What kind of landlord would you be if you keep letting your temple be vandalized? Or, throw one at him like, you're supposed to strive for your full potential and do wondrous things in the lord's name. Ya can't do that, if you're lying on the ground." Nick smiles at JD's reaction to his last statement. "I know those are two contrasting statements, but my point is that you won't ever know what you are supposed to say, until you initiate the conversation." Nick stands up abruptly and offers JD a hand. "Come on, I have something for you." Nick heads back to his office, making his way over to his "storage" room. Before deactivating the locking mechanism, Nick pays homage to his Master, bowing in front of the old man's portrait.

JD follows Nick inside the small room, for the first time. In the almost three years that JD has known his mentor, no one has ever gone inside this room except Nick. Finally, JD gets to see the treasures of Nickolas Landry. He too bows in front of Masamoto's portrait, believing it to be the right thing to do. The interior of the room resembles a Japanese shrine, complete with another smaller portrait of Masamoto. In the corner is a mannequin wearing the garb of a Japanese warrior of mythical proportions. It's the costume JD recognized on TV last night. The walls are decorated with weapons and tapestries, but none are more dazzling than the center piece of the room; the dragon statue. "Ya know, you never did tell me how Master Masamoto's father was able to split the talisman in half. I mean, you did say that the pieces of the key couldn't be destroyed, right? So how do you break something in half that can't be broken?"

Nick removes the talisman from around his neck and drapes it around the dragon statue. "According to Masamoto, his father had the village blacksmith attempt several times to split the talisman in half, but it couldn't be done. The blacksmith however, refused to give up. There wasn't a metal on the planet that wouldn't bend to his will. So, he devised a plan and built a machine that would do the job. To make a long story short, it was a cross between a guillotine and a catapult. When the hatchet blade swung around and made contact, the talisman was split in half, but the energy released killed the blacksmith and the other workers present. This also alerted Masamoto's brother to what had happened." Nick turns away from JD and retrieves a package wrapped in traditional rice paper. "Now, I want to give you this as a memento of your success." He hands it to JD, motions for his student to exit the room, and then locks it securely before heading over to a beat up gym locker on the corner of his office.

"Dude, this is so tight!" JD exclaims, ripping the paper open to see a new gi, complete with split toed tabi boots. "I've never seen a gi designed like this before. He holds the martial arts uniform up and looks it over thoroughly. Then, he folds it up neatly and stacks the uniform over to the side, and goes out to get his uniform that he has worn for nearly two years. Nick just stares at his student when he returns, wondering why he would choose to wear his old worn out handed down gi, instead of the new one. JD sees the confusion on his teacher's face, and happily offers an explanation. "No offense, Teach, but I just thought I should wait to try it on after I pass the final test you have for me."

"Not a problem," Nick replies, slipping on his split toed tabi boots, and then waits for JD to get dressed. "In that case, choose two weapons for the first two phases of the test." Nick plays the first hand, motioning to the swords and weapons on his office wall. JD, as well as every other student knew that the weapons in the dojo don't have sharpened edges. These in Nick's office do. "What's it gonna be? Swords, Naganatos, Bo staffs, Sais, whichever you like.

JD pulls his shirt over his head and then looks the wall over. He doesn't want anything to do with the Naganatos. To him, they are the most absurd weapon he's seen. Whoever thought that putting a broad bladed sword at the end of a five foot spear was a good thing, definitely had issues. "I choose the katana and the bo staff. Now, what did you want to talk about?"

Nick chuckles at the question and retrieves the weapons from the wall. "Do you remember the day we met?"

"Yeah, how can I forget? You seem to find a way to remind me every chance you get." After tying his belt JD accepts the weapons from Nick before they head out into the main room of the dojo. "You really spooked me with all of that good and evil mumbo jumbo. Shoot, I almost didn't come to see you the next day, because I wasn't sure which way you were coming from." JD points the tip of his katana at Nick, challenging him to the upcoming duel. "To be honest, I still don't know if I've got you figured out."

"Watch it, smart guy." Nick draws his sword and accepts JD's challenge. The student and teacher charge at each other with swords held high. Nick stops first accepting the role of defense as JD comes in to attack. Their blades clang together again and again, as JD pushes himself to his limits to prove himself worthy of Nick's test. Finally, the two combatants come together with the blades of their swords holding each other at bay. "Had enough, Teach?"

Nick uses his lightning fast reflexes to deliver a kick to JD's leg, giving him leverage to push his student away. "We haven't even started yet, kid." Nick raises his sword and takes the offensive, driving JD back across the mats. "So, do you still have questions for me?" Neither opponent holds anything back as Nick continues his offensive attack on his student. JD wants to prove he is worthy of the test, and Nick wants to push his student to his limit to prove his student is worthy. Their blades slice through the air and come together, ringing out the sounds of steel against steel. Neither falters, neither concedes to the victor.

"How long do you have to carry out this duty of yours?" JD takes the advantage away from Nick by spinning around and delivering a kick to Nick's back while blocking his series of blocks and parries. The sword is not JD's first choice of weapons, and he has to admit that he's surprised at himself for lasting against Nick this long. It's not like he's had a choice in the matter. There were a few of Nick's moves that JD was sure would have taken off his head, if he hadn't come through with the blocks.

Nick staggers forward, surprised and impressed with JD's move. He can see that his student has had enough, but isn't ready to concede just yet. He's taken Nick's best and is still standing. "My duty as Guardian will last my entire life. Should the necessity end before I do, then so be it." Nick jumps back away from JD's attack sending the young man sprawling to the floor. JD quickly rolls over to collect his sword and find his opponent. To his surprise, Nick is standing still with his sword raised in front of his face, as if saluting JD's accomplishment. "Good job, my son." Nick lowers his sword and bows to JD.

JD returns the gesture and bows to Nick, knowing that he has passed his first portion of the test. "You're a hell of a man, Nickolas Landry. That's all I've got to say." He walks over to the weapons wall and returns his sword to the hooks that hold it on the wall. "In the midst of the closest thing to a family crisis that you can have, you're here with me to uphold your agreement with me. I'm honored by that, Teach. I want you to know that I consider you my best friend, and I am proud to call you that."

Nick tosses a Bo staff at JD. "Don't think you can sweet talk your way out of this. We still have some testing to complete." Nick bounds across the floor, using his staff to vault over closer to JD to make his attack. His student is ready for Nick this time. This is JD's weapon of choice and he is highly skilled with the five foot long piece of wood. The wooden Bo staffs clack and crack together with the repetition of an automatic weapon. The attacks come high and low with each man doing all that he can to fall the other. Now it is Nick who is beginning to tire. He must change the variables of the battle. "Do you think you've got what it takes, to take my place should I fall?"

"Huh?" JD freezes, completely stunned by Nick's question. The distraction does its job just as Nick had planned. With a jab to JD's stomach, Nick spins around and sweeps JD's legs out from under him, sending the student to the floor. Nick steps back and laughs, while shaking his finger at his student. "Don't allow yourself to be distracted. Your mind controls your actions. If it stops, so does your body. Thus the opening for my attack is given."

"Oh man, you are dead!" JD charges his teacher with a smile on his face and his staff spinning and twirling all around. Nick has taught him well the tactics of battle. If Nick is stooping to use distraction as an ally, then he is obviously tiring of battle. He takes the offensive to Nick and never relinquishes it again. From the moment his staff makes contact with Nick's, the student sends the teacher backpedaling from the onslaught. JD never lands a blow to Nick, but it takes everything the teacher has to prevent it from happening. Once he is backed up against the wall, Nick has no other choice but to concede. The student has bested the teacher. JD leaps back, performing a flip in the air, to give Nick room to kneel before him.

The teacher doesn't go that far, but he does give up his weapon and bow to his student. Looking up and smiling, Nick is proud of JD and the hurdles he has overcome. "You are my finest student, Jefferson, who has embraced his own destiny by learning all that I have. I am proud of you and proud as well to call you my friend." Nick walks over and puts his arm around JD's shoulder. "To be honest, I like to think of you as the son I'll never have." With that said, Nick legs sweeps JD, catching him completely off guard and sending the student to the floor.

"What the hell was that for?" JD asks, looking up at Nick from the flat of his back.

"Just to make sure you never get to cocky." Nick reaches down and takes JD's hand to help him up. "You are my only friend, Jefferson. I wish you all the best as you take this next step in life. College life gave me a lot of good times and a lot of good memories. Go make some of your own, but always remember that my door will be open to you."

"Aw, come on Nick; don't go getting all mushy on me." JD becomes a little melancholy with the feeling that they were saying goodbye for good. Not to mention JD was a little embarrassed by Nick boasting about JD's success. His own father has never given him such honorable accolades.

"I agree," Rawson interjects, stepping into view as he lights a cigarette. "I was beginning to wonder if the two of you were going to kiss or not." The Detective takes a long drag off his cigarette and blows the smoke into the air. Nick is highly insulted by Rawson's actions. Using his lightning fast reflexes, Nick flings his body up into the air with a twist and a spin, to hurl his staff at Rawson, removing the cigarette from between the Detective's finger, and snuffing it out against the concrete block wall behind him.

JD nudges Nick with his elbow. "I told you that you should change up the front entrance to this place. Ya never know what will wander in unannounced."

Nick doesn't reply. He just stares down the Detective that keeps interfering with Nick's life. "You're trespassing."

The Police Detective has never seen anything more

incredible than what he just witnessed. Of course, the action was disturbing enough to cause Rawson to pull his weapon and point it at Nick. "Does this bother you, Landry?"

"Not at all, Detective, I've had bigger guns than that pointed at me. The only difference is that I would usually kill the man holding the gun before he could squeeze the trigger." Nick doesn't back down a bit. How dare this man come in here uninvited and disturb what Nick and JD were doing?

"Okay, things just got too crazy for me." JD walks over to grab his bag. "Nick, I'm gonna let you deal with Dirty Harry. As for me, I'm heading on home where guns aren't so freely pointed at people." JD starts towards the Detective and stops a few feet from him. Again Nick is impressed by the cool confidence that JD is displaying. "Do you need me for anything? If not, I'm right the hell outta here, and away from your ass." JD turns away not waiting for a response, and heads into Nick's office to change clothes.

"No, I already know everything I need to know about you, creampuff. You're free to go." Rawson laughs as JD gives him the once over. "Get outta here, kid, before I shoot you in the leg for the hell of it." Rawson holsters his pistol and walks on over to Nick. "Cute kid," he says sarcastically. "Now, let's get back to you. See, I was thinking about writing a biography, or autobiography, I can never get those two straight. Ya know what I mean? I've been doing my job investigating you, and man, have I come up with some shit that would make a best seller. Slip back in time with me to Nov. 10th, 2005. Megan Kennedy and one Japanese National, Hiro Masamoto, were killed at the rehearsal dinner for your wedding to Miss Kennedy. Did you know that I searched high and low and could not find any record of Masamoto coming to this country, but low and behold, there he was, dead in the chair next to yours?"

Rawson pauses for a minute as JD exits the office. "It

was fun Nick, until Deputy Dickhead crashed our party. I'll catch up with you later on tomorrow, okay?" The young man walks passed Rawson giving the Detective the cold shoulder before heading out the front door.

Once JD is out the front door, Rawson turns to face Nick one more time. "Do you really think he was buying that load of bullshit that you were selling him?" Rawson reaches for his shirt pocket for another cigarette and then remembers that he is out. Obviously, this confrontation between him and Nick will have to be cut short.

"I don't know who you are accustomed to dealing with, Detective Rawson, but unless you plan on charging me with something, I suggest you back the hell off of me, before I am forced to give my lawyer a call." Nick casually walks over to Rawson and stares into his eyes. "By the way, if you hadn't noticed, you're standing on the wrong ground.

Suddenly, the storefront window explodes sending the shattering glass flying into the dojo. JD screams out with panic, "Nick!" The young man stands outside the building held hostage by the enemies of light. The obvious man in charge motions for his henchmen to charge the room, as JD passes out, sending them heading straight for Nick and Detective Rawson. Nick doesn't hesitate and charges right at the oncoming warriors of darkness, while Rawson takes the easy way by pulling his pistol from its holster. Diving to the floor, Nick retrieves his sword and meets the dark warriors, quickly dispatching their demonic possessions. Rawson on the other hand takes the easy way and drops two more ninja clad warriors with a bullet for each. Before he can take aim on his next target, he is hit in the hand by small dagger causing him to drop his weapon. Rawson knows that he doesn't stand a chance against these guys, especially unarmed. Gritting his teeth, the middle aged Detective grabs the handle of the dagger and pulls the blade from between the bones of his hand. At least now he has a weapon, for all the good it will do for him.

"Landry, behind you, look out!" Rawson flips the blade around and slings it across the room, hitting one of the henchmen, who were charging towards Nick's position. At the same time Nick spins around, heeding Rawson's warning, and hits the other two warriors right across the belly with the razor sharp blade of his sword. Rawson looks around and watches as the battle continues. No matter how many of Nick's opponents fall, they are quickly replaced by twice as many more. One would think that this many ninja clad warriors standing on a city street would draw the attention of someone.

A short whistle brings the battle to a sudden halt, with Nick standing against twenty or more opponents poised to attack. Nick looks back to check on Rawson, and then quickly refocuses on the front of the dojo. There, outside on the sidewalk is the true villain, holding up an unconscious JD hostage. The leader stands there using JD as a human shield, while clapping his hand against JD's shoulder in a slow procession, almost as if he was taunting Nick's valiant effort. Nick's eyes narrow, mapping every inch, every detail, of his opponent. The jet black hair slicked back, the black sun glasses; even the simple black three piece suit doesn't hide the man's identity, Yukio Masamoto. Nick knows who this is, recognizing the young man's voice, and sees him as a true enemy threat. The young man nods his head and gives Nick a devious smile. "So Guardian, you do remember me. The last time we met, you were at a loss for words."

"So you have decided to resume your futile quest. That's fine by me. Let the boy go, and you and I can dance all night." Taking a defensive stance, Nick points his sword at his adversary, challenging him on. "What was it you called yourself, Nightfall? That's right, and your sister calls herself

Twilight, right? How's that little bitch doing now a days? I've got something special for that little lady."

"I have to say that I am honored that you remember my given name." Yukio Masamoto appears to be in his late twenties, but he and his twin sister have been on this earth much longer than that. In fact, it has been almost fifty years since they swore allegiance to their uncle's cause, forsaking their father, Hiro, for all times. Under this cool façade of a Japanese mobster is a monster ready to strike. Yukio leans in over JD's shoulder. "As for your student, I think I would like for him to stay right where he is for the time being." The mob assassin gives Nick a devious grin and lays the edge of a blade against JD's throat. "This is how we will play the game. I will take your protégé to Japan, where my Uncle awaits your arrival. There, you will hand over your half of the dragon's ring to Master Seko in exchange for your student's life."

"You know I won't give up the talisman, Yukio, and I don't think you can take it from me. Drop the boy and give it a shot. Maybe you can prove me wrong!" Nick takes another step towards his enemy, only to be stopped by Yukio's blade being pushed up tighter against JD's neck. Time is running out, and too much of this is being displayed out in the open. Not to mention, Nick's new best friend is standing behind him memorizing everything that is taking place and being said.

"No, the honor of stripping you of the treasure you possess belongs solely to Master Seko. You will come to Japan, and you will try to save your young friend. The only way for you to do so is by handing over your half of the Dragon's Key. All of this is true. If you do try to prove me wrong, we will turn your student against his teacher and send him back here to you. Or maybe, I'll recruit that lovely roommate of yours. I've taken quite an interest in her as of late. In fact, I think she would make a fine addition to my ranks."

"You know what? You talk too much. Let the boy go, and I'll give you the chance to take me back to your so-called uncle. Miss your shot, and I'll beat you bloody with my bare hands, right where you stand!" Nick's threat is interrupted by the arrival of a police car, responding to a 9-1-1 call. For a split second, Nick lowers his sword giving Yukio the opening he needed to hit Nick in his sword arm with a throwing star.

Yukio Masamoto motions for his men to gather their fallen comrades. "Explain yourself to your Police, Dragon's Fang. Then come to face us in the land of the rising sun!" The mobster/assassin known as Nightfall turns and faces the approaching police officer's who were screaming for everyone to drop their weapons and put up there hands. He tosses a small spherical orb to the ground causing it to erupt into a large cloud of smoke. In seconds, the entire street is clouded from view, blinding everyone present. Nick staggers back and collapses against Rawson, before he is able to remove the star from his arm. He has a strong suspicion that the shuriken was dipped in some poison designed to slow Nick down. No, it isn't meant to kill him, just slow him down enough to give him a cold trail to follow.

Rawson tugs on Nick's arm to pull him up from the floor. "Hey man, are you gonna be alright? If so, you need to get moving if you're gonna catch those clowns!" Rawson lets go of Nick's arm and gives him a slight shove to start his momentum. The thick smoke cloud was keeping the police at bay, for the moment. Rawson knows that the officers outside had probably fallen back to the safety of their squad cars and are awaiting back up. This should give Nick a very small window for a chance to make an escape. "Go man, and use some of that hoodoo voodoo shit and get outta here. Oh, and when you catch up with the fat mouth, punch him right in his head for me one time. He's the one who hit me in the hand with the blade."

"I'm surprised at you, Rawson. I thought you weren't the type to give up your man like that." Nick tries to shake off the effects of the poison and regain his senses.

"Yeah, well I'm not. The way I see it; you're the only one who has a chance to stand up to those guys and save your teacher's pet. Now get outta here before the cops outside come crashing through the door." Both men turn and look at the shattered store from of the martial arts dojo, where the smoke was filling the room from the outside. "Shut up, you know what I mean. Now move, Sailor, I've got enough explaining to do." Rawson turns away from Nick, doubting his own actions and judgment. The badge tells him to hold Landry for questioning. It's more than obvious that Landry holds all the answers about what is going on. When you consider all that Rawson has personally seen, he doesn't know if there is anyone on the Police Force who would believe any of it. As far as he is concerned, Rawson came by here tonight and was the victim of an attack meant for Landry. It's the truth and he's sticking to it.

Nick studies Rawson for a second and then bows to the Detective as a sign of gratitude before hurrying off to his office. The smoke is so thick inside the dojo now that Rawson has no idea which way Nick went. That's fine with him. What he doesn't know shouldn't hurt him. Nick stops at his office door and kneels to look back at Rawson one more time. He can see the apprehensive officers slowly entering the front of the dojo, and knows that his time here is at an end. Slipping silently over to his inner sanctum, Nick lays his hand on the palm reader and disengages the locking mechanism. Once inside, he pulls the heavy door shut and reactivates the lock. His actions are methodical, almost rehearsed, as he gathers his belongings in a matter of seconds. With the small room stripped bare of anything pertaining to weapons, or Nick's identity, he lifts a plate in the floor and slips down into short tunnel that was a project of his, hand dug, years ago. Twenty feet outside the building, Nick's tunnel exits into a storm drain in the middle of the building's parking lot. From there he follows the pipe to the next inspection cover, where he exits and heads for home.

There are too many questions to worry about at the moment. He doesn't know why, but he is pushed to go against everything that Masamoto had taught him about his duty. Rule number one; never to go Japan. Rule number two; no one life is worth the risk of losing the talisman. Nick knows about the severity of the warning and what will happen to the world should he fail. But for right now, all he can think about is how to get to Japan and what to do when he gets there. The rest will all be sorted out when the time comes. He isn't sure where he stands with Rawson, but for the moment the Detective seems to be willing to help Nick's cause. Without knowing how long that help will last, and assuming that it exists, he has to take advantage of the offering. One thing is for sure, Nick has got to get out of town as quickly as possible.

"What do you mean you're not sure? Damnit, Rawson, you were standing right here in the place of business, of our suspect, in this investigation!" Captain Charlie Russo is a man who feels like he is about to lose his mind. He's holding four separate reports in his hand, of what happened at Nick's dojo, and none of them coincide. "I want you to start from the beginning, as in what were you doing here?"

Rawson stands up and walks away from the paramedic who was tending to the Detective's hand. "Come on, Captain, give me a break. I'm a wounded man, here." Rawson looks back at Russo to see that the Captain's demeanor is unchanged by Rawson's remark. "Okay, I was checking out some leads that pointed me in this direction. I stopped in to question Landry, but he wasn't in." This is where the lying starts. Reaching into his pocket, Rawson remembers that he's out of cigarettes. "Anybody got a smoke?"

"Yeah, I do Detective." The young rookie hurries over to brown nose the Detective by supplying Rawson's demand. "Here ya go, Detective Rawson."

"Thanks, kid, now go take care of crowd control, and keep the people back."

"Uh, Sir, can I have my cigarettes back?"

Rawson gives the rookie patrolman an irritated glare. "No, you're too young to be smoking any way. Wait until you've been doing this shit as long as I have. Then you'll have a reason to smoke." The overbearing detective lights his cigarette and exhales, accidentally right into his Captain's face. "Sorry Cap'n, but as I was saying, his assistant said that Landry was due back at any moment and that I was welcome to hang out. The next thing I know, the front window of the place shatters and somebody sticks me in the hand with a knife. I got off a couple of warning shots, but the next thing I knew, the room was filling with smoke, and the assistant had vanished." Rawson offers his Captain a cigarette before dropping the pack into his shirt pocket. "Want a smoke?"

"No I don't want a cigarette! I want you to tell me how to I'm supposed to believe that shit you just spit up!" Russo looks outside to see the news vans pulling up to the scene, before turning beck to face Rawson. "Gomez and Silva said that they saw someone inside the building with you before the smoke bomb went off, and that the perpetrators were dressed in Ninja costumes. Silva said that there was some kind of sword fight going on in here and you had ringside seats." Russoo snatches the cigarette from Rawson's mouth and takes a long drag off of it, before handing it back to the Detective. "Care to explain that one to me, Detective?"

Rawson holds the cigarette up and looks at it before flipping it out the open window and lights another one.

"Hmm, Ninjas and sword fighting in Miami; sounds like the rookie's got a great idea for an action movie, Cap'n."

"It's a God damned bad movie Rawson, and the worst part of it is that you and I are in the starring roles! I want the ending credits rolling on this one, like right now, Detective! Do you understand me? Find Landry and lock him down, and while you're at it, see if you can pinpoint the location of his roommate. It seems that the hospital has either misplaced a comatose patient, or she just got up and left on her own accord. Lock this city down and have some strong answers for me by sunrise, or there will be hell to pay!"

Rawson watches the Captain make his way over to the awaiting news people to give them as little as possible before dismissing himself from the scene. Looking around, and really not understanding everything that happened here, Rawson flips his cigarette butt to the curb and walks over to his car. "Okay Landry, I hope you've got your shit together, because I can't do any more for ya." Rawson looks around one more time before climbing into his sedan. He starts up the car and looks into his rear view mirror to back up, and sees a young oriental woman sitting in the back seat. "Holy shit lady, where the hell did you come from?"

In her homeland, she is known as Twilight, sister of Yukio Masamoto. "All that matters, Detective Rawson, is that you ensure Nickolas Landry the opportunity to join my brother and me in Japan. Do this and you will live, for a while." Gesturing with a nod, she adds, "Look, your Captain is coming back to talk to you again." Yukia points to the front of the car.

Rawson takes his eyes off the young woman for a split second, "What are you talking about, my Captain…" He looks back in the back seat to find it empty. Rawson jumps out of the car and looks all around, but there is no sign of his back seat mystery guest. "I'm getting too old for this shit.

All in favor of a stiff drink say I, I." He climbs back into the car and takes off down the street to find the nearest watering hole.

# CHAPTER XI

"There you are Mr. Landry, one coach ticket to Japan. The flight departs from gate thirty four, at eight fifteen. That gives you about twenty minutes to get through security. We have you a seat on one of our big boys that will head on to China and Thailand, after a little stop in LA to drop you off. Your connecting flight from LA to Tokyo will be boarding forty five minutes after you land at LAX. Are you sure you wouldn't like to book a later connecting flight to Japan. That's not a lot of time to maneuver your way through Los Angeles' busiest airport. I do have another flight that leaves out two and a half hours later." The ticketing agent bats her big blue eyes at Nick and offers him a pleasant smile.

"No thanks, this will do just fine." Nick takes his ticket and checks his bags. He tries not to come across as nervous or impatient, but he knows the stakes being played. Law enforcement officials frown on their key suspect taking flight right in the middle of their investigation. Nick knows that he has to be the exception to the rule. What he is doing is above the laws of mortal man and the outcome of his actions balance the fate of mankind. He cannot be hindered and will not answer to no one, until his duty is fulfilled.

"Alright then, here's your boarding pass with your claim stubs for your luggage pasted to the back. You will be flying on flight 669 to LA where you will transfer to flight 506 to Tokyo. Have a nice flight and thank you for flying International Airways." The ticket agent looks passed Nick to call on the next person in line. "Can I help you, Ma'am?"

Nick walks away from the ticket counter and gives the terminal the once over. The crowds are surprisingly thin for a Friday night at Miami International. Usually the main terminal is packed with People either coming to South Beach for the next big thing, or they're headed off to catch the next big thing in some exotic locale. There is no one in sight waiting to kill or apprehend him, so Nick heads off to his departing gate. The anticipation of boarding the plane is killing him. Nick can't help but think about the police storming the terminal just as the plane pulls up to the gate, to stop him from leaving. He sits down at his assigned gate, and scans the gathering crowd waiting for the plane to arrive. Five years ago, Nick thought that the death of Megan and Masamoto was the turning point that Masamoto warned him about, where his duty as Guardian would change his life. Now he can see the truth to his Master's warning of how the Talisman would change his life forever, with said life unraveling all around him.

Most people in Nick's position would probably take advantage of this down time and try to get some rest. Not Nick; he constantly scans the crowds for any signs of present danger. Part of him believes that Masamoto would have his men staking out the airport in Tokyo to keep tabs on Nick's progress. Who's to say the madman doesn't have his agents in Miami's airport as well? He doesn't believe they would make a move on him before he reaches Japan, but his SEAL instincts are alive and well, and they won't let him dismiss anything. At first, he becomes unnerved by the growing number of oriental passengers, wondering if one or more could be Masamoto's men. Then he calms himself a little by reminding his paranoid mind that he is flying on an airplane that is headed to Orient, so of course there would be more Orientals on the plane. Just to be on the safe side, he weighs the pros and cons of each scenario just so that he could dismiss the possibilities. "Flight 669 to LA is now boarding at gate 34. First class passenger may now line up at the gate. Have your tickets and ID ready for the flight attendant."

Nick is actually relieved to here the call for his flight to board sound out over the airport's intercom. He scans the crowd one more time to see if there is any sign of threat poised against him, as he walks over to get in line. Rationally speaking, it doesn't make sense for anyone to make a move against him before Nick reaches Japan. Masamoto once told him that Doomsayer's demon soldiers were instructed to never take the talisman. The Guardian had to be returned to Japan where the dark Lord would remove the talisman himself, breaking the spell that land locks him to Japan. This alone should ease Nick's paranoia, unless his plan fails. Besides, he's too public for anyone to make a move against him right now, isn't he? Being the first in line, he wants to go ahead and get to his seat so that he isn't out in the open any more sitting around the airport terminal gate. The first thing he needs to do is put his paranoia to rest. He's laid out every possible scenario of what could happen to him before the flight, and even a few scenarios of what could happen in LA. None of them makes sense. Nick has to accept the fact that the first confrontation has already taken place outside his dojo and there won't be another until he reaches the land of the rising sun. Still, he can't help but scan the crowds one more time to look for anyone who appeared to be a threat. So wrapped up in his thoughts while looking around the terminal, Nick doesn't notice the young woman standing behind him with a cat's paw tattoo on her cheek. Relieved to not see any more of Yukio's ninja assassins, Nick heads down the ramp and boards the plane where he is quickly greeted by a cute flight attendant who helps him to his seat and stow his bag. "There you are, Mr. Landry. My name is Julia, and if there is anything I can do for you, just give me a buzz, okay?" She gives Nick a smile, and then especially for him adds a wink and a slight puckering of her lips to blow him a kiss, as she walks away to greet the rest of the passengers. Nick actually chuckles at her actions, easing the tension in his mind for a second. If the circumstances were different, Nick might consider asking her out. He ponders for a moment the idea of dinner and the night out on the town with the young lady, and then dismisses the whole ordeal altogether due to the uncomfortable circumstances of it all, when he realizes Miss Julia reminds him of Megan. Her cheek bones are high with her nose slightly turning up, with big blue eyes that you could get lost in. Megan had a cute little nose, and blue eyes that Nick would get lost in every chance he got. I sure do miss our times, Meg," Nick thinks to himself as he settles into his seat.

As he tries to make himself as comfortable as possible in his seat, Nick feels that he will need some help with the comfort ability in his head. The infamous headache is attacking him, most likely due to the overwhelming stress and strain of what's transpired over the past few days. Reaching up, Nick turns on the call light for the flight attendant, sending Julia running right over to him. Okay so she didn't run, because they are on an airplane, but Nick was impressed with how quickly she responded to his needs. "Yes sir, Mr. Landry, how can I help you now?"

Nick looks up, but before making eye contact, he notices how her whole body seems to jiggle, almost like a cell phone on a kitchen counter. He quickly closes his eye and reopens them to see everything back in focus. "Julia my dear, I think I have one of those brain splitting headaches coming on. If I don't get something for it now, my head will probably explode before we reach thirty thousand feet."

"Not a problem Mr. Landry. I'm really not supposed to do this, but you're cute, so I'll help you out." Julia gives Nick another big smile and hurries off. Again Nick's visual focus gets the jitters as he watches her walk back up the aisle. He's concerned about his welfare, but still has to laugh to himself in a sarcastic way, watching her walk away with a vibrating jiggle to her appearance. Again he closes his eyes and tries to relax the anomaly out of his eyesight. Nick needs to be focused on what he is doing. No more thoughts about cute flight attendants. No more wasted minutes worrying about Sonny. Obviously she's alive, but Nick still doesn't know her status. He can only assume it to be true, based on Yukio's statement back at Nick's dojo. For now, he has to keep his mind on rescuing JD. When the two of them return from Japan, then and only then, can Nick pick up with Sonny's situation. Situation; it sounds cold, even if he's the one thinking it. Hang in there Lieutenant. I'll be home soon."

"Here you are, Mr. Landry." Nick opens his eyes to see Julia's hand in front of his face holding two small pills. "All I have is Tylenol extra strength. I hope it does the job for you."

He reaches up and takes the medication from her. "Thanks darlin', this will do just fine." Nick pops the pills into his mouth and then accepts a cup of water to wash them down. He's glad to see that his vision jitters are under control, but his headache is still increasing. His best course of action at the moment is to close his eyes and try to get some rest. If he is going to save his friend, Nick will have to be at his very best, and knows that he will need a clear head to do so. He doesn't pay attention to the conversations going on around him. He doesn't flinch when a young child bumps him as the youth walks down the isle. Nick doesn't see the young woman with the tattoo stand and walk to the restroom. He doesn't hear the flight attendant ask the young woman to return to her seat. Nick's asleep by the time the young woman gives her polite reply.

Once inside the confined quarters of the restroom, she quickly pulls out her cell phone and "Hello, yes Miss Masamoto, We are on board flight 669. The plane is due to land in Los Angeles in four hours and forty seven minutes. I have men stationed throughout the plane and have more reinforcements planted amongst the ground crews in Los Angeles." The young woman smiles at the praise coming through the phone. "Yes, that is so, but the advantage to using my service is that I have people under my employ on both coasts of the US that can be mobilized at a moment's notice. At any rate, there is no way Nickolas Landry can escape us before, or after, arriving in Los Angeles. Upon arrival, we will apprehend and deliver him to you, as you have requested. If you don't mind me asking, why don't we wait to make our move until he reaches Japanese soil? "

Yukia Masamoto sits back in the darkened room and stares out into the LA nightlife. "I am beginning to think that I might like it here, in Los Angeles," she states, hearing the crime and violence outside her window, in concert with the emergency sirens passing by. "If you must know, I wish to take possession of Landry before my brother has the opportunity to claim him in Tokyo, so that I am the one to regain my Uncle's good favor, before the plane lands at Tokyo International. By the time Yukio realizes what has happened, I will already be back in Hokkaido giving my Uncle what rightfully belongs to him, and cause my arrogant brother to fall from grace. Remember, you are authorized to use whatever force necessary, but Landry must be alive when

I hand him over to Master Seko. Only my uncle may have the privilege of taking Landry's life. Do not fail me, Siam. I see the two of us having a prosperous future together." Yukia Masamoto hangs up her cell phone, pleased with how her plan is working out.

The young woman on the plane is equally pleased with the telephone conversation. The money she stands to earn from this job alone could return her to the prominent standing she deserves in the terror/ assassin circles of the world. She is known throughout the orient as Siam, a blood thirsty Mercenary for hire who usually keeps to her Asian roots. She looks at the phone and folds it closed. With her newfound allegiance to Yukia Masamoto, Siam believes that she will sit at the right side of the new reign of the world. For Yukia, Siam is the perfect Lieutenant to carry out her ultimate plan. "It will always be a pleasure doing business with you, Ms. Masamoto." She returns to her seat and instructs her comrades accordingly, before closing her eyes for a nap of her own.

Nick opens his eyes, hearing the sounds of celebration all around him. He recognizes the image in front of him, but he is no longer in the cabin of the airliner he boarded. The image where he has awakened is his old house five years ago, right before his marriage to Megan. The disturbing part of it all is that he is staring at himself and his three best friends as they celebrate their reunion.

"Check it out, Nickels, I made it, babe!" Sonya Richards yells out from the front yard as she kicks the door of the cab shut. She leaves her bags sitting out in the front yard and rushes into the house and into the arms of her dearest friend. "Check you out, man, you look too sweet!" The former Navy SEAL pulls away from Nick as Megan walks out of the kitchen, taking her place at Nick's side. Seeing the competitive side of Megan, Sonny gives her a cordial smile, to hide her taste for competition. "How are you doin'? You must be Meg. I guess I should give you congrats, right?" Before Megan could respond, Sonny turns her attention to Charlie Steiner and leaps into his arms and gives him a long, firm, hug.

The fourth member of this formidable foursome steps forward to make his presence known. "Damn girl, you've been keeping yourself in good shape." Jorge reaches over and wraps his hand around Sonny's bicep.

"Yeah, well I've had a lot of time on my hands, and didn't like the idea of being another woman's girlfriend, so I spent my time on my back, working out on the weight bench." Sonny gives Charlie a harmless kiss on his cheek. "It sure is good to have the old team together again."

Nicole steps up and taps Sonny on her shoulder. "If you don't get off my husband, I'm going to have to charge you by the minute." To make a show of unity, Nicole takes Charlie's arm, signifying that he belongs to Nicole.

Never one to concede politely, Sonny gives Nicole a devious grin and replies, "Really? So, between you and me, how much is that minute to minute charge, just so that I can budget my money?"

"Okay, you two, that's enough for now." Charlie pulls Sonny's arms from around his neck and takes a step back. The last thing he needs right now is Sonny starting up shit with Nicole. "Come on, everybody, let's go get something to eat and have a few drinks, and catch up on old times."

Suddenly, the images of the past begin to swirl and blur, causing Nick to looks around and try to regain his focus. It is then that he sees his Master standing beside him. "I'm not on the plane any more, am I, Master?"

"Yes, and no, Nickolas, now see the past not as you remember it." Masamoto doesn't turn to face Nick. Instead, he waves his hand in the air out in front of himself causing the vision to focus on another time. "Pay attention and see the past not as you remember it."

The vision clears again, replaying the events that lead up to Masamoto's death. Charlie, Sonny, and Jorge crash through the front door of Nick's house, searching for the groom to be. "Nick, where are you, LT?" The threesome searches the house quickly, only to find no one at home. The sound of two pieces of wood hitting against each other catches Jorge's attention. Motioning for his friends to follow, they start back through the house towards the back yard. Playing around, Sonny and Charlie pretend to be reliving a mission from their combat days, complete with imaginary assault rifles. At the back door, they see their friend in a sparring match against a little old man who seemed to be giving Nick everything he could handle.

"This is down right pathetic!" Sonny charges right out the door, to state her distaste for Nick's shortcomings against the stranger, with Charlie and Jorge following close behind. "Nickels, are you seriously letting this little guy get the best of you, or are you holding back so that you don't break anything?"

Nick and Master Masamoto halt their exercise and lower their weapons. "Sonny, guys, I'm glad you're here, I want you to meet someone." Nick turns and bows to his Master before stepping away to greet his friends. "What are you guys doing here, any way? The rehearsal doesn't start for another five hours." Nick throws his arms around Charlie and Jorge's shoulders while Sonny leads them over to Masamoto.

"Who's your playmate, Nickels," Sonny asks as she circles Master Masamoto. "You've lost your touch, Landry, if this guy can best ya."

Master Masamoto bows to Sonny and replies, "perhaps you would like to test your skills, Sun Dragon?"

Right away, Nick knows that this could be a recipe for disaster, and quickly steps in to intervene. "Whoa, hold on a second there, so that I at least have the chance to get the introductions out of the way, before this turns into a free for all." He knows that Sonny has no control or self discipline needed to face off against Masamoto, and the old Master has no reason to fear her as a threat. If they squared off against each other, it would be like two pit bulls, Sonny not knowing when to stop and Masamoto unwilling to concede to the likes of her. "Hey I know, does anybody want something to drink? I know I could go for a bottled water right about now.

Sonny smiles at the challenge, believing she is about to take the old man apart. "No, you heard him Nickels, we're just gonna feel each other out." She lunges at Masamoto, trying to draw a reaction from him. Her only problem is that her action brings her in too close to the old Master. Before Sonny can withdraw out of reach, Masamoto already has her in an arm bar that he uses to flip over Sonny's back, before he slings her out into the yard. With no intention of offering injury, Masamoto directs her path to the center of the lawn, where she hits the ground on the softest, thickest, grass. He didn't want to hurt her, just shut her up. The one injury that couldn't be avoided was to Sonny's pride.

The outcome of the brief encounter causes Charlie and Jorge to burst out in laughter at their friend's unfortunate receipt of humble pie. Masamoto turns and faces the two men and bows to them. "You mock your friend, as if your capabilities could produce a different outcome, and yet you do not step forward to prove yourselves. Is it out of respect for the better adversary, or do you fear the suffering of the same outcome?" Masamoto opens his eyes and smiles at the two Navy men.

Charlie, always wanting to clown around, begins to mock Nick's teacher, by performing exaggerated martial arts moves as if he was warming up for battle. "Hey, no disrespect, Charlie," Nick warns his best friend.

"Don't sweat it, Nickels. We're just having fun, that's all. Lighten up a little, will ya?" Both Charlie and Jorge turn and look at Nick with disbelief painted all over their faces. Did this old man just challenge the both of them, at the same time? Nick just throws his hands up in the air, as if saying to them, "do your worst." At the same time, the two men charge at Masamoto with the intent to show that they fear no challenge, but at the same time didn't want to hurt the old guy. In a matter of seconds, both Jorge and Charlie find themselves lying on the grass next to their fallen comrade. Masamoto bows to the fallen and waits for them to give it another try.

"Come on, boys, he can't take all three of us at the same time." Sonny jumps to her feet and forces her friends into another round with the Master. Masamoto invites the challenge, taking the best they have to offer before he sends the three back out into the grass again.

"Master, forgive my friends' shortcomings. They don't know who you are, or when to admit defeat." Nick bows to his teacher as a show of respect for the Master's abilities, with Masamoto returning the gesture to his student.

Sonny sees the opening and decides to take it. She doesn't need Nick speaking for her, believing her actions speak louder than words. There is no way she is going to be bested by an old man who looks like he already has one foot in the grave. One step sends her back up onto the deck. The next sends her right at Masamoto as he bows to Nick.

The old man moves like a cat, eluding Sonny's attack and quickly gains the upper hand, when he grabs her around her neck with one hand. "As I said, Sun Dragon, you will never best the Guardian, ever!" Using his other hand, Masamoto presses his knuckles into the side of Sonny's neck. Instantly, her body is temporarily paralyzed, causing the female upstart to collapse to the deck. Later on, Nick and his friends would pose with Masamoto for the photo hanging in Nick's office.

Again, the images begin to blur as Masamoto moves Nick to the next Vision. "Why are you showing me all of this, Master?" These are all memories of good times, but painful just the same. The vision coming into focus is even more painful than the last. "I don't want to see this."

"You must."

The images appearing in front of Nick cut at his heart and soul, now wanting to relive this again. Unable to look away, Nick stares at himself and Megan, as they ready to rehearse their wedding vows, Five years ago. "We're ready to begin." The preacher announces as he joins the wedding party on the front steps of the church. After ushering everyone inside, the preacher leads Nick, Sonny, Charlie, and Jorge to the front of the chapel. Sonny seemed peculiar, demanding that she wear her tuxedo for the rehearsal. After all, Nick was proud to call her one of his best men for the wedding. The wedding march begins to play forcing Nick to quickly turn around to see his fiancé walking up the aisle. Later on before the rehearsal dinner, Charlie would make comment about how Nick looked to be the proudest man in the world, when Megan joined him at the altar.

The preacher explains each step of the service as they move through the process. When they reach the part where the two would exchange vows, both Meg and Nick recite their lines without a hitch. "Do you take this man to be your lawfully wedded husband?"

"I do."

Do you take this woman to be your lawfully wedded wife?"

"I do."

The preacher gives them an approving smile. "Then by

the power vested in me, I now pronounce you man, and wife. You may kiss the bride," He announces as he closes his bible. The preacher then clears his throat to break up the passionate kiss between the bride and groom. When that doesn't work, he gives Nick a tap on the shoulder. "Okay, you two, there will be enough time for that tomorrow." The preacher faces the audience and addresses the friends and family of Nick and Megan. "Thanks for coming tonight for the rehearsal. It helps us prepare better for the real thing when there is an audience. We'll see all of you tomorrow for the real thing."

Megan wipes her mouth, and blushes a little at everyone in the congregation laughing at the preacher's remark. "Nick, I'm gonna run to the restroom and change. I'll meet you out front in a few minutes." She starts to walk away, only to be stopped by Nick, as he pulls her back to him. "Come on, ya big lug, let me go so we can get outta here."

"Baby, I'm never gonna let you go." Nick gives her a big cheesy grin, toying with his bride-to-be. Off to the side, Charlie and Jorge laugh at Sonny's reaction when she sticks her finger in her mouth to throw up.

Unable to produce the effect, Sonny opts for the alternative of grabbing Nick by the arm to lead him out of the chapel. "Come on, you two; let's get a move on here. I'm dying to get some good food in my stomach." The trio of best men, including Sonny, leads Nick to the chapel doors when Sonny suddenly stops their march out of the building. "Ya know what? You guys go round up Nicole and the others, while I go cop a squat and squirt. I'll catch up with you in a minute. She struts away proudly, knowing that her abrasive personality is sure to rub at least one person a night the wrong way. Nick and the guys are immune to her charms, so that means there is still a target out there somewhere for the night.

Megan enters the restroom with her bags in her hands, following an eager Sonny who rushes into the first stall. There is something about that lady that makes Megan feel very uneasy around her. Lady; Meg is sure that term is definitely used loosely when it is a reference to Sonny. Still, this is supposed to be one of her future husband's best friends, so she has to try to make a connection, doesn't she? "Ya know I'm so glad I got to finally meet you. Nick is so happy that you were able to make it to the wedding. He looks so alive having his old team back together again. I just want you to know that there will always be a special place in our lives for you and the others, Sonny." There, Megan has laid out the groundwork, and no one can say that she didn't try to meet Sonny half way.

A flush of the toilet seemed to come across as a reply to Megan's statement. If that was too subtle, Sonny storms from the stall and moves in right behind Megan. "Cut the shit, sister. We both know how you feel about me." Sonny looks at Megan's reflection in the mirror and gives her a sinister smile. "To you, I'm nothing but the hot tiger that is treading on your territory. What you need to keep in mind is that me and Nick shared something that you will never have. In fact, I think that's what is eating you up inside, isn't it?" Sonny starts to play around with Megan's hair, as if imitating a salon stylist. "The thought of your man depending on another woman just eats you up inside, don't it?" Pulling down and around on the back of Megan's hair, Sonny turns the bride-to-be's head around to look her in the eyes. "Here's a little friendly advice; don't ever hurt him, or I'll peel your pretty little face off of your skull."

Megan pulls away from Sonny and turns to stare her down. "Empty words, Sonya, you should keep in mind that it's not your job to worry about him any more." Megan pulls her jeans up and returns her shoes to her feet. "Besides, why would he want to tap that, when he's had this since high school?"

Sonny's demeanor suddenly changes from cold blooded killer to that of a sweet and caring person. "Ya know what, Megs, you're alright. I guess Nickels really has found a keeper. It'll take a woman like you to keep him from getting bored." Sonny straightens her coat and looks at her self in the mirror. "Now let's go spend your daddy's money. I'm starved, and we've got some celebrating to do!" Megan is already out the door and headed to the limousine. Sonny just smiles at the mirror, knowing that she had stated her case perfectly.

The images begin to blur and swirl around Nick and Masamoto. "Master, I don't remember, hell I didn't even know that little confrontation took place. Why did you show me that?"

"Because, you must know the enemies in your past, if you are to confront the ones in your future."

"So, what are you trying to say? Sonny isn't a cause of my problems right now, Master."

Masamoto ignores the remark and refocuses the vision. Nick sees himself standing at the banquet table beside Sonny, as his friend lays Megan down on the floor. Sticking in her chest and neck are thin metal spikes that were thrown at Masamoto and Nick, only Nick wasn't in his seat. Nick reaches up and grabs his Master and lays him in the floor beside his dying bride. In doing so, Nick is able to collect the talisman from his Master, hiding his actions with the chaos that was enveloping all around them. One look from Nick to Sonny, tells her what his plan is. The two leap to their feet and join Jorge and Charlie in the battle taking place at the center of the room.

The villains who have interrupted this blessed event quickly focus on Nick as he charges into the fray. His true talents are on display as he bounds over Charlie and takes out four opponents before touching the ground again. Charlie, Sonny, and Jorge fall in behind their commander leaving the odds standing at twelve against four, with Nick and his friends having the unfair advantage. In all honesty, it is Nick that gives them the unfair advantage, which he quickly demonstrates by eliminating six more opponents, before the battle is halted by a mysterious man and woman at the front doors. Wanting their shots in too, Sonny and Charlie take out the other six just for good measure. Even though they have never been introduced, Nick is sure he knows who they are. Master Masamoto told Nick the story a long time ago about how Doomsayer killed Hiro's family, save the twins, who were spared and then corrupted by darkness to serve Doomsayer's bidding.

"Come face us, Guardian, and surrender what rightfully belongs to our Master." The brother motions to his sister for them to exit the building, challenging Nick to follow them outside. The two villains turn and use their dark power to shatter the glass doors to make their way outside. Charlie, Jorge and Sonny expect Nick to lead them on, but are shocked when he turns and runs back over to the table to collect his master's cane. Most would find it disturbing to see Nick leave his fallen loved ones behind, in order to take chase after the vile killers who have disrupted his life. Charlie and his friends are shocked when Nick leaves them standing in the center of the banquet hall, taking chase on his own.

Sonny was heard making comment about how she liked Nick's idea of beating the bad guys with a big stick. When she and Charlie reach the front door, they see that Masamoto's cane actually concealed two short swords that nick was using to slash up more of Yukio's men. Charlie is awestruck watching the friend he thought he knew, slice and hack his way through the men who seemed to run right at Nick as if it was their duty to die. Soon, the numbers become overwhelming, sending Sonny into the battle yelling, "Wait any longer and there won't be any left for ya!" She was right, as Nick hacks and carves his way through the men who hurried to the deaths.

Once allied with his friends in this battle for vengeance, Nick gains the upper hand and is able to break through the line to get to the big prize. The brother and sister waste no time rushing in to meet Nick's approach. One on one would be an uneven match for anyone to stand against the Masamotos. For Nick, it took everything his Master taught him, plus some adlibbing of his own to fend off these two. His swords worked through the air like a twin engine airplane, defending their assault from both sides. Occasionally, Nick is able to deliver a brief offensive but never enough to gain the upper hand over one or both of the siblings. That is, until Sonny and the others finished off Yukio's men. When the threesome joins Nick to take the offensive together, the twins see that their window of opportunity has closed and bow out of the conflict. "You have proven yourself worthy of the task, Guardian. When the time is right, we will return to collect what rightfully belongs to our Master." Yukio and Yukia bow to Nick, and then vanish in a cloud of smoke.

The visions blur again leaving Nick and Master Masamoto standing together in pitch, black, darkness. "Why? Why are you bringing all of this back up?" Nick is completely and positively irate for being forced to watch the painful event that haunts him. Nick has had enough of this little dream, and is ready to wake up.

Masamoto begins to look around in the darkness in all directions but focuses on nothing at all. Nick can tell that something is wrong. "Go back, Nickolas, I sense that you are in great danger!" Master Masamoto hits Nick in the chest with the palms of his hands, ending the dream and causing Nick to wake up aboard the airplane.

# Chapter XII

Nick opens his eyes to find a thin airline blanket laid over his lap, and the feel of cold steel around his wrists. Something is definitely wrong, but he doesn't want to let anyone who opposes him to know that he is onto their game. He will soon learn that his efforts are in vane. "Good evening, Mr. Nickolas Landry," A quiet voice says from the next seat over. Nick looks towards the aisle to see a young man, clean cut and in his early thirties, sitting in the seat next to Nick. "The name is US Air Marshall Deputy Jason Dockery. Now that we have the introductions out of the way, I'd like to say how much I would appreciate it if you would remain calm, cool, and collected, and here me out." The deputy shifts his ball cap up onto his head, off his brow, and then looks at Nick over the top of his mirrored sun glasses. "Here's what I can tell you, at this point in time. In the great state of Florida, there resides the Miami/Dade Sheriff's Department. Now, I'm sure you can imagine their disappointment when they discovered that you had left town without saying goodbye. Evidently, you have become their number one suspect in a number of cases, including the murders of two Detectives that were found gutted at your home." The Deputy looks around the cabin and then nods to the flight attendant as she walks by. "Now I know what you're thinking; I sure do know a lot for an Air Marshall Deputy. Let's just say that they wanted me to know what, and who, I was dealing with. Just so you and I are clear, they gave me a brief summary on your background. You were a Navy SEAL, right? Yeah, they said you were some kind of Billy bad ass. Know this; if you try anything with me, I'll tazer your butt in a heartbeat, if you so much as breathe wrong."

"Actually, I have a friend named Billy who's a bad ass, but this has nothing to do with him," Nick mumbles, and then sits back in his seat and decides to remain quiet. His mind is working a thousand miles a minute trying to come up with as many possible scenarios on how to better his situation. Obviously, the connecting flight is now out of the question. Once he gets out of this little mess, he'll have to find another means of transportation to Tokyo. First task, he must get out of this mess and get away from Deputy Dawg, and then get out of the airport without being seen.

"Ladies and Gentlemen, this is your Captain speaking." The voice comes through the intercom resembling that of a Vegas crooner in some off strip casino. "We have now entered the flight pattern for Los Angeles International and have been given clearance to land. You will notice that I have turned on the seat belt sign, and request at this time that you return your trays and seats to their locked and upright positions. For those of you getting off in LA, on behalf of International Airways, I'd like to thank you for flying with our airlines. For those of you who will be continuing on to China with us, we will have an hour delay before starting the next leg of our journey. We want to make sure they have enough time to fill up the gas tanks. Thank you, and pleasant journeys."

Deputy Dockery leans over to Nick as the Captain's little

228

speech is translated and broadcast again. "Now, don't go getting all antsy or anything. We're going to wait for everyone else to disembark, before you and I even think about standing up." Dockery looks around when the Captain's joke about fuel is repeated in Chinese, causing the passengers to laugh out in unison.

Nick ignores the Deputy's statement, and dismisses the rest of the passengers who were beginning to ready themselves for departing the plane. He's watching for his opportunity to make his move. The people who hold JD aren't going to wait around for Nick to sort all of this out, with the Authorities. They'd just as soon kill JD and begin design on some other way to get to Nick. One thing is for sure; he knows that JD would prefer it not come to that. For now, all Nick can do is watch and impatiently wait for his chance to show itself.

Across the cabin a call lamp lights up, calling for the attendant's assistance. Julia is quick to respond, as Nick watches out the corner of his eye. To his surprise and then worry, Nick recognizes the young woman with the cat's paw tattoo. Years ago, he happened across a file on her terrorist cell working in the Orient. For her to be on this plane is not good at all, not one bit. She's as blood thirsty as they come, with no regard to human life whatsoever. Nick read in the file that she once blew up a hospital and orphanage in Taiwan, because the local Magistrate wouldn't release her partner in crime and terror. Evidently, there was some kind of double cross that had taken place, and she was unhappy with the outcome. The local officials and two hundred and forty seven other people died that day, all because one man's greed caused him to disregard the contract between his office and Siam. "Deputy Dockery, I understand your position and respect it, but I need you to hear me out for a minute. Across the cabin, the flight attendant is talking to a known terrorist. I can't tell you how she got into our country, or what she's doing on this plane, but whatever it is can't and won't be good for us or the passengers."

"Dockery pulls his hat down over his face and doesn't even bother to look at who Nick was talking about. "Come on, Landry, you've got to come up with something better than that."

Nick looks back at Julia and becomes uneasy, when Siam and the flight attendant turn their heads and stare at Nick. Deputy, you really should take this warning to heart." Nick becomes even more unsettled when the passengers seated around Siam all turn their heads to look at Nick and begin to stare at him as well. Suddenly, all of their eyes flash, and then glow with an ominous red tone, and then their bodies jiggled slightly, as if they were out of sync with the rest of reality. "Man, you really need to listen to me, pal, or the chances of either one of us getting off this plane are going to be slim and none." Nick looks back over at Siam to see her and her colleagues all facing forward ignoring Nick's presence. Julia has returned as well, to her seat to prepare for landing. All of this begins to make Nick wonder if he was suffering from hallucinations, due to his extreme fatigue. No, he' sure that this was happening, and the threat that Siam poses is real. That's okay, because he is ready for her to make her move. There is no doubt that what Nick has seen in the past few minutes is all real, and tells him that she is here for him, and he has and he has no choice but to be ready for anything.

The plane swoops in over the runway of LAX, and drops down to bring the landing gear to the concrete surface. Nick watches Siam like a hawk as the plane settles down and rolls along taxiing to the gate. As the passengers begin to off load, he does his best to keep his eyes on her. Passengers move about the aisles, collecting their carry on luggage and wait in line to exit the plane. It is during this time that Siam and her associates make their move, standing up to walk towards the front of the plane. Deputy Dockery raises his hat to look around, and determines that the plane has cleared out enough for him and Nick to take their leave. "Come on, Mr. Landry; let's see about getting you back to Miami." Nick stands and watches Siam halt her departure to cross the cabin through the center row of seats.

"Get behind me," Nick instructs, handing the Deputy back his set of handcuffs. At this time, if for nothing else, Nick would rather have the Deputy's life listed as saved, instead of a casualty of this war.

Deputy Jason Dockery is amazed and alarmed that Nick had somehow freed himself from the handcuffs. Panic sets in on the officer, causing him to jump ahead of Nick in the aisle and quickly pull his pistol to draw down on him. The last thing Dockery needs, or wants, is to have Nick's escape on his official work record. After years of trying, Dockery just earned this position two months ago. The last thing he wants is to watch his career run away. It is then that he sees Siam making her move and draws down on her to stop her approach. He looks back at Nick, as if saying he should have listened to his prisoner. "Everyone freeze! I don't want another person to move until we are off this plane!" The remaining passengers scream and fall back in their seats, not understanding what was taking place, or who Dockery is. "Let's go, Landry!" Distracted by anxiety and fear, Dockery doesn't see Siam pull a small dagger from her coat. He doesn't see her lightning fast reflexes fling the blade across the cabin to hit him in the shoulder. The action causes Dockery to reel back, squeezing off a few rounds taking out two of Siam's associates, and an innocent bystander in the process.

Siam produces a pistol of her own, posing in a standoff with the wounded Deputy. "If you and the rest of these people want to live, release Landry into my custody at once, or I will begin to kill these passengers, one at a time." Her men quickly block the exit and take control of the plane.

Nick stands frozen in his place, assessing the situation with the speed of a genius. In seconds, he has the entire scenario mapped out and is ready to make his move. His opportunity is on the rise. Nervous and frightened passengers scream with each little movement of the aggressors. Nick needs this chaos to cover his escape. What he didn't expect was Julia adding to that chaos. The flight attendant appears behind Dockery and produces a handful of nine inch claws at the ends of her fingers. Before Nick could give the warning, Julia hits Dockery across the back of his neck, removing the man's head and sending it into a woman's lap. Blood trails cover several other passengers, as Julia follows through, swinging her arm around. More screams of terror and panic send several men scrambling over the tops of the seats to try and get away. Siam's men show them the severity of their actions by shooting the two innocent men dead. The chaos has now erupted into full effect, revealing to Nick his opportunity. It's a shame that these people have lost their lives, because Dockery didn't heed Nick's warning. For Nick, this has become another reminder of how his involvement with humanity has, and always will end with a body count.

His move is made; Nick casts a small sphere to the floor at his feet, causing a small explosion to envelope the entire cabin with a cloud of smoke. He can hear the panic in Siam's voice as she screams for her men to find Nick. She is already too late, as Nick makes his way into the galley and climbs into the dumbwaiter. Yes, believe it or not, this was the plan that he came up with, a few minutes ago. There are necessities in his bag, that can not, must not, be left behind. To get to his duffle bag, Nick must get into the lower level of the plane. For Nick, this is the closest, quickest, most accessible way available to accomplish this task. As he reaches up to activate the dumbwaiter's controls, he sees a young boy lying on the floor under a row of seats, staring at Nick through the thinning smoke. Nick holds his finger up to his mouth, telling the young boy to keep quiet, and then presses the button to send him deep into the plane's belly.

Only a few seconds pass in the time it takes for the smoke to clear. "Where is he?" Siam looks at her men demanding an answer. Looking around, she takes notice to the young boy, who couldn't help but stare at the galley, hoping Nick was on his way back to save the day. Siam hurries in to the cramped area of the galley, and flings open the door of the dumbwaiter. She pulls her radio from her belt and keys up the mike. "Wake up down there, you lazy dogs. The Guardian is down in the forward section. Check the food locker and report back to me at once!"

"Hey Yiu, the boss said that the American is headed down here. Keep your eyes open and call me if the guy shows up." This man is another low rate thug hired by Siam specifically for this job. You see, like Yiu Ling, Sammy Lee is expendable. The gunman stops, sensing that something is wrong with his comrade, Yiu. "Hey, are you awake over there?" Sammy walks over and gives his comrade a nudge, sending Yiu rolling over into the floor. "Oh shit, he's killed Yiu!"

"He's not dead, just unconscious like you." Nick hits the gunman twice in the chest, once to the side of the neck, and another to the side of the man's temple, all happening so quickly that the man is unconscious as well, before the pain of the first strike sets in. Nick catches Sammy's lifeless body and pulls him over to the side. After securing both men, he starts for the luggage hold, to retrieve his duffle bag. Certainly, the odds are stacked against him for accomplishing this feat. First, he has to get into the luggage and determine where his is located. The main hold should be divided up for specific luggage to specific destinations. He knows that one section will be dedicated to passengers getting off in LA. There has to be a compartment for his connecting flight to Tokyo, but how many more connecting flights for this one are there, and where are they headed? Process of elimination has to be his only course of action.

Retrieving one of his ceramic throwing stars from the pouch strapped to his leg, Nick uses the sharpened edge to slice into the first canvas divider separating the luggage. With just one inspection of the bags' tags tells Nick that this group of luggage is heading to Thailand. His bag is still somewhere else, sending him climbing through the suitcases to get to the other side. Once at the next canvas divider, Nick performs the same act again, slicing into the material to create his own passage way. To his surprise and relief, this luggage is heading to Tokyo. With the first step accomplished, he sets out to find his own bag, and collect what he needs. Lucky for Nick, he only has to go through two bundles of luggage before locating his own.

"Hold it right there, Guardian. Drop the bags and turn around real slow. You don't want any of these nice people to get hurt, do you?" One of Siam's men pulls the bolt back on his automatic weapon, to emphasize his threat. "I know you heard me, Guardian. Turn around real slow, and show me your hands, and do it now!"

More lambs for the slaughter. "There's no problem with my hearing, pal. You just ease back on that trigger and we'll get along just fine," Nick replies, as he slowly turns around. "See, nothing in my hands." With a quick flip of his wrist, Nick hits the gunman right in his chest above the heart with the ceramic throwing star. The downed man falls back out of the luggage and lands on the floor of the cargo area, right beside another of Siam's men. Nick takes the advantage of the situation and dives through the opening to tackle the surprised gunman, and take him to the floor. The two are separated by the impact giving Nick the chance to stand up and take the offensive. Nick's newest opponent shows his own skill by flipping himself up into the air to land on his feet, to defend Nick's attack with ease. A well placed defensive blow sends Nick passed his target, allowing the man to step in and grab Nick, and then throws him across the belly of the plane. Nick rebounds quickly, flipping his body around so that his feet hit the wall first, before he springs back towards his opponent. The man struggles to free his gun hanging over his back, as if he realizes that it is his only solution. His efforts are in vain as man's attempt is halted by Nick flinging his dagger across the small cargo bay. The blade finds its mark pinning the gunman's arm to his chest. Two more of Siam's men leap to the center of the confined area, and challenge Nick to battle. The former Navy SEAL shakes his head and accepts the challenge reluctantly, knowing that time is not on his side, at the moment.

These men are nothing but casualties of war, to him. Nick has now has regressed into a person that has laid dormant deep inside of him for many years. Very few people alive know what the capabilities of Nickolas Landry truly are. These men will learn soon enough who and what Nick is. His actions are swift and his blows deadly, as Nick crushes one man's chest with a single punch, while leaping into the air to grab the other opponent. Snaring the gunman's neck with his feet, Nick falls to the floor and slings the man head first into the framework of the fuselage. He quickly recognizes these two thugs hanging around the departure gate in Miami. Crazy thought; what if everyone on board is actually working for Siam? It would be overkill for sure stacking the odds against Nick like that, but it would definitely change his outlook on who should, and shouldn't, be saved.

Staying focused on the event of the moment is a vital thing in situations like this. His thoughts wander. This is something uncharacteristic about Nick, and if he had a few hours, he would probably meditate to uncover what it is that has him distracted. Years of habitual training should be so easily dismissed. He is trained to be aware of his surroundings and what transpires, at all times. These hired thugs, are no match for Nick, and yet his distractions seem to keep his opponents in the fight. There are two events taking place at the moment that catch Nick's attention, right off the bat. One; the cargo hatch on the side of the fuselage is being unlatched from the outside. The second is a last ditch effort of the dying man as produces a small incendiary device from his coat pocket, about the size of a golf ball, and throws it at Nick. "Are you insane!?!" Without any consideration about anything except self preservation, Nick leaps into the air and kicks the small explosive on a line drive right back at the pitcher. Nick drops to the steel panels of the floor and leaps towards the luggage bays, as the timer activates the detonator, built into the small grenade. This works in coincidence as the grounds crew opens the side cargo hatch and is quickly eliminated when the explosion rushes out the side of the plane. Now, there is no doubt that the rest of the airport will know what is happening.

One moment Nick is clambering over the piles of luggage, seeking refuge from the blast. The next, he feels a pair of clawed hands grabbing him from behind, and flings him further into the luggage bay. His forced flight sends him right at one of the canvas dividers that separated the loads of luggage, tearing it from its hooks. Wrapped up in the heavy material, he is unable to get free before his attacker is on him again. The claws of Nick's opponent slash and tear at the canvas trying to get in at Nick. Once the attacker's weapons hit skin, Nick is snapped out of his dumbfounded stupor and forced to retaliate. "Come here, Guardian," The assassin commands. "My job is to render you lifeless without killing you. I can't do that with you hiding in there."

"Who said I was hiding?" Nick reaches up from under the luggage and stabs his opponent in the leg with the ceramic throwing star he had used to cut his way into the luggage. Siam's partner howls out in pain as Nick takes the advantage and kicks him squarely in the chest. The assassin is sent flying back into the cargo bay where the emergency crews are trying to enter the plane to assess the damage. Again Nick receives the opportunity to make his move. Taking said opportunity, He leaps for the open hatch, seeking the safety outside the plane. He doesn't know what awaits him out there, but it's got to be better than the cramped surroundings of the cargo bay. Mid air, Nick learns that the chance had been missed, as his opponent rebounds and slams into him, driving Nick into the inner wall of the fuselage. "We've gone through too much trouble to find you, just to let you slip away again. The name is Pang." With that said, Pang flings Nick up against a fuselage girder. He hits the steel plating and falls to the floor head first, suffering his first serious wound. Blood runs down his face from the deep laceration to his scalp, but Nick can't be concerned with that right now. He focuses on his new adversary who gives Nick a salute, before the killer leaps across the cargo bay. "Help me." His mind's voice cries out. The fire and smoke burns and chokes the oxygen from his lungs, sending Nick to the floor seeking fresher air. For a second, Nick is able to catch his breath, plunging his head between the suitcases to find clearer air. With a replenishment of oxygen, he can better assess his situation. It sucks. Where is the mystery man? There is movement over to the side of the cargo hatch, but Nick can't be sure who it is.

Then, Pang hits Nick with the ferocity of a charging rhino, raking his claws through Nick's flesh, and sending him up against the fuselage wall again. The expected attack sends the former SEAL into action as he tries to block out the pain of his most recent wounds. He thinks about how Sonny would be more suited for a battle with this guy. They're both pretty much out of their minds. Nick pulls his short sword from its sheath and points the blade at his opponent. Pang accepts the dare and leaps at Nick, only to meet the heel of Nick's foot that sends the assassin flying back across the plane. He had hoped to drop his opponent out the open cargo hatch with that move, but ol' Pang is too agile for that. He collects himself, and then leaps at Nick again, displaying his animalistic nature for Nick to see. The two grapple for a short time that simply ends in a standoff, with the two men pushing away from each other, only to attack one more time. Nick makes his move again, trying to reach the open hatch. Outside, he can hear the approaching emergency vehicles responding to the explosion. Unfortunately for Nick, it is Pang this time, who gains the upper hand, delivering a crushing blow to Nick's back and ribs. The oriental opponent is awesomely strong, far more than Nick, which causes the SEAL to rethink his options.

Nick has to end this as soon as possible. The sounds of emergency sirens tell him that the vehicles are approaching outside. Pretty soon, the entire area will be will be locked down and crawling with more officials than Nick cares to face. Despite all of that, Nick still feels the urge to continue this fight. "Help me." His own blood drips into his eyes, reminding him of the wound to his head. Pang takes the advantage as Nick appears to be blinded, but misses with his kill shot, when Nick leaps clear at the last moment. Pang spins around to face Nick, and readies to strike again. But the Guardian stands ready too, pointing his sword at the villain. "Okay tough guy, you wanna have some fun, let's have some fun." How did all of this wind up so inside out and upside down all of a sudden? It started out plain and simple. All he had to do was fly to Japan, save his best friend, and take on a mad man who wants to cast the world into eternal darkness. It seemed pretty cut and dried at the time. Now, Nick has these egomaniacs to deal with first, before he can continue with his crusade around the world. The one question he can't put an answer to is why are these maniacs intervening?

To his surprise, Siam and six of her men appear from the tail section of the plane, adding to the numbers standing against him. Suddenly, five armed men appear at the open hatch, all pointing automatic rifles into the belly of the plane. "Freeze!"

Nick grabs the talisman and renders himself invisible, causing Pang to leap at Nick's last known position, to avoid losing his target. The armed TSA agents open fire at Pang's attack, hitting him and several more of Siam's men who were in the line of fire. Nick sees the demonic possessions leaving their bodies, as he leaps through the hatch to escape. For the moment, he believes that Siam and her threat to him, has been eliminated, or at least long enough for him to make his getaway. With no time to lose, his path sends him right through the emergency crews rushing in. His chosen path forces him to bound and leap from one direction to another, to avoid the vehicles and men in his path. By the time they enter the plane and subdue the fires, Siam and her men have vanished, including their fallen comrades. The only one who could offer any light to what happened is Nick, and he is now standing at the edge of the runway. But, even he can't figure out why this attack took place. It doesn't make sense no matter how Nick looks at it. If Yukio wanted to take him out like this, why did he bother with all of the posturing at Nick's dojo? Certainly it wasn't because of Rawson's presence. So, why bring in this outside interference? Even Nick deduced that the prime location to make their move would have been the Tokyo airport. All that this has done is add more attention to Nick, making it even harder for him to get out of the country. If they want Nick to go to Japan, why make it more difficult for him than it already is. Yukio would have been better off subduing Nick when he had the chance, instead of this.

Nick watches the activity around the plane, as the pilots and flight crew proceed with the emergency evacuation of the rest of the passengers and tend to the injured. Minutes seem like hours as he scans the scene intensely from the edge of the runway from behind a service shed, as the emergency crews fight the fires and search for any more survivors. The sound of dripping water catches his attention, reminding him of how he needs to clean up some. The dried blood caked on his head and face would certainly stand out in public. Not to mention the condition of his clothes. Taking a second away from his observation, he turns to investigate the dripping water. A water truck sits abandoned beside the service shed, waiting for the next time it is needed. The water is frigid from the cold night's temperature, leaving Nick sure he is going to regret what he is about to do. He opens the gate valve on the back of the truck until the water is pouring out the pipe works at a nice easy flow. Then, without any hesitation, he shoves his head under the running water to wash the evidence of his previous battle away. Invigorated by the eye opening experience, Nick directs his attention to the ground crew who were beginning to unload what's left of the luggage and cargo from the plane. The only reason he is still here is his duffle bag. He can't leave here without it, and can't afford to have the Federal boys going through his bag. The incriminating evidence could have Nick answering questions for weeks. After all of this is over, the last thing he wants to do is sit around in some Federal building, answering redundant and unnecessary questions. Not to mention the fact that it would be nice to have a change of clothes. So, he has no other choice but to stand in the shadows and wait. He has the means to move in and claim his bag, as soon as he can locate it. Each piece off loaded from the plane is taken over to a man wearing Black pants and a black and yellow windbreaker, checking the luggage to the passenger manifest. Once checked off the list, then and only then, is it taken to one of the luggage trams to be carried away to the terminal. Nick has to intercept his bag before it reaches this man or it will be lost to him.

To his surprise, Nick sees his duffle bag loaded on the back of another luggage tram driving around the back of the plane. Nick starts for the tram, hoping he could skirt the area and catch the tram on the other side. As he makes his move, the head lights of another emergency truck crosses Nick in the back, warning him of its approach. He grabs the talisman and renders himself invisible once more. For a split second, the driver thought he saw someone and hits the brakes, sending the vehicle into a slide and forcing Nick to leap out of the way. Is it too much to ask for a guy to get a break? Cloaked by the darkness of night and the power of the talisman, Nick sprints over and runs along beside the vehicle until he can grab the bag. The presence of demon spirits encircling the plane is in full view for him to see. The sooner his belongings are in his possession, the better. Then, it's off to the perimeter fence and away from this place as fast as possible. For now, Nick must focus on his new dilemma of where does he go? His name is going to be the talk of the town, nationwide, before the sun comes up. He needs make his own departure from the scene, and find anther means of travel. Yeah, good luck with that one, brother.

Siam and her men kneel before their new Master with Yukia looking down on them with disgust. "Before I pass judgment, would you like to state your case for your failure?"

Fearful of Yukia's transformation taking place, Siam begins to plead for her life. "Master, I beg you to have faith in your choice for my service. Landry has not left the region. Allow my men and I to carry out your command, and I guarantee you our success." Siam doesn't look up or try to determine Yukia's position. It is an action that shouldn't have been dismissed so easily.

The Masamoto daughter reaches out with a demonic clawed hand and slices off Siam's head. "That will not be necessary my dear. I shall handle this matter myself, from here on out." Yukia walks into the darkness as two bestial creatures move in to finish off Siam's men. In a matter of seconds, all that is left of the terrorists are a few large blood stains on the maintenance parking lot. "Come my pets," Yukia pats her hand against her thigh. "We have a guardian to hunt."

# Chapter XIII

"No ma'am, I'm telling the truth! I saw the guy ✦ ✦ ✦ that saved us! He beat up the bad guys, made 'em all jump out of the airplane! And then he saved us when we crashed. I don't know what he did, but I'm sure we're alive because he did what he did!" The young boy rambles on about the spectacle he had seen, and even filled in some blanks using his own imagination. He doesn't care; he's getting his fifteen minutes of fame with this interview. For his parents, they were hoping that their little Johnny could lead them to their cash cow with his story.

The reporter stands and faces the camera, recognizing that the boy was now adlibbing. "So, there you have it. Was there a guardian angel on board this flight that prevented a catastrophe? Or did our little eye witness here just see another one of the hijackers trying to escape. One thing is for certain; YWTK is on the case and we won't stop until we have the truth. I'm Bethany Phelps saying, when we know, you'll know. Goodnight America." The camera man signals to Beth that the feed was cut and they are off camera. She relaxes and slumps her shoulders slightly, before turning around to thank the child and his parents for the interview and begins to roll up her microphone cord. "This is going to be the big one," she thinks to herself. "Here I was doing some crappy winter vacation bullshit gig, only to have the story of my career fall into my lap, while I'm here at the airport! I did it! Bethany Phelps scooped the story." She hurries over to the news van and hands her camera man the microphone and cord. "Here Tommy, take this and then get me over to the ticket counter, pronto."

"Yes, Ms. Phelps. Is there anything else ol' Tommy can do for ya?" Tommy hands his cell phone to Bethany and gives her a devilish grin. "Walter is sending us to Hawaii," he explains, gloating the entire time.

"What? Give me that!" Beth holds the phone up to her ear. "Hello, Walter?" Beth listens to the phone call for a second before becoming agitated and defiant. "No! I'm onto something big here, and you're not going to take this one away from me this time! You owe me one, Walter, for all the other times you've stolen my thunder before. No, I don't want double owesies! Twice as much of nothing is still nothing. If Hawaii is so damned important, why don't you send that doofus brother-in-law, of yours, Chad Savage? I for one, think he's deserves a trip to the islands, if you consider the royal ass kissing that you get from the guy on a regular basis. Anybody that puckers that much deserves a day on the sandy beaches, don't they? Hey, maybe we'll all get lucky, and the islanders will sacrifice his ass to appease the volcano Gods." Beth hangs up the phone and tosses it back to Tommy. "Come on, camera boy, I want the full low down on this whole story a.s.a.p."

"Aw, come on, Beth, you're passin' up Hawaii?" Tommy's shoulders slump as he closes the rear doors of the news van. Just to make sure his feelings on passing up Hawaii are well stated, He mopes all the way back around to the driver's door. This could be his only chance to fly to the Islands on the company's dime, and Queen Bethany just shot it out of the sky.

"OH, don't be like that, now. Forget about the grass skirts and fruity drinks, and trust me. You've got the eye for the camera, but I've got the nose for the story. I'm telling ya, Tommy, this one's gonna be big." She climbs into the passenger seat and closes the door. "I'm talking award winning big," She adds trying to swat her partner's outlook. "Now get me over to the ticket counter so I can bribe someone for information and a passenger manifest."

Tommy climbs into the news van and plops himself down in the seat. "You know, I've been meaning to talk to you about that nose of yours." He knows that his comment comes across as mean or hurtful, but he feels she deserves it.

Beth spins to the side to face her partner. "What about my nose?" Her tone is defensive, which is what Tommy expects, since her nose job cost her thousands of dollars to look this good.

Tommy starts up the van and gives her a coy smile. "You have a tendency to stick it into other peoples' business, which usually results in us in deep piles of…"

"Yeah, yeah, just get me over to ticketing, ya big cry baby." Bethany goes through her ritual of checking her makeup and making sure her hair has that just left the salon look for the camera. "Ya know, if you drive a little faster, we could probably get a trailer shot for tonight's eleven o'clock show."

Nick moves through the streets of LA using his training and talents to blend and hide in the California nightlife, instead of using the power of the talisman to cloak his presence. To be honest, his body is so exhausted, Nick isn't sure if he could produce the concentration needed to do anything with his trinket. He needs to rest, but knows that he has to keep moving, he has to get away. Once he is as far away from the airport as possible, rest can be sought out. But time is short, and his destination, and JD, still awaits him. Finding a five dollar bill in his coat pocket, from his bag, gives him a little more maneuverability, or at least set a pace faster than walking. Limited funds and great distances require the cheapest solution, being public transportation. Train stations usually have their own transit police officers. If the city police are looking for him, then they probably have the transit police watching the stations. This leaves the buses, but unless you're near a main terminal, you're standing at a bus stop, out in the open, like Nick is doing at the moment.

For the past few minutes, he has worked his way down the street, avoiding patrol cars to reach the closest bus stop that is soon to be loaded. He's actually back tracked down the street a ways just to keep from being in one spot for too long. Slowing his movements is the number of police cars swarming through the area. They're looking for someone, and Nick has assured himself that it is him they're looking for. Another patrol car speeds around the corner with its lights flashing, racing passed Nick's position, where he waits with a group of people for the bus that's less than a block away. Nick completely dismisses the patrol car's presence. He doesn't move, he doesn't turn to walk away. Hell, Nick doesn't even look out the corner of his eye to track their course. Then the car stops. Its lights cast red and blue flashes against the walls of the buildings on both sides of the street. The one cop in the passenger seat jumps out of the car with his hand on his pistol and starts walking towards the bus stop crowd, as the driver backs the car up. Nick doesn't flinch. Both officers are shocked to find Nick nowhere in sight. They question the bus stop patrons, but no one noticed Nick or saw him walk away. Dissatisfied with the outcome, the cops climb back into the patrol car and drive away, having nothing else to go on.

Nick watches them leave from across the street, and even

waits for the bus to load its passengers and pull away before he decides to resume his trek. Maybe this is what Master Masamoto meant when he said that the talisman would ruin Nick's life. Let's see, in the past five years he has lost his bride, his friends, his dojo and business, maybe Sonny, and is in great danger of losing his freedom and/or his life. His standing with the Navy and the community are now shot to hell. And to top it all off, his finest student, friend, and protégé, has been kidnapped and taken to another country. Nick has no choice in the matter. He must seek JD out and rescue him, all without compromising his duty as the Guardian. How much worse could it get? Rule number three in Nick's laws; do not tempt the Gods against you by asking that question. They will always show you how bad it can really be.

Nick pulls his collar up around his neck, and slings his duffle bags over his shoulder and steps back into the LA nightlife. His destination is the home of Lt. Commander Ken Mitchell who now lives in the area, is still living out his life married to the Navy. At one time, Mitchell was one of the best field operatives to serve in this country's military. Once, he was the Field Commander of Nickolas Landry, while serving in the SEAL teams together. If Nick is going to find any assistance with his situation, Mitchell would be the person on this side of the country that could give it to him.

Sitting in the shadows waiting for a bus gives a man time to think. In situations like this, a man might weigh out the pros and cons of his past and future, to determine the path he takes. Not Nick, or at least not in a philosophical point of view. According to Masamoto, he should simply keep on walking and let the Gods of fate run their course. The thought gives him a cold shiver and causes him to look up to see the bus pulling up to the bus stop. There hasn't been any sign of the cops in the past few minutes, leading Nick to believe that they have moved on, spreading out their numbers away from the airport. He may be headed in the same direction, but the further the police spread out, the more holes open up for Nick to slip through. This isn't the first time he's been caught behind enemy lines. Nick knows exactly what he has to do. First, he needs to get on this bus and take it as far south as it goes. Then, he'll find the next bus and repeat. He sure wishes that Charlie and Sonny were with him now.

"Sorry bud," the uniformed officer says, as Nick pushes past him to get on the bus. It was completely an accident, completely uncalled for. What made Nick break and run up onto the bus like that? For one, it is completely out of character; especially with the way he has tried to avoid confrontation until now.

"Sorry about that, Officer," Nick mumbles, but continues onto the bus without looking back. He pays the fare and takes a seat on the driver's side of the bus. Now he's down to a couple of dollars and a bus transfer. Nick starts to wonder how far it will get him, and then gets the feeling that it doesn't matter any more. He looks back as the bus pulls away, to see the cop still standing there looking back at the bus.

"Central, this is Carson."

"This is Central, go ahead Carson."

"Yeah, I'm off duty, but I think I just ran into the all points bulletin getting onto the 619 heading south on Sepulveda Blvd. I just wanted to let you know."

"Roger that Carson, I'll alert RTD to let their driver know, and then dispatch the nearest patrol cars to intercept.

Nick is losing that steely control that makes him who he is. Paranoia has set in and is starting to thrive in his psyche, worrying what he should do. For whatever reason, he clutches the talisman as he worries about his situation. "One thing is for sure; I don't want to be on this bus any more." Suddenly, Nick finds himself standing in the middle of the street, staring at the hood of an oncoming taxi cab as the bus drives away. The cabbie slams on the brakes, unsure how Nick suddenly appeared in front of the car.

The cabbie need not worry, because Nick is as shocked by the current event as the cab driver, with full blown fear and panic setting in. Run, that's what he needs to do; it's what he has to do. After he quickly renders himself invisible, Nick takes to the nearest alley and then the next, and the next, putting as much distance between him and the bus. The police officers will stop the bus and search it thoroughly for any sign of Nick, but he will be far away by then.

Now he must deal with another problem on this run through hell. The longer he goes under the cloak of the talisman, the more stress and strain builds in his mind. And yet, he refuses to release his hold on the talisman. The landscape around him is shrouded in gloom and misery, as winged demons and ghostly spirits torment and terrorize the populace of the land, who are simply trying to make their way through this miserable existence. Nick knows that this is not his own reality, but a possible one should he fail at his duty. That little fact doesn't make this any more bearable to see the gruesome sights he sees. For some odd reason, Nick begins to feel like the demons in this possible reality are beginning to follow him now. More and more he begins to see pairs of red and orange glowing eyes appearing in the shadows, watching his every move. The number of little glowing eyes continues to increase as he makes his way through the desolate streets of this alternate LA. Ten, a hundred, a thousand eyes, maybe more, can be seen in the darkness, all staring at Nickolas Landry.

Finally, he finds an alley that isn't littered with dead bodies and homeless dreg suffering a miserable existence. His problem has been that there is no way for him to tell if the suffering masses that he encounters really exist in his reality or not. The last thing he needs, or wants, right now is anyone else seeing him using the talisman's power, or in this case, stop using the power to render him self visible again. The strain of what he sees is becoming too much for him to bear. He releases the talisman and closes his eyes trying to purge all of the horrific images he has sees from his mind. After a few seconds and a couple of deep cleansing breaths, he reopens his eyes and looks around. The smoke filled air, decaying buildings and demonic presences, are replaced by star filled skies and the empty surroundings of the industrial complex.

Nick drops his bag and sits down to take a quick rest break. There are several things he could be doing at the moment to make his task easier. In his bag is a portable GPS that he planned to use in Japan, to locate JD. He could break it out and use it to pinpoint his location as opposed to the Mitchell residence. He could, and probably should, but first he wants and needs to catch his breath for a minute.

"Hey, amigo, what's in the bag, bitch?" Nick turns his head slowly, really finding it hard to believe that he can't have just a few seconds of me time. Walking towards him from the end of the alley is four street punks following the mouth asking the question. Out the corner of Nick's eye, he sees three more hoodlums walking towards him from the other end of the alley. "Ya know, I don't know how you got in here, homes, but this is private property so we're gonna have to take your stuff and rough you up real good for trespassing in our alley."

Why can't he be left alone? All Nick wants is a few minutes to catch his breath and get a little rest. He stands up to face the gang of eight as they move in around him. Eight against one, for a split second, Nick wonders how his upstart friend, Billy would handle this situation. No, that's just not Nick's style. "Do yourselves a favor and walk away right now."

"Amigo, you don't just come into our house and tell us what to do." The eight gang members leap at once, believing Nick's warning to be an insult, to who they are, and how they live. How was one lost tourist going to stand up against the eight of them? Frustrated and fed up, Nick lashes out in another way that isn't his style either. "Leave me alone!" With that, a blast of black mystical energy is emitted from the talisman in all directions obliterating everything around Nick. Power line transformers explode, steel dumpsters burst into flames, and all that is left of the eight hoodlums is charred remains and smoldering heaps of bones littering the trash strewn alley. This is a whole new aspect that Nick never expected, and detests. Part of him believes that the gang members had it coming. His morality and his teachings tell him that their lives should have been spared. Wanting all of this to be over, Nick gets his bearings and heads off for his destination.

Bethany Phelps stands off to the side of the airport terminal with her eyes fixed on a certain door, just down the way from the International Airlines ticket counter. For the past forty five minutes, she has watched a number of high ranking airline officials accompany just as many Federal Agents in and out of the room. Then she sees her nightingale exit the door and look around the terminal. This nightingale is a young woman who just so happens to work for the airlines and is in league with Ms. Bethany Phelps. "Tommy, wake up, here comes Carly." Beth grabs her bag and walks over to meet her friend half way. "Quick, what have you got for me, girl?"

Carly looks around the terminal nervously, before she speaks to her friend. "The only passengers who are unaccounted for is twelve Chinese nationals and one

American, a Mr. Nickolas Landry." She pulls an envelope from her pocket and nonchalantly hands it to Beth.

Before Bethany has a chance to take the envelope from her friend, Carly has the envelope snatched out of her hand, sending the contents of money flying into the air. The brash FBI Agent who confiscated the envelope peers inside to read a slip of paper. "Why, this is nothing but a grocery list!" The female agent exclaims, sure that vital information about the case was being passed around.

"Well, hello, Kimberly," Bethany replies in a cheerful but forced tone. "Of course it's a grocery list. That's why I'm here, unless you would like to do our shopping for us."

Agent Kimberly Andrews motions for her lackeys behind her to pick up the money, and then forcefully shoves the envelope, Money, and grocery list against Bethany's chest. "That's Agent Andrews, to you. What are you really doing here, Phelps?"

This is just the icing on Bethany's cake tonight. Bethany and this uptight, equal rights activist, Federal Agent have butted heads before. "Why Agent Andrews, you're not still mad at me for that little incident a few months ago, are you?" Beth sticks out her hand demanding the money that has been collected by the other agents.

"Mad? Now why would you think that?" Andrews lets her facial expressions state her distaste for Beth. "Your interference only cost me six months of surveillance and two agents their lives!" Andrews pauses for a minute to collect emotions and regain her composure. "I want you to listen to me good, Phelps. I don't want to see you anywhere near this case, or this airport, for that matter. If I do, I swear to God that I will lock you up for obstruction! Do you understand me?"

"Well, if it puts your pretty, but aging head at ease, I was here doing a segment on vacation destinations, when

Carly here, called me up and asked me if I would pick up a few things for her, at the store. Evidently, she can't get off at her normal time because you people are making her work a double." Beth gives her friend a sly wink, telling her to play along.

Agent Andrews snatches the money out of Beth's hand and shoves it back into Carly's possession. "Go do your own shopping. You're off the clock as of right now, and until this investigation is over," she declares, before turning to face Tommy and Beth. "As for the two of you, I don't want to see your faces around anything connected to me or tonight's incident. You can count on one thing for sure. No one will get anything on this until I deem it so. I won't have the two of you leaking any information before I have my suspects in custody. Then, and only then, will the media line up for the story. Beth, my dear, you will be the last in line."

"Can I at least quote you on that?" Beth shoves her recorder in front of Andrews' face, just to piss her off a little more.

"No comment," Andrews replies, slapping the voice recorder out of Beth's hands before motioning for two of her agents to escort the reporter and her cohorts out of the building. Agent Andrews and her fellow agents turn and walk away, as Beth spouts off amendment rights trying to antagonize Kimberly Andrews as much as possible.

"You are a miracle worker, baby girl!" Carly can't believe the luck. "Do you have any idea how long I have been trying to get some time off? Now I know what to do. Next time there is some kind of incident here, I'll just proudly step forward and state that I am Bethany Phelps' best friend, and I must go home for security reasons."

"Yeah, well I'm not sure how far that will get you, but thanks for everything on this one." Beth takes the time to wave at her favorite FBI Agent, who was watching them talk outside the terminal. There's no surprise on Beth's part, when Andrews looks around before giving Beth the middle finger. "I'll talk to you later, Carly. I need to tap your brother's data base for information." The two ladies hug, and then part ways, with Bethany grabbing Tommy by the arm to lead him away. She is oblivious to the world around her when she gets like this. Tommy grabs Beth by the arm and stops her from walking out in front of a taxi, while searching her purse for her cell phone. Ignoring his effort and remarks about carelessness, she dials her boyfriend's phone number, Carly's brother.

"Hello, this is Detective Rosa."

"Hello yourself, lover boy," Beth blows a lip smacking kiss into the phone. "Did ya get that? It should have knocked you out of your chair." She motions for Tommy to go get the van, so that she could have a little privacy. "Honey," she asks with a sugar coated tone.

Detective Manuel Rosa shakes his head and turns away from his fellow Detectives. "Don't give me that honey crap, Bethany. Any time you start off a conversation by blowing a kiss into the phone, it usually means that you want something that somehow could possibly cost me my job. So, I love you, the answer is no, but tell me what you want, any way."

"Well, any time you call me Bethany, it means you're mad at me and won't help any way. So why should I even bother wasting my breath." Beth goes as far as pouting, even though Rosa can't see her through the phone. "I guess I'll see you later, oh wait, I think I might have a headache by the time you get off."

Manny sits up in his chair, suddenly willing to change his stand. After four days and nights of surveillance, in a little apartment with three other police officers, Manny was looking forward to an intimate evening with his lady. "Hold on there a minute, baby. I can't think of one good reason why you would want to be like that. Tell me what you want, and I can probably bring it over when I get off tonight."

Beth grins as the van pulls up to the curb. "Hold on a second," she asks, before climbing into the passenger seat of the vehicle. "Okay, but you better produce, mister, or you won't be getting off tonight." Beth drops her phone into her lap and unfolds the slip of paper that Carly had slipped her when she handed Beth the grocery money. She grabs a cigarette from her purse and lights it before picking up the phone. "Are you still there?"

"Are you smoking a cigarette? Beth you know I hate it when you come home smelling like an ashtray."

"Oh no, don't even think about it," she replies, rolling down the window to air out the van. "Now, are you ready for this? The guy's name is Nickolas Alan Landry. Check for any ties to Miami. That's where he got on the plane. "

Manny jumps up out of his chair and opts to leave the room. "Beth, are you talking about the shit going down at LAX? Oh, baby, you really do want to get me kicked off the force, don't you?" Slipping into a vacant office, Manny sits down at the computer and types in his access and security codes. "This will take a little time, but it'll give me something to do. While I have you on the phone, you should know that I'm going to be a little late. I've been asked to hang around a little longer tonight, while our guys are down at the airport handling the crowd control." Manny stares at the computer screen as the history of Nickolas Landry starts to come up in front of him. "Hey Beth, you're not gonna believe what there is on this guy."

"Print it, and bring it to me, babe. I need to go, so I can call Walter and tell him what I've got. You think it's good, don't ya?"

"Good enough to get me locked up for life, for giving it to

you." Manny hits the print command, knowing he is going to regret this. "You better rock my world tonight."

"Love ya," she replies, before hanging up the phone and dropping it into her purse. Her mind is working at light speed trying to come up with as many possible options that she might have. One last drag from her cigarette, and she flips the butt out the window, before exhaling the smoke after it.

"You said you were going to call Walter," Tommy points out, looking over at Beth as he tries to navigate the traffic leaving the airport. "Do me a favor and tell him that you kidnapped me or something, okay? I don't want him to think I was a willing participant in whatever you are planning." He looks back at the road to see who or what a car was honking at before looking back at Bethany again. "Well, you are going to tell me what we are going to do aren't you?"

Bethany gives her friend a big cheesy smile. "Here's what I want you to do. Drop me off at the office and I'll go in to see Walter, personally. You go home and pack up your travel cam and gear. As soon as I see Manny, and have time to go over what he's got for me, I'll call you and tell you when we're leaving."

"Well, are you at least going to tell me where we are going?'

"Hell son, we're going to South Beach," Beth replies, wearing a big smile. Her statement revives her partner's faith. Miami is a much better destination than Hawaii, since he didn't have to fly over an ocean to get there. Tommy steps on the gas pedal, and drives as fast as he can to the production office.

"This whole world is going to hell." Former Lt. Commander Keith Mitchell closes the door and locks the dead bolt before heading back to the living room of his house. He pats his leg with his hand trying to call his faithful mutt over for some attention. The dog gives him a grumbling growl not willing to give up his spot on the couch. "Terrorist threats are becoming second nature, boy. The damned government is falling apart and nobody gives a shit any more. And to think this is what I served my time to protect." Mitchell picks up the dog's dish and walks over to the kitchen doorway. "Here Nickels, get max some water and quit hanging out in the dark."

"Evening, LT, How'd you know I was here. Your dog didn't even know I was here." Nick turns on the light and walks over to the sink. The kitchen reeks of spoiled food, and is littered with empty take out containers and dirty dishes.

"Max doesn't even know that he's here."

Nick exits the kitchen with the water dish and sits it down in the floor. "You're not surprised to see me?"

"Let's see, three cops show up here, asking all sorts of questions about you," Mitchell flips one of the Detectives' business cards over at Nick. "I figured that if they were here asking about you, I'd be running into you, sooner or later. It only makes sense." Mitchell looks over at Nick with a concerned expression. "What are you doing bringing your problems here, Landry?"

"To be honest, I need to call in my old markers, LT."

# Chapter XIV

Japan, the land of the rising sun of the orient, it is a place of wonder, and dark mystery. "What? What do you mean there was interference?" Yukio Masamoto paces back and forth in his Tokyo condominium, irate with the news that he is receiving. "If I didn't know any better, dear sister, I might start to think that you plot against me. Let me explain this to you. If your man aboard the plane verified Landry's presence, and he wasn't found as a casualty, then he must have arrived at the airport. Remember what the Master taught you, and use the darkness around you to pinpoint his location. If he used the power of the piece, which he obviously did to exit the airport, you should be able to pick up some kind of energy trail leading to his location. Find him and finish this once and for all. I leave for Kyoto with our guest at dusk. I will begin to prepare our forces should you fail me again."

"Why dear brother, have you no faith in me? I told you that this plan of yours was too intricate for my taste, in the first place. If we are going to rule this world in darkness, then I say let us get on with it. My way would have been much quicker and simpler."

"Yes," Yukio replies, "but it would have been much more noticeable to those who we don't want interfering."

Yukia hangs up her phone and drops it in her pocket. "Come my pets, find Nickolas Landry for me." Her two demonic looking canines move to her side and sniff the night air. A low growl from the beasts informs Yukia that they have his scent. She spreads her arms wide and arches her back, causing a pair of reptilian wings to protrude from between her shoulders. Yukia takes to the air and soars over the LA nightlife so that she tracks her demon dogs' progress unseen. This turn of events works in her favor, more and more. It is more evident proof that her brother is not fit to stand beside the Master. If she is able to right the wrong, it will prove her worthy over Yukio. This gives her even more incentive to find Landry and take him to Japan.

"Oh Lucy, I'm home!" Manny Rosa enters the front door of his girlfriend's ritzy apartment carrying a stack of files and a sack full of greasy tamales. Once inside, he kicks the door closed with his shoe, leaving a scuff mark for Beth to complain about later, and hurries off straight for the master bedroom. "Baby, you are here, aren't you?" He loves that the place has her special woman's touch. What drives him crazy is that they never use the rest of the place. The condo would actually make a great place for a gathering or party. That would be great, except for the fact that Beth would have a nervous breakdown before the night was over, worrying about her clean, pristine, never been used appearance of her home.

Bethany charges out of the bedroom wearing one of Manny's long sleeve shirts. "Ya know you need more of a Cuban accent to pull off a good Ricky Ricardo impression." She gives her fiancé a kiss, and then snatches the folder out from under the sack of tamales, almost spilling Manny's dinner all over the floor. Without apology, she hurries back into the bedroom and jumps up onto the plush king size mattress and goes to work. Within seconds, she has already rifled through half the paper work, pulling out articles of interest. "This guy is definitely one hot mess! Did you see any of this stuff?"

"Of course I saw it, well at least some of it. It wasn't like I took the time to study each page as it printed out. I was in a little bit of a hurry, not wanting to get caught," Manny adds sarcastically, before he takes a bight of his tamale. When he lays the unwrapped morsel on her dresser, to get undressed, Beth is quick to take notice.

"Oh honey, don't do that! Those things are so greasy. It's gonna mess up the finish."

He quickly pulls his shirt over his head and retrieves his dinner to stop her complaining. "You want one of these? Angela's mother made up a whole batch and sent them to the precinct. Nobody else wanted any more, so I brought the rest home for me and you." He kicks his shoes off beside the bed and drops his pants. When he doesn't get a response, Manny just shakes his head and walks around the bed to the master bath. "I'm getting in the shower, but I expect a full body massage as payment for getting that stuff for you."

"Yeah, yeah whatever," Bethany replies at the moment, not realizing what she was agreeing to. Her mind is working in overdrive, trying to process all of this information to determine which way she should lead with the story. Never in her life has she read such an interesting file on someone. "This Nickolas Landry is the story of the year." She reaches over to the nightstand and grabs her phone and speed dials her boss, Walter. It only takes her a few minutes to convince him that what she has could be an award winning story. With Walter's blessing, Bethany hangs up the phone and starts to get dressed. She is the master of multitasking. While sitting on the edge of the bed, she slips her shoes on, logs onto the internet on her laptop, while scribbling a note apologizing to Manny for running off. A minute or two later, Beth is dialing another number on her cell phone, as she collects a prepacked bag from the closet. "Yeah, Tommy, were you asleep? Well get dressed, we're headed to Miami. I've got a cab headed to your house as we speak. Meet me at the Southwest departure gates in thirty minutes. Okay, an hour, but you better not miss our flight screwing around to get through security."

"And where do you think you're going, young lady?" Manny stands at the bathroom door, disappointed to see his lady readying to leave.

"Sorry babe, but Walter wants me in Miami before the sun comes up."

"Oh come on, you've gotta at least give me tonight before you run off to the other side of the country!" Manny drops his towel hoping to entice Bethany in staying. "What about my massage?"

"As soon as I get back, I promise." She hurries over and gives him a quick kiss. "Oh don't cry, honey. It's the nature of the profession." One more kiss and she is out the front door.

Manny flops down on the edge of the bed and turns on the TV. "Hello, Mr. Leno," he says to the image on the screen. "You want a tamale, Jay?"

JD watches his captor pace the floor of the Tokyo condo. This is where Nick's teachings come into play. Rule number one: Know your surroundings. Okay, there's a lot of hi-tech stereo and TV equipment. Modern design furniture in the room is strategically placed for optimum view of the door. This tells JD that his captor is either a man of high power or severely paranoid of the world outside. If it is the first, then the second could still be in play. What gives JD the biggest clue of all, is the strong colors of red, black and white that make up the interior design. The guy is a power trip with a strong ego. Still, it is a weakness that can be exploited. JD just needs to come up with a way to take the advantage, in his condition. Stripped of his shirt, pants, and shoes, he has been placed in a very vulnerable situation. Even if he could escape, where would he go wearing nothing but his underwear? As much as he hates to admit it, JD realizes now that he has become a part of a chess match between Nick and his opponents. The scary part isn't that the winner of this duel could rule the world in darkness. The scarier part is that the only thing JD has at risk is his own life, and he doesn't have a say in how or what happens. If JD had any doubt about Nick's destiny, it has been laid to rest hours ago. The recent events involving him is more proof than JD could have ever wanted. This is that moment in time where JD finds out if he's really got what it takes. "Ya know pal, toying with Nick like this is going to get you nothing but hard times."

Yukio looks at JD as if he doesn't have a care in the world." There is much more to all of this than you realize, young one." The Japanese mobster starts to walk casually towards his captive. "There is so much more than your innocent little mind can fathom. Would you like a taste to satisfy your curiosity?" Lightning fast, Yukio moves across the room and lays his finger against the side of JD's head. "You speak with bravery in your voice, but I know there is fear in your heart." Instantly, murderous visions of entire races being tortured and killed are shown all around him. JD looks around at the miserable landscape of the apocalypse, developing a fearful feeling of dread. All around him is agony and suffering, as nomadic tribes are continuously assaulted by demonic warriors. Cries of anguish and screams of fear and pain fill the air and echo in JD's ears. Buildings burn but are not consumed. People are slaughtered, but no one dies. He can't help but believe that this is truly hell.

He's forced to witness this horror as black warrior knights ride on demonic steeds passed him, to mercilessly attack a band of fleeing nomads seeking refuge. If you are evil, you are possessed by evil. If you are good in light, you are the ones suffering in this dark world. The doom riders have the duty of enslaving the children, and raping the women, so that they will bear offspring for more dark warriors to serve their Master. JD looks up and sees an ominous figure riding towards him, wearing armor of regal red and black. This darkest of Lords sits perched on the back of a wingless dragon, the size of a small elephant. He is the one called Devastator, leading his council right up to where JD is standing. His General on his right is a warrior in armor of Purple and black, The Dark Lord rides atop a steed that looks like it climbed right out of the belly of Hades. Behind him are four more massive knights in armor, riding four more hell steeds of their own. JD can see their faces behind the masks and helmets, and can see the joy in their eyes. The Dark Lords watch idly by at the torture and suffering taking place. They find joy in the actions taking place, as their armies conquer the lands. Where is the joy in this? There is none.

Tears well up in JD's eyes, with his heart crying out for the lost souls he sees. It is not his world, but the suffering is all the same. The vile being known as Doomsayer removes his helmet and stares into JD's eyes, giving the young man more of a reason to fear this witnessing. As Doomsayer's eyes begin to glow brighter and brighter, he points a finger at the young warrior of light, and releases a ghastly scream. Then with a flash of brilliant white light, the images vanish, leaving JD with only the pain and suffering he had seen, while under Yukio's trance. The mental agony applied to JD's mind renders him defenseless. His thoughts are void and he has no idea what he should do. In some ways, he would rather die now, than suffer the example he has just witnessed.

"You're not as brave as you proclaim, are you, soldier of light?" Yukio laughs at JD's tears, believing that this soul is now lost to the cause. "Tell me, was that more than you expected to see?" JD drops to his knees, surrendering to his fate. Now, Yukio is sure that JD will bend to his will and serve his cause against Landry. "Tisk, tisk, I didn't expect to break you so quickly. Maybe I should look at it with an optimistic view. Maybe, you are simply more intelligent than I gave you credit for." Yukio reaches down and grabs JD's face with his claw bearing, deformed hand, and lifts him from the floor. "Surrender to me now, and I assure you that the past you saw will never be your future to suffer."

He is a young man, who has experienced a lot, and has learned that much more. His one weakness is that he is human, as displayed by his emotions. The strength of a man is tested in moments like these. Sometimes, it's just a matter of how fast or slow you regain your composure. JD has found his. "Actually, I was hoping that I could get you this close." Before Yukio realizes what is happening, JD hits him in the nose with a head butt and deploys his force field, sending Yukio flying across the room. JD is surprised when Yukio produces his own set of wings, like his sister, and gains control of his predicament. He flies back over to JD and lands a few feet away. "Cute trick, hombre," JD commends, letting his force field drop as a show of strength and arrogance. "I don't know what you've been drinking, but when Nick gets here I'm gonna watch him kick your ass all over Japan!"

"Your faith in your Sensei is honorable, and yet misplaced." Yukio turns away, sensing another presence. His action confuses JD a little, but it's enough for him to drop his guard. He relaxes a little, and then feels a sharp pain in the side of his neck. Seconds later, he falls to the floor unconscious to the world. Yukio walks over to the middle of the floor and stops. "Load him in the car, Shade," Yukio commands as his assassin materializes in front of him. "We leave for Kyoto within the hour."

Lt. Commander Keith Mitchell sits on his sofa staring at Nick, wondering what he should believe. He has just sat through the most outrageous story he's ever heard. He's heard some whoppers before, but Nick's definitely takes the cake. "Well, how is Sonny? Is she, you know, alive?"

"To be honest, LT, I'm not sure. The last I heard, she was stable, but I haven't had any way to find out for sure." Nick stands up and starts to walk around the room. He takes notice to the drab and dreary interior and broken down furniture. Even with everything Nick has going on in his own life, he has the time to feel sorry for LT, seeing how his former CO has fallen on bad times. "LT, I've seen shit that I don't understand, so don't think I would blame you if you can't wrap around all of this. This much I am certain of; the people holding my friend have gone through a lot of trouble to lure me to Japan, and have done everything possible to make it difficult for me. They are very deadly, and his life is in danger more and more, the longer he is in their custody." Nick pulls the talisman out of his shirt and holds it up for Mitchell to see. "This is the only proof I have to offer. It's the reason they hold JD. It's the reason I have to go to Japan." Nick slumps down on the sofa next to his former field commander, stirring up the unmistakable odor of dog. He wants to say something, but knows that the last thing he wants to do is offend the guy that could help him out.

Mitchell leans over and puts his arm around his friend. "First of all, you need to ease up there, bud. You're wound up tighter than a three dollar watch." Mitchell reaches out and touches the talisman, thumping it with his finger. "You

265

read about this shit in fantasy novels, or see it…" Mitchell's statement is cut short as dark visions flash in and out of his mind.

"LT, are you okay?" Nick tucks the talisman back into his shirt and lets his concern show for his friend.

"Y-yeah, I'm okay. I guess I just had a brain fart or something, that's all. You hang tight for a second or two, and I'm gonna go make a couple of phone calls to see what I can do. You try to relax a little. I'll be back in a minute." Mitchell stands and pats Nick on his shoulder. The effect of the talisman still lingers with him. Even in the brief moment of touching his friend's shoulder, the Lieutenant sees an image of Nick in a battle for his life, with the agents of darkness he had seen in his little vision before. Walking to his bedroom, he contemplates what he saw, or thinks he saw, or was his mind playing tricks on him based on Nick's story? There's only one way for sure for him to figure that one out. Mitchell opens his nightstand drawer and retrieves a bottle of whiskey. If nothing else, maybe this gut rot can wash the images of cruelty and suffering from his mind. He grabs a shot glass from the top of his dresser and empties the cigarette butts out of it into the trash can, and then pours his drink. Mitchell's not one to drink straight from the bottle. He's got more class than that. Obviously, it's not a lot more, but it's enough. "Hello gorgeous how's my girl?" Mitchell asks, holding the bottle up in front of his face, before he pours himself a shot and gulps it down. "You never let me down, darlin'," He adds, giving the label a kiss before returning the bottle to his drawer. After staring at it for a couple of seconds, debating on whether or not he should pour another one for good measure, Mitchell takes a deep breath and exhales hard trying to clear his system of the bad mojo he's feeling. With phone in hand he dials out a number and holds the receiver to his ear, hoping he is doing the right thing for his friend.

"Hello, Pickens, I've got a buddy here at the house that is gonna need some special attention."

"Hey, LT, what in the hell are you doing calling here at this time of night?"

Mitchell closes the bedroom door, "I've got somebody here that is in need of some assistance." Mitchell lights a cigarette and walks around the room trying to come up with a good story. "Okay, here's the deal; I've got this friend who's stationed in Sapporo. The guy went and got married while he was on furlough, and took too long consummating the marriage and missed his flight back to Okinawa. Do you have anything headed that way that he could piggy back on?"

"I've got two questions for you, LT. Why is it that all of the screw ups always wind up at your door? The second is; where the hell is this guy going, Okinawa, or Sapporo?" Pickens looks at his flight chart for a second. "I do have something leaving for Sapporo in about three hours, but nothing flying out to Okinawa for at least two days."

Mitchell cringes, recognizing his mistake. "Did I say Okinawa? I'm sorry, Bruce. I guess the old mind is starting to slip. Either that or I'm having a flashback to my time in Japan. Naw, the guy's in dire need to get to Sapporo, can he do it without confrontation?

Pickens pops his bubble gum in front of the receiver just to aggravate the old man. "Yeah, that shouldn't be a problem. There aren't any big shots on base so security will be bare minimum. I'll call down to the east gate and tell them to expect him. What will he be driving?"

"My car, and who's working the gate tonight?" Mitchell retrieves the bottle and shot glass from his nightstand, feeling the need for another drink.

"Rodriguez."

"Good, tell him I'll be down tomorrow to pick up my car, and that I said hello to him and Maria." Mitchell starts to hang up, but he is halted by Pickens screaming into the phone.

"Man, you can't hang up without telling me the guy's name!"

He looks around his room, searching for a quick answer. If Nick is really in as much hot water as he said, he can't be Nickolas Landry. On his bedroom wall hangs a picture that has a name tag and rank hanging below it. "The guy's name is Steiner, Lt. Charlie Steiner." He takes another swig of whiskey and hangs up the phone. This uneasy feeling keeps growing inside of him by the minute. He beginning to see how tonight could end up being another sleepless night. Mitchell takes a drag off his cigarette, looks at the butt, and then drops it into his shot glass and sets it on the table.

With a heavy heart, he walks over to the picture on the wall and stares at the faces in the photograph. Nick, Charlie, Sonny, and Jorge, were certainly four of a kind to draw to. Charlie's gone, and Sonny maybe, as well. Mitchell starts to wonder if he'll outlive Nick and Jorge too. After what he's heard tonight, the odds seem to be in his favor when it comes to Nick. "Sorry about this, Charlie, but your amigo needs to borrow these for one last mission." Mitchell walks over to his closet and retrieves a dress uniform and heads back out into the living room. "Have you gone and paid your respects to Charlie and Nicole?"

"To be honest, no," Nick replies, feeling ashamed about his answer.

"Here, put these on and get out of here." He tosses Nick the clothes but hands him the rank and name tag out of respect for Charlie. "Here are my keys; I want you to take them and drive my car to the airfield in San Diego. Your plane leaves in three hours. I told the night officer that you missed your flight because of your wedding. You'll be piggy backing on a C-130 into Sapporo. When you're done with all of this, take the insignias to Charlie and pay your respects. He was your best friend, once." Mitchell walks over to the sofa and grabs his smokes. "Security on the base may be light weight, but you'll need to watch your ass with everything that's going on over there with Korea. You never know when the Pentagon is going to put a base on alert. Good luck Nickels," He pauses to light his cigarette, "cause you're damn well gonna need it."

"Are you gonna be okay, LT?"

Mitchell gives Nick an unconvincing smile. "You just go do whatever it is you're gonna go do, and don't worry about me. I can still take care of myself." Mitchell stands up and waits for Nick to put on the officer's uniform, and then escorts him to the door. "We're even up now, Nickels. I don't think I want to see you on my front step ever again." Mitchell turns his head to blow out the smoke. "Goodbye, old friend."

Nick understands where Mitchell is coming from with the statement. He has put Mitchell in a very serious circumstance simply by coming to his house. What Nick's friend has done may have cost him his own freedom for helping, all because of a stupid debt that should never be owed. "I understand, LT. I hope you believe me when I say that I'm not the bad guy here, but somebody has to be. If they come back here looking for me, or tie me to your car, I borrowed it, no questions asked. I'm a friend, why would you not loan it to me? They haven't released anything on the news, so you have no reason to suspect me. Stick to that story no matter what. After I take off, call the night officer to spread the word that my presence should be forgotten for everyone's sake. Tell them whatever you want, but stick to it. There's no need for you to stick your neck out any further for me than you already have." Nick turns away from his friend, believing that this has to be the most painful goodbye he has ever experienced.

"Watch your six out there, Nickels." Mitchell closes the door and locks it shut. This is a sad moment for him as well. He always knew Nick would do something with his life. Mitchell never imagined anything like this. He looks around the living room and decides to hold off straightening up, until morning. Right now he requires the comfort found in the bottle, in his nightstand. Before retiring to his room, Mitchell walks over to turn the lights off like every other night, but then decides to leave them on. He checks the door again and then the kitchen door as well, before walking back through the house. "Max, are you coming with me?" The old dog moans and groans for a little bit before finally pulling itself off the couch and walk to the bedroom as if it was killing him with every step. "You're a sad sort, Max."

Mitchell sits down on the edge of the bed and grabs the remote to turn on the TV. There has to be something on that would take his mind off what has happened. "Here we go; Jon Stewart always knows how to put a smile on my face. Thank, Comedy Central." Mitchell slides back on the bed and reaches into his nightstand drawer to retrieve his best friend. After a swig of whiskey, he wipes the whiskey from his chin and is ready to settle into some good comedy to ease his attention. Just for comfort's sake, he reaches around behind his pillow to make sure his 9 mm Beretta is where it belongs. One more swig of bourbon and Mitchell is over the edge.

The humor of "The Daily Show" skits, do the trick to take his mind off of tonight. By the time the "Colbert Report" is on, Mitchell can't remember Nick being at his house. So drawn in to what he is watching, or too drunk to care, Mitchell ignores the low growls coming from his faithful dog, and doesn't flinch when Max jumps off the bed and walks out of the room. A bumping sound does catch his attention, but it sounds like it is coming from the roof. "Well I know that's not Santa. He's not due for a few more weeks." Mitchell finally notices that Max is nowhere around. "Max, where the hell have you gone off too, boy?" He starts to get up when he hears a light yelp from his dog, somewhere else in the house. Mitchell immediately grabs his pistol and loads a shell into the firing chamber. Staggering to the bedroom door, he tries to make a cautious approach, or at least as much as a drunk can muster. He slides along the wall until he comes to the door jamb where he stops to take a slow deep breath. Then, he jumps out into the hallway, checking both directions for intruders. With his pistol held chest high and out in front of him, he heads out into the living room with his Beretta leading the way. What he sees in the middle of the living room floor is more than he can bear. Mitchell falls back against the wall, knocking pictures from their hangers, as Yukio calmly strokes the fur of Max's headless corpse. "Who the hell are you, and what did you do to my dog?" He pulls the hammer back and points the pistol at the young woman with a trembling hand.

"Good evening, Lt. Commander Keith Mitchell. I'll have you know that I did not do this." Yukia Stands up and calmly walks around as if his pistol was no threat to her at all. "He did," she explains, pointing at her demonic hound that was chewing the fur and skin from Max's skull. The beast looks like a Bull Mastiff on steroids that is waiting for the opportunity to get at Mitchell. "It would seem that we have a mutual acquaintance that I'm just killing to find."

Mitchell laughs at her remark, but never takes his eyes off the hell hound on the other side of the couch. Without any hesitation, he squeezes off a round, hitting Yukia in the chest. The force sends her flying back over the love seat and out of sight. The demon dog reacts, but Mitchell doesn't hesitate to give it the same treatment. The first bullet doesn't seem to phase the beast, but the next six takes it down with no problem.

To his surprise, Yukia appears at his side and drives her clawed hand in between his ribs. His blood begins to flow freely as the pain causes him to drop to one knee. "Save yourself the agony of prolonging this, and simply tell me where Landry is." A twist of her fingers snaps a rib, adding to his suffering. She then retracts her fingers and lets Mitchell fall to the floor. "As you can see, Lt. Mitchell, you are outmatched and outclassed."

You wanna know where Nickels is? Sure, I'll tell ya. He's headed to Japan on one of thirty different aircraft. From what I understand, he's headed to meet your boss and give him some of this." Mitchell empties the pistol into her torso and replies, "as for outclassed and outmatched, I don't see it that way." Suddenly, Mitchell's life flashes in front of his eyes, as the next attack comes from behind. Yukia's other demon dog was laying in wait, concealed by the darkness of the kitchen. Its oversized mouth closes in around Mitchell's face before slamming shut like a bear trap. Yukia stands and walks over to Mitchell as if nothing had happened to her. She kneels beside his twitching body and lifts him effortlessly with one hand. "Fool, did you really think that you had a chance to survive?" She leans her head over and sinks her fangs into his neck, and begins to suck and slurp at the puncture wounds created. Instantly, she knows all that Mitchell knew about Nick's destination. "Leave him my pet. There will be other for you to feast upon." A few seconds later, the alcohol in his blood sends her rocketing through the roof and into the night, driven by an intoxicated rage.

# Chapter XV

Nick pulls up to the east gate and calmly waits for the portly officer to exit the guard shack. "You must be Mitchell's hard luck case. Welcome to the fraternity, man. If it wasn't for Mitchell, me, and my best friend, would be out of the Service the hard way. It's nice to know that there are still guys like him around, to help out guys like us." Pickens motions for Rodriguez to open the gate. "Follow me over to motor pool. I'll show you where to park LT's car, and then I'll take you over to the hangar." Pickens heads over to his jeep and starts the engine. Seconds later, he is driving across the base like a bat out of hell.

Once at the motor pool, Nick follows Mitchell's instructions and drops the keys to the Buick Apollo into the trunk and closes it. He looks around and then climbs into the jeep where Pickens was waiting to shake his hand. "How ya doin'? I'm Bruce, Bruce Pickens. It's really an honor to meet ya. I recognize your name from some of Mitchell's stories. He said that you and some guy named Landry really tore it up over seas." Pickens puts the jeep in gear and speeds off again. "I'll tell you this much, ma an' ol' Mitchell are gonna have a talk tomorrow. Now, I don't mind paying my debts to people, but this is way over the line, no offense. I mean, a guy should be fair enough to give another guy fair warning about something like this coming down the pike. Do ya know what I mean?" Pickens looks over at Nick and adds, "Do you have any idea how much trouble I could get into if someone finds out about this?" He looks back to the roadway and then to Nick again saying, "You don't talk very much, do ya? That's alright though, because knowing Mitchell, the less I know the better off I'll be."

The rest of the drive to the hangar was pleasantly quiet for Nick with him preferring it that way. In fact, it was creeping Pickens out so much that he was becoming uneasy in Nick's presence. To him, the sooner this is all over, the better. "Here ya go, sport, this is your stop. Oh good, here comes your pilot. I'll introduce you to him." Pickens jumps from the jeep and waddles over to the approaching pilot and points back at Nick. "Major Michaels, this is Lt. Charlie Steiner. He's gonna stow away on your flight to Sapporo since he missed his own flight out."

"That's okay with me. Glad to have you on board, Lieutenant. I hope you can handle the bumpy ride with the rest of the cargo." Michaels looks at the name tag on Nick's shirt. "Steiner, Steiner, hey I remember, you were in the SEALS, right? I thought you looked familiar. I flew your team into the Gulf on a high altitude jump. You remember, don't you? I was the one who thought that you guys were insane for jumping out of a perfectly good airplane at those heights." The Major salutes Nick, who actually forgot to salute the higher ranking officer, to keep his cover intact. "Any way, the rest of the cargo is being loaded onto the plane now and my copilot has already begun the preflight check list. If you'd like, you can wait in the hangar break room until we're ready for takeoff. In fact, why don't you just kick back for about twenty minutes and I'll have somebody come get you when we're ready."

Major Michaels opens the man door to the hangar and motions for Nick to enter first. "Come on, I'll show you the secret to a free cup of coffee from the vending machine." Nick watches as Pickens drives away, and suddenly feels all alone in a fish tank full of piranha. Sitting in the middle of a military airfield, while the whole country is looking for him, is not Nick's first option of choice. Then again, sometimes the best place to hide is right under the noses of the people who are looking for you. The two men enter the hangar and make their way through a crew of service men working on a shipment for the next plane. Michaels leads Nick to a small room where there is only a soda machine and automated coffee machine occupying the room with two chairs. "Through that door over there," Michaels points out, "is a TV and a couple more chairs. Go ahead and make yourself as comfortable as possible and I'll have someone come get you when we're ready for takeoff." The pilot drops a quarter into the coffee machine while holding onto the coin return lever. Out drops the quarter and the machine begins to produce a cup of coffee. "We'll see ya in about twenty minutes," Michaels gestures towards the fresh cup of coffee. Nick gives the pilot a nod and a nonchalant salute with Michaels returning the gesture before exiting the hangar.

Nick's thoughts are quickly diverted to his mission at hand. For the first time since he boarded the plane in Miami, Nick actually feels like he can relax a little in this small room of solitude. Too much has taken place over the past few days, giving him reason to believe that his life is never going to be the same after this. On the TV is the late night news recapping Nick's earlier episode at the airport. He sees this as proof to his earlier thought, and quickly dismisses it wanting to stay focused on the one who is in need. JD has to remain Nick's top priority until he is safely returned to the US where he belongs. Only then can Nick worry about his own situation and find a way to reclaim his life.

Suddenly, his thoughts are interrupted by two of the service men from the work crew, when they come crashing through the plate glass window that separates the room from the hangar. Nick jumps to his feet and quickly takes the defensive, hell bent on being sure that no one was going to blow this, his last shot at getting to Japan. Nick lets a short sword slide out of the sleeve of his coat, knowing that the true danger is still on the other side of the wall. He goes from defensive posture to offensive motion leaping right through the shattered window. Nick is shocked by what he finds. There are bodies, and body parts, scattered all over the hangar that is covered with the blood of the fallen service men. Who could have done this in so little time? These men died horrific deaths unnecessarily. Nick knows that this is a message for him, but why the morbid extremes?

"So Guardian, you do possess some measure of bravery. That will definitely make this more sporting." Yukia points to her hell hound, and then directs her finger towards Nick, telling the demonic beast to attack. It charges towards Nick, as he stands his ground, while the demon dog gnashes its teeth ready to bury them into Nick's flesh. At the last second, Nick spins to the side avoiding the attack and lops off the beast's head. Before the demon dog has the chance to hit the floor, Nick has already wiped the beast's blood form his blade and is pointing it at Yukia. The beast hits the concrete floor already beginning to decay. "I'll kill you!!!" She slings her hands down to her side causing long claws to extend out the ends of her deforming hands. Nick stands his ground and waits for the moment. As she runs, her wings begin to sprout from her shoulders again, lifting her feet from the floor. This is the moment. He flings his ancient short sword into the air where it severs a steel cable attached to an overhead hoist. On the other end is a crate full of munitions and supplies, being readied to load for the next plane. The tons of equipment crash down on Yukia just as she takes to the air, burying her under the awesome weight and eliminating her as a threat.

"Sorry toots, but I've got a plane to catch." Nick sheathes his sword and quickly retrieves his bag. He isn't sure if anyone heard the crashing noise of the large crate falling on Yukia, but isn't willing to take a chance on someone investigating until he is well on his way to Japan. He checks the mountain of destruction in the middle of the hangar floor, on more time, before locking up and exiting the hangar. He had to check one more time to make sure Yukia was down for the count. On his way out, Nick sees a clip board hanging by the door with a stack of paperwork clipped to it. He grabs the papers and heads out the door as quickly as possible. Once outside, he comes face to face with the copilot of the C-130.

"Ah, very good, I was just coming in to get you. We're on a very tight schedule, so if you'll go ahead and get on board, I'll grab the cargo manifest from inside."

"Nick grabs the copilot by the arm and produces the paperwork in question. "Is this what you're looking for? The guys inside asked me to give it to you. Something about turning around and coming back for it being out of the question?" Nick hands the papers to the copilot and holds his breath as the officer looks through them. Then comes a sigh of relief, when he gives Nick a nod and motions for him to move on out to the plane. A change is taking place deep inside Nicolas Landry. Once, there was a time when the lives of the innocent were not so easily dismissed. Seven servicemen died inside that hangar tonight. At one time, he would have considered them brethren even though he's no longer in the Navy. Now they are merely casualties of war. A war that is brooding far worse and far greater than any the US forces have ever faced. His focus has now been narrowed to JD and the talisman. His life back in Florida, the complications with the Law, even Sonny's demise are nothing more than forgotten memories of a life that no longer exists.

Once aboard the plane, Nick settles into one of the crew seats in the cargo area away from everyone else on board. Within minutes of takeoff, Nick falls fast asleep. His body is exhausted from the toll placed on it by recent events. There is no dream sequence of him being visited by his former Master. The only thing coming to him is the need rest to rejuvenate his body and spirit. The crew of the plane knows nothing about the investigation taking place in the hangar back at the airfield. No one is warned about Nick being on board impersonating a dead Naval Officer. The plan is to apprehend him as soon as the plane lands in Sapporo. There he will answer to Military, and then the Feds, about everything from all of the killings, to the missing Chinese nationals from the airline flight, and the murder of Lt. Commander Mitchell. That is why no one on the plane can know what's going on. The last thing any of the Military Brass wants is to put any more people in danger.

"Excuse me, Lieutenant Steiner, sorry to wake you, but we're going to be landing soon and we need you to strap yourself in." The radio officer suddenly jumps back as Nick leaps up from his seat, caught off guard by the sight of the officer standing over him. His name is Bob Hansen, and ol' Bob has never seen anyone move that fast in all of his life. "Whoa, big guy, I didn't mean to spook you like that." The man steps away from Nick a little, becoming uneasy with Nick's sudden movements and appearance.

Seeing the fear welling up in the man's eyes, Nick backs down and apologizes to him. "Dude, I'm sorry about that. I was in the middle of a bad dream when you woke me, that's all," Nick explains, knowing that his words are all bullshit, but it's the best he could come up with. Sitting back down in his seat seems like the best course of action at the moment. He gives the radio officer a goofy smile as the man returns to his station. Just as Nick is about to buckle his seat belt, something slams into the side of the large aircraft, sending Nick flying from his seat. Bob isn't as lucky as Nick since he was sent into the framework of the C-130. Nick knows that it would take something pretty powerful to cause this bird to roll over like that. Whatever it was, it wasn't military ordinance that hit them. Anything that the military has to hit them with like that would have blown the plane apart. Whatever it is, it strikes again this time from above.

Nick does his best to maintain his balance as he hurries over to help the radio operator as the plane is jarred again. The Navy man has made over a hundred flights in this big bird, and has never experienced anything like this. "What in the hell was that?" Bob asks, taking Nick's hand to pull him self up from the floor of the cargo area.

"I don't know, but you should get on the horn and find out if anyone is out there that could give us a hand," Nick suggests, as he helps Bob stabilize himself, and then motions for him to return to his radio and get busy. For whatever reason, Nick knows that this too is connected to him and the talisman. His proof is delivered by Yukia's fully extended claws rip into the top of the fuselage. The plane has already begun its descent, so the damage that she has produced is not life threatening. These birds can fly with their tail ends hanging open. Still, the entry she has created causes the plane to buck and shudder. It is Yukia's head appearing in the hole that makes Nick wonder whether or not the plane would survive the landing. Bob sees the sight as well from his vantage point, and it disturbs him much more than it does Nick. "Michaels, you're not going to believe this," Hansen screams into the intercom! "We're under attack by some kind of woman who is climbing in through the top of the plane!" His eyes are full of disbelief as Yukia enters and crawls around on the ceiling. This is too much for him to bear. Hansen takes off running towards the front of the plane, fearful of what he has seen. Yukia stops his progress by hitting him in the back with four daggers.

"What did you do that for?" Nick lets his short sword slide from the sleeve of his coat. "If it's me you want, then come on and dance with me!" Nick points his blade at her, and starts for her position as if initiating the challenge.

"That's it, Guardian, you are almost ready. What I think you need is your confidence knocked down a notch or two, and then you will be mine." Yukia leaps through the opening in the fuselage and disappears from sight.

"Come on, Bobby, answer my call!" The pilot is now concerned about his radio man who is communicating with the rest of the crew. Michaels looks over at his copilot who was just staring straight ahead. "What the hell do you think he was talking about, Bernie?"

"M-maybe he was talking her." Bernie responds, pointing at the female warrior who appeared to be sitting on the nose of the plane. She gives the two men an evil grin and then leaps through the windshield, removing the pilot and copilot's heads with the leading edge of her wings. Once through the cockpit, she exits into the main body of the plane expecting Nick to meet her half way. Nick stands there waiting for her to make her next move. Judging by the Japanese coast rushing up to them, he doesn't have a lot of time to wait.

Yukia stares at Nick standing twenty feet away from her, allowing her rage to expand and grow. "You buried me under that wreckage and killed my pet. For that, I will beat you within an inch of death, and happily hand you over to my Master. When he is through with you, I will be given the chance to end your life as I see fit." Yukia produces two short swords of her own, and begins to slice through the wiring and control panels, crippling the plane and its systems, as she makes her way towards Nick. "Where are you hiding the piece? Tell me now, and I will promise you a quick ending to your life when the time comes.

Nick surprises Yukia, by throwing down his sword and just looks at her with complete disgust. "Ya know what? I am so sick and tired of all of this shit!" Nick could see the surf along the coast getting closer and closer. This has to be quick and precise, or he won't survive to protect anyone or anything. "If you want it so bad, it's locked up in that secured cell over there, but you'll need the pilot to open it for you. That safe in there is bomb proof and there isn't anything including you that can get into it," he adds, betting the fate of the world on whether or not Yukia's arrogance and greed can be his ally.

A play like this in Vegas would net him a fortune if it paid off. He's happily surprised when Yukia leaps to the security cage and climbs inside and enters the vault to start ripping open the security boxes with her claws. She's quick to realize that there is nothing in here that is beyond her means. Then she realizes that her arrogance and eagerness to succeed has doomed her. Yukia spins around just in time to see Nick closing the vault door. Her scream of anger is sealed quiet inside the steel tomb, as Nick locks it shut. Then, just to be on the safe side, he locks the cage as well.

Timing is everything and Nick has to be on his mark. The plane is less than ten thousand feet above the surf and dropping fast. He takes off to the rear of the plane and finds his bag before he activates the tail ramp controls. The rear of the plane starts to slowly open up like the mouth of a giant whale, as Nick hurries over to a locker and grabs an emergency parachute. By the time the plane is opened up, Nick has the harness strapped on and his bag tethered to it, running towards his last chance of survival. One great leap and he is in the grasp of the night air. As a SEAL, he made plenty of jumps out of the back of a C-130, but never this close to the ground before, or to watch it plummet from the sky. He pulls the rip cord on the chute and is snatched up into the air.

From his perch floating on the air currents, Nick watches the plane heading for disaster. His focus is the plane, but he watches for Yukia to see if she gets free before it impacts with the Hokkaido surf. His concern is the fact that he is hanging in the air like a piñata to swat at if she does get free. Anticipation builds more and more until the plane makes contact with the surf. The C-130 is obliterated as it tries to bury itself in the beach. He never saw her clear the plane, so Nick has to assume that she is somewhere under the wreckage and flames. One thing is for certain; this plane didn't go down without someone else knowing about it. Nick knows that ATC was alerted about five minutes ago when the plane first veered from its flight path. That means a spotter plane should be flying over the area any minute. He has to get out of sight, but must also verify that Yukia is down for the count.

Nick guides the chute in over the crash site and scans the wreckage for her body, before drifting in over the jungle tree line. It appears that Yukia is no longer a threat to him. The question now is; how many more Yukias are there waiting for him? He knows that there are overwhelming odds for him to face by meeting his opponents on their home turf. If he had any other choice he would have taken it for sure. He knows that this event is the final straw that seals the fate of his life. There will be no explanation that will clear him of what has happened. His life has forever been changed, or destroyed depending on your point of view. Before he hits the ground, Nick comes to the decision that he no longer matters in this outcome. If this is how it is to end, then so be it. He has lost everything else because of this destiny of his. If he is going down because of it, then he's going to take as many of them with him as he can.

Once on the ground, he quickly packs his chute and gets his bearings. According to his portable GPS, Asahigawa is about a hundred and fifty miles away. By vehicle, he could be at his destination in a couple of hours. By foot, it could take him a couple of days. Nick is sure to opt for the first choice, the first chance he gets. Off in the distance, he could hear the whine of an F-4 fighter heading towards the coast. He looks one more time to the wreckage on the beach before entering the cover of the jungle. He's happy to see that there is still no sign of the Masamoto daughter. Still, something feels different to him, ever since he laid foot on the island soil. The talisman feels warm lying against his chest, and his heart seems to beat a little stronger as he enters the unknown territory. Shadows seem to begin to move around, making him wonder if his head was starting to play tricks on him. Then out of the corner of his eye, Nick sees a dark spirit moving through the trees. He stops and watches as the dark spirit stops as well, and looks at Nick with glowing red eyes. Why is he able to see this demon without using the power of the talisman? At the last second, Nick drops to the ground as another dark presence swoops in from overhead. Without any other altercation, the two demons fly off through the trees, leaving Nick feeling very alone.

# Chapter XVI

"**S**onofabitch, somebody really did hit me with some kind of tranquilizer dart!" JD states in his mind, as the effects of the narcotic finally wear off. The question on JD's mind now is where has he been taken? He opens one eye, but doesn't move another muscle. First analysis of the situation; he's sitting in a chair, with four post legs, flat back, square wood seat, resembling something standard in an old school class room. He can feel the ropes that bind him to the chair, rough, maybe weathered. There are sounds of someone moving around on the other side of the room, but whoever they are; they're out of his line of sight. He can smell the wood burning, and hear the pops and crackling of the logs in the fireplace. It, the fireplace, is behind him considering the cooler temperatures on his face. The rest of the décor tells him that the room is old, really old, but yet in pristine condition. Nick taught him this. "Awareness is your greatest ally. Be aware of your surroundings at all times, and the people that occupy those surroundings." Nick taught him well.

Seko Masamoto portrays the feeble old man as he hobbles into view. "So, my young warrior of light, you have returned to the living. Would you like to know the progress of your Guardian?"

When JD sees the two dark spirits encircling the old man, he can't help but move, startled by the ghostly presence. When he does jerk back in his chair, it causes something beside him to let out a low rumbling growl of disapproval. JD slowly turns his head to see an oversized Rottweiller staring back at him. Its glowing eyes and three inch teeth are more than enough to make JD reel away in the opposite direction. "Tell ya what, why don't you just keep it to yourself, and we'll make this book a mystery!" He's scared to death, but is hell bent on not letting it show. "Now, do us both a favor and call off your poodle here, before its breath kills me."

Seko Masamoto laughs at JD's statement, and then waves his arm in the air, causing the demon dog to vanish from sight. "Well, well, haven't you grown the long spine in such a short time?" Seko Masamoto walks over to JD and stares into the young man's eyes. "Your Guardian is here on this island. Unfortunately for you, that means that your role in this tragic epic is soon coming to an end." Masamoto slowly walks over to the desk behind JD and presses the intercom button. "Yukio, get in here, at once." The ancient looking man then turns and walks towards the door. "Farewell warrior of light," Masamoto says, as he turns to look back at JD. "You possibly could have been a worthy opponent, if the circumstances were different." He meets Yukio at the door and instructs him to dispose of JD. It's easy to understand why JD becomes a little unnerved by Seko's command. This however is what makes Yukio perfect for the role as Seko's lackey. He is a killing machine with no remorse, who's only purpose is to inflict pain by serving his Master.

Yukio bows to the man possessed by Doomsayer's spirit, happy to carry out his orders. JD knows that he has to think fast. What would Nick do? He knows what Nick would do. Nick would get free and kick the shit outta these guys. Unfortunately, JD doesn't have a knife, or anything else sharp hidden in his underwear to accomplish that feat. This means that he will have to improvise. Yukio is coming. JD has to get free if he is going to make a stand. His only option; talk his way out. "Good dog, hey old man, how much did it cost for obedience training? Can you make him roll over and fetch a ball too?" JD stares at Yukio defiantly as the Japanese killer casually walks across the room. "Yeah, come on ya crazy sonofabitch! You'd better take your best shot while I'm tied up. It seems like it's the only way you can win a fight. An infuriated Yukio speeds across the room and leans over to stare into JD's eyes. He smiles at the young man, and then back hands JD, driving him and the chair to the floor. This results in a violent collision between JD's head and the hardwood surface. The side of JD's face throbs with pain as he sprawls around on the floor with his legs tangled up in the toppled chair. "Block out the pain and maintain your focus," he thinks. JD knows that he has touched a nerve. Now the question is; will Yukio let his ego control his actions, or will his rage just finish JD off? He decides to put his money on the first option. "Sonofabitch, you're pretty quick! I wonder how well you'd fare against me if I was untied."

"Isn't it I who should be asking you that question?" To explain himself, Yukio produces razor sharp claws at the ends of his fingertips and slices the ropes free from JD's arms and legs. "Now then Gaijin; come show me what you've got." Yukio lunges at JD testing the young man's stand. JD doesn't disappoint, leaping clear of the attack and lands next to a display of Samurai swords to take a defensive stance. He looks at the swords and figures that it is now or never. He grabs two from the rack and slings their sayas, or scabbards, away and flips the swords around so that their blades are pointing behind him. Yukio chuckles at the action. "Oh my, now you've got me scared." The killer draws his own swords from his hip and points the tip of the blade at JD. Do you know the traditions of the swords? One is that once you've pulled the sword free the saya, it cannot be returned for safe keeping without drawing blood. Do you think you can do that, Gaijin?"

"I don't know. What'cha say we find out together." JD changes his stance, encouraging Yukio to attack. The young man's display of arrogance only enrages his opponent to the boiling point. JD has mastered Nick's teachings. Now he is about to find out how well that will help him against someone who has trained with a sword all of his life. Yukio strikes fast using his experience with the blade to shatter JD's weapons just above the hilt. JD just steps back against the wall, dropping the broken swords and raising his fists.

Yukio stares at JD and then tosses his sword aside. "Now do you wish to pray to your god, and ask him to receive you when I send you to meet him?" Yukio extends his claws to full length and clicks the razor sharp tips against each other.

Seko Masamoto steps into the room, drawn back in by the conflict between Yukio and JD. "Yukio end this now!" The Dark Master demands, as he starts to walk back across the room.

"Don't worry about my God, freak! Worry about your own self. It's obvious that you can talk the talk, but can you walk the walk?" At the moment, JD is wondering if he can answer his own question. He has his ace in the hole, but knows that it is a one time deal if he is able to use it again. He's about to find out, as his boastful question sends Yukio into a blind rage running straight at JD. This is what JD was waiting for. Nick had told him once that if a man's emotions could be provoked, it would give his opponent the upper edge. As Yukio lunges at JD, he finds his young adversary is much quicker than Yukio anticipated. After leaping into the air, JD kicks Yukio in the back, sending him slamming into the nearby desk. Against his father's beliefs, JD takes the offensive for the first time in an actual conflict. He can't explain why, his body just acts. JD lands on top of Yukio, driving the dark warrior to the floor, where JD delivers an onslaught of punches to Yukio's back, head, and ribs. He holds no dark desire in his heart for what he's doing. There is no rational how or why, but something has taken control of Jefferson David Johnston. It is that little voice in the back of a person's mind that speaks up saying, "no, you're not going to do that to me any more." This moment has been denied from him all of his life, trying to live by his father's wishes. Yukio Masamoto just happens to be the unlucky recipient of the pent up frustration and anger of it all.

Unable to take it any more in his present form, Yukio surprises JD by sprouting a pair of reptilian wings from his shoulders as his body takes on a scaly appearance. The force of the wings shooting out of his back sends JD soaring into the air before coming down on top of the desk nearby. His pummeling of Yukio only lasted five or six seconds before JD could be fended off, but it was long enough for JD to inflict enough damage. He rolls off the desk and lands on his feet in a squatted position but quickly stands again to face his opponent. Now his adrenaline level is peaked and confidence is fueling him on. "Who, or what, are you supposed to be? I have to warn ya that there is a guy in Gotham City who already holds the franchise on bats." On the desk is a small one foot baton that JD quickly picks up to use as a weapon. Yukio will have to get in close for JD to use it, but at least it's something. To his surprise, a trigger is activated when he wraps his hand around the short shaft, causing it to extend out in both directions until it is a full five foot length Bo staff. "Yeah, this is more like it," He says as he twirls the staff around like an oversized cheerleader's baton. He brings it around his head and stops the motion pointing the end of the staff at Yukio. "Come on, hot shot, you made it sound like I don't stand a chance." For the first time in his life, JD faces the choice of dying as a warrior, or lying down as a coward. He has had his fill of the second.

Yukio has had enough of this upstart's boisterous attitude. He reaches over to the desk and presses a button on the intercom system. The buzz produced summons eight ninja garbed men rushing into the room, lead by their leader Shade. JD quickly uses the staff to pole vault himself over Yukio's head to avoid being caught between the proverbial rock and a hard place. "Boast now, Gaijin. As you can see, you are outnumbered and outclassed." Yukio motions for Shade and his men to move in on JD and take care of the dark warrior's dirty work.

The ninjas rush JD's position, shrinking his bravado, but he still has his ace. Yukio may not be considering JD's force field, but it's always on JD's mind. He leaps into the air and with but a thought produces his defense mechanism and extends it outward with such velocity that the impact drives Yukio and his henchmen through the exterior wall of the office. Of course the pain inflicted resembling a mental spike being driven through his brain, causes JD to stagger a bit as he tries to focus his vision. Everything around him was disturbed from its position, including Seko Masamoto. Right now, all JD is concerned about is escaping. He has no idea where to go or which direction to take, but he knows that he needs to satisfy this incredible urge to run, as fast as he possibly can. He hurries over to the opening in the wall and looks down at the ground below. The sight of Yukio's clawed hand thrusting upward out from under the pile of bodies on top of him is the sign for JD to make his next move. Without any consideration for the height of his jump, JD leaps from the second floor office and lands on the mound of bodies, driving Yukio back to the bottom of the pile.

In a split second, JD has the full layout of the courtyard. Over to his left is what looks like a temple, and the only observers are dressed in Kendo uniforms, conducting their sparring sessions on the temple's front patio. That is, until JD blew a hole in the wall behind him. Now, several of the kendo warriors are moving over to investigate the disturbance. "Well, at least I know what that clack, clack, clack, sound was that I heard earlier. The little voice in the back of his head tells him to run, run as fast as you can. "That actually worked out better than I planned," he thinks as he breaks out into a full sprint. His path takes him straight between two buildings and past the farm shed, heading right out into open ground. The only thing between him and the nearby tree line is about ten acres of crop fields.

Yukio explodes from under the unconscious bodies as a dozen more men rush to the scene. "There goes the prisoner! Find him and kill him, once and for all!" He reaches back down and snatches Shade up from the ground. "Fail me again, and I will devour your soul." Yukio throws Shade away and turns to face his dark master, who was joining his minions outside the building. Yukio bows before the old man, showing respect, or begging for mercy, depending on your point of view. "Master, my men will catch and kill Landry's student. They will not fail me."

Seko Masamoto draws on all of his strength to slap Yukio across his face. "Fool, serve me best by seeing to the task yourself!" Seko stares into Yukio's eyes, as the defiant attitude of the warrior shows itself on the younger man's face. "Landry is near. I can feel the pull between the two halves needing to be rejoined. Destroy the student of the Guardian and display his body on the perimeter wall for Landry to see!"

"Yes, my Master, as you command." Yukio spreads his wings and takes to the air, being made well aware of the damage to his ribs by JD's assault. Covering more ground by air, he quickly catches up with his men moving through the fields, and heading across the soy fields.

The wind blowing in off the mountain cuts at JD's bare skin like knives flying through the air. He tries to block out the pain of the elements by ignoring the numbing effects, but he hasn't conditioned his mind to that level just yet. This takes a lot of focus and concentration, which are both broken when he trips and falls face first in the flooded crop field. "Geez," he screams out, as he stands up shivering from the sudden drop in body temperature. He turns and sees Yukio joining his men some two hundred yards away and closing fast. His pursuers move at a speed not normally achieved by an ordinary man. This eliminates JD's advantage of being a runner. Even if he could maintain this pace indefinitely, Yukio's men still have the upper hand of greater speed. Eventually, they will simply run him down. The stakes in this game have definitely been raised, and JD is now beginning to wonder if he can keep up.

Yukio points to JD, "There he is! Spread out and sweep the trees all the way to the gorge. I want his body at my feet within the hour!" He snatches a bow from one of his men, and demands an arrow from the man's quiver. Smartly, Yukio is given three. He then turns, nocks all three arrows and lets them fly. "There, that should make your job easier."

JD claws his way up the muddy slope at the foot of the tree line. Before he is able to find his next foothold, he hears a faint whistling sound that warns him to get down. Following his instincts, JD drops to the ground making him self as small a target as possible, when two arrows bury themselves into the soft muddy soil beside him. The third finds its mark grazing his shoulder, before entering the surface of the mud under him. The razor tip arrowhead only slices a quarter of an inch deep, but the wound is two inches long, allowing a curtain of blood to cover his arm. He knows that time is slipping away from him, and Yukio would be on him soon to deliver the death blow. Something has to be done, but his thoughts are clouded by the pain of his wound and the anxiety of the situation. "Damn, after watching Rambo a thousand times, I shouldn't have a problem remembering what to do in this situation." A reminder of his plight hits the tree beside him in the form of another arrow, urging him onward.

Into the trees he moves, finding a more firm ground to traverse. At the top of the tree line he stops to look back to see Yukio and his men entering the trees. Beside him, tangled in the overgrowth of limbs is a cloth banner weathered by time and the elements. JD rips off a piece of the cloth and ties it around his shoulder and takes off down through the trees. The landscape quickly forms a gulley running down the side of the hill towards the nearby cliffs of the river gorge. He looks to the left and sees a large rock outcropping on the ridge of the hill that had been exposed by centuries of erosion. This could serve as suitable coverage but he knows that he needs a diversion, something to make his pursuers think that he is still moving downhill, instead of back up. He scrambles as fast as he can towards the natural hole under the outcropping, but stops half way to pick up a basketball sized rock, and gives it a toss down the hill through the trees. The large rock tumbles down the gulley, knocking down small trees and stirring up enough dirt and underbrush that it appeared to be someone moving down the hill. Yukio's men pick up on this and take chase. It's the first break JD gets since this whole mess first started. He climbs in between the rocks and huddles up in the fetal position trying to stay as warm as possible. All he needs now is for Nick to come along and save the day, before JD freezes to death.

An hour earlier...

Morning has come with the sun on the rise. Nick has made his way to the upper Ishikara River Valley with no hurdles to overcome. He had caught a ride on a farmer's truck that was taking his wares to the river for transport, to market down stream. That in itself was an event. Nick scared the old man half to death, when Nick broke through the tree line to come face to face with the hood and grill of the truck. Needless to say, it was hard to tell who was more shocked by the meeting. Nick, who was in full dress complete with swords, looks like someone who had stepped out of ancient legend. At first the old man is hesitant about getting out of his truck to confront Nick. Then, as if he understood Nick's position and purpose, the old man drops down and bows in front of him paying homage to the Guardian.

After a long Deliberation in badly broken Japanese dialect, Nick is able to convince the farmer that all he needs is a ride. It's something that Nick almost regrets, having to ride in the back of the truck with the baskets of vegetables and pigs that are heading to slaughter. The cab of the truck was out of the question as far as passenger transportation. Riding in the cab of the truck was out of the question. The old relic of a vehicle no longer has a seat, with the farmer using an old five gallon bucket to sit on, with the passenger side of the cab converted into a chicken coop. The only problem Nick has left is determining if the smell in the back of the truck was better or worse than the one coming from the cab through the broken window. That is, until he is given the deciding factor, when the truck hits a rut in the dirt road that causes one of the pigs to relieve itself. Now, Nick is willing to climb into the chicken coop just for fresher air.

The old truck rattles along the rural countryside until it reaches a side road that makes its way down to the river. Before long, Nick can see the outlying buildings and sheds of a small river village that appears to be the farmer's destination. As the rust bucket rattles to a stop, Nick leaps from the truck bed, startling more people with his presence. The farmer quickly takes Nick by the hand and leads him over to the village elders. In seconds, the old man had explained Nick's position as the Guardian, and sought the elders' approval for assistance.

"Welcome, Nickolas-san, we have awaited your arrival for some time now." The ancient man looks like he has lived in the backwoods of Japan all of his life and it hasn't been an easy one at that. Judging by his attire, this old man is probably the village shaman or religious leader. Whoever he is, there is something about him that Nick trusts. "Come, walk with me, Guardian. There is much to be done and little time to do so."

"Excuse me, sir, but I'm not here for a tour of the lands. I thank you all, but I have to…" Nick pauses for a second and thinks about the situation, and then uses his thumb to lift his sword from its scabbard, an inch or so. This is a sign of preparation for battle, instigated by Nick's sudden apprehension. "You speak pretty good English, old man," Nick points out, slightly confused by the way the old man's lips and words seemed to be out of sync.

The village elder bows to Nick as if apologizing for offending Nick. "Master Guardian, we are but humble servants to your cause. You hear the English language being spoke, because it is what you understand." The old man turns away from Nick and starts to slowly walk towards the river. "You were once told that you will encounter agents on both sides of this war. This village serves as an alliance for your benefit. Walk with me now, Guardian."

Curious, Nick quickly takes chase, wanting to learn exactly what it is that the old man knows. He doesn't sense any danger from the people of the village. Everyone around him bows out of respect for his position as they move about with their daily duties. How do they know who Nick is? Masamoto never said anything about this village or Nick being connected to it. "Excuse me," Nick says, trying to get the old man's attention. "How do you know all of this? How do you know who I am? You speak to me as if you knew I was coming, which bothers me to no end in so many ways." Tired of walking, Nick steps in front of his so-called ally and forces a confrontation. "Yes, what you said is true, but then you should know that I was also told never come to Japan, so why would I need any alliance here?"

"You were told to never come here, and yet here you are." The old man's reply is obvious, but somehow seems philosophical at the same time. Why are you here, Nickolas?" The old man just stares out across the river as if his question had no value.

Nick doesn't have time for this. JD is waiting for him to come save the day. The last thing Nick needs right now is a history lesson on his past. "Look, I'm sorry if I came across as a little skeptical, but I've been through a lot lately. Master Masamoto never said anything to me about you, this village, or anything else about this place. To be honest, I'm winging this on my own, and really need to be moving on."

"Hiro Masamoto could not tell you about our meeting, or my existence for that matter, because he is forbidden to influence your actions." The elder turns around and reaches out to touch Nick on his shoulder. "Nickolas-san, only you can discover your destiny. What you were taught, what you were told, was for the benefit of you finding your own path to enlightenment. Now, before you go any farther, it is I who must give you a warning." The village elder motions for Nick to take a seat on a rock beside the river. He then takes his own place on a rock beside Nick at the edge of the water. "You cannot succeed in your quest as you are right now. For you to move on, you must first give to me the pain that you suffer."

Nick stares at the old man for a second and then chuckles, "oh, is that all? For a second there, I was worried that you wanted me to give you the talisman, or my soul, or something else that you'll never get." Nick looks around at the nearby villagers, seeing that none of them were paying any attention to what Nick and the old man was doing. "Sure, Sport, if you think it would make things better, then have at it. You can have all the pain and suffering there is. God knows that I've got enough to go around for everyone."

"I know," the old man replies, as he reaches out and touches Nick's chest. "Now give to me what I seek from your heart and soul." The old man suddenly becomes stiff and rigid on his perch as his eyes roll back in his head. His lips move as if he is silently chanting some kind of ancient incantation to perform the rights. Nick finds his eyes suddenly close as if he is being forced to look inward at what is taking place. It's like watching every painful memory being closed and removed from his mind. Everything, from the deaths of his parents, to Megan and the others, all is taken from him and replaced with a thought of serenity. The agony of being shot is gone forever. The anxiety and guilt of Sonny's imprisonment is ancient history. The anger of JD's abduction, and the sorrow of Sonny being shot, is nothing but faded images gone from his mind.

Nick opens his eyes feeling cleansed, as if he hadn't a care in the world. Years ago, the sight of the old man's eyes glowing while he sits on the rock trembling, might have disturbed Nick. But now, it's almost as if he sees this as the natural order of things to come. "Who are you?"

The old man closes his eyes and then reopens them to

focus on Nick. "Seventy two years ago, I was the best friend of Hiro Masamoto." The old man strains to remove himself from the rock and motions for help from the villagers who had moved over to the old man's location. Overburdened by all of Nick's pain and sorrow, the former friend of Masamoto stumbles and then collapses to the ground as Nick is lead away by several other men.

Minutes later, Nick is escorted to a boat and given directions to his destination. The well wishers see him off and return to their lives as he begins his journey upriver. For the first time in his life, Nick has total clarity for life, destiny, and what he must do. There is no doubt in his mind. There is no doubt in his heart. He sees his purpose and recognizes his goal knowing what he must do to succeed, without any hesitation or apprehension. He accepts the fact that this is no longer about JD's safety, and that it's about his destiny being fulfilled, and upholding the safety of the world as the Guardian.

A mile or two upriver is where his journey gets rough. The natural order of the water flow has carved a canyon with steep cliff walls over the centuries that made any assault from the river on the Masamoto stronghold difficult at best. This is the path of Nick's choice. With his weapons secured, he ties off the boat to a tree at the water's edge and crosses the narrow shoreline at the foot of the canyon wall. The climb is difficult for him, but not impossible, due to Nick's training and experience. After everything that has happened on this little journey Nick almost expects his enemy to look over the edge at him, as he reaches up for the top of the cliff. Needless to say, he is relieved when he pulls himself up over the edge and scans his surroundings to find himself alone. There is something though, nearby, that is giving him an uneasy feeling. He stays low, slithering through the tall grasses between the cliff and the tree line. Once at the trees, he stands up using their height and girth to conceal his own.

Nickolas Landry of Miami Florida no longer exists. He is no longer the Martial Arts instructor, or friend of everyone. He is now the Guardian, facing his destiny and upholding his duty. This is the end of his charge that threatens his life. Nothing else matters, nothing else exists. Those who stand with him will be spared. Those who stand against him will fall by his sword. Without regret, Nick heads into the trees towards his destination.

A snapping of a twig behind him causes Nick to freeze. It is a sentry making his rounds on guard patrol. This is easy for Nick to see, due to the automatic rifle the man is carrying. It's just not a typical farming utensil, for any region. Nick sidesteps up to a tree and waits as the sentry moves on. The problem is that he notices how the grasses were disturbed along the cliff's edge. He starts to walk towards the cliff, and then suddenly stops and gasps. Looking down the gunman sees the tip of Nick's sword protruding from his chest. A second later, the man vanishes from sight without a sound.

Nick takes to the trees, moving like a phantom spirit that appeared to be floating just off the ground. His arms sweep back away from his body, with a sword in each hand, slicing through the chilled morning air like wings of death. The fog of a hot breath being exhaled appears from the trees ahead of him. He has already spotted the man's weapon hanging at his side, as Nick runs silently passed the tree. The gunman is unaware of Nick's presence, as the Guardian moves like silent death. Nick's progress is not halted, a detour is not made. His right arm comes forward, and then back again slicing through the man's neck, removing his head without a sound. Nick stops, none the less. It is a rumbling sound that has caught his attention, with the sight of a small boulder rolling down a shallow gulley a few feet away. It's an odd spectacle, but it warns Nick of Yukio's men moving through the trees, down the hill towards him. To make a stand against this many opponents amongst the trees would be suicidal. He has to seek open ground which means backtracking to the cliff once more. It's a move in the wrong direction but the right one for Nick to make. Back through the trees he runs, moving like the wind retracing his path. Several more sentries are encountered, following his path up the hillside. They fall by his swords before they even realize his presence among them.

Once clear of the last tree, Nick turns to face the opposition. Ready, he sees fifteen or more men charging his position. By the time the first three exit the tree line, Nick has already dispatched the demonic presence that possesses the dead men's bodies. Before he can take another life, Nick is surrounded by the minions of Yukio, whose numbers seem overwhelming. Nick steps back and accepts each attack as the men begin to simultaneously lay down their assault against the Guardian. Their motions send them crossing the circle from one side to the other, striking at Nick as they passed. Most, not all, but most suffered wounds from Nick's retaliation, but none land a strike against him.

JD sits in the outcropping of rock watching the battle of swords through the trees. He can see that Nick is outnumbered, and he knows that if that invisible sonofabitch is around, he can tip the scales against his friend. JD has to be the ballast of the equation. The question now is, how does JD deal with the supernatural aspects of the conflict? This is the one thing Nick never mentioned. So far, Nick has managed quite well against the dark warriors, but JD knows that this is nothing but a stall tactic to keep Nick occupied until the head honcho shows up. Down in the conflict, Nick turns to face two opponents moving in, and sees JD rushing down the hill wearing his underwear, and nothing else. It's a peculiar sight to say the least, but not enough to distract Nick from his challenge. With his opponents distracted by JD's arrival, Nick steps forward eliminating the two men permanently from the equation. As the next selection of combatants move up to face him, Nick surprises them by diving to the side. Before the three men could get a fix on Nick's new position, JD launches himself through the air with a body block that sends six of Nick's opponents over the edge of the cliff. "Man, am I glad to see you!"

Before Nick can respond, JD is snatched from his stance and lifted high into the air. Nick looks up to see Yukio hovering overhead with JD in his clawed clutches. "Put him down!" Nick commands, sighting in on Yukio and JD, down the blade of his sword.

To prove JD's worth, Yukio simply flings him up into the air higher, sending the young adversary out over the river below. Instead of watching JD disappear over the cliff, Yukio should have kept his eyes on the Guardian. With a flip of his wrist, Nick sends four daggers hurling towards the demonic Masamoto. Each finds its target somewhere in Yukio's body, with one ripping through the skin-like membrane of his wing. The dark warrior howls out in pain and rips one of the daggers from his chest. "Finish Landry and bring him before me. Find the body of his student and bring it as well. Landry will watch as his charge is painfully converted to serve our needs."

This time it is Nick who is distracted, if only for a split second, but it's long enough for him to notice that one of his adversaries was no longer in his midst. Using the power entrusted to him by his dark master, Shade lives up to his name, rendering himself invisible to make his attack. With speed and reflexes rivaling Nick's, Shade moves in and delivers several well placed punches and a spinning wheel kick that sends Nick flying. To make it worse, the men in the direction that Nick is traveling decide to take advantage of the situation and attack him with their swords as well. To avoid personal injury, the other opponents step away from Nick as he hits the ground hard, with his swords flailing about in defense. Before he can pick himself up and wipe the mud from his eyes, Shade moves in and delivers a crushing stomp to Nick's ribs. To the assassin's surprise, his attack falls on nothing but cold ground, as Nick has already cleared away from the attack. He trained for this scenario long ago. Nick didn't understand its significance at the time, but now it does make him wonder if Masamoto really did know that Nick was coming to Japan. He listens as Shade moves around behind Nick. Isolating out the back ground noise, he can hear the subtle grinding of Shade's sword sliding out of its scabbard. Closing his eyes, Nick can feel the moving air as the invisible warrior makes his move to strike. At the last second, Nick spins around and slashes above the open ground beside him with the blade of his sword. First, a spray of blood is produced out of thin air, before Shade is rendered visible again by the pain of the wound breaking his concentration. Nick stares up at Yukio, and then as if giving a warning, he spins around and lops off the head of Yukio's lieutenant.

By the time Nick spins back around, Yukio is gone along with the rest of his men, hiding somewhere in the trees. The dark warrior has suffered lethal wounds from Nick's daggers. He must return to his uncle and beg for salvation, all the while not wanting to give up the severity of his wounds. "Save the world Guardian, but to do that you must come to face my Master and defeat him." With that, Yukio takes to the sky, erupting through the tops of the trees heading home.

# Chapter XVII

JD's adrenaline rush from earlier has now been replaced with a severe fear of falling. He knows for sure that this is not what Nick meant when he said, "put him down!" JD can't deny that this whole scenarios sucks. As he descends towards the tops of several large trees growing along the river, JD can see Nick's boat and several people moving around in the water beside it. He deploys his force field and concentrates as hard as he can, as his energy field makes contact with the tops of the trees. Limbs snap, and leaves are sent flying, as he descends through the canopy. Finally, he is able to slow himself enough that he reaches out and grabs one of the larger branches to stop his fall. "See Nick, I was paying attention," he says, as he pulls himself up onto the branch. To his surprise, a ninja garbed man; one of Yukio's dark warriors is also occupying the same branch, hugging the tree trunk to avoid JD's descent. Before the man could react to JD's presence, this recently proclaimed warrior of light gives the man a swift kick, pinning his head between the tree and JD's foot. While holding the man in place, JD looks up to the sky and says a silent thank you prayer, for his force field, and for Nick. If it wasn't for Nick's training, JD might not survive this experience. Of course, if it wasn't for Nick intervening that fateful day, when he and JD first met, JD wouldn't be in Japan in the first place. JD grabs the ninja who was about to fall out of the tree and quickly begins to undress the man, doing all of this while trying to maintain his balance on the tree limb. He isn't sure if the guy is out cold, or out permanently. Either way, JD has already decided that he needs the man's clothes more, no matter what the fallen man's status is.

There are more of Yukio's men climbing and falling down the cliff. The ones that are bouncing off the rocky terrain are not to be worried about. Obviously, they were sent over the edge by Nick's help, based on their uncontrolled descents. The ones who are moving about on the ground have to be JD's main concern. For whatever reason, the hired killers don't seem to be concerned with his entry into the treetops. Then, he sees another one of Yukio's soldiers falling to the bottom of the cliff, and realizes that Nick is handling his situation well. These guys probably think that JD's plummet from above was just another one of their comrades meeting an untimely demise. Of course, there is the water fall, and the rushing river, that is creating a lot of noise that could have drowned out his entry into the tree tops. He has a plan, not a very good one, but he has a plan. Wearing the clothes he took from the man in the tree, JD plans to exit the tree and make his way back up to the Masamoto complex. It works in the movies, right? In JD's defense, this is his first goat rope.

After a deep cleansing breath, JD climbs out of the tree and drops to the ground at the water's edge. He's spotted right away and waved over to Nick's boat by one of these ninja warriors, which isn't all that much of a surprise to him. The whole reason he put on this Halloween costume was to blend in. It's obvious that he's accomplished that, by the fact that the other men were waving him over, instead of charging his position with swords held high. A question comes to mind as JD starts to walk over. What is with all of these traditional warrior ways? JD's seen movies about modern day Japanese mafia people using traditions from long ago, but this place is like stepping back in time. As he makes his way over to the boat, he has to believe that everything is going to plan, so far. What he doesn't count on, is his victim in the tree regaining consciousness. When the warrior starts to come around, he shifts his weight on the tree branch causing him to fall to his death on the rocky shoreline below the branches. The demonic spirit inhabiting the body pulls itself from the broken host and hisses at JD, as he turns around to see the result. Finding it hard to believe what he witnessed was real; JD quickly turns back around to face the dark warriors standing right in front of him. Like the spirit that had just left the dead body, these warriors' eyes are glowing deep red, with a slight jitter to their appearance. Needless to say, it is a very unholy sight to JD.

The men who were at the boat were already a little skeptical about JD's appearance, noticing how the uniform he is wearing was made for a man about six inches shorter. When the body of their dead comrade floats down to join them beside the boat, several of these dark warriors go to investigate JD's presence. This results with his smooth sneak attack plan blowing up in his face. JD smiles behind the hood, and then delivers two forward thrusts to the warriors' throats, incapacitating the human hosts for a moment. The other four men around the boat leap to the rocky shoreline of the river, drawing their swords. He knows that his cover is blown, so JD slowly starts to back away, still wondering if he could outrun them. Still with some distance between them, JD turns to make his getaway. It is then that he sees the rest of Yukio's men, who were coming down the cliff of their own free will, to search for JD's body. Unfortunately, he isn't making it hard for them to find. The numbers against him have grown to ten, all brandishing their swords. The time has come for JD to even up the odds. He waits until the last possible moment before he deploys his force field, and then does so with such force that the imitation ninjas are sent slamming into the cliff face, or flying out into the river, to be found later on, downstream. He is disturbed to say the least, when the demonic spirits that possessed the warriors' bodies exit their dead hosts, and make for the top of the cliff. For the first time, since all of this madness started, JD is not in any apparent danger. Still, he staggers over to the boat where he collapses from the mental strain applied by his force field. With the pain too great, he passes out in the boat, on top of his own uniform that Nick had brought with him.

Nick breaks the tree line just in time to see Yukio flying over the massive complex that represents the Masamoto Empire. Between Nick and his goal, is ten acres of soy fields. The same ones JD had traversed earlier. Since JD's peril is no longer a condition, Nick opts to take the more concealed, less traveled route, to reach the perimeter wall of the complex. If he's going through with this, Nick isn't going to make it easy for the opposition. A part of him is crying out for Nick to rush back to the cliff, hoping to find JD safe from harm. This desire is denied by Nick's newfound state of mind, allowing him to remain diligent in what he must do. It is all perfectly clear to him now. Every moment for the past seven years has lead to this point in time, sculpting and molding him for this task, this destiny. He can see that everything that has happened until now has done so to guide Nick here to this place, for this reason. Accepting this is what's changed his outlook on why he's in Japan. No matter what Nick believed, it was never about Jefferson at all. He hopes that JD somehow survives all of this, and follows his own destiny, but this is where their paths together separate. The only thing that sticks with Nick now is a warning Masamoto gave to Nick, when the old man was dying. He said, "The world will die if you fail with your attempt." According to Masamoto, if Nick was not properly prepared, there was no way he could succeed. Nick shakes off the effects of the flashback, as the image fades from his mind.

Along the south side of the soy fields is a thick row of evergreens that separate the crop fields from the tiered rice patties on the hillside. This is Nick's choice of approach to the distillery complex. He finds it kind of funny that if things go wrong here today, the world's supply of Chinese takeout restaurants will have to find a new soy sauce supplier. Suddenly, Nick stops as a field hand staggers out of the evergreens in front of him. Judging by the odor of the smoke being exhaled by the man, he has just finished off a session of some high grade opium and is lost in a narcotic haze. When the man turns to face Nick, he reveals that his attire is simply for show. The short sword on the man's hip isn't so out of place, but Nick doesn't know of anyone who uses an automatic rifle for farming, like the one hanging on the man's shoulder. It's obvious that the man is one of Doomsayer's warriors, but Nick doesn't sense an overwhelming feeling of danger. The worker shows no sign of sensing the presence of the talisman. This could only mean that there is no dark possession residing in this man, which could explain the man's drug use. Still, this doesn't make him any less dangerous at the moment.

By the time he realizes Nick is standing in front of him, there is no time for the man to react. Nick is already on him, using the man's inability to distinguish reality to take the offensive, twist the man's head around, and then lays him down quietly with silent fluidity. There is no second thought, or time for remorse. Nick has been in this situation many times before while serving with the SEAL teams. Just about every mission had something to do with him and his team infiltrating some compound or outpost, to retrieve some information or free some captive. When you get right down to the nuts and bolts of the scenarios, it's all the same, except this time, Nick is alone. He's not ashamed to admit that he would welcome a little help from Charlie, or Sonny, with this one. Sometimes, there are some things that have to be done on your own.

Yukio staggers into the main building of the complex, moving upstream against the exiting dark warriors, departing to carry out their Master's command. Nick was right in assuming the wounds from his daggers landed more lethal wounds than first expected. One of the daggers' tips severed the dark possession that inhabits Yukio's heart. He is actually dying, and fearfully knows this. That is why he has returned to his uncle's side to beg for a second chance. "Uncle Seko, Landry has landed a lethal wound and I fear that I will not survive without your help. I beg of you, please see fit to give me one more chance to bring Landry to you."

Seko Masamoto moves across the room with his feet just inches above the floor. The frail looking old man reaches out and slaps Yukio down with the ferocity of a giant. "I ask you, servant of mine, at this final hour, do you finally see that your role in this has come to an end?" Seko gestures with his hand and lifts Yukio up into the air and throws him across the room, without ever touching the Masamoto heir. Yukio's path takes him through a timber support column, breaking it in two, and Yukio as well. "Your job was to bring the Guardian, to me. You have done that, so your task is now complete. The only thing I need from you is the spirit that you possess, to add to my own strength. Surrender it now, or I will be forced to take it from you." Again, Seko waves his hand in the air, sending Yukio flying through the wall into the next office. "You must know that I will have no regret on how it comes to me."

Yukio rolls over, reaching up to his Seko, "but Master, you said that my sister and I were chosen to serve you and your quest. Why does that change now?" He is helpless, trapped by the Dark Lord's will find that he can be cast aside as refuse at this hour.

"Your purpose has been served, time and again, Yukio, but you were never meant to be more than what you are, a guard dog. You do know that your Uncle ceased to exist many, many years ago, don't you?" The Dark lord walks around Yukio's broken body as he gives his explanation, while pondering what his next move should be. "But, do not despair in your final minutes. You can die knowing that you were part of a greater success. For eight hundred years I have waited for this day. With the other half joined to the piece I possess," Seko raises his half of the talisman into the air, "I will finally be able to leave this wretched land, and thwart my mother's attempt to rule this world once and for all. Then, I will hunt down the remaining pieces of the scepter and finish what my mother started centuries ago. Alas, it is unfortunate for you that you will not be around to witness the end of times. So sayeth the Doomsayer." The Dark Lord reaches down and buries his hand into Yukio's chest, and then draws his hand back, snatching the demonic spirit free from inside. After letting the creature of darkness go, it soars around the room and then flies right into Doomsayer's chest. He walks over to the open balcony and watches his warriors preparing to take a stand against the Guardian. "Remember, your task is but to channel him to me. I will be the only one to take his life. Once he is inside the complex you are to seal the perimeter to ensure he does not escape."

Nick waits in the trees beside the perimeter wall as the foot soldiers of Doomsayer move out from the complex to take their positions in the fields. At first, it seems like they are sweeping the grounds, but when the Dark Lord gives them the ability to seek out the talisman, they all turn and face Nick, heeding the call of the talisman's dark power. Nick charges from his hiding place and rushes for the opened gates of the compound. With no time to spare, he slips inside and slams the gates closed to bolt them shut as the dark warriors reach the other side. Believing he has time to catch his breath, Nick slowly turns around to see that he is dead wrong. The group of warriors dressed in Kendo armor has not abandoned their post. Their leader, Kenso, was once a childhood friend of Yukio Masamoto. It was that friendship that duped Kenso into sacrificing his soul for power and wealth. Now he is nothing more than a servant to the Dark Lord, until he dies. Death is something that he welcomes, to be rid of this ongoing curse.

"<Attack!>" Kenso screams, as his men rush Nick's position at the gate. These warriors offer Nick no lethal danger, unless they plan to beat him into submission with their Shinais, or practice swords. Still, they are the enemy and Nick acts accordingly. The traditional Doh, or breast plate, of their armor gives no resistance to Nick's swords as he slashes his way through them to get to their leader. Designed to protect the wearer from the blows of the opponent's shanai, the armor doesn't offer any protection against the blades of Nick's swords. Within seconds, Nick has made his way through the Kendo warriors, sending their demon spirits flying off into the building in front of him and their leader Kenso crawling to his Master.

"Pitiful Americans, you always think you can run in to save the day." A goliath of a man steps into the open and reaches out to grab Nick by the throat, with reflexes faster than light. Before Nick can react, he finds himself gasping for air in the crushing grasp of the attacker. The former sumo wrestler was once a Nation's champion, Sake Tanaka, until he was taken from the limelight to serve the Dark Lord. In a futile attempt to try and break Tanaka's grip, Nick draws back and delivers a crushing blow to Tanaka's nose. "Fool, don't you know who I am? I am Sake Tanaka! You cannot hurt me!" The big man squeezes his arms tighter around Nick's ribs, doing his best to break the Guardian in half.

"Oh really, I thought you were the Pillsbury Dough Boy!" JD follows his exclamation as he descends from the trees along the courtyard with his Bo staff pointed right at Tanaka's head. At the last second, JD deploys his force field, concentrating it at the end of the staff. On contact, the psychic energy blows a hole through the big man's head, in one ear and out the other. All signs of life instantly fade from the goliath, as the massive body collapses to the ground taking Nick with it.

"Well, don't just stand there! Get this big sonofabitch of me!" Nick commands of his student, spitting snow and mud from his mouth. He struggles to no avail, but the big man is immovable from Nick's position. He suddenly halts his attempt when he sees a rush of wind and snow blowing directly towards them. "JD, watch your back!"

Nick's warning comes too late. JD is swept from his feet and raised high into the air. Before he has time to react, the mysterious force sends JD flying across the courtyard, until he collides with a stone statue and falls to the ground lifeless. A female warrior appears in the wind and blowing snow, hovering over JD's body. She points her hands at him and produces what looks like fluid ice that solidifies around JD on contact. Now she can focus on the Guardian and succeed where the others have failed. "Guardian, I am Sunaki Masamoto. I am your next opponent." Sunaki floats over to her fallen ally and lands beside the oversized carcass. With a mere touch of her hand, she freezes Tanaka's body solid. Holding her hand there a little longer continues to freeze the bone and flesh until it shatters. Sunaki expects to find her prize underneath. She is shocked to find Landry gone, and very disappointed to be wrong. She's shocked even more when two arrows find their mark in Sunaki's chest from twenty feet away. Seeing Nick standing across the courtyard, she throws back her head and releases a blood curdling scream. Seizing the moment, Nick lets fly one more arrow, using her open mouth as the target. Sunaki quivers, and then falls to the ground as the demon spirit begins to claw its way out of her dead body and return to its master.

Kenso rushes into the main office and right up to Doomsayer and bows. "The Guardian is on his way here to face you. I will serve as your frontline."

The Dark Lord gestures with his hand, lifting Kenso from the floor. "That will not be necessary, my faithful one." Doomsayer points his finger at a button on the desk, and then thrusts his hand into Kenso's chest to retrieve the demon spirit within. On the desk a red light begins to flash, pulsating at a slow pace but gradually increasing in speed. "However, I will need this for my own benefit." Doomsayer discards Kenso's body and welcomes the spirit into his fold.

Once again he accepts that this is the moment he has spent past seven years training for. This is his destiny, and he embraces it fully. It is time to begin. "Boy, it really sucks to be affiliated with you, don't it?" Nick stands at the open double doors of the office after witnessing Kenso's demise. He points the tip of his sword at the Dark Lord and says," I'm assuming that you're the next in line, right?"

Doomsayer chuckles at Nick's statement with full arrogance in his voice. "No, Guardian, you have it all wrong. You are the next in line." Doomsayer waves his hand in the air, using the power of Sunaki's demon to create a blizzard in the middle of the office. This is merely a diversion to disorient Nick, as Doomsayer uses the power of the talisman to create fireballs to hurl at Nick's position. This is all to no avail, as Nick avoids attack after attack with ease. Charging in, Nick brings both of his blades to bear on the Dark Lord's chest. Doomsayer swats the assault away with a gesture of his hand, and waits for Nick to make his move again. Nick takes the offensive, and surprises Doomsayer when he uses the power of the talisman to fend off Doomsayer's advance, and then brings his sword in to cleave off the Dark Lord's head. Taking the advantage from Nick, Doomsayer produces a large double edged sword from thin air and blocks Nick's assault, at the very last second. It is the surprise of the sword suddenly appearing that gives the point to Doomsayer. Bringing the heavy blade around to bear on Nick's position, it takes everything Nick has to keep the massive blade from cutting him in half. One of Nick's swords is snapped in two, and Nick himself is sent flying across the room. He's down for the moment, but he's still alive and uninjured. Losing the blade of his katana, Nick draws his Wakizashi, or short sword, and readies for battle again. "I have to admit, Guardian, I haven't faced a foe of your caliber in over eight hundred years. All that he stood for, all that he sacrificed is about to come to an end. Take heed from this and see the futility of your actions."

"Here's what I see. I see you in front of me, telling me that you are over eight hundred years old. Now, we both know that's not completely true, but never the less, it's time to put you in the ground." Nick sidesteps Doomsayer flying across the room, but is able to strike the Dark Lord across his ribs with the tip of his sword. It's not a lethal wound, but it's enough to prove to both combatants that the body is very much mortal. "So this guy, eight hundred years ago, did he have a name?"

"Why does it matter?" Doomsayer asks, holding his hand over the wound, and then revealing the blood on his palm and fingers.

"Because I want to be sure to honor this guy, when I put you down for good," Nick declares, as he rushes Doomsayer's position, calling on the power of the talisman to increase his speed. At the last second, the Dark Lord raises his sword and blocks Nick's attack with such force that the Guardian is sent flying backwards across the room.

"Can you not see that your efforts are futile?" Everything that has transpired has done so according to my design." Doomsayer brings his sword around wielding the weapon with eight hundred years of experience. Any attack made by Nick is defended with ease, each time with the Dark Lord driving Nick away. Then, it is Doomsayer who takes the offensive, believing that Nick is weakening from the battle. He rushes to meet the Guardian in the center of the room, and attacks with vicious blows with his broad sword, shattering both of Nick's blades. "Look at you, Guardian. You have no idea what power you possess." Doomsayer raises his hand and hits Nick with energy drawn from the half of the talisman that he possesses. Nick is blown from his stance and sent crashing into the wall. "Look at you," Doomsayer says, as Nick looks around for another weapon. "Of course you don't, and you never will! Masamoto didn't tell you everything you needed to know, because you are incapable of controlling the power you possess. That alone should be enough for you to see that your efforts are pointless."

Grabbing a sword from one of the fallen warriors, Nick raises the weapon to defend himself, showing Doomsayer he isn't ready to lie down just yet. He can feel himself beginning to tire from the day's battles, but can't let his opponent know.

Trying to draw strength from the talisman is useless because he can't offer the concentration needed to perform the task. "Master Masamoto didn't need to tell me anything else than what I know. Maybe, he figured that I was capable of taking out your sorry ass without using the talisman." That should antagonize the megalomaniac. Nick charges the Dark Lord, holding Kenso's Yachi, or long sword high over his head. Surprising the Dark Lord with this sudden burst of energy, causes Doomsayer to take a quick defensive, but it isn't quick enough. The first blow by Nick is defended as expected, but when Nick rolls his blade with Doomsayer's blocking thrust, Nick is able to spin around behind the Dark Lord, and land another attack across Doomsayer's unprotected back.

The Dark Lord howls out in pain from the wound. This Guardian is not worthy of his success. He calls on the remaining dark spirits that possess his foot soldiers stationed around the complex. Spirit after dark spirit heeds the call and joins the growing force of darkness inside of Doomsayer. Enraged by Nick's success, the Dark Lord calls on this newfound power, and then extends his arm and clenches his fist. Nick is suddenly gasping for air as his feet are lifted from the floor, while Doomsayer raises his arm higher. Then, with no effort, Doomsayer slings his arm outward, sending Nick flying head first into the plaster wall. Slowly, the Dark Lord strolls across the room as Nick falls from the hole in the wall. It is more than obvious the Guardian has met his match, and then some. "Here at the end, can you see that you have failed in your duty? You were warned to never come to Japan. As long as I was exiled on this wretched island you could serve as the Guardian, and you would have served the purpose well. But, even with all that you know, all that was warned, it was still your destiny to come face me here. Now that I think about it, I would say that perhaps you have served your purpose fully."

Nick rolls over with blood running down his face, and partially blinding his vision. He reaches around on the floor trying to find his blade as Doomsayer raises his broad sword to deliver the deathblow. "I'd say that you shouldn't have wrote me off so easily," JD replies, landing in front of Nick wearing the suit Nick had given him, and deploying his force field as Doomsayer brings his sword down with all of his might. When the blade strikes the energy field, Doomsayer suffers the most being blown from his feet by the equal but opposite reaction of the strike. The force of the Dark Lord's attack sends JD reeling back, and falling over his friend, but unharmed. Both he and the Dark Lord stand at the same time, realizing that somewhere in the impact, Doomsayer was separated from his half of the talisman. There it is, lying on the floor between them, with Doomsayer making the first move as he dives for his most precious treasure. JD proves that his reflexes are quicker, as he simply extends his force field out around the talisman, putting it out of Doomsayer's reach. The Dark Lord collides with the energy field, sending him toppling to the floor in front of Nick. The Guardian now demonstrates that he is also as quick, and not quite out yet, by reaching up and grabbing a war axe from the wall that he uses to remove Doomsayer's head.

"Could it all be over that easily?" JD thinks, as he watches Nick collapses to the floor. "Nick, catch," JD says, tossing the other half of the talisman to his teacher."

"JD, no…"His warning doesn't come in time. Nick's only choice is to catch the piece and do all he can to prevent the two halves from rejoining. But, it is too late, and he is too tired to fight it. The two pieces of sculpted gold collide together and release a shock wave that disturbs the entire building right down to its foundation. JD picks himself up from the floor and looks around, wondering where the sound of a maniacal laugh was coming from. To his surprise, and fear, it was Doomsayer's head lying on the floor a few feet away.

"Everything has taken place as I have foreseen. You have not won anything. You will die, and this complex will be destroyed, but I will live on. And one day soon, curiosity will get the better, and someone will pick up the talisman that you have now made whole. When that happens, I will take possession of that body and I will resume my quest with victory in my grasp!" With his declaration made, Doomsayer's head explodes, releasing the dark spirit within to roam the world once more.

"What do we do now, Teach?"

Nick scans the room, and sees the flashing red light on the desk pulsating faster and faster. "We run!" Nick shoves JD towards the hole in the wall that JD created earlier and takes chase after his student. Both men leap to the ground, landing at the same time on the courtyard walkway. Nick understands full well what Doomsayer meant with his last statement. If Nick is blown to bits before he can leave the complex, there will be nothing to stop the Dark Lord from claiming the talisman. With the two halves reconnected, the spell cast to keep Doomsayer land bound is broken. This isn't over yet, and Nick isn't ready to be served up as the main course of a Bar-B-Q. He gives JD a shove towards the gates, as a series of explosion begins to topple the stone columns of the building's main entrance. To avoid the toppling spires, Nick takes to the air leaping and bounding off the collapsing structure, trying to get to JD. His student can't help but watch his teacher, remembering the excerpt from the journal about Nick's training field. This forces Nick to drop down just in time to pull JD clear of the danger.

After freeing the bolt, Nick throws the gates open wide, wondering what manner of opposition awaits them on the other side. JD doesn't wait for another shove from Nick. He takes the first two steps of his sprint, with Nick right beside him, as the entire complex erupts in a massive explosion. Both Nick and JD are sent flying out into the crop fields as debris begins to rain down around them. Nick grabs JD by the arm and pulls him to his feet, sending the both of them off running, as fire rains down from the sky on their position. They sprint passed the fallen warriors and straight through the crop fields, heading towards the river as fast as they can. Both men are exhausted, wanting so much to stop and catch their breath. Both also know that they don't have that luxury.

As they reach the tree line, JD suddenly turns to Nick and leaps at him, tackling his teacher to the ground. Before Nick can question why, JD deploys his force field as the trees erupt in a ring of fire around the complex. By the time the fires subside, JD is showing signs of a headache coming on, from using his force field so frequently. "That's twice now, young man. Are you going to be alright?"

"Yeah, and, if it weren't for you, I wouldn't be able to do what I did to save your butt either time." After sitting there for a minute, JD gives his head a shake or two, trying to clear his mind and focus. "Can we go home now?"

"Yeah, buddy, let's get the hell out of here." Nick takes the lead, meandering through the brush fires and burning tree trunks to make his way to the top of the hill. "I guess you can say that it's all downhill from here. I'll see you at the bottom, Sport." Believing that the end was near, and feeling a little rejuvenated by it, Nick slaps JD across his chest and takes off down through the trees. Not to be shown up, JD is right on Nick's heels, which is how Nick wants it. The sooner the two of them are on their way, the better. Without any hesitation, Nick clears the trees and runs right off the cliff, diving to the river below.

"Oh no you didn't!" JD follows suit, this time feeling

more comfortable about controlling his descent to the river this time. His dive to the water is flawless. His entry into the frigid waters is heart stopping at most. This propels him to swim as fast as he can to shore and join Nick at the edge of the water. It isn't until he's standing beside his teacher that JD sees what Nick sees. "Uh Nick, tell me these guys are friends of yours.

"Your involvement in this is that you were kidnapped to draw me here. You don't know why, and you don't know anything else, got it? Stick to that story JD, no matter what." Nick drops to his knees and laces his fingers together behind his head.

One of the soldiers in futuristic armor points his rifle at JD motioning for the young man to raise his hands. JD follows his teacher's lead and drops to his knees as well. This patrol of hi-tech soldiers is quickly joined by their Commander, a group of Navy and Japanese officials, and the rest of their patrol. JD takes notice to the fact that these soldiers aren't military by the Darkside Command insignias on their uniforms. These are the guys who are called in to clean up international incidents. The Commander steps forward and looks at both of the men kneeling in front of him. "Landry, Johnston, my name is Major Brad Delaney, of Darkside Command. Just so we are all on the same page, if either of you try to pull any of that shit you did back at that distillery, my men have orders to cut you in half. Now, I don't like to waste ammunition, so I hope you won't try anything stupid." To emphasize the Major's statement, all of the soldiers take aim at Nick and JD, as if daring the two men to make a move. "Nickolas Landry, you have a whole lot of people standing in line to get their hands on you."

# Chapter XVIII

Nick and JD sit quietly in the back of the helicopter as it makes its approach for the Sapporo air field. At the moment, JD is more afraid about this outcome than anything he faced earlier. He wants to say something to Nick but doesn't know if that would warrant one of these goons to open fire. "What do we do, Nick?"

"You stay calm and remember what to say. I'll make sure that you are cleared of any wrong doing, as long as you stick to the story." Nick doesn't look at JD, or show any signs of emotion as he speaks. Instead, he just stares forward as the helicopter begins to land at the air field. JD looks out the window to see armed troops, both Military and DSC alike. He has to admit that he's a little confused about all of this. Is the US really that pissed about Nick coming over here to save JD?

The helicopters circle the tarmac once and then moves into a hovering position to land. Again, Delaney has been pulled back into the field where he doesn't want to be. Still, regardless of what he what would like to keep locked in the closet, the Major has a job to do. As the helicopter touches down, Delaney leans forward. "I'd like to say that you'll

319

receive a warm welcome, but that isn't going to happen. Wait for everyone to get off the chopper first, and then the two of you will be escorted to the base's detention center for holding until we are ready to leave." Out on the pavement waits at least twenty armed troops, a mix of Military Police, and DSC operatives, awaiting their arrival. The looks on the Marines' faces tell Nick that they aren't happy to see him exiting the helicopter. Nick ignores the disgruntled faces, knowing in his heart that no innocent lives were taken by his hand. What happened between him and Doomsayer at the distillery is above the laws of man and will never be explained. This is how it has to be.

Major Delaney and the Japanese officials exit the second helicopter following the Navy Brass and make their way to a nearby building, while Nick and JD are escorted to the detention facility. Several airmen passing by spout threats at Nick, blaming him for the lives of the C-130 crew that crashed last night. At the door, the DSC guards step aside and allow the Marines to take the lead the rest of the way. Their path takes them through two high security doors about fifty feet apart, and down a long hallway that had several debriefing rooms along one side. Nick has seen places like this before. Basically, when a Seaman, jarhead, or any other military wild ass gets into trouble, they usually spend a little time in a place like this between flights. This is a memorable occasion being Nick's first time in this situation.

Down at the end of the hallway, it intersects with another wider corridor with offices at one end, and cells at the other, behind another security door. The parade of guards and prisoners stop at the first cell where JD is shoved inside. The Sergeant in charge slams the iron door shut and gives JD a smile through the bars. Then, Nick is shoved forward as the guards continue to the last cell at the end of the hall. Nick casually walks into the cell offering no resistance whatsoever.

Once the cell door closes, the Sergeant of the detail leans against the bars and just stares at Nick. "I don't get it. You were once the pride of the Navy, a highly decorated officer. I sure hope that doesn't earn you any leniency, during your trials. Too many people have died because of you. What did they, or their families, ever do to you?" The Sergeant stares at Nick hoping for some kind of response. "You Bastard!" Angered by Nick's silence, he slaps his hand against the iron bars of the door and walks away.

"Nick," JD calls out from down the hall. "What are we going to do? Can't you use the talisman…"

"Shut up, JD!"

"Do you still have it?"

"Damnit JD, I said shut up!" Nick walks over to the cell door, feeling like a heel for yelling at JD. "Listen, Sport, I want you to do something for me. No matter what you hear from this moment on, I want you to deny everything, forget about me, and move on with your life. This event has damaged me, and the last thing I want is for you to be pulled down the toilet with me." Nick walks to the back of his cell and sits on his bunk to try to get some rest. It's going to be a hard thing to do with his mind racing through memories of recent events. The sergeant's accusations have basis, but the accusations are falling on the wrong man. Circumstantial evidence points the finger at him, but how can he prove otherwise with the real killers already dead? Nick knows that if anything happened to LT that it had to be Yukia who did him in. She was the one who confronted him at the airfield. The only way she could have known where Nick was, is if she found out through Mitchell. In an offbeat sort of way, Nick's the cause of Mitchell's death, since Yukia followed Nick to Lt's house. The same goes for the airmen in the cargo hangar. If Nick hadn't followed the path he took to Japan, those people would still be alive, maybe. When the time comes, he'll be willing to take the responsibility for their deaths, but not as the death dealer.

He still has the talisman, but he's not going to tell JD, one way or another. He has managed to keep it out of sight, and reach, of the security detail. He doesn't understand why, or really care at the moment, but for whatever reason, it hasn't been much of a mental strain to impose his will. The only deduction he can come up with for an explanation is that he now has the entire talisman. Of course, the jury is still out, on whether or not that is a good thing.

Nick looks up when he hears keys rattling at the cell door. Three rough neck Marines are standing there with police batons in their hands, staring at Nick as a form of intimidation. "Hello, tough guy, we're the welcoming committee." Through the power of the talisman, Nick could see the demon spirits that inhabit the Marines' bodies and realizes that even though Doomsayer is gone, he will always be plagued by the agents of darkness, as long as he possesses the talisman. The first Marine unlocks the door and allows the other two Marines to enter. "We just wanted to stop by and show our appreciation for gracing us with your presence here in Sapporo."

He doesn't move, he doesn't flinch, and he doesn't rise from his seat on the bunk. "All I can say is bring it on, guys." He may be handcuffed and shackled, but Nick is more than capable of handling these goons. Whatever happens next happens because they came into his cell looking for trouble. He's a little surprised at the confidence being displayed, especially with the reports circling about how many that have already fallen by Nick's hands. He rights it all of this off as the dark possessions urging the Marines on. It is the evil in their hearts that allow the men to be controlled. One thing is always for certain; there's always somebody out there that thinks they can do what others couldn't.

Two of the Marines step over in front of Nick, tapping their batons in their hands while wearing devious grins. The two grunts look at each other, and then draw back to offer Nick the beating of a lifetime. Nick lets one of them land the first blow. That way the security cameras will have him on tape defending his self. A trickle of blood runs down Nick's brow from the only blow delivered. Before the second Marine could bring his baton down on its mark, Nick lunges off the bunk and delivers two crushing blows to the Marines' knees. As the two jarheads crumble to the ground, Nick rises up like a rocket, driving his shoulders into the Marines' chests. The two men fly up into the air and back against the concrete wall. As they fall to the ground, the third Marine rushes in to avenge his fallen comrades. Nick ducks below the wild swing of the baton, and crushes the Marine's ribs with a knee lift as the two men pass. With all three men down for the count, Nick reaches out his hand and summons the demon spirits from the Marines' bodies. The security camera doesn't record the dark presence; it can't register the beam of energy that is projected from the talisman that destroys the dark spirits. Nick didn't know he was capable of doing that. He just felt like it was the right thing to do.

JD can only imagine what is taking place in the cell at the end of the hall. There has to be some way he can help Nick, whether his teacher wants the help or not. If Nick is kicking the shit out of the Marines, that's okay. If it's the other way around, his friend is in a world of trouble. "Hey, somebody get in there and do something before they kill him!" JD jumps up and down in front of the video camera, hoping to get someone's attention on the outside. To his surprise, a gang of security officers come charging down the hallway. JD can only watch as they file by and wonder who had the upper hand in the cell down the way. Then, one by one, the Marines are carried out and down the hallway, with

Nick bringing up the rear with his own personal guard. "Hey, where are you taking him?" JD rushes to the bars of his cell, but quickly steps back as one of the security men jumps at the bars. "Whoa, easy there, big guy," JD suggest. "If you look at the file, I'm the one listed as innocent victim/bystander."

The security officer laughs at JD's statement. "If I've learned one thing in all of the years that I've been doing this; it's that anybody who professes to be innocent is usually guilty of something. Don't worry about your friend. We saw the whole attack on video, and know that the jarheads are the ones who are guilty this time. We're just taking Landry down to the infirmary to get his head checked out, that's all."

On the other side of the world, Bethany Phelps climbs out of the passenger seat of the rental car, and looks up and down the Miami suburb street one more time. The only thing that seemed out of place was an ordinary carpet cleaning van sitting on the other side of the road, across from the home of Nickolas Landry. It seems strange for a carpet van to be sitting in front of an empty lot, but Beth is sure that there is probably a hundred other reasons besides a police stakeout.

Tommy exits the driver's side of the car, hoping to persuade Beth to change her mind. "Come on, Beth; let's go check out a few more leads first. That Detective Rawson said for us not to push this one. Besides, I've got a bad feeling about this place. You don't want the cops pissed at us on both sides of the country, do ya?"

"Andrews is a Fed, not a cop. Any way, that Rawson sounded like he was giving us more of a friendly warning than an official notice. Not to mention the fact that he said he had been taken off the case. Chances are we won't ever run into him again." Beth turns on her recorder and drops it into her purse. After slipping her sunglasses onto her face, she looks in the reflection of the car window to check her hair. "Now go over there and run interference for me, just in case that van really is a stakeout. I'm just gonna go up and see if anyone is in the house. The cops said that Landry's roommate hasn't been seen since she left the hospital. Besides, the way our luck has been running, there's probably no one home," she adds, agreeing with Tommy's earlier statement. That worries Tommy even more, knowing how Beth has a tendency to go into places uninvited.

To him, she was just patronizing him to the fullest by repeating what he had said. "I'm telling ya, Beth, I've got a bad feeling about this," he declares as he walks across the street. It's not unusual for Tommy to talk to himself when he gets nervous. Especially since Bethany never listens to him. "We could be sitting in Hawaii right now, enjoying the sunshine and interviewing drunken tourists. But no, she has to chase the so-called story of the year across the country." His paranoia for Beth getting the two of them in trouble knows no bounds. Even now he entertains thoughts of obstruction, and yet he carries out his orders, because his commander always seems to pull it off by the skin of her teeth. If God loves him, Tommy will be long gone when Beth's luck runs out. "You be careful, girl," he warns as he watches Beth walk up to the front door of Landry's home.

Fighting down a queasy feeling in her stomach, Beth looks around the neighborhood one more time before knocking on the door. Maybe Tommy was right? Why wasn't anyone trying to stop her? Supposedly, this guy is the target of a nationwide manhunt, and she just walked up to the front door of his house. Through the glass in the front door, Beth could see the darkened interior of the front room, but there is no sign of life. Once she swallows her own fear, Beth raps on the glass pane with her knuckles. The glass rattles in the door making more noise than she expected. This causes her to look out into the deserted street to see if anyone heard the noise. Out the corner of her eye, she sees movement inside the house. It was a flash, or a blur really, nothing of form or distinction. Beth presses her face up against the glass trying to see if anything is there. Suddenly, Sonny's face appears on the other side of the door, causing Beth to stumble backwards, falling to the porch.

Sonny quickly opens the door and rushes out to help Beth up. "Oh you poor dear, let me help you up," Sonny offers apologetically, and then snatches the reporter up to her feet. There, are you okay, now? I am so sorry I spooked you like that. Those pesky police detectives keep coming around here at all hours of the day and night. It really makes it hard for a girl to get her beauty sleep, if you know what I mean."

"Yeah, you look like you haven't slept in days," Bethany replies.

Sonny stares at Beth's face for a second, as if studying the young woman's features. "Hey, I know who you are! You're that reporter from the TV tabloid show! Girl, I love to watch you give the cops a hard time. I guess you can say that it's something that you and I have in common." Sonny throws her arm around Beth's shoulder as if she wanted to buddy up to the reporter. "Why don't you come on in for a minute, and let me make it up to you for the scare tactics a minute ago." She gestures towards the door with her hand inviting Beth into the darkened house. "Please tell me you're here to do a piece on what's happening with Nick. If so, I know I can shine the light of truth on the subject"

Bethany Phelps quickly loses all of her inhibitions about the situation, when she sees her angle handed to her by this estranged young woman. "You have no ideas how refreshing it is to hear you say that. I have found the Miami police Department to be uncooperative, to say the least." Beth opens up her purse and pulls out a tablet and pen, and then purposely sits her bag on the table so that her voice recorder could get the entire conversation. "Okay, obviously, you want Nick to be seen in a good light, so why don't you tell me what makes him so good. Give me something that would make me say, gee, maybe this guy is getting railroaded here."

Sonny stands up and walks to the kitchen. "The best place to start, is always the beginning, she replies. I mean, I never pick a book up and start reading from the middle, do you?" Sonny peaks her head around the corner. "I'm getting some water. Do you want anything?" She disappears back into the kitchen before Beth could politely decline. "Any way, the only thing I need to know is which beginning do you want me to start from?" Sonny appears out of the hallway on the opposite side of the room, catching Beth completely off guard. "There's Nick, and then there's me and Nick, and even the beginning to how all of this started a couple of days ago. You pick the starting point, toots, and I'll take it from there." Sonny hands Beth an unwanted bottle of water and sits down on the sofa beside Beth.

"Thanks, Beth replies before sitting the bottle onto the table. She was beginning to see what Detective Rawson meant by Sonny being a touch off normal. But hey, who is he to judge. His statement was based on hearsay. Beth on the other hand is working with first hand proof that seems to be building a strong case against the former Navy SEAL. "Well, the beginning sounds like a great place to start. Let's go back to the first choice. I want you to tell me about Mr. Nickolas Landry, so I can build an accurate bio on him. From there, you can bring me up to current events by filling in the highlights."

Sonny gives Beth a confident smile. "So you want to know about Nickels, do ya? Alright, let me tell you about the man." She takes a drink from her water bottle to wet her mouth. "When I was first signed on with the SEALs, Nick had just been promoted to the status of Field Commander. He was a good leader who cared about his men, always putting their lives ahead of his own. Me and Nick hit it off right away. He tried to keep it professional, but sometimes that is hard to do when the attraction is so strong." Sonny jumps up and grabs a framed photograph from the fireplace mantle. "Here, this was taken after one of our missions." Sonny intentionally grabs this photo, because of the way she is posing in it, giving Nick a kiss a kiss on his cheek.

"So, Nick was a devoted Service man, caring, honorable, and loyal to his men." Bethany flips back a couple of pages in her notebook and scans through the pencil scratch. "Now, would you care to talk about his involvement with your incarceration? From what I've gathered, he's been quite influential with your rehabilitation."

Sonny stares at Beth with a painted on smile, trying to figure out which way the reporter was heading with her change of direction. "Yeah, Nickels has stood beside me through thick and thin. When I got busted down, he gave up his own career with the Navy, to crusade for mine believing he couldn't serve a system that was so unjust." Sonny takes another drink of her water and looks at the reporter with a determined expression. "Let me ask you something, Ms. Phelps. Would you expect any less from your lover?"

Beth looks up from her notes, surprised at Sonny's question. According to what Beth had already gathered on the couple in question, they have never been more than close friends. "So, you and Nick were a couple? Why don't you fill me in on what happened when you were busted down. Help me build a profile by telling me more about what he did to help in your time of need."

"Well, it all started when this ass clown of a commanding officer blamed me for a failed mission. A foreign ambassador and his family were killed when the terrorist that held them learned of our attempt to free the hostages. Somebody had to

take the fall, and our superior elected me. Nick stood up his team, pointing out that the Intel on the mission was flawed and inaccurate, but that wasn't good enough. The blame had already fallen to me, so while Nick proceeded to take the case to a higher authority, I decided to handle it my way. The superior officer hated the fact that he had the first woman to serve with the teams, under his command. I proved my worth over and over, but could never change the fact that I was a woman. So, to prove him wrong about his opinion, I challenged him to one on one, hand to hand, contact. With his Lieutenant as a witness, I told the Major that if I beat him, he would drop the charges and leave me be. If he beat me, I would resign from the teams, and the Navy. Needless to say, I beat that man within an inch of his life, in every direction. Of course, when it was all said and done, he, and his Lieutenant, conspired to say that I attacked the Major, because of his allegations against me. He spent six months in the hospital, while I spent three years of my life in prison."

Beth becomes a little nervous watching Sonny's expressions as she described her story to the reporter. It was more than obvious that Sonny enjoyed telling the story, as much as she enjoyed participating in this delusion of grandeur.

Flipping through her notes, Beth finds the page she's searching for and looks back at Sonny, who was trying to read Beth's notes upside down. "Okay, now while you were away, Nick returned to Miami to start a new life, with a new wife, right?" Immediately, Beth can see that she hit a nerve with that one. Sonny's somewhat friendly demeanor suddenly disappears, as her distaste for the question shows all over Sonny's face.

"That prissy little bitch, Megan? I assure you that she was a down point in Nick's life. You see, when Nick left Norfolk, he actually came back home, to Miami. Nick and Megan's

infatuation with each other was an item all through high school, but when Nick was accepted into the Navy, Megan chose the plush, posh, lifestyle that her parents had to offer. When she found out that he had returned to Miami, she couldn't wait to sink her claws into his back again."

"They say that she died before they were married. Do you know what happened to her?"

Sonny gives Beth a smile, as if saying she enjoyed the thought of her answer. "Nope, I was still in prison. It's a damned shame too, because I got out two days later and would've loved to have been there to see it. That rich little bitch was nothing but a parasite that would have sucked the life right out of Nick, and tried to change him into something he could never be."

Now Beth is disturbed by Sonny's change of attitude. In Beth's years of experience as an investigative reporter, she has learned how to read people to tell if they are telling the truth, or hiding something. Right now, every little red flag in Beth's mind is waving frantically, warning her that something is wrong. She already knows that Sonny was at the rehearsal dinner when Megan was killed. That was public knowledge that Beth had found in the newspaper archives on line. Judging by Sonny's mannerisms, it's a topic Beth wants to move on from as quickly as possible. "Okay, let's fast forward a little bit to the other night. Why don't you tell me about Nick's involvement with you being shot at the nightclub, okay?"

Sonny stands up and takes on a dark maniacal look about her face. "I don't think I like your tone of voice, Ms. Phelps. In fact, at the moment, you sound like those cops who keep implying that Nick is somehow involved with everything that is wrong! You know what? You look like that bitch Megan, a little bit around the nose and eyes. You glory hounds are all alike, aren't you? You want, want, want, until it doesn't suit you any more, and then it's on to the next thing! Tell me something, Ms. Phelps, what is your interest in this story, any way? Maybe you thought Nick could add a little excitement to your life as well?" Sonny starts to step forward towards Beth, never breaking eye contact. "Right now, the best thing for you to do is leave! Shag your pretty little ass back to LA, before you wind up in something that you don't want to be a part of."

Bethany Phelps may be hard headed, but she isn't stupid. In all honesty, she was ready for this to be over a couple of minutes ago. "I'm so sorry, Ms. Richards. In no way did I mean to upset you. I'll leave if that is what you want, but there is no need for any threats."

Sonny steps right up to the reporter, trying to intimidate Beth with her height advantage, as Beth stands up. Sonny breathes hard in Beth's face, almost causing her to gag from the smell of death that's produced. Now her fear sets in, sending Beth stumbling around the sofa to get to the front door as fast as she possibly can. Sonny follows her to the door but stops just short of stepping out onto the porch. "Know this, sweet ass, if you go after Nick in any way, I'll come after you and rip out your heart through your throat!" Sonny slams the front door shut as Beth hurries from the porch.

Tommy leans against the van across the street while finishing his cigarette. It was more than obvious that there was no threat to their presence inside the van. Surely the Miami police department wouldn't let a famous reporter walk right up to their prime suspect's house, in the middle of the investigation. He just didn't feel like walking back across the street until he had to. Yes the great Bethany has duped him again, sending him on a wild goose chase while she gets the scoop. That fine by him in this case, because he's got the heebee jeebees about this whole thing.

His cellular phone rings in his pocket, making it hard

for him to man his cigarette and answer the phone, while holding a water bottle at the same time. One has to go, so his water bottle falls to the gutter, allowing him to reach into his pocket without breaking his smoke. "Yeah, hey Beth, did you get what we needed?"

"More than I could've ever wanted! Hurry up and meet me at the car. I want to get away from here as quick as possible." Beth exits the driveway and turns down the sidewalk, double timing her trek to the rental car.

"Alright, I'll be there in a second." Tommy takes a long drag from his cigarette and smiles. This is the first time he and Beth have actually agreed on anything, this entire trip. Wanting to leave as well, he hangs up his phone and flips his cigarette into the gutter in front of the van. Grabbing the door handle on the van's side door, Tommy uses it to brace himself as he bends over to retrieve his water bottle. To his surprise, the door opens slightly from his weight pulling down on the handle. A couple of flies exit the vehicle and circle Tommy's head as he stands up with his bottle. The insects don't bother him at all, but the foul smell coming from inside the van is enough to turn his stomach. With Beth already at the car honking the horn for him to hurry, Tommy closes the door and hurries across the street. He never looked inside to see the dead police officers. He's too far away to hear anything, when the radio inside the van comes to life.

# Chapter XIX

"Lt. Commander Nickolas Landry, you have a long list of people waiting in line to get their hands on you," Delaney declares, as he enters the infirmary and walks over to stand in front of Nick. "Of course, the ones I'm talking about will be much more civil than your Marine buddies in the next room." Delaney motions for the guards to uncuff Nick from the examination table. "I saw the video of what happened in the cell. You are one lethal sonofabitch, aren't you? Tell me something, what's the deal with you and the kid? The Japanese say that he's as illegally in their country, as you are. We found his passport in your bag on the river, which makes me wonder how you planned to get the two of you out of Japan without raising suspicion?"

With the circulation returning to his hands, Nick rubs his wrists and faces Delaney. "JD's involvement in all of this is simple. These people came to my dojo and said that I had something that belonged to them. I didn't have it with me, so they abducted JD and brought him to Japan, ordering me to bring their property to them, in exchange for JD's life. Things went bad, they blew up, me and JD got away. You know the rest," Nick adds, leaning back on the table as he touches his mouth, assessing another secondary wound he received in the scuffle.

"Buddy, I don't think I know anything about any of this. One thing is for sure, I don't think I can ever recall where one man was connected to so much trouble in so little time."

"Let me ask you something, Major Delaney. Actually, it's two things. What is your stake in this, and what exactly does Darkside Command do? Humor me for a few minutes." Nick touches a rag to his scalp to check the wound on his head to see if it was still bleeding.

"That's a fair enough request to grant a condemned man," Delaney replies as he relaxes a little. Confident that Nick doesn't pose a threat at the moment; the DSC Major dismisses the guards so that he can speak candidly with Landry. "My, or should I say, our job, is simply to act as a taxi service to take you back to the States for prosecution. As for Darkside Command, we are privately funded, and the only nonmilitary organization acting under the authority of the United Nations' Peace Council, and in cooperation with the United States Government. Basically, to put it into terms that you understand, we are an internationally based sweeper team that takes out the bad guys who oppose world peace. Delaney stares at Nick for a moment and then asks, "why?"

Nick stares back at Delaney, trying to determine what is true, and what is bullshit.

"A friend of mine was killed last year, it's my understanding that one of your teams was on the case. Do you know anything about it?"

"I don't know. Who was your friend?"

"Lt. Charlie Steiner," Nick replies. It isn't that he's probing for anything specific. Nick would just like to know about Charlie's case, maybe just to have some sort of closure with the subject.

Delaney looks up at the ceiling for a second as if

contemplating the name. "Oh yes, I think I remember something about that coming across my desk. He was wrongfully accused of weapons hijackings I believe." At this moment, the last thing Delaney wants is his past connections to the Callistone crime family coming into light. "You aren't connected to that too, are you? Any way, getting back to the matters at hand," Delaney wants nothing more than to change the subject. "I've been asked to see if you want to press charges against the Marines."

"No, they weren't acting with their own free will. I can't hold them responsible for what they did. How could anyone else?" Nick lays back on the examination table, if for nothing else but to rest and relax for a little bit.

"You're not going to be trouble for me, are you?"

Nick gives Delaney a smile, but doesn't open his eyes. "No, Major Delaney, I'm not here to give you any trouble."

Delaney feels like he's swimming around in chaotic mud. Nick's response about the Marines came from deep left field. He wants to ask the question, but isn't sure if he'd like the answer Nick would give him. "Alright then, I have a transport on its way, so we'll be heading out of here within the hour." Delaney walks over to the door and gives it a rap with his knuckles. When the guard opens the door, Delaney instructs him to escort Nick back to his cell.

JD watches Nick walk by the door of his cell, and is confused at why Nick is acting this way. "He didn't even bother to look at me, when he walked by. Why is Nick trying to cut himself off from me? At the moment, I seem to be the only one in his corner." JD doesn't want to betray Nick's wishes, but he can't just stand by and watch Nick be wrongfully accused. How can he help without Nick finding out? The voice of reason tells him to follow Nick's orders and never look back. JD doesn't feel that he is on speaking terms logic and reason.

Returning from depositing Nick, the guard stops at JD's cell and unlocks the door. He motions for the young man to follow the guard to a small interrogation room, where JD sits down at a table and waits. The questions quickly start to well up in JD's mind, wondering what this is about. "Okay, Johnston," Delaney starts, as he walks into the room, "I think your fearless leader is trying to sell me a bill of goods. In fact, he's adamant that you are some kind of poor, innocent bystander that was pulled into this mess. I don't suppose you would want to elaborate on any of that, would you?" Delaney sits down at the table across from JD.

"Yeah, first of all, I'm not some dumb, poor, black kid from the projects. My IQ is higher than yours, and I have the knowledge that enables me to take you out, at any given moment." You give up too much information, JD. Nick said for him to keep it plain and simple. He writes it off as a funny way of anxiety showing itself. "So, do me a favor and show me a little respect, and back off with that guilty until proven innocent attitude, alright?" There, maybe that will calm the moment down.

Delaney laughs at JD's remark, and looks up from the papers in front of him. "You've got spunk kid, I'll give you that. Still, when I see you sitting here, in Japan, wearing a similar Halloween costume as your friend, I can't help but wonder how innocent you really are."

JD looks at Delaney for a second, and then starts to laugh. "So, what do you think, me and Nick are like some international Batman and Robin? I'm gonna do you a favor and tell you everything I know. Nickolas Landry saved my life once, took me in under his wing and taught me not to fear the world I live in. He is my teacher, Mentor, and friend. In fact, he's the closest thing I've had to a father in eighteen years. So," JD leans back in his chair and laces his fingers behind his head. "I'm sure you can understand why you can't or won't get anything out of me that would or will incriminate Nick." JD drops the legs of the chair to the floor and quickly leans in over the table. "Saturday night, I was wearing this gi, because Nick had given it to me for my birthday present and as a token for my accomplishments in his class. I don't expect you to understand what it means to earn an honor like this, so if you want, you can ask the cop that was there when I was taken hostage."

"Don't sweat it, kid. We've already got his statement."

JD sits back in his chair. "Okay, then the next thing I know, I'm sitting tied to a chair, half way around the world. Nick showed up, I'm free, that's all there is to it." JD stares at Delaney trying to determine whether he bought the story or not. He should, after all most of it was true."

Delaney shakes his head and logs off his handheld computer. "Well, if that's your story, then that's your story. If you and your buddy stick to that, you should be able to carry on with your life with no hassle." Delaney stands up and gathers his papers and then surprises JD by sitting back down. "Hey, off the record and just for personal curiosity, do you know what the ransom was?"

JD leans forward with an enthusiastic look on his face, and says, "No, do you, because that one has really been bugging me. A guy kinda wants to know what his life is really worth, right."

"You tell me, kid. You were the one who was bragging about how smart you are." Delaney shakes his head and gives JD a smug look. "Any way, just so that you have bragging rights, your friend was involved with one of the biggest mob syndicates in Japan."

"They're called the Yakuza." JD adds.

"Yeah well, the Japanese Government would like to thank Landry for single handedly taking out the entire operation. Of course, then they would like to lock him up for a hundred years for his tactics used on Japanese soil. Meanwhile, the Military and the Federal boys are standing in line fighting over who gets their hands on Landry first. So, unless you have something that you can add that can save your friend's life, I'm afraid that this is the end of the line for Nick Landry."

"Nice try, pal, I will tell you this much; if there is one thing I do know, it's that the only one who can save Nick Landry, is Nick Landry. One thing you can count on, when that time comes, he will do whatever he has to do to make things right."

Delaney stands back up again, not sure how he should take JD's comment. He walks over to the door and presses the buzzer. "I'll be escorting you and Landry back to LA. From there, the Feds will take you back to Miami, where you will be released, and Landry incarcerated. Keep your nose clean, kid. We have a habit of keeping an eye on special cases like you." Delaney stops at the door and gives his orders to the guards. Looking back one more time at JD, he says, "Go with these men and they will take you outside to the shuttle, while I go get your friend. It's time for you to go home."

Outside the interrogation room, Delaney motions for two guards to follow him as he heads for Nick's cell. He stops at Nick's cell door and stares through the bars at the man sitting calmly on the bunk. It only takes a second or two before Nick becomes annoyed with the act. "What are you looking for, Delaney?"

"Let's just say that I'm trying to see if there is some kind of hero in there, trying to stay hidden, or if it's a mad man trying to get out. Tell me something, Landry. Was one boy's life worth all of those who died?"

"One day, when you least expect it, you will look back on this day and say yes it was worth it all." Nick's reply makes no sense to Delaney, but neither does Nick's calm cool collected attitude. Knowing that time is short, Delaney opens the cell door to allow the guards to enter. Without any hesitation or interference from Nick, the guards shackle the prisoner for transport. He looks at the handcuffs and then at Delaney. "Judging by the fancy jewelry, I take it that we're ready to start this grand adventure." Nick starts for the cell door after a nudge from one of the guards. The guards take their place in front of Nick with Delaney falling in behind the prisoner, as Nick short steps it down the hall. Once outside, Nick quickly takes a tally on whom, and what is present. First and foremost, is the truck waiting to deliver him to the air field. There are more of Delaney's DSC troops, but what is troubling Nick the most, are several dark spirits that seem to be hiding in the back of the truck. As Nick moves closer, the spirits flee, adding to his discomfort. It's not so much that they left, but that he doesn't know why the spirits are watching him.

The DSC troops motion for Nick to climb up into the back of the truck as Delaney climbs into the passenger seat of the cab. Once in the back, Nick is directed to sit between two DSC guards while the rest sit on the other side of the truck. Once settled in, the entire group sits quietly with none of the DSC troops making eye contact with the prisoner. Nick can only wonder how painfully monotonous this trip will be. As they pull out onto the service runway, Nick can see JD standing outside the awaiting plane with an escort of guards to keep him company. Again he sees the troubling sight of dark spirits encircling the plane and troops waiting outside. As the truck stops the guards inside quickly exit to form a corridor between the troops for Nick to walk through. At the plane, the troops form another corridor that leads to the stairs of the shuttle. Nick is more concerned with the presence of the spirits. He knows that there are other agents of darkness besides Doomsayer. Nick also knows that these vengeful spirits could just be faithful to the Dark Lord, and want to return the talisman to him. This brings him to his next question. Was the Dark Lord really destroyed? Doomsayer said that he would come back to claim the talisman. The unknown is how would these dark specters aid the Dark Lord?

Nick watches intensely as the spirits pass through the guards searching for suitable host. The anxiety of it all is becoming too much for Nick. His shackles and the heavily armed troops prevent him from defending himself, and keep him from offering any kind of defensive assistance. In between the two corridors of troops is an open expanse of about ten to fifteen feet. Every guard watches his every move with their weapons pointed at Nick. If the Dark Lord's minions made their move now, there would be nothing he could do without jeopardizing any more lives.

If Delaney and the others could see what Nick sees, they probably wouldn't be so critical of his sanity for what he is about to do. As he reaches the center between the two columns of soldiers, Nick decides that this is where he will make his stand. He tenses up every muscle and yells as loud as he can, "be gone!" A wave of energy is expelled from the talisman in all directions, obliterating the demon spirits and end Nick's torment. Several of the guards chuckle at Nick's actions. To them it must have seemed like a last ditch effort of a condemned mad man to get free. If the guards and Delaney could've seen the spirits and wave of energy, they probably wouldn't doubt his sanity so much.

Delaney walks up to Nick, looking around as if he suspects something else was still to come. "Are you trying to get yourself killed? Because the last thing I need is to fill out a mountain of paperwork for one of my guys shooting you for pulling some bullshit like that!" Delaney leans closer to Nick, and asks, "What did you do? I felt something, I know I did."

"Just consider your shuttle blessed for a safe flight." Nick continues his walk of humility as the guards laugh and mocks his previous action. Just before he reaches the shuttle, one of the guards gives Nick a shove to hurry him along. "Easy jumbo," Nick warns, looking back over his shoulder. "I can only move so fast in these shackles." Nick looks into the guards' eyes and sees the one of the demons was able to find safe haven in this soldier's dark personality. "Delaney, you better get this guy out of here before you have another incident on your hands!" Nick drops to the concrete surface of the runway as the guard brings his weapon to bear on Nick's head.

"Freeze!" Delaney can't believe that one of his own men was turning against him. The guard lets out an animalistic roar at his superior, and then prepares to execute Nick. Several shots are fired, but by the other guards and Delaney, ending the threat to Nick's life. Delaney then rushes up and grabs his prisoner by he arm and hurries him onto the shuttle. "I've seen some crazy shit before but this definitely takes the cake!" Sitting down beside Nick, Delaney straps himself into the seat, and adds, "I hand picked every one of my team for this mission. These men are the best at what they do, trained for any situation. I can't believe he turned against me like that."

"Delaney, I'm sure he was as surprised about it as you were." Nick sits back and closes his eyes after acknowledging JD boarding the shuttle. If nothing else, Nick has the comfort of believing that the flight should be an uneventful to say the least.

"Tina, yeah it's Beth," Beth replies as she throws her purse onto the hotel bed and then switches her cell phone to loudspeaker and sets it on the bed. "Yeah, I just got your message. Please tell me you've got something for me," Beth pleads, as she begins to undress. Feeling the cool air of the ocean against her bare skin sends her hurrying over to the balcony door to close it. There she stands for a moment, believing she had seen something out in the black night sky over the ocean. Still feeling uneasy about her encounter with Sonny, Beth locks the door and closes the curtain.

"Beth, I just got word that your man of the hour has been captured in Japan, of all places, and is being returned to LA by DSC operatives." Tina slurps down the rest of her smoothie and tosses the cup over by the trash can. "This guy is big time, Bethany. Walter said that you'll get your corner office, if you pull this off and get the scoop."

"You're the bomb, Tina! Get me a flight booked to LA as soon as possible. I should be able to get to LA before they get there from Japan." Beth leaps into action heading over to pack her suitcase for the trip, and realizes that she needs some of those clothes to cover up her bra and panties she's wearing.

"Hold on there, girl. He's coming to you. As soon as the DSC guys deliver him to the Feds, the Feds are high balling him straight to Miami, where all of this started. You just hang tight and think about window treatments for your new office. By the way, there is a Detective Rosa who keeps calling for you. Do you want his number to call him back?"

"No need, girlfriend, I'll talk to him when all of this is said and done." Beth hangs up the phone and plops down on the fresh linens of the bed to relax. Her plans have changed with Nick being returned to Miami. After doing the math, she figures that she has plenty of time to follow up on a couple more leads before the guest of honor arrives.

As usual, Tommy stands outside Beth's door, looking at his watch for the fourth time in three minutes. Why does she always do this to him? After finally developing enough back bone, he knocks at the door. They were supposed to be hitting South Beach about fifteen minutes ago for dinner. Needless to say, Tommy is a hungry man who does not want to be kept waiting, any longer. Unlike most men, Tommy is not a happy boy when she opens the door, wearing nothing but her underwear. "You're not ready to go down to South Beach, are you?" Tommy slumps his shoulders and pushes his way passed her into the room. "Why aren't you ready to go, Beth? You know I've been starving all day."

"Because, Tommy boy, we've got work to do. I'm gonna take a shower, while you order us up some pizzas. Order whatever you want. It's all on me tonight, to make up for your mistreatment. I want to go over everything we've got so far, and make sure we've covered the bases up to now. After we eat, we can go down to Landry's martial arts studio. I also have an address for the Aunt of one of Landry's students. Evidently, he is missing, and I think it's connected to our story."

"No," He has had enough. "You are going with me to South Beach, we are going to eat dinner, and that is all there is to it. I'm tired of this crap, Beth. All you care about is your story. Well, let me enlighten you about something. The whole reason I stayed with you was for the exotic locales, so get your butt ready so we can go enjoy this one."

This time it is Beth who pouts. "Fine, but it's going to be a working dinner, and afterwards, we are still checking out these other places."

JD stares at Delaney, trying to get a read on the guy. He sees the Major as the typical Military/Government stiff who seems to keep a lot of unwanted luggage in the closet. "So, Delaney, would you want to talk a little? I'm going out of my mind with the boredom and anxiety of this flight." Hoping that Delaney feels accommodating, JD doesn't take his eyes off of the DSC Officer.

"You know, son, I'm not at liberty to talk to you about your friend's case." The Major hopes that his reply is enough to deter JD's curiosity. After all, Delaney pulled that one right out of the DSC operations handbook. What Delaney wants at the moment is a little sleep as well. Nick is exhausted and snoring up a storm.

"No, I know enough about sleeping beauty over there. I was actually talking about some of that crazy shit that you were talking about earlier. Come on, man, there's got to be some really cool declassified stories that you can share, right?" JD stands and walks over to sit down beside Delaney, drawing the attention of the guards.

Delaney waves his soldiers off as his hidden paranoia subsides. He recognizes the young man's curiosity and enthusiasm as genuine. Allowing his ego to take control, Delaney seizes the opportunity to brag a little. What he doesn't realize is that he is about to open his mouth about everything he's been trying to cover up. "Yeah well, in my line of duty, I've seen a lot, that's for sure. Let's see, I've seen the aliens from the Roswell crash, but that's elementary school level compared to our own planet's evolution. Let me ask you something. Have you ever heard of our team Omega Corps?" Delaney pauses and waits for JD's response so that Delaney knows which way to go with the story. With an enthusiastic nod from JD, Delaney smiles and continues. "To be honest, I was actually against the whole concept from the beginning."

"Why?"

"Some of my Superiors believed that we should fight fire with fire against these super villains and free lance vigilantes. Did you know that the United States Government pushed for the scientific community to give out a new label to the next generation of the human species? Son, let me tell you the President was pissed when they came back with the genus: Homo Superior." Delaney laughs at the memory flashback, for a second. "Any way, the team, Omega Corps, is lead by one of the original members of DSC's first covert ops team, code named Task Force Zebra. His name is Commander AC Cannone, and one of the biggest thorns in my side. Basically, this so-called team started out as a bunch of juvenile delinquents, with Cannone serving as their Probation Officer.

"Okay, Delaney, now you're talkin'. What was it that made these juvenile delinquents so special?" JD slips up to the edge of his seat waiting for Delaney to spill.

"Let's just say that they are gifted. I've seen one outrun a Camaro in the quarter mile. Then there is this girl, who has a tendency to cause things to spontaneously combust. The leader of the group, Cannone, this guy doesn't look it, but he could pick up a greyhound bus without a problem." This is the point where Delaney crosses the line. "Kid, about eight or nine months ago, me, and my boys tangled with this creature from the deep. I'm telling ya, if I wasn't so scared at the sight of the guy, I would have been awestruck. He was blue…"

JD sits up straight in his chair and gives Delaney a confused expression. "Hold on there a second, Major. Did you say the guy was blue, from the ocean?"

Delaney acts as if he is insulted by JD's doubt. "No, no, no, I'm tellin' ya kid, this guy was like half man and half fish, and all bad ass. He was tougher than a shark, and meaner than a barracuda. In fact, I think the case file was titled Cuda, but it was closed when the creature was presumed dead." Delaney suddenly cuts the story short, when he ties his story in the Caribbean, to the conversation he had with Nick earlier. Nick is asleep, but the names of Steiner and Richards part his lips, making Delaney feel a little uneasy.

"Oh, don't sweat him," JD explains. "He talks in his sleep all the time about his old SEAL buddies. Believe me, it can get annoying. I remember one time, we went on this survival camp trip and he would not shut up. Every night it would be the same thing. Ten minutes after he fell asleep, it would be blah, blah, blah."

Yeah, sure kid, now let me ask you something. What are you going to do, now that this is all over?" Delaney wants to change the subject fast, hoping that it would ease his tension about his choice of topics. He has severed his ties to the mob, as of late, and doesn't want to bring up anything else that is tied to that past.

"Well, I guess I'll be heading off to start college. I've been accepted into Auburn University, which is cool because it's only a couple of hours from my mom's place."

"That's nice. Well, I think I wanna follow your buddy's lead and try to get a little rest. You should try to do the same. We'll be landing in LA in a few hours." Delaney leans back in his seat and closes his eyes, only to look at JD one more time. "Do us both a favor, sport, and go take your seat. We don't want any of my trigger happy goons getting an itchy finger. He closes his eyes again, wanting so much to block out the past that keeps revealing itself in his life.

JD takes his seat and strap himself in. He looks over at one of the guards next to him and asks, "You don't want to talk, do ya?" The guard shakes his head no, and sits back in his seat. This is going to be a long three hours. Fortunately for JD, it isn't as hard for him to fall asleep as he thought it would be. He was able to finally calm himself down after the day's excitement, while he talked to Delaney. This gave his body time to assess his situation and determine that sleep is what he needs most. Later, it will be food and a lot of it.

# Chapter XX

"Bethany, it's me, Tina. Yeah girl, your prize winning story is landing at LAX as we speak. No way, girl, they can't keep this one under wraps. There are activist groups already forming their petition lines around the airport to protest. You better be stepping fast and putting your story together, because this story is breaking open."

Beth stomps her feet under the table, angered by the fact that she wanted to be at LAX, but is sitting in a restaurant three thousand miles away. "Tina, I told you I should've come back to LA. Why did I let Walter talk me out of it?"

"Don't be so down, little lady. I'm about to hand you one righteous piece of information. Of course that is figuratively speaking, since you are in Miami, and we we're talking on the phone. Any way, the Feds are flying your boy to you. Only, they want to avoid there what they face here, so they're flying him into Palm Beach with some teenager named Jefferson D. Johnston, and then driving him down to Dade County. That's a good thing to know, right?"

Looking across the table, Beth gives Tommy a smile before answering her friend's question on the phone. "Girl, I'll tell you that this is the kind of information that could earn you a Champagne dinner! When is all of this taking place?"

Tina watches her supervisor walk by and waits until she is gone before continuing the conversation. "As soon as they go through the song and dance here in LA, they're flying out from a private hangar headed straight for Palm Beach. Agents will be waiting to transport Landry down to Miami. My best guess is that you've got about five hours to get your butt to West Palm Beach so that you can find a good seat..." Tina quickly hangs up the phone as her Supervisor's face appears over the top of her cubicle beside the face of Agent Andrews' unsmiling face. Tina knows that her next move is to clear out her desk, without anyone even saying a word.

Into her bag goes the cell phone, with Beth retrieving her wallet to pay for dinner, without a wasted movement. "I think we just lost our information source at Homeland Security," she explains, looking across the table at Tommy.

"So, that's no reason to stomp on my foot like that!" Tommy stuffs another butter soaked morsel of lobster into his mouth to try and forget about his throbbing toes. "What did Tina say?"

After wiping her mouth with her napkin, Beth throws it on her plate and waves to the waiter for the check. "She said for you to hurry up, so that you can drive me to Palm Beach to meet a plane. You've got five hours to get me there before Landry arrives."

Tommy shakes his head in full defiance. "That's tough shit, Miss I don't eat a lot, because I'm gonna sit here and eat steak and lobster until I can't any more," he declares, waving the waitress over for another steak and two more lobster tails. "Now I know it will only take us an hour and a half to drive up, so why don't you just kick back and relax for a little while. Isn't this place too cool, or what? Check out the way the vines grow in from outside, and lace their way around the ceiling."

Tommy looks away from his meal to see Beth staring off into the distance. "Beth, did you hear a word I was saying?"

Distracted by someone she saw, Beth was beginning to wonder if Sonya Richards was stalking her. There have been times all day where she has felt like someone was watching her and a couple of times where she thought she had seen Landry's roommate. "Huh? Oh, yeah, you go ahead and finish hoarding, Tommy. I need to go satisfy my curiosity." She adds, validating her actions. Looking around again, Beth is unable to locate the mystery woman of topic. The woman couldn't have gone far, and Beth just wants to know if it is Sonya following them or not.

"What is it, Beth? Where are you going?"

She stands up and pushes her chair away from the table. "No sweat, Tommy, you just eat to your heart's content and I'll be back in a minute." Beth meets the waiter half way to the door, and hands him her credit card and gives instructions to leave the card with Tommy. She exits the out of the way restaurant and starts out into the dark street. There are tourists and locals alike making their way up and down the historic boulevard, but Beth doesn't see anyone resembling her stalker. She can't explain why, but her intuition takes her down the less busy end of the street. As she passes a darkened alley, Beth hears the sound of someone kicking an aluminum can across the pavement. She is startled by the noise, causing her heart to race, but she stops and stares into the darkness of the alley all the same. "Hello, is anyone there?" Then, like at Landry's house, she thinks she sees movement in the darkness. "Ms. Richards, is that you?" Beth asks, walking into the alley. "If you have more information to offer, I'd be happy to listen."

Once into the darkened passage, Beth begins to hear small, faint noises coming from all around her. There's a scratching sound of fingernails against concrete behind her, the sound of fast moving fabric in front of her. With her bravery quickly shrinking, Beth reaches into her purse and retrieves a canister of pepper spray. She hears the sound of someone moving right behind her and spins around, only to see the alley is empty except for her presence. Again, she hears movement above her, and then a woman's laugh deeper in the alley, sounding slightly maniacal, and somewhat evil. Something falls to the pavement landing in a puddle of rainwater, causing Beth to spin around again. Slowly, Beth walks deeper into the alley until she comes to the graffiti covered block wall of a building, with the harsh and violent artworks making the dead end seem even more ominous. Again, she hears the faint laugh sounding as if the person is right above her. Fearing the possibility, Beth takes a deep breath and slowly looks up. Suddenly, a hand falls across her shoulder, causing her to spin around as fast as she could to unload the contents of her pepper spray canister. The stream of fiery liquid hits Tommy square in the eyes.

"Oh Jesus, girl, what are you trying to do? Are you out of your mind!?!" Tommy drops to one knee and begins to cry in agony as the liquid fire burns at his eyes and nose. "God, I can't even breathe!" He exclaims as the fumes cause him to gag and choke.

Beth is so frightened now that every little thing is making her jump. "Did you hear that? Did you hear it? Come on, Tommy, we've gotta get outta here!" She takes her friend by the hand and quickly leads him out of the alley and back into the public eye.

"Did I hear what? I can't even see at the moment, and you're worried about me hearing stuff?" Tommy staggers along as Beth leads him to a garden hose attached to one of the corner buildings. She turns the water on and hands the hose to Tommy as she continues to scan the alley for any signs of life. "Man, I swear I'm gonna kill you for this, Bethany!"

His threat is sputtered by the flow of water hitting Tommy in the face, but it's still sincere to him, as he tries to wash the painful deterrent from his eyes. Minutes seem to pass like hours to Tommy before the effects of the spray finally release their hold on him. As his eye sight slowly returns, he is able to see the anxiety on his coworker's face. "Damn girl, what's got you all stirred up?"

Beth looks back down the alleyway one more time, only to see what looked like a pair of red eyes glowing in the dark, looking back at her. "I want to go, Tommy. Let's get out of here, now!" Tommy can see that Beth's fear is genuine, and enough to make Tommy a little uneasy as well. The two person news crew makes their way back down the street to their rental car, finding the vehicle with a flat tire. "Oh great, now what do we do?"

Tommy pulls off his shirt and throws it in a nearby trash can to be rid of the pepper spray once and for all, and grabs a t-shirt from his bag in the back seat. "The first thing we need to do is calm your ass down and see about getting this tire changed." Pulling the fresh shirt down over the rolls of his belly, Tommy takes notice to a large silhouette passing overhead. It happens so fast that he has no time to verify what he thought he saw, which adds to his nervousness brought on by Beth's actions. "Now see what you've done? You've gone and made me jumpy too! As soon as we change this tire, we'll be out of here as quick as possible. Are you alright?" He asks, as he makes his way around to the trunk of the car.

Bethany appears to be caught in a full blown bout of anxiety as she continues to scan every face in every crowd. "I'm telling you, Tommy, that crazy bitch from Landry's house is messing with my head. I'm almost positive that it was her I seen when we went to the student's aunt's house, and I know I saw her in the restaurant a little while ago. It was her in the alley playing her game, and the reason I sprayed you with pepper spray!"

"Yeah well, if she can sprout wings, it was probably her that flew overhead, just a second ago too." Tommy's input lets his sarcasm flow freely about the way Beth is acting.

"Are you serious?" She quickly looks to the night sky to see if there was any sign of Sonny. Tommy may doubt her, but Beth has a bad feeling that Sonny is a danger to both of them. Her coworker on the other hand believes that Beth is the only one he has to worry about, as usual. "Listen, I'm gonna sit in the car while you do this, okay Tommy?" The sight of the three slashes in the sidewall of the tire is enough to make her climb into the car and lock the doors. Tommy just shakes his head at her antics as he pulls the spare tire and jack from the trunk of the car. He knows that the sooner he gets this chore done, the sooner she will calm down and they can continue on the next leg of their journey.

"Good evening, this is Sandra Brown of YWTK, reporting for Bethany Phelps outside the Los Angeles International Airport. As you can see, there is a large crowd gathering behind me, but it is not for your typical Hollywood celebrity or Political Dignitary. No, this is for the arrival of the now infamous mass murderer, Nickolas Landry, who will be arriving here in a few minutes. Landry is being flown back here from Tokyo Japan where he fled to avoid the charges facing him here. Several accomplices have been connected to Landry's activities but deny an involvement. Federal officials believe that they have enough evidence gathered already for a strong conviction even without any outside testimony. Do you want to know more? Catch our show by Bethany Phelps this weekend to see her full expose on Nickolas Landry, the man and the life. That's all for now, from LAX, I'm Sandra Brown, saying Goodnight America."

The camera man cuts the feed and waves his fingertips in front of his throat, signaling it a wrap. "That's it, Sandi."

She tosses her microphone to the camera man and starts for the van. "Hurry up and get me home, Mike, so I can figure out what that bitch owes me, for this one."

"Wake up, Mr. Landry. We have arrived at Los Angeles International." Delaney gives Nick a gentle nudge to the shoulder as the plane comes to a stop. The guards jump to their feet and stand at attention as JD and Nick begin to wake up from their restful sleep. Both men feel refreshed and ready to take on the world again, until they remember their current situation. The guards begin to exit off the plane in single file as Delaney gives Nick and JD the update to what's going on. "Okay, you two, evidently it has leaked out about you coming home. So to avoid the masses of hysterical people, we're offloading on the runway, where Federal authorities will be taking over to deliver the two of you first to the Federal Building downtown, where you will be readmitted into the country, and debriefed before continuing on to Florida. To avoid a situation in Miami like the one we have here, you will be flown back to West Palm and then driven down to Miami." Delaney walks away from the detainees and stands at the door watching for the vehicle to arrive.

Looking over to his sensei, JD takes notice to how passive and compliant Nick is being with his current situation. "Nick, what are we going to do? You can't stand trial for what's happened, not when it wasn't your fault."

"JD, you are going to do exactly what I told you to do. I have to ride this out alone. The last thing I need is for you to become involved in this affair any more than you already are. I can't focus on what I need to do, if I'm worried about you screwing up your chances at a normal life." Nick hangs his head, knowing that JD is sincere in what he wants to do, but

Nick has to stay this course. It hurts to turn JD away, but it is what he has to do.

"Okay you two, the car's here. Let's move out and make it quick." Delaney motions for Nick and JD to follow him out of the plane. Delaney is more than ready for this mission to be over. For whatever reason, there are too many ties, and loose ends, connected to Nick and some of Delaney's questionable associations. The sooner he is away from all of this, the better. His men line up in two columns as Delaney, Nick, and JD exit the plane. "I'm Major Delaney of DSC," he explains as the female agent exits the SUV. "By order of the US Government, I deliver these two into your custody."

"Good evening, Major Delaney, my name is Special Agent Kimberly Andrews. I accept, and relieve you of your duty," she replies, motioning for Nick and JD to get into the vehicle. "You've had a long day, Major. Is there anything I should know about these two?"

"Only that Landry shouldn't give you any trouble. I think he's already done what he's going to do. The kid, he's a cream puff. Just remember the two of them just escaped from a Yakuza stronghold, leaving over a hundred men dead or dying. So, I wouldn't lock the safety on your weapon, just to be safe." Delaney turns and faces JD, giving the young man a farewell salute.

Agent Andrews climbs into the SUV and motions for the driver to take off as she closes the door. With two more cars in front, and two more in the back, the caravan exits the airport only to be swarmed by the groups of protestors who were trying to get a glimpse of the mass murderer. The scene is really too much to bare. He was a decorated officer, having served this country to protect the people that live here, these very same people that crowd around the cars cursing and swearing at Nick as they drive slowly by. Now, he has the second duty accepting his destiny to save the world from darkness. He does this for these very same people as well. The problem is that all it has brought him is pain and suffering. His life has been destroyed because of it all, with the public eye seeing him as nothing but a criminal lowlife. Gratitude sure has a funny way of showing itself.

The drive through LA is a little more enticing for JD than the rest. This is actually his first trip to the west coast, and he is anxious to see what all the hype is about. Unfortunately, the glitz and glamour of it all isn't anywhere to be seen at this time of night. Maybe it'll look better in the morning.

The SUV pulls up in front of the Federal Building downtown, where a cast of twenty Federal agents await their arrival. Andrews steps from the vehicle first, followed by Nick and JD who are quickly whisked away into the building. Not a word is said as the group of Agents crowd around Nick and JD as they wait for the elevator. JD can't stand the awkward silence. He has to say something. "So, how about them Lakers? Are they gonna get another championship?" Everyone turns and looks at JD, as if warning him that they would shoot to kill if he opens his mouth again. The elevator doors open with a "ding", signaling everyone to enter the lift. With the doors closed, the elevator takes off at a rapid speed, having them arrive at their designated floor in no time at all. Agent Andrews is the first to get off and leads the group down the hall to a secured room. After unlocking the door, she motions for two of the guards to escort Nick and JD inside, and then dismisses the rest of the agents. "And, somebody get these two clowns a couple of sweat suits or something, before I have to parade them through town again." Andrews then heads off down the hall, once her prisoners are secured with the door closed and locked. The two men take their assigned positions on either side of the door, while Nick calmly takes a seat with JD walking in circles around the table. A minute or two later, another agent arrives with Department issue sweat suits for Nick and JD to wear.

The sound of keys hitting the lock again causes both men to look at the door. Nick does this slow and easy, while JD is more unsettled and quick. The door swings open revealing Agent Andrews with a stack of files over three inches thick. My name is Special Agent Kimberly Andrews," she declares as she drops the stack of paperwork onto the table. "You sit down," The Agent commands, pointing her finger at JD. Andrews then takes her seat across from Nick and waits for JD to sit down at her left. "Do you know what these are? These files are all that's left of your victim's lives." Andrews is quick to notice JD's surprised look about her statement. It was a test, a harsh one, but it gave her the answer she needed. Before continuing with her interrogation, she motions for one of the guards to take JD out of the room. "So, why don't you tell me where we should start with all of this? That way, we can sort all of this out, so we can find you a nice cell, until your execution."

"Why did you put on that little show for JD?"

"It was a test to see how innocent he really is. Now, answer my question."

"Nick's expression goes unchanged. He looks as if he is innocent with nothing to worry about, or he is so guilty that he doesn't even care. "My dear Agent Andrews, we both know that there is no hard evidence that links me directly to these deaths as the culprit. This truth like all of the rest will come out in the end. I assure you."

Andrews lets out a grunt and slams her hand down on the table. She isn't sure if it is confidence or arrogance, but his display pisses her off just the same. "Okay, tough guy, let's start at the beginning then." She rifles through the files and pulls out her selection. "Okay, here we have Sonya

Richards, former Navy SEAL, your roommate and current whereabouts unknown. Where is she, karate man?"

Nick's calm demeanor slips a little with Andrews' accusation hitting too close to home. "Hold on a minute, sister, but you need to recheck the facts. Sonny was gunned down by the men who robbed the nightclub, and the last time I tried to get in to see her, I was stopped at the nurse's station. So, where she's at is hard for me to say. My best suggestion for you is to pick up her trail at the hospital and see where it leads you."

Andrews opens another file and continues, "Here we have one Calvin R. Brewster. He was a small time thug, until the night Richards was shot. Witnesses at the nightclub fingered him as the ringleader of the robbery. Later he's found dead on board a yacht that ran aground in Biscayne Bay. Would you care to elaborate about this?"

Nick responds quickly, catching Andrews off guard. "Tell me about the part in there of how a lone vigilante foiled the robbery and took chase in my car. Maybe you should be asking him about Mr. Brewster's demise."

"How did he get your car?"

"I gave him the keys when he asked for them. I didn't want any more trouble than I already had with Sonny being shot." Nick sits back to see how this hand will play out.

Andrews laughs sarcastically at Nick's statement. "Yeah, we know about this so-called vigilante. You wouldn't know how to get in touch with him, would ya? He's facing a whole butt load of charges of his own, back in Atlanta. But, let's move on and try to stay on track, shall we? Now, while you're under investigation for conspiracy, murder, aiding and abetting, and one count of piracy, you flee the country, making yourself a wanted felon. Your alibi is that young Johnston out there was kidnapped and taken to Japan, where you had to go to pay the ransom demands. Ya know, I don't see in here anywhere what those demands are…" Andrews flips through the papers one more time, "…No, it isn't in here anywhere. Would you care to elaborate on that?"

Nick gives her a confident smile. "Sure Agent Andrews, I can do that for you. You see, a long time ago, my Master, or Sensei if you will, came to America and brought with him a family heirloom. It meant everything to the Masamoto family, so much so that when they found out he had died, they came to me for it. When I refused to release it, because of my Master's last wish, they took JD hostage to force me to return it. Thus I went to Japan." Nick loves the hand he has just played and sits back to see how Andrews will counter.

"So, you're saying that you killed all of those people, risked the lives of countless more, and hijacked a military plane just to save one boy?"

"No, what I'm saying to you is that I made my way to Japan. Those people killed were not so by my hand."

Andrews pulls out a note pad and jots down a few notes about what Nick had said. "According to the Japanese authorities, you are responsible for single handedly dismantling one of the largest Yakuza families in Japan. Of course, they are pissed as hell at how you went about it. According to the numbers, you left behind one hundred and twenty seven bodies, but that's not a total. Evidently they are still pulling bodies out of the ashes and trying to match up some body parts before releasing a solid number." Andrews leans in over the table a little. "I knew you SEAL guys were good and all, but damn! Tell me something; was the boy wonder in on that blood bath, or are you going to take the fall for it all." She looks up to see that Nick's smile was gone, and he was staring at her with a straight face. "You're right, that's not my problem. That one belongs to you. Getting back to your problems, why did you kill you former CO? First you go to him to catch a flight to Japan, and then kill him to cover your tracks, right? Be warned, the Navy is pushing to get their hands on you first for all of the service men you killed at the airfield."

Nick sits up and leans forward, placing his hands on the table. "Lieutenant Commander Mitchell was my friend. He repaid a debt to me by getting me on that flight. What happened to him after I left is, and was, out of my hands? I will tell you this much. The person responsible for his death, and the deaths of the servicemen at the airfield, was the same person who was trying to stop me. Her body will be found in the wreckage of the C-130." Nick leans back, not wanting to give the wrong impression.

"So, you're telling me that a woman is responsible for killing fourteen servicemen and boarded a Navy plane without being spotted?"

"Oh, come on, Agent Andrews; don't try to come off like your male counterparts. I'm sure you can be a badass when you want to be. Sure a woman is capable of doing what I said, especially when the woman is Yukia Masamoto. She trained all her life to kill." Nick leans back in his chair and crosses his arms again.

Suddenly, Kimberly Andrews becomes a little uncomfortable with the situation. "How did you get out of those restraints?"

Nick reaches down and retrieves both sets of shackles and lays them on the table. "You mean these? They were starting to hurt my wrists and ankles. I don't see a need for them any way, if I can get out of them that easily." Nick leans forward again and looks Andrews in her eyes. "Look, I'm innocent, but more importantly, I need a ride home. So, that makes me more than willing to cooperate with you completely." Nick leans back again to wait for her reply.

"Well, if you're willing to cooperate completely, would you mind putting them back on?"

Nick just smiles at her. "Do you really think it would help?"

Kimberly is more than capable of seeing his point. "I'll tell you what I'm going to do. You wait here while I go check on our transportation, and get the paperwork I need for your friend to legally reenter the country. You relax for a minute, and I'll be right back." Kimberly Andrews can't get out of the room fast enough. Being in a locked room with a guy who is accused of killing over a hundred men doesn't bother her, but when she found out he was unrestrained, she became very nervous. Nick has somehow set off her early warning system and she doesn't know how to take it. It's not that he seems dangerous. It's more like he knows something that no one else should know. "There is something spooky about this guy. Shoot him if he moves." She orders before leaving the room. Once out of the room, she walks to the end of the hall where she hides around the corner to try and regain her composure. This case seems to be getting more and more eerie by the moment. There was more to the deaths of the servicemen than she was willing to divulge in her conversation wit Nick. Mostly because the descriptions of how the bodies were torn apart, as if they were savagely attacked by some kind of wild animal. Yes, there is more to this story, and Nick for that matter. The good detective inside her wants to find out what it is. Her desire for self preservation may have a different outlook on the situation.

Just as she is about to head back to Nick's room to face the music again, a late night shift assistant comes rushing out a nearby door, startling her and surprising himself by running into her. "Oh, Agent Andrews, I'm so sorry. I was actually coming to tell you that your car is waiting for you down in the motor pool. They are prepared to take you to a private airfield, where a plane is waiting to take you and the prisoners to Palm Beach International." When you land in

Florida, Agents from Miami will be waiting to escort you down to Miami. Your contact there is a field agent, his name is Wallace Alexander. The young agent follows her all the way back to the interrogation rooms where he sees JD and his attire, causing the young agent to give the young man an odd look. Andrews taps the agent on the shoulder trying to regain his attention. "Good boy, now go tell them that we are on our way." Andrews looks over at JD who was staring back at her. "Let me ask you something, kid. How well do you know that man in there?" She asks, pointing at the room holding Nick.

JD stands up and faces Agent Andrews. "I know this much, Nick is a stand up guy that has helped more people than you could ever imagine. I trust him with my life, and he is my best friend. Because of that, and what I've seen in the past few days, there is no way I could ever believe he's done anything that you hold charges for."

"Well, I hope for his sake that his lawyers can prove you right. We'll be moving out as soon as I gather up the star of this traveling side show." Andrews enters the room to find Nick demonstrating a meditation exercise to the two guards in the room with him, while he sits on top of the table. "Okay Buddha, let's move out."

Nick doesn't open his eyes, but he does reach out and lift the stack of files and hands them to her. Then he grabs the shackles and chains and lifts them, "Should I put these back on?" He asks, finally opening his eyes. His question doesn't come across as sincere, but she can appreciate him asking.

"Do you think it will really matter?" She motions for him to move out after accepting her files from him. "Besides, if you try anything, I will have every agent accompanying us to shoot to kill not only you but your friend as well."

"That's pretty harsh, don't you think?" Nick asks, trying

to get an idea on where she was coming from with that statement.

"Let's just say it's another test, to see how much the kid means to you." Andrews takes the lead out of the room and motions for JD to follow as well. His chaperones fall in behind him as the caravan of agents and prisoners make their way downstairs to the motor pool. Once in the underground garage, they climb into a waiting unmarked sedan that pulls out of the motor pool as soon as everyone is inside. The drive is short when you consider LA traffic, mostly due to the early morning hours. Andrews just stares out the window as they drive through town. She can't help but wonder if anything else will come to surface connected to this case. Nick's calm, cool, demeanor only makes her that much more uncomfortable. Deep down inside, she shares Major Delaney's desire for this to come to a speedy end. Four and a half hours flying across country is not going to make that happen any quicker for her. She can't explain why, but she is beginning to question herself about Nick's guilt and innocence, and what is true involvement is with all of this.

# Chapter XXI

Nick and JD wake up as the small jet lands on the runway at Orlando International airport. Neither one of them can believe that they slept the entire flight across country. Well rested, both men are ready to face what the morning had to offer.

"Oh good, the two sleeping beauties have finally woke up." Agent Andrews walks back to Nick and JD's seats. "I've got some good news and some bad news. The good news is that we didn't crash in the Tropical Depression that is pounding the southern half of Florida right now. The bad news is that we had to reroute to Orlando, to avoid flying into the storm. This also means that we will be driving right through the center of it all."

"So, we're not in West Palm Beach right now? That's cool; I've never been to Disney World before." JD stands and stretches his arms, and moves his head side to side, cracking his neck."

"Yeah, but like I said, we were rerouted. Now stop doing that, it sounds disgusting. And, by the way, I've got some more bad news for you. You're still not going to see Disney World, except from the Highway, if you're lucky." Andrews turns away from Nick and JD to escort them off the plane. As the trio reaches the exit hatch leading to the stairs, a black sedan pulls up in front of the Agents, stationed at the bottom of the stairs. One agent opens the door, allowing Andrews to walk straight down the stairs and into the car, with Nick and JD following close behind her. The transfer happens in seconds with no problems or delays. This makes Andrews a happy girl. As soon as the door is closed, two more sedans pull up to collect the other agents assigned as escorts. The three vehicles accelerate across the runway and head for a maintenance access, away from the crowded terminal. As they approach the fencing, stationed police officers open the gates allowing the three cars to disappear into the city unseen. Their route has already been predetermined to take them straight to the Florida turnpike, headed south for Miami.

Once settled in for the trip, everyone sits back and remains quiet for the drive. The last thing JD wants is to try and start up another conversation with anyone, so he just stares out the window at the storm they are heading into. Suddenly, Kimberly sits up in her seat and turns to face Nick. She's kind of surprised to see him sitting there with his eyes closed, and yet he responds to her movement. "Yes, Agent Andrews, is there a question?"

"Stop doing that stuff, before you freak me out, but yeah, I've got a question for you. You said that you went to Japan with a valuable family heirloom, to use as ransom for Junior's life, right? If this heirloom is so valuable, and your master didn't want them to have it, where did it go?"

"Just for the record, Agent Andrews, that was two questions. As for the second question, to be honest with you, I'm not sure of its exact location. You see, in all of the chaos of freeing JD, I was separated from it, and it is now lost to me. Yes, it was probably very valuable, but obviously JD's life was worth more to me than a chunk of gold." Nick lets a half smile curl the sides of his mouth. This is brought on by the knowledge that she is easily unsettled by what she doesn't understand. He never opens his eyes, but knows that she is staring at him intensely, to see if his eyes are truly closed tight. After a moment or two, he then senses her sitting back against the seat and picking up her files.

Miles, and minutes, pass as the cars fight the weather down the roadway. Kimberly's phone interrupts the silence, signaling that she has a message. "The name you gave me checks out. According to Interpol, Yukia Masamoto once killed thirteen Buddhist monks and then vanished while in Japanese custody. I guess the only way to know for sure if you were telling the truth, is when they dig the rest of that plane out of the surf." Kimberly looks over at JD as he squirms around in his seat, trying to be as inconspicuous as possible. "What the hell is your problem, Johnston?"

JD opens his eyes and looks at Agent Andrews with a sympathetic stare. "Sorry lady, but I haven't had a chance to go pee since we got off the plane in LA. I really gotta go, so can you have a little mercy?" To emphasize his necessity, JD crosses his left leg over his right, and leans forward a little.

Andrews leans forward too, tapping the driver on the shoulder. "How long before we reach Miami?"

The driver looks back over his shoulder before answering, "Three or four hours on a good day, but in weather like this, you better add a couple more hours to that. There's a service center coming up in about twenty or thirty minutes. By then, the sun should be up and might clear out some of this weather."

"Good, try to get there as fast as you can without killing us, before we have an accident back here on the upholstery." Andrews looks over and gestures with her thumb, pointing JD out as the possible culprit.

"I can't believe the luck I'm having!" Bethany stands out in the pouring rain, staring at their rental car that is buried in the mud, up to its axles on the side of the road. "First they reroute his flight to Orlando, then you drive right off the road and get us stuck!"

Tommy has had it with Beth's Pompous, self serving attitudes. The time has finally come for him to dish out a little of what he's been receiving all of these years. "Now you listen to me, Ms. Bethany Phelps. I have taken your shit for far too long, and it is going to stop right now! You're the reason we're standing on the side of the highway, instead of laying on some beach in Hawaii. You're the reason I've been driving through a hurricane instead of sleeping in my hotel room, just so you can get your scoop. So, when I tell you that I swerved back there to avoid someone's gazebo, I did it to save both of our lives. Ya know, the other guys were right. I've been a fool to play the role of your lackey. Sure the perks were great, but how many times does a guy have to be pepper sprayed, or locked up, before he takes a stand." Tommy just throws his hands down and starts to walk up the side of the turnpike.

Feeling really humbled, Beth takes off after her partner to beg for forgiveness. She knows that what he said was true, and she knows that she hasn't given Tommy the credit that was due. She always believed he was happy enough with what was given, and took him for granted. It is an arrogant thought, being that little was rarely handed out. "Tommy, please wait for me." Beth slips in the mud along the emergency lane and takes a step up onto the asphalt, when a truck passes by showering her with the runoff from the road surface. Tommy turns around just in time to see karma bite her on the butt, as she is drenched by the passing truck. He laughs at her reaction to the onslaught of water, and walks back to her with his anger already subsiding. "I'm sorry for spraying you in the face with pepper spray," she sobs. "And I'm sorry for blaming you for my bad luck, okay?"

Tommy moves her matted wet hair off of her face to reveal her makeup melting down her cheeks. "Jesus girl, you look pathetic. Come on, there's another one of those service centers just up the road. Maybe they have a tow truck that can pull the car out."

"Was it like a wooden gazebo?"

Tommy smiles, even though he is now soaked to the bone. "No, it looked like one of those yard tents, with the framework all twisted up by the wind. If you weren't so wrapped up in your work, you would have seen it heading right for the windshield."

The small fleet of southbound sedans takes the off ramp to the service center located between the north and southbound lanes of the turnpike. It's designed to service both and maintain the separate flow of traffic. All three cars pull over to the side of the parking lot, away from the buildings, where four of the Federal Agents exit the cars and make their way over to the service center to assess the situation. A few minutes later, two of the agents return and approach Andrews' window. "Everything is clear. We're ready when you are, ma'am."

Kimberly looks over at JD. "Make it quick, son. I don't like being late." Andrews dismisses her man standing outside in the rain and opens the door to let JD out of the vehicle. Of course, she has to get out, to let JD out, which becomes comical when JD tries to rush out of the vehicle, needing to relieve his bladder. Kimberly was trying everything she could to try and keep dry, and the two of them dance around trying to get out of each other's way. Even with one of her men holding an umbrella, for her, she is still soaking wet before she can get back into the car. JD just shrugs his shoulders at her stern look, and pulls the hood of his sweat shirt up over his head, and heads towards the building.

The parking lot is sparsely occupied with random cars and trucks that had pulled in to wait out the storm. Just then, a big rig races down the turnpike, throwing up a wake of rainwater off the roadway from under its tires. It doesn't startle JD, but the flash of lightning and the roar of thunder, causes him to jump.

Once under the awning of the entrance, JD starts to shed the rain water from his arms and legs, slinging it all over the agents who were hurrying over to keep up with him. He opens the door and then gestures for them to go first. Both agents frown and insist that they follow JD wherever he is going. Inside, the doors open up to a large corridor that runs between the service bays and the truck stop style convenience store, with shelves littered with knick knacks, snacks, and 70s country music CDs. Patrons meander through the aisles looking at the dime store novelties while waiting out the storm. Judging by the looks on their faces, they are bored, tired, and sick of traveling. JD knows exactly how they feel.

Above his head is an information sign pointing the way to the restroom at the end of the corridor, on the left. With his chaperones pointing the way, JD heads straight for the restroom, ignoring the agents' requests for him to wait. At the door of the men's restroom, he finds two more agents standing guard. "Geez, if you guys are here for assistance, you're standing at the wrong door. I've got this completely under control."

"Just get in there and get this over with," one of the men commands.

"Ya know, I think I'm gonna call you mirrors from now on." JD declares before heading into the restroom. His remark was aimed at the agent's desire to wear his sunglasses even in the early morning hours, but the agent didn't catch on, or care.

"Hold on there a minute," One of JD's escorts demands. Did either of you check out the facilities to make sure that everything is clear?"

"Yeah, but if you feel the need to do it again, go ahead." One of the other agents replies.

The overzealous agent motions for JD to wait a minute while the agent enters the restroom, one more time. A few seconds later, he opens the door and waves JD in. "Okay, it is all clear in here."

"Oh, thank you sir, I feel so safe now, to piss." JD rolls his eyes at the way the agent was acting like a prick. He rushes passed the agent, blocking his path to exit the stall as JD hurries into the first stall. Not wanting to be a spectator, the agent exits the facilities, only to be called back in again by JD. "Hey Mirrors, do a guy a favor and bring me some toilet paper in here. This stall is empty. Hold your breath though, because it smells like something died in here!" The agent at the door drops his head, and pushes the restroom door open, bracing himself for the worst. To his surprise, and relief, JD is standing in front of him, smiling proudly. "Gotcha," he declares, exiting the door and drawing a couple of smiles from the other agents. "You weren't watching me, were you?" His question frustrates the agent even more, giving JD a little satisfaction for the way this is being handled. He's sure that if these guys really knew what happened in Japan, they would all see Nick in a different life. They head back outside to find that the storm is still as mean as ever. Once inside the car, JD looks over at Kimberly and says, "Thank you, ma'am."

Nick looks to Andrews, "a little mercy for me too? Meditation can only do so much for a guy."

Andrews rolls her window back down to stop her men from getting in their cars. "Hold on guys, the star of the show needs to go now. I want eyes on him at all times, understand?" She waves at the driver, telling him to unlock Nick's door. "You get out over there. I'm not getting back out there again."

Nick gives her an understanding nod and exits the car on the other side, as the agents move around the trunk of the car to accompany him into the building. There is no urgency on their part any more. None of them believe their suits could get any wetter. Nick enters the service center and runs through the same scenario that he taught JD. "Always be aware of your surroundings, and everyone in it, at all times." The same moping faces look back at Nick and the Federal agents as if surprised to see a second man in a grey sweat suit, being escorted by men in black suits. When the patrons begin to whisper to one another, Nick turns away slightly to conceal his identity, and moves on to the restroom. One agent motions for his coworkers to wait at the door and for one other agent to follow him and Nick into the restroom. A young boy walks over and stares at the agents with wide eyes. "Sorry, but this restroom is temporarily closed. You'll need to come back in a few minutes."

The child never changes his expression. "Is that the President in there?"

"Beat it kid, before I arrest you for obstruction."

Shocked by the agent's reply, the boy's mouth drops open as his sticky bun falls to the floor. "But I'm only nine years old!" Quickly he is snatched away by his mother, who was disturbed by the agent's threat.

One of Nick's chaperones walks over and pushes open the first stall door to inspect the closed space, and then motions for Nick to use it. "Hurry up and no funny business in there." Nick calmly walks into the stall and closes the door. He then sits down and relaxes for the first time in hours, and relieves his bladder. The whole reason he was meditating in the car was because of the strain he was under, keeping the talisman hidden from view. He reaches into his shirt and pulls out the gold chain, revealing the talisman in all its dark glory. "Master Masamoto said that you were going to ruin my life. He sure was on about that, wasn't he?" Nick drops the medallion back into his shirt, back in his shirt, once he realizes that he said the words out loud.

"What did you say in there?"

"I said there isn't any toilet paper in here." Nick flushes the toilet and exits the stall to see the agent wearing a sour expression. "What?"

"Your buddy already tried to get me with that one," The agent explains. "The two of you shouldn't use the same jokes all the time. But then again, he won't be going where you're going, now will he?" Suddenly, the lights flicker, and then flicker again a few seconds later, before going out completely. "Don't move a muscle, Landry."

"Man, are all of you Federal boys, this jumpy. It's probably just the storm messing with the electricity." The emergency lights come on revealing Nick standing exactly where he was when the lights went out. The agent, on the other hand, was showing his true courage by moving towards the door, with the other agent pointing his gun at his partner. Outside the door, they hear yelling, and then the sound of leather soled shoes running away from the restrooms. The overzealous agent looks at his partner and then at Nick. "You wait in here with him, while I go see what's going on." He turns and hits himself in the face with the door, before running out into the service center to investigate what's going on. Nick and the other agent stand in the bathroom looking at each other, and then the flickering illumination of the emergency lighting.

Jones exits the restroom and catches fast movement in the food court, out the corner of his eye. The lights flickering in the dining area add to the eerie feeling about the place, as he walks through the death scene. This is not because of the storm. Someone, no, some thing, has slaughtered these poor people, and could still be in the building. Suddenly, he is snatched from his feet and lifted high into the air. A cascade of blood begins to flow, falling to where Agent Jones was standing. His scream echoes through the service center before everything goes deathly quiet.

Agent Kimberly Andrews flips through her files on her lap top computer, trying to pass the time. She looks at her watch, and then looks outside wondering how much longer Nick is going to take in there. "Your friend sure is taking his time. What's he trying to do, delay the inevitable?"

JD slowly turns his head to face Andrews, trying to come up with something witty to say. Before he can answer, he sees Kimberly's eyes grow wide with terror as one of her agents slams against the car window, before slowly sliding down the blood covered glass. JD quickly locks the door beside him and drops down into the floor board of the back seat.

"Landry, you son of a bitch!" Kimberly climbs across the seat, and JD, to get out on the other side. She stops for a moment and stares into JD's eyes. "If you so much as think about getting out of this car, I swear to god I will shoot you myself!" Andrews pulls her pistol and pushes the door open, only to fall out onto the wet pavement. She looks back at JD to make sure he understood her, and then runs off to join the other agents rushing from the other two cars. She directs them to different locations, and then heads for the main entrance with another agent. Immediately, the two Federal agents see the carnage that has taken place. One of her own agents was spread out across the entry's floor lying in a large puddle of his own blood. Over to their right, in the convenient store section, innocent patrons are laid out where they were standing, with their belly's slit open. The cooler doors are splattered and streaked with the blood of the bodies shoved through the glass. Merchandise and shelving are toppled and spilled, accentuating the mayhem that has taken place.

The employees behind the counter didn't weather the chaos any better than anyone else. One attendant was slumped over the cash register with his throat ripped open, with the other seated on the floor where she bled out. Everywhere she turns, there is nothing but death. Her men are everywhere, literally everywhere. Half of Jones is leaning up in the corner. His legs and lower torso is lying on top of the counter beside her. "How could Landry have done all of this so quickly?" One thing is for sure, self preservation is quickly moving up her list of priorities.

"What's going on, Agent Andrews?" Her partner looks around at the horrific scene. Never in his career has he been exposed to such a nightmare.

"I don't know, Johnson. Just keep your eyes open." Out the corner of her eye, Kimberly sees a pair of feet disappear around the counter of the fast food court. She takes off running, leaving her partner standing alone and feeling abandoned. As she reaches the food court, Andrews loses her footing, slipping and sliding on the blood covered tile floor. Dead bodies hang from chairs, and lay face first over the tables. Blood seemed to be dripping from everything and everywhere. Kimberly can't help but wonder how this was all possible for one man to do. Her head starts to swim, when the sight of it all becomes too much for even this seasoned veteran to handle. Her stomach heaves slightly, sending the burning taste of bile up into her throat. No amount of training could prepare anyone for the likes of this.

A sound of something falling back in the kitchen, takes her mind off what has happened out in the dining area, and gives her reason to exit the company of dead bodies. Her partner, Johnson, is even more eager to depart the death scene, leaping over the counter to disappear into the kitchen, before Kimberly has the chance to stop him. Just as she is about to take chase after Johnson, she sees a sign of life over to the side of the dining area. Curious, she hurries over to verify what she thought she saw. There at a table, a truck driver lays over his food with his throat viciously ripped out. Using his finger and his own blood for ink, he uses the rest of the life in his body to write three letters onto the Formica surface. Andrews stares at it for a moment, wondering what it is that the man was trying to say. "Wom? What the hell is wom?"

A man's scream from the kitchen demands her attention. "Damnit, Johnson." Across the food court she runs and stops at the order counter to look into the darkness of the kitchen. "Johnson," her voice is quiet and timid as she calls out his name. Her actions are slower, and more cautious as she climbs over the counter. Death is all around her with more workers brutally slain and left to litter the kitchen floor. The smoke of burning food blinds her vision as she steps through the bodies, to make her way to the rear of the kitchen. At the end of the row of burners and fryers is the cooler for frozen products, giving her only one option, to turn right at the end of the food prep station. She rounds the corner letting her pistol lead the way, only to see a gruesome sight in the doorway some fifteen feet away. There, hanging upside down in front of the door was Johnson. Gruesome, because his belly had been split open with his entrails hanging down around his neck, like a deer that had been field dressed by a hunter. The sad thing is that Johnson appears to still be alive, and in a severe state of shock with his eyes open wide. On the floor behind her, a can mysteriously rolls out into view. This is the catalyst that sets Kimberly Andrews off. Fear takes total control of her, sending her running to the back door, having to push Johnson aside to escape with her life.

Nick leans back against the sink counter and stares at the agent who is staring back at him. "Dude, tell me you heard that scream," the agent asks. "What do you think is going on?" The agent walks over to the door as if contemplating going out to investigate. "Listen, I read your profile and what is going on doesn't fit you or your style, so I don't think you've got anything to do with it. I just wanna know what you think we should do?"

Nick senses danger, but doesn't want to let on right now. For one, he doesn't think these rookies could handle what Nick expects. "Right now, the only thing we don't want to do is get all worked up over the unknown." Nick could tell that the young agent has never been in a situation like this. The last think Nick needs at the moment is a nervous man with a loaded gun, waving it around in close quarters.

"Yeah, well that's easy for you to say. You were a Navy SEAL for Christ's sake! I'm sure you're completely right at home with death, murder and people disappearing!"

Nick knows that he is starting to lose this guy, and he has to act fast. "What's your name, buddy?"

"Walters, my name is Eric Walters," the agent replies, while staring at the door.

"Okay, Agent Eric Walters, wouldn't you say that it would be wise for us to use my experience, to better our chances and see what's going on out there?" Nick doesn't know what is actually going on, but the best way for him to get any cooperation from his estranged associate is to cater to the man's thought levels. For Nick, this is a simple task of speaking softly to strengthen the man's spirit.

Walters snaps his head around to face Nick. "No, you have to stay here. I'll go check on Barber and the others. You just stay here, until we come back for you." Walters swings the door open and darts out into the service center.

Nick thinks about the situation for about a millisecond, before he reacts. There is something going on and the only way he can find out if it is connected to the talisman is to leave the restroom. As he reaches for the door, a report of a pistol being fired sounds out. This is the last straw, as far as he is concerned. He opens the door slightly and peaks outside. With the power of the talisman, he could move through the building unseen. He hears Walters scream off in the distance, giving Nick the sign that it was clear for him to exit the facilities. Rendering himself invisible, he starts out into the service center and quickly sees the horror of what has taken place. The corridor is filled with a cloud of smoke and steam originating from the food court. The smell of death is strong in his nose. He sees the condition of the convenience store area and wonders how could all of this have happened in such a short time, without him or the agents in the restroom hearing it? What manner of creature could possess such a bloodlust? He has no other choice but to believe that this is some dark creature seeking out the Guardian. If he's right, how did this demonic presence find his location so fast? He could, and probably should, go out to check on JD but morbid curiosity prompts him to see what lies around the next corner. Movement on the other side of the food court catches his eye, but once in the dining area, all he finds is more death. The storm pounds against the window, accentuating the mood of the scene. A body shifts in a chair, where the person was killed, rolling off onto the floor. Contact with the tile surface sounds more like raw meat falling, rather than a person's body, living or dead. Ready to give up, he turns around just in time to see the silhouette of a human form running past the windows outside. Nick takes chase, leaping into the air and diving out through the plate glass window. He hits the ground and rolls up to his feet, but there is no one around. Then, a shadow darts into one of the service bays, but stops at the door to look back at Nick. He realizes that in all of this, he had broken his concentration on the talisman and is visible again. A hundred feet away, and poor visibility, doesn't stop him from keeping with the chase. Whoever that is intentionally stopped to look at Nick, as if daring him to keep the chase going. "Be careful what you wish for, pal."

To Nick, this was a challenge, and it's one he isn't about to turn down. What has happened here will only complicate his life even more. This time, he was going to do all that he can to make sure the villain lives, this time. He takes off at a full sprint, covering the distance in seconds. He is weaponless save one, the talisman. Focusing on it again, Nick renders himself invisible once more, before entering the service bay. Once inside, he begins to scan the area for potential exits and hiding places. To his surprise, there is no sign of life, anywhere. Quietly he walks along the side of the service bay, trying to keep him concealed even though he can't be seen. One thing is for certain, he needs to clear his own name of involvement here, just to keep the list of casualties he's blamed for, from growing any longer. Beside him, a tall metal rack of automotive tires is ripped loose from the floor, and sent toppling over onto Nick's position. His instincts serve him well, recognizing the danger, and giving him the ability to leap clear of the danger. He dives across the floor and rolls up to his feet, just as the heavy metal structure slams against the concrete floor.

Nick is able to take one step before a blow to his back levels him. He was able to avoid the rack, but the tires that were stored on it are now bouncing projectiles heading straight for Nick. He tries to stand, only to be hit by another, and then another and another, until he finally collapses under the weight of it all. One more tire comes in to finish Nick off, clipping him in the head and knocking him out cold.

Kimberly Andrews is now a hysterical wreck. She has searched this entire facility and hasn't found a single person alive. Her trek has taken her from the south bound side to the north bound, with her now skirting the wall of the building. Her pulse races as her heart pounds in her throat. The fact that she is an armed Federal agent eludes her at the moment, authority, jurisdiction, all of that has gone out the window, now. There isn't even any concern for her job, or duty, as far as Nick Landry is concerned. In fact, in her paranoid and terrified delusions, Landry is the one she is trying to escape.

Looking towards the north bound off ramp coming into the rest stop, Kimberly sees two people walking towards the service center through the rain. They have to be warned! As a Federal agent, it is her job, and duty, to keep innocent lives safe from the potential dangers that are involved with her job. Not to mention the fact that she would love to have someone around her that isn't bleeding profusely, or dead. Andrews looks around the parking lot, and then bolts out into the storm, running right towards the two unsuspecting people. "Stop, go back!" She yells through the rain as she approaches the pedestrians. "You don't want to go in there!" She adds before seeing their faces.

"Why, Agent Andrews, what are you doing all the way over here, in Florida?" Bethany is disturbed by the sight of Kimberly, but it is due to the blood splatters on her clothes and the sketchy mental state that is being displayed.

"You! I don't know what you're doing here Phelps, but you need to go somewhere else!" Andrews can't believe the luck she is having. If there is one person in the world that Kimberly Andrews does not want to see at the moment, it is

Bethany Phelps of YWTK. "Both of you need to get out of here now, if you want to keep living!" Kimberly develops a surprised look on her face and then suddenly goes quiet, as her chest is slightly shoved forward toward Beth and Tommy. To the surprise of the two reporters, Sonny suddenly appears behind Agent Andrews as the Federal Agent convulses again. "You shouldn't talk to her like that. Bethany Phelps is my friend!" With that, Sonny pulls her hand from inside Kimberly's back, removing her heart with it. She looks at Beth, and then at Tommy, and back to Beth again before asking, "Who's the fat boy?"

Beth faints at the sight of Sonny taking a bite out of the warm, steaming heart in her hand. Tommy just stands there, paralyzed and pissing all over himself. "Oh, I guess it doesn't matter." She reaches out and slashes his throat so fast, that poor Tommy doesn't even realize that he has been struck, until he collapses to the ground.

# Chapter XXII

Nick opens his eyes, finding himself under a mountain of vulcanized rubber, staring up at the ceiling, through the gaps and holes between the tires. He can see wisps of smoke moving around the rafters of the roof. It takes him a second or two for him realize that these wisps of smoke are moving about in a determined manner. Then, one puff of smoke defies all manner of reason and descends to the floor. The closer it gets, the more Nick realizes that it isn't smoke, but a spirit.

It swoops down onto Nick's position, this spirit of white, with the face of a woman appearing before Nick's eyes. This is one of the people who were killed in the food court. Why does Nick see this? He isn't using the power of the talisman, so how or why he can see them is unexplainable. The woman's spirit moves down through the tires and then passes right through Nick's body. The sensation is painful, but what hurt the most was hearing the woman's voice in his head saying, "You are to blame! You are to blame!"

Before he can recover from the first encounter, another spirit performs the same act, and then another, and another, until all of the white spirits are attacking him exclaiming,

"You are the reason, you are to blame!" Each attack offers more pain, but no explanation as to why this was happening. Why, why are they attacking Nick? He isn't the one who took their lives. His tolerance is quickly diminishing until finally, he retaliates by using the power of the talisman. By simply thinking the thought and focusing, the talisman wills the act to happen. Within a flash, the tires are blown away from him, and the spirits are obliterated by a wave of energy. Seconds later, after the last tire rolling falls over; there is nothing but silence. Nick picks himself up and looks around one more time, wanting to avoid any other chance happenings that might be coming his way.

With his thoughts gathered, Nick uses the talisman again, this time to render himself invisible before exiting the building. The last thing he needs right now is to walk out in plain view without knowing who or what is out there. As he suspected, several travelers have already stopped on the north bound side, and discovered the carnage left on display. The man from one car is hurrying his wife to get back in the car, while she vomits on the front bumper. Another family had already loaded back up, and was making like a bat out of hell to get away from the horror. A trucker is playing the Good Samaritan, directing traffic away from the crime scene. He had seen the bodies lying beside the off ramp due to his advantage of riding high in the cab of the rig. This should make Nick's departure from the southbound side a little easier with no witnesses.

Back through the service bays he runs, checking the status of the southbound side. With the storm moving north, southbound traffic is basically nonexistent. Remaining cloaked from view, Nick's first move is to grab a new battery from the rack, a pair of wire cutters and a roll of wire and electrical tape from a work bench. Then, he heads out the service door headed straight for Andrews' car, building his plan along the way. One thing he doesn't need, or want, is to find JD as a casualty of this macabre event, but he has to know one way or the other. His collection of items is for the next leg of his journey.

He reaches the sedan and finds the agents dead, lying where they fell, but there is no sign of JD anywhere. Nick looks back at the service center wondering if his friend was back inside the building somewhere. If there is a clue for Nick to follow, the first place for him to look is in the car. Opening the door, he sets the car battery on the floor over the transmission, and begins to thoroughly scan the interior of the vehicle. The keys are still in the ignition. There's a half a tank of gas. The driver smokes, or did smoke, having a pack of cigarettes stashed above the visor. One of the agents brought along a copy of yesterday's LA Times, now shoved between the front seats. A cup of coffee is sitting in the passenger seat cup holder. Nick tastes the cup of coffee to check the temperature of the drink. Based on when they left Orlando where the coffee originated, and the tepid temperature, he does the math to determine that he might have been unconscious for about thirty minutes. Moving to the back, Nick turns and looks over the back of the driver's seat where he sees the biggest clue of all. There in the middle of the seat is one of Andrews' files, with a note written in someone's blood, "Hurry home, Nick."

It's all that the note says, but it's enough for Nick to figure out his next move. On the end of the wire cutter's handles are two screw drivers that fold out. Nick claims the Phillips head bit and climbs under the driver's side dash. In a couple of seconds, he has a small black box unfastened from the firewall and pulls the wiring harness down so that he can work. For step two, Nick cuts off two strands of wire about twelve inches in length. He attaches one wire to each terminal post on the battery and secures it with electrical tape. Then he takes the black box and studies the wires for a second. This model has a built in antenna mounted on the side of the box, so all he needs are the power supply wires. Once they're located, Nick uses the wire cutters to strip back the insulation on the selected wires. Then, one at a time, he connects the wires from the battery to the bare spots on the wires to the black box. Nick takes care to wrap each connection with electrical tape to prevent the crossover from shorting out. Successful, he clips the wires one at a time from the dash, freeing the black box from the car. He mounts the box to the battery with a couple of wraps of tape, and then sits it onto the curb beside the car. Now the car can't be tracked through its GPS system. Nick starts the car and puts it in gear, spinning the tires on the wet pavement. As he pulls out onto the turnpike, his mind becomes cluttered by questions and theories about what has happened. One thing is for certain; he alone must find the one responsible for the service center massacre. Otherwise, he'll be spending the next twenty years trying to explain his innocence in the ordeal. Of course, having the hows and whys to his questions answers would be nice too.

His biggest question is who could've done this? It's more than obvious that this is all connected to him, thus the note left on the back seat. The first thing he needs to do is compile a list of suspects. Topping his list should be any and all agents of darkness that is seeking out the talisman. This doesn't help much. When it comes to chaos and madness, his friend, the rebel vigilante comes to mind. Billy can be scratched off his list as quickly as his name is written down. He may be a little crude with his tactics, but Billy's no mass murderer. Besides, what would Billy have to gain by coming after the man who saved his life? No, this was someone who took JD, again, and was sending a personal message to Nick. Thinking about home, for a split second, Sonny crosses his mind, causing him to wonder if she's alright, or even alive. "I sure could use your help right about now, Sunshine."

Driving past the West Palm Beach toll station, Nick takes notice to the fact that it isn't staked out by SWAT or the FBI. He has to get off the turnpike before the Highway Patrol locks down every exit to make things even more difficult for Nick. Knowing what the other side is doing sure would be helpful right about now, and then it dawns on him that his wish could come true. What can make that happen is mounted under the dash, in front of the passenger seat. Switching the car's radio on, Nick hits the channel scan button to hear what's going on.

It doesn't take him long before he hears how the FHP is on the scene and shutting down north bound traffic. Obviously, they were expecting the perpetrator to head north, instead of south, towards the dead end of the country. The FBI are in route, but what he finds troubling is the all points bulletin that's been put out on the sedan with government plates; the one he is driving.

Up ahead, he can see the lights of the next service center coming into view through the down pour. Adapt and improvise, Nickolas Landry. It's what you did best in the Navy. With no other cars around him on the road, Nick drives the car down into the center median and buries it in a thicket of small trees and underbrush. With his mind set on what he has to do, Nick takes off running towards the service center.

His first move is to find a vehicle that he can get a ride in, or at least stow away in, to get off the turnpike. Then it's just a matter of continuing his trek to Miami, and then getting home. That's where the note told him to go. That's where he will find his next clue about what's going on. Once he has that, he can plan out his next series of moves.

Of course, he could've picked his target a little better. Two cars and a U-haul van occupy the service center parking lot, with a tractor trailer sitting off at the end of the parking lot. First, he needs to lose the giant badge that is screen printed on the back of his sweat shirt. Walking inside wearing this would be a death sentence for sure, or would at least draw unwanted attention to him. His first option is strapped to the top of one of the cars. With unrivaled speed, skill, and ability, Nick quickly pulls the first suitcase down, and scores. Inside, right on top, is a larger sweatshirt and a ball cap. He isn't happy with this situation, but drastic times require drastic measures.

With his clothes changed, Nick checks his surroundings one more time before he walks over to the building. Along the way, he finds himself second guessing his actions before he walks inside. Now, he has stooped to stealing. What will be next, a series of blatant lies? Has he reacted too soon? Should he have traveled a little further down the road? The car was okay on gas, so it wasn't like that was a concern. Maybe he could have made it to the next service center.

Nick quickly dismisses all of it, knowing that self doubt is his worst enemy. He opens the door and enters, running into a family leaving the cash register. Nick heads straight down the corridor to the restrooms to avoid the kids. He doesn't want to put any children in harm's way. Suddenly, the women's restroom door opens, revealing a heavy set woman wearing a cowboy hat, probably in her late forties, early fifties. "Well, hey sugar, if you're waiting for someone else to come out of there, you're out of luck. If you're waiting for me, then my luck is definitely changing for the better." The lady lets the door close, causing it to push her just a little closer to Nick.

Nick gives her a courteous smile and backs up a little. "No ma'am, to be honest, I'm not sure what I should be doing right now. Me, and my girlfriend, had a big argument, and she took off in my car, with my wallet, and all of the money still in the glove box."

Man that hurt more for Nick than anyone could know. Mr. Honesty feels like the lie left the worst taste possible in his mouth. Even a little white lie to aid his dire situation troubles him.

The overly friendly woman offers Nick a huge smile. Well damn, darlin', if you need a ride, all you have to do is ask? Hell, I'm heading all the way into Key Biscayne. You just tell me where you want me to drop you off. It's as simple as that!" The lady trucker sticks out her hand after forgetting her manners. "The name's Shirley, by the way. What's yours?"

"Nick," he replies, not thinking about what he is saying. To make himself feel better, he can blame the lapse of intelligence on the fact that he was distracted by the guilt of lying to the lady. It still doesn't change the fact that he has just identified himself as the Nation's number one most wanted man.

"Are ya hungry, Nick? I was gonna grab a couple of sandwiches for the road. It's my treat, if you're hungry." Shirley walks away headed for the food court, with Nick remaining behind. Standing in front of the restroom seems out of place to him, but he can't help but just stand there, wondering what his next move should be. Hanging out in the public eye is not his first choice. Shirley can give him a ride, but the longer he waits, the tighter the noose will close in around him. His decision is simple. The best thing for Nick to do is go back outside and wait for Shirley by her truck. There's only one in the parking lot, so it shouldn't be too hard to figure out which one is hers. "I figured there had to be a reason why you were lollygagging. Since you were standing in front of the bathrooms when I met ya, was because you needed to drain the pipes like all the rest of us. I woulda' helped you with that if ya needed it. Any way, I just doubled my order, and figured that beggars can't be choosers, right?" Shirley declares, handing Nick the sack of sandwiches and drinks. Proud of her good deed, Shirley then turns and heads for the door.

The odd couple exits the convenience store and walks passed the service bays ignoring the rainfall. One of the mechanics walks over to an open bay door and looks out at the dreary weather. "It looks like it might clear up soon. You be careful out there, Shirley. Something happened up the road at another service center. FHP is shutting down the turnpike all the way to Orlando." The mechanic looks Nick over as they walk by, suspicious of his association with the truck driver. "Who's your friend, Shirley?"

"Who, this guy," She spreads a wide grin across her wider face. Why, he's my new love toy, Carl. Are ya jealous?" Shirley turns to Nick and gives him a wink. "Say hello to Carl, and then get on up into my truck." She gives the mechanic a tip of her cowboy hat and continues on to her rig. "You try to stay dry, Carl. You don't want to get sick again. Not when you've got eight mouths to feed"

Nick looks up at the truck and almost drops the sandwiches, "aw man!" There in all its glory, sits a long nose Peterbilt painted as pink as it could be. If Nick can't see that he is having the worst kind of luck, then he needs to reconsider his point of view. "I bet the astronauts in the space shuttle can spot this thing from space," he thinks to himself. "So much for finding an inconspicuous ride to Miami," Nick climbs up into the passenger seat of the cab, closes the door and leans his head on the cold window glass. If this ends any way but bad, Nick will be happily surprised.

Shirley doesn't shut her mouth the whole trip into Miami. The woman even talked while eating her lunch and dinner. It was Nick's assumption that Shirley was combining the two meals. There's no way he could eat two foot long deli subs and still be hungry again for dinner. There's no doubt at all that Shirley has been without any companionship for quite some time, and she was making up for it with Nick. It got so bad that at one point, he actually tried to drown her out by forcing down one of the sub sandwiches. Nick swears that he could feel his arteries hardening as he swallowed the oil soaked, heavy meat sandwich. It probably wouldn't have been so bad, if it was food that he was accustomed to eating.

The exit from the turnpike was uneventful, but Shirley has just about driven Nick to the point where a police confrontation could be a welcome thing. The truck rolls to a stop at an intersection, causing Nick to look out the window. He was hoping for something, anything that would take his mind off of Shirley's ongoing babble. What he sees is far better than a distraction. "Whoa, hey we're here. Shirley, you've been a gem. I'll just say my goodbye and get out here. There's no way you could get this big rig in and out of my neighborhood streets." Nick gives her a smile and opens the door.

"Are you sure? Well, I hope everything works out for you and your girlfriend." Shirley gives him a salute goodbye and down shifts the transmission.

"Yeah, sorry I hit you with that one," Nick replies, apologizing the best way he can, for lying to her.

"No problem, darlin', sometimes it's better to talk things out. You take care now, ya hear?"

Nick closes the door and steps down off the truck to the curb as the traffic light changes to green. Shirley honks the horn of her truck and rolls on down the road. Some day, she'll brag to other drivers how she picked up the infamous Nick Landry on the Florida turnpike, and survived to tell about it.

Standing at the intersection, Nick watches her truck disappear around the corner two blocks away, and makes a mental note that she has to be one of a select few who haven't died because of Nick's presence. The rain has passed through Miami, but the low clouds make for a dark, dismal, and dreary day. This could make it easier to get into his house, or it could make it more difficult. With the bad weather threatening, there are fewer eyewitnesses on the streets. But, then again, it also means that he'll stand out being the only one moving about. This will take some time, but he needs to reconnoiter his entire block to know who and what he could be dealing with.

One of the deciding factors for him and Megan to build here was the large park that bordered two sides of his block, complete with jogging trail that meanders through the entire neighborhood. It's the same jogging trail that runs along behind the fence of Nick's back yard. Suited for running, he pulls the hood of his sweatshirt up over his head, and enters the park. Heading in the opposite direction of his house, Nick jogs the entire two mile trail through the neighborhood to end up back at the park.

He stops for a second to catch his breath, and takes the time to look around while getting a drink of water, to see if anyone looks out of place. Then, he takes off again. As he gets close to his house, he spots a car that he can't remember seeing before. The problem isn't the car, but the two men inside it are. If he crosses the street, they are sure to see him. What he needs is a diversion.

To his blessing, three young ladies have come out to run in the fresh air, complete with tight fitting spandex outfits, informing Nick that they are out more for the show, than physical exercise. Nick stops to tie his shoes as the girls reach the other side of the street, slowing to cross safely, in front of the mystery car. While the two men ogle the young ladies, Nick slips around behind the car, and heads on down the jogging path unseen.

Once down the path between the fenced back yards, Nick stops at a section of redwood planking, and grabs the end of the fence and pulls, revealing a gate hidden in the planking. Once inside, he closes the gate and secures it, to make sure no one else comes in this way. A blind man could see that there has been a full on assault on his residence. The evidence of it is everywhere. His hand stacked waterfalls and coy ponds are toppled and running dry. Nick walks over to the largest of the ponds and feels around in the bottom to retrieve a water tight package, six inches wide and three feet long. Now that he is armed again, he can feel better about hurrying home. He looks at the condition of his house and is disgusted by what has happened. Doors and windows are broken out, revealing the multiple points of entry that were used. Cautiously, Nick walks up to the patio door to the kitchen, where the barricade tape warns him to keep out. Someone else has already ignored the warning, so why shouldn't he?

The inside of the house is dark, lacking the usual sunlight that illuminated the rooms. Instead, pale beams of light try to brighten the interior, but the thick overcast skies outside hinder the effort. Still, it's enough that Nick can still see what happened, not too long ago. Standing in the doorway, he can see the moved and toppled furniture. Kitchen drawers have been dumped, and his organized kitchen desk has been ransacked. This is not the way he left his house before going to Japan. Sure the Police are probably the ones who went through here like tornadoes. Hell, Nick's sure that the FBI did their fair share of damage, as well. But, what troubles him enough to use the power of the talisman to enter his own house, is the bloodstains washed across every wall. Whose blood is this? This isn't from one person, so how many people have been killed in Nick's home?

Compelled to see the extent of it all, Nick stumbles

through each room to see body outlines on the floor and the walls painted with innocent crimson red. All he can see is the evidence of death and horror, but there isn't any sign of his mystery nemesis from the service center, or any clues to point him in a different direction. Finally mentally and physically exhausted, Nick slumps down onto the floor of his room and leans back against the wall. Whoever it is that wanted Nick here, here he is. The destined Guardian has reached his breaking point, and he is willing to give his adversaries the opportunity to come to him for once.

It seems like it was only yesterday, when he and Sonny started off their day with their jog on the beach. It's hard to believe everything that has happened in such a short span of time. He wishes there was some way he could find out about Sonny and her condition, but he can't think of one that wouldn't alert the authorities to his presence. For now, he has to stay the course. He was told to come here. This is where he'll stay until he is instructed to go somewhere else. Once he knows JD's situation, then he can move on to find out about Sonny.

Minutes turn to hours with Nick steadfast in his seated position. The sound of a vehicle pulling up out front catches his attention. He cautiously moves to the window and peeks out through the blinds. The vehicle is a local news van, delivering a reporter and camera crew for a live feed on human misery. Nick is miserable right about now. With the news crew out front, it's more than apparent that his reputation has suffered lethal blows from all of this. Even if he is proven innocent, his standing in the community will never recover. Nick remembers again how Masamoto warned him of the dangers of his destiny, and how it will destroy his life as he knows it. Nick always believed that the change his Master spoke of took place, when Yukia and her brother first attacked five years ago. Only now does he see the true devastation of it all.

He tires of waiting, and begins to doze off. Nick tries to fight off the urge, knowing that he would be defenseless, should he fall asleep. Ultimately, he succumbs to the need for rest and closes his eyes to drift off to sleep. If it is his destiny to keep fighting this crusade when he wakes up, then so be it. If it's his destiny to fall to his enemies while he sleeps, then that's fine too. Almost immediately, flashes of images begin to rush through his subconscious, forming plots that dreams are built upon. Then, everything goes black.

# Chapter XXIII

"**W**ake up!" The sound of Masamoto's voice causes Nick to sit up with a start, and take notice of his surroundings. He is no longer sitting on the bedroom floor of his room. Nick is now in another realm, and Masamoto is sitting in front of him with his eyes closed. "Nickolas, why did you go to Japan?"

Nick quickly sits down to respect is Master. He looks around, mapping his new environment. Masamoto had what looked like a ceremonial campsite set up on an ancient battle field. The ground is covered with decayed bodies from battles a thousand years ago. Focusing on his Master, Nick looks at Masamoto as his frustration with his destiny begins to surface. "I did what I had to do. Remember, Master, you were the one who chose me for this destiny. Don't go around questioning my motives!" Nick stares at his Master looking for some kind of response. When one doesn't come, he adds, "Why didn't you come to me sooner? Why didn't you tell me about your friend in Japan?"

"I couldn't."

Why is Masamoto meeting Nick this way? The last time one of these little gatherings took place, it happened in front of the council. Perhaps the old man is trying to give .Nick a little assistance without the head spooks knowing about it. The chain of thoughts actually calm Nick down a little, seeing a glimmer of hope for his faith in Masamoto. "Master, why have you brought me here this way?"

The old man finally opens his eyes and looks at Nick. "Nickolas, you have passed your first two tests, of honor and duty, but the third still waits. I have summoned you to warn you that pursuing this final test will force agents of our cause to move on you. They are poised and ready to strike, with their only goal being the removal of the talisman from your possession."

Nick gives Masamoto a confident smile. "That's easy, Master, thanks for the warning. I'll just write it up that two out of three isn't bad, and drop the whole thing."

"You cannot stop what has already been put into motion."

Nick bows his head for a second. "It's because of JD, isn't?" Nick looks up to see Masamoto's reply. "Hell, why don't I just give it to them, then? In fact, I don't even want it anymore!" Frustrated to no end, Nick stands up and turns away, tired of playing a game where the rules are constantly changing.

Masamoto reappears in front of Nick and shoves him back, to keep him from leaving. "If you step outside the circle of light, you will be lost to the darkness forever!" The old man's frantic demeanor quickly subsides to a more calmed nature. "To take the talisman from you now means that you will be killed in the process. You are now part of it and it is part of you. There will come a day when you will willingly give the talisman to an unlikely ally. He will be the betrayer of the world. Only he possesses the power to destroy the scepter. But, be warned, Nickolas; because of the choices you have made, the council now sees you as a threat to their cause, and sees fit to eliminate that threat, by eliminating you."

Nick has had enough. "Let me get this straight. It's my destiny to safeguard the talisman, and because I have done so, now your friends want me dead? You know, you should have warned me about JD. You should have warned me about it all. Maybe this council of yours shouldn't have dropped the ball on this one, and should have clued me in on a few more things instead of keeping me in the dark!" Masamoto suddenly, becomes frantic again, and begins to look around in all directions.

"Nickolas, you must go! She has returned to seek her vengeance!" Masamoto gives Nick a shove to his chest to send him back.

"No!" Nick takes notice to how he was able to resist Masamoto's demand. "Tell me who has returned! Is it Yukia?"

"Go!" Masamoto hits him again with more force, sending Nick back to his realm. His vision goes black, and then returns just as quick as images and visions begin to flood his mind, showing the history of the talisman, and what waits in the Devastator's realm. The images become so graphic that they force Nick to open his eyes again. At first, his vision is blurry, and he's mentally drained from his encounter with Masamoto. So much so, that he doesn't realize that he is lying on his bed, instead of sitting in the bedroom floor. He tries to shake out the cobwebs from his mind, and rubs his eyes to focus. When he opens them, he sees the grisly images reminiscent of the Service Center massacre.

"Damn Nickels, you had to go and see the old man, didn't ya?" Sonny drops down from the blood stained ceiling and lands on top of Nick's chest. "That just blows my whole surprise I had for you, all to hell and back!" Sonny grabs Nick and rolls off the bed, slinging him across the room to collide with the wall on the other side. "Get up, you son of a bitch! I want you to face me like a man, so that I can kick the shit out of you fair and square, for what you did to me!"

Nick stands and faces his opponent with mixed feelings. This is Sonny, and he holds love in his heart for her. She's also the most lethal person Nick knows. Something has sent her over the deep end, and she's already killed because of it. He's always been the one who could get through to her. Now is the best time for him to give it all he's got, to stop this killing rage that she's caught up in. "Tell me what's going on, Sonny. I need to know what has happened, so that I can help you. Do you know where JD is?" Nick looks at the two detectives hanging from his ceiling. He's seen the same kind of wounds inflicted on these men, at the service center massacre. Everything about the killings is starting to lean towards Sonny, but how she could've pulled it off, is unknown to Nick. His Master had warned him that "she" had returned. In Nick's frustration and panic, he assumed that Masamoto was referring to Yukia. Right now, Nick would rather face the daughter of Masamoto, instead of Sonny. "Who are these men, Sonya?"

"That's you, huh Nickels? You've always gotta be worried about other people's welfare instead of your own!" Sonny dives across the room, covering the span in a second. Right before she reaches Nick, Sonny spins her self around and kicks him square in the jaw. Nick is sent sprawling across the floor of the doorway. "Now pay attention, so I don't have to do this twice." She back flips over to the two men and lifts the first one's head. "This is Detective Frank Moreno of Miami's finest. Today, he leaves behind an ungrateful bitch of a wife and three little spoiled brats." Sonny lets go of Moreno's head, letting his chin bounce off of his collar bone. "Now, this fine specimen," She says walking over to the other man. Nick recognizes him as the driver of the mystery car parked down the street. "This is Moreno's partner, Frank Holmes. Ya know, this guy actually confessed to me that he was having a tawdry affair with Mrs. Moreno." Sonny puts her hand up to her face, as if trying to keep the dead men from hearing what she's saying. "Evidently she's a kinky little bitch. Any way, I forgave him for his sins before I gutted him, so that he can move on with a clear conscience."

"That's so noble of you."

Sonny smiles at Nick, "Yeah, it is, ain't it?" She shoves Frank's head backwards, causing the dead man to look upwards with is mouth open wide. "Your friend, Rawson has been spreading nasty rumors about me. These two ass clowns thought that they should start their own investigation on me." She looks over at Moreno and asks, "How's that working out for ya?" After slapping the dead man's face, Sonny turns and starts to walk towards Nick, slow and methodically. "You know, you should be thanking me right about now. If it hadn't been for me, they would've walked right up on your dumbass!"

He tries to stand, but Sonny drives Nick back to the floor by delivering a round kick to the side of his head. He's quick to take notice of her strength and agility, but wishes he didn't have to receive the demonstration first hand. The confusion of the situation makes him vulnerable to her attacks. The question keeps running through his mind, why has Sonny turned on him? "Sonya, you have to talk to me. I need to know why you're doing this, whatever it is, so we can work this out, just you and me."

"Don't try to use that psyche babble on me, Landry! Did you ever stop to think that maybe you can't fix everything? Maybe you should think about the possibility that some things aren't supposed to be fixed, it's just the way they are. Maybe I don't want your help, and never did! Face it, Nickels; you've been my patsy from the beginning!" Sonny lets Nick stand and then leans in close to him almost touching nose to nose. "You want to know why I'm doing this?" Sonny takes a half step back. "Do you really want to know? Let me show you why, you bastard!" Reaching out, Sonny hits Nick in the chest with both hands. Her reflexes are so fast that he doesn't have time to block her attack. The force of the blow sends him crashing through the bedroom wall beside the door, to end up in the living room floor on top of the drywall and wood frame debris. Nick writhes in pain as he looks back through the hole expecting her attack. Sonny just stands there in his room tensing up every muscle in her body. The result starts to show itself as her skin begins to ripple and contort, until her body is covered with bony plate armor, just below the skin. She lets out a cry of pain that resembles an animal's roar, as bony protrusions exit the skin at her shoulders, elbows and ankles. To finish the transformation, Sonny arches her back and then slumps her shoulders forward to allow a set of reptilian wings to stretch out from her back to touch the ceiling.

It is all clear to him now. Nick recognizes the greatest mistake of his life, standing in front of him, on the other side of the wall. Before he can react, Sonny leaps through the hole in the wall and slaps Nick across his face, letting her clawed finger tips rake the skin of his cheek, drawing first blood. "Now do you see what you did to me? Isn't it glorious?" Her question comes across with a jubilant air, as if asking Nick for his approval, and yet there is a sarcastic overtone that lingers. Then, her demeanor takes an opposite turn. "Because of what you did to me, I plan on turning your world into a living nightmare, just like you did for me!" She punctuates her statement by stabbing her claws into Nick's side.

Even through the shots of pain rushing to his brain, as Sonny pushes her claws deeper into his flesh, Nick is still able to fill in the blanks about what was happening. It was the egg, and how he tried to save her life. It had to be, what else could've done this to her? Yukio did make comment about approaching Sonny. Is it possible that he did this? No, Sonny is blaming Nick. Masamoto told him once that the egg could be used by the Devastator's minions to heal the fallen. Again, more important information has been left out of the conversation. "My God, what have I done?"

"Come on, Nickels, you mean to tell me that you figured it out all by yourself?" Sonny pulls her fingers from Nick's flesh and delivers an upper cut that floors him one more time. "Get up ya puss! How are you supposed to save the world, when you can't even save yourself?"

Nick picks himself up off the floor and tries to clear his mind so that he can focus. "Sonny, you have to believe me. I never wanted anything like this to happen." He fights his inner urges and tries to remain calm as he faces off against her. This isn't some stranger off the street. This is his best friend. "You took a bullet for me, and probably saved my life. I felt obligated to do whatever I could to help!" His sincerity is genuine in his voice and compounded by the sorrowful look in his eyes. "My God, Sonny, do you really think I would have used the egg, if I had any idea that this would happen? I love you, kid."

"News flash, Nickels, you failed miserably! As for your goddamned love, if I want it I'll rip your heart from your chest and feast on your love!" Sonny steps back and looks wildly around the room. Nick can see that this animalistic rage growing inside her is separating her from rational thought and actions. Now, her movements are starting to resemble that more of a wild predator, rather than a human being. Maybe this is a weakness he can exploit.

"Where's JD, Sonny, and why did you do this?" Nick stands up straight, ignoring the pain of it all and focuses on Sonny's face. Here eyes dart around, as if her mind is questioning why Nick has changed the subject so abruptly. "Whose blood has been spilt here? How do you want this to end? Why did you kill all of those people at the service center? Do you want to kill me too, Sonny?" He hopes that the barrage of questions will confuse her enough to give him the opening he needs.

Sonny quickly regains her composure and focuses on Nick's face, studying his every feature for a determination of his tactics. Then, out of the blue, her personality changes to that of a school girl, reciting the answers to his questions. "Okay, hold on a minute, I think I can do this. He's my guest, and because he always occupied your time. It was really kind of weird. Any way back to the answers, everybody's, to the death, because they could've jeopardized me getting to you," her expression quickly changes again, "and I swear to God Nick, with my bare hands!" Sonny then looks up and counts the questions and answers to make sure she didn't miss any. Then, her personality becomes even darker, as she holds her hand up and waves her index finger at Nick. "I bet you're disappointed that I got 'em all right, aren't you?" Then in a psychotic twist, she looks at her blood soaked finger tip, and then displays all five digits, wiggling the claws at the end of her fingers. "Oh, I just realized that my hands aren't so bare any more.

Nick knows that he has to make his move now, or he won't get another chance. "Cool, it sounds like you've got all of your bases covered. Let me ask you this; how will you deal with these guys' buddies who are pulling up out front?" Nick gestures towards the front door. "It looks like someone is taking an interest in their disappearance," he adds pointing at the two detectives. For half a second, Sonny falls for his ploy, turning her head slightly. Nick dives over to the wall adjacent to the kitchen and produces two swords from behind the sofa. He knows that he just used the oldest bluff in the book, but it was all he could come up with at the moment. "Don't force me to use these, Sonny."

She continues with her jocular attitude, responding as if she and Nick were just joking around. "Nice try, buddy, with that 'guy behind me' gig. That's a classic, and nearly worked on me that time. I guess I must be slippin' in my old age." Again her personality distorts, becoming cool, calculated and deadly. "Besides, if there was anyone behind me, I would know it." Sonny takes a step closer to Nick causing him to raise his swords a little higher. "Here's the skinny on how this is going to go down, Nickels. You and me are gonna have a race. You try to catch me, and kill me, before I make it to your star student and his new friend. Just to be a good sport, I'll even give you a hint to where we are going. It's my domain. Get there quick or otherwise you'll get to watch both of them die, before I end your pathetic life, too!" Sonny takes a deep breath and then sprays a fluid from her mouth that bursts into flames from the contact with the air. The flames spread like wildfire, igniting the floor and walls to build a barricade of fire between her and Nick. "Sonya Richards is dead, Dragon's Fang. Long live the Sun Dragon!" Sonny takes two steps, bounding towards the front door, and then explodes through it to fly off into the evening sky.

Nick hurries to his room and gathers more weapons, appropriate for what he is about to face. One is a twelve gauge assault gun loaded with full slugs. This is a last ditch effort weapon compared to his swords, but he believes it is a necessary evil for this situation. Ready to exit the house, Nick notices that the door to his safe in the closet is standing open, slightly. "Why would she have taken the egg?" This is an unknown that Nick never would have expected. Now is not the time to be worried about it, or the fact that his house is burning down around him. JD's safety has to remain Nick's top priority. Right now, he needs to focus and prepare for the fight of his life, against one of the most deadly people to ever walk the face of this earth. And, that was before her ungodly transformation took place.

Detective Bill Rawson pulls his car up to the curb in front of Nick's house, slowly inching it to a stop. The rain is starting to fall again, but it looks like the worst of it has already come and gone. Of course, with the gloomy skies all around, Rawson would rather be pulling up in front of his home, any home, instead of this one. Parked in front of him is Moreno's sedan, but there is no sign of the detective or his partner anywhere. "Man, I've got a really bad feeling about this. In the past few days, too many cops have died in this house, and Rawson is bothered by the fact that he has been sent out to investigate two more disappearances. After all, it's dark in there and the sun is going down.

Rawson shuts off the car, when coincidentally, his phone rings at the same time, causing him to jump. Afraid of being noticed, he quickly answers it to silence the ringer. Then he laughs at himself for working up a severe case of paranoia. "Hello? Oh, hey Captain, no I haven't located Moreno and Holmes yet. I'm gonna check on a couple of places connected to a case that they were working. I'll check in when I have something more solid." He hangs up the phone and timidly exits the car. While hurrying over to the sidewalk, seeking shelter from the rain under the trees, Rawson stops for a moment thinking he heard noises, no voices coming from Nick's house. This gives him just cause to pull his pistol from its holster, but before he can wrap his fingers around the pistol grip, Sonny explodes out the front wall of the house, shattering the front door and tearing the siding from the entry way. Fearing for his life, Rawson dives into the bushes along the sidewalk. It would seem like a cowardly act to most, but ol' Bill was just trying to avoid the shower of splintering wood and debris flying through the air. He was already safe from injury, being twenty feet away from the front door of Nick's house, but he figured why should he take the chance? By the time the event subsides, Sonny is long gone. Rawson couldn't see who it was from his vantage point, just that it was some sort of winged creature taking to the sky. After all, he was twenty feet away. Looking towards the house, the detective sees the smoke from the fires inside, already starting to billow out the opening in the front of the house. Then, he sees a familiar face inside in the smoke and flames.

Nick rushes out onto the porch, and then stops for a second when Megan's expensive imported sofa erupts in flames. After shaking his head with disappointment, Nick leaps from the side of the front porch and runs to the corner of the house. There awaits his trusty steed. He pulls the cover off of his racing bike and looks up to the rain falling from the sky. Part of him wishes it would rain harder, hopefully to put out the fires in the house before it's a total loss. The more rational side of him realizes that the wet pavement will make his ride a little more risky. The last time he seriously rode this thing, was with Charlie several years ago. He and Nick had bought identical motorcycles five years ago right before Nick left the Navy. That doesn't mean that the vehicle hasn't been prepared for him just in case he ever needed to use it while serving as the guardian. He drops his swords into two pipes that are strapped to the bike's framework, hangs the twelve gauge around his back, and then presses the electric starter button on the motorcycle's handlebars. Nick looks back at the house one more time, as he hears items inside popping and exploding from the heat. He knows that the house will be a total loss, just like everything else in his life. His and Megan's dreams are literally going up in smoke.

"Landry!" A familiar voice calls out from the shrubs behind Nick. "You hold it right there, mister! I've got some questions for you," Rawson declares, finally pulling his pistol free.

"Relax that itchy trigger finger, Bill. You've got my attention, but right now is not a good time!" To show no ill will, Nick releases the Tsuka, or handle, of his long sword, allowing it to drop by down into the section of pipe again. He doesn't have time for another confrontation like this. Sonny is a whole different breed of killer who will end JD's life if Nick delays his arrival.

"I swear to God, I'll put a bullet in your back if you try to ride away." Rawson motions for Nick to get off the motorcycle, with short gestures waving his pistol back and forth. "What in the hell was that thing that just came flying out of your house?"

Looking over his shoulder at Rawson, Nick can see Sonny hovering overhead. She lets fly a hellish screech, and dives towards the meddlesome detective. Distracted by the sound, Rawson looks up to see Sonny rocketing towards him. With Rawson frozen with fear, Nick makes the move to save the detective's life, leaping backwards off the motorcycle seat to tackle Rawson to the ground. This doesn't please Rawson, being shoved to the muddy ground, but he quickly concedes that Nick had just saved his life, by causing Sonny to miss her target.

"Why don't you ask her yourself," Nick replies as he points at Sonny rising back up into the air. Fearing another attack, Nick rolls away from Rawson and rises to his feet in one fluid motion to take a defensive stance for her next assault.

"Let's go, Nickels. Any more delays could be detrimental to your friends' welfare!" To punctuate her statement, Sonny showers their position with demonic fire, sending Nick and Rawson diving for safety in opposite directions. Then, she simply changes direction and flies off to the west.

"Nick jumps onto his motorcycle and restarts the engine. Rawson stares at Nick with a dumbfounded gaze as Nick rushes off to face Sonny. He isn't sure if Nick is the bravest, or most stupid man, walking the face of this Earth. "Hey what about me," Rawson asks? He runs over to Nick, hoping that he might reconsider his next move and not leave Rawson behind, "what about your house?" Rawson stands next to the motorcycle holding on to the bike's handlebars, waiting for a reply, but Nick offers no answers for the detective's questions. Instead, he puts the bike in gear. Once Rawson releases his grip, Nick decides to give him a bone, believing that it might not be such a bad idea to have some kind of back up. "She's headed for a junk yard, two blocks north, and five miles west." Without another word, Nick pops the clutch standing the motorcycle up, and rides a wheelie from the yard and out into the street.

Rawson holsters his pistol and leaps over the dying flames and runs as fast as he can to his car. Slipping and sliding on the wet pavement, he scrambles around to get into the driver's seat to take chase after Nick, who is now pursuing Sonny. He isn't sure what's going on, but he's sure that the best way to get his answers is to follow Nick. It's more than obvious that Detective William Shepherd Rawson has stumbled into something that is not of this world. Finding out what that is, compels Rawson to start the car and takes chase. The problem is that he isn't sure where he's going, or what to expect when he gets there.

Why is he doing this? All Rawson needed to do is finish out another year and a half, and he could retire from the force with a full pension. Things were going good for Rawson, until this past Saturday night, when he got the call for a robbery involving multiple homicides. He had cleaned up his act, climbed up on the wagon, and mended the fences between him and his ex-wife and kids. All he had to do was keep his nose clean for fifteen months and he could reap the benefits of his efforts. So what is he doing now? He throwing it all away, because the cop inside him says that there is so much more to investigate, before saying case closed, that's what he's doing. The problem is that he can't seem to come up with a way to justify his actions. The political aspect dictates that he should ignore intuition and allow due process to run its course. Deep down inside, he knows that this is something bigger than the laws of man. Rawson is beginning to believe that this is as something of biblical proportions, like heaven and hell. It's not an easy thing to do, for a man who isn't religious.

# CHAPTER XXIV

Bethany opens her eyes, unsure of how long she was unconscious, or what has happened in the mean time. To find that she was tied to a stack of demolished cars, sitting in the middle of an abandoned junk yard is not what she was expecting. She's held in place by a strand of steel cable fifteen feet off the ground. Frayed wires of the cable dig in to her ankles and wrists, as gravity pulls at her weight. Nervous, scared, and in a lot of pain, Beth tries to block it all out by striking up a conversation with her fellow captive. "This is just a long shot, but your name wouldn't happen to be Jefferson D. Johnston, would it?"

JD opens his eyes, surprised to hear a stranger's voice speaking his name. "Yeah, how are you doin'? I would offer to shake your hand but I'm a little tied up at the moment." He looks around to get his bearings. At first, he has no idea where he is, but then recognizes the faded name on the bill board sign at the front gates. Rusty's, it seemed like a poor choice for a junk yard's name, the first time JD saw it. Nick had brought JD here, a few years back, to run an endurance test with his student. JD remembers that it was the first of many times that he impressed his Sensei. "Listen, I don't mean to be rude, but I've got two questions for ya. How do you know my name, and how long have we been here?" He listens to the sound of the coming night, realizing that he and Beth are not alone in this morbid captivity.

"My name is Bethany Phelps. I'm a reporter, who was doing a story on your buddy, until everything went south on me this morning." Beth scans their surroundings, hearing the same sounds that JD heard. "What do you know about your teacher's roommate, Sonya Richards?" Before JD can answer her question, a beastial, savage, man runs over to the bottom of the stack of cars, growling and snarling at the conscious captives. The demonic presence leaps at Bethany, wanting to devour her flesh, but JD is too fast for the man. Extending his force field out below Beth, the man's leap ends abruptly sending him plummeting back down to the ground with a thud.

The mental spike stabs at JD's mind from deploying his force field in such a reckless manner. One day, his defensive mechanism could be his undoing if he doesn't learn to control it. If he survives this, JD vows to learn to develop a more regulated approach to govern the strength of his force field, if for nothing to avoid these migraine-like headaches. There are more noises coming from all around the junk yard leading JD to believe that there are more of these abominations running around the yard. Howls, growls, and snarls, echo between the stacks of cars, and are growing closer and closer to Beth and JD by the second. The best thing for him to do right now, is try to keep Beth's mind off the apparent danger roaming around them. "So, how do you know Nick and Sonny?" Good question, JD. That will really take her mind off of her problems. Sometimes he wishes that he could kick himself before his mouth opens, instead of after the fact. If nothing else, it could keep him from looking like an ass.

"H-how did you do that?" Beth can only assume that

JD was the one responsible for foiling the attack on her, seconds ago. "Y-you did do that, right?" With JD giving her a humble nod yes; Beth stifles her frightened emotions for a second. Looking at the young man beside her, Beth shows her panic all over her face for the situation, and yet seems to be a little relieved to be in JD's company, even in their current situation. "Personally, I don't know either one of them. Like I was saying, I was assigned to do a story on your friend." Beth pauses for a second, realizing how her self serving ways cost her good friend Tommy his life. Knowing then what she knows now, Beth would have definitely pursued this differently. "Actually, I assigned myself to this story, searching for my next big break. My friend died because of that. As far as Landry's roommate goes, I would give anything for the chance to go back in time to stop myself from ever walking up to Landry's door." Off in the distance, movement on the other side of the yard catches her attention, causing her pulse to quicken as her heart begins to race. "I need you to do me a favor, Jefferson. Tell me how all of this started, off the record and just between me and you, so that I have some way of knowing what's going on, and why I'm going to die."

JD looks up to the sky and then back down to the ground before he tries to answer. "Okay, but you've got to do me two favors yourself," he replies, stalling for time. "Call me JD, and forget all of this crap about dying, okay. I don't know how much of this you're going to believe, but it all started over eight hundred years ago. Way back then, there were three great battles between armies of good and evil. The forces of evil wanted to enslave the world of humanity, by opening a portal to what was called the Devastator's realm. This being would then be able to cross over to our realm, enslaving the population in darkness and literally bring hell onto Earth. The armies of light fought for humanity's survival all three times, and they won the wars, but not without suffering great losses. It was after the third battle for earth that Nick became involved with this out of control merry-go-round, eight hundred years later of course. You see, after the second battle, the forces of darkness were so weak with power that they set out to collect all things of darkness, to reenergize their dark magic. Sculptures, statues, anything used in rituals of dark arts and religions were melted down to create pieces of a scepter. Each piece retained the dark power, or magic, within the gold that was used. When the pieces were assembled, the scepter would work like a key to open the portal between Earth and the Devastator's realm. Once opened, the armies of the Devastator would come to earth and enslave humanity, and like I said, bring hell onto Earth for all times." JD is beginning to get as jumpy as Beth, seeing movement out in the open, but unable to distinguish what it is. He knows that he needs to remain calm for Beth's sake. If he loses his cool, Beth is sure to have a meltdown. "Any way, after defeating Doomsayer and his armies, the forces of light took the scepter and scattered the pieces to the corners of the Earth. Seven years ago, Nick was approached and told that it was his destiny to be the guardian of the most powerful piece of the scepter. I was abducted and taken to Japan by these warriors of darkness, who has spent centuries seeking out these pieces of a scepter of great power. The talisman that Nick possesses was to be the ransom for my freedom.

Beth hangs on the side of the stack of cars with her mouth wide open. That had to be the wildest story that she has ever heard. The sad part is that there's none of it she could use in a story without becoming the laughing stock of the journalistic world. "So, you mean to tell me that all of those people died and all of this has taken place, because Nick is in charge of saving the world? No offence, Jefferson, but it doesn't look like he's doing a very good job." A car rocks side to side over to her left, catching her attention. The movement was subtle, but enough for her to see. Was someone on the car? Was it something that jumped off the car? Her fear grows stronger by the minute. "To be honest with you, I wouldn't have believed a word you just said, if I hadn't lived through the past two days to see what I've seen."

"Yeah, well that makes two of us, reporter lady. Since we're getting so close and chummy, do me that other favor and call me JD, okay?" He pauses for a moment and tries to use his force field to break free from the cables that bind him. His efforts are futile not having the focus required to get the job done. The strain his body is taking while hanging there makes it hard for him to breathe, much less concentrate. For now, he is helpless until his situation changes. "You just hang in there, Ms. Phelps. I'm sure Nick is on her way." JD wishes that he had a mirror hanging in front of him, just so that he could see how convincing he looked at the moment. JD can't even start to think about where Nick is, or what he could do to help. The last time he saw his sensei was half way up the state when Nick walked into the service center. Obviously, he's still alive, or JD and Beth wouldn't be tied to the side of these cars as bait. "Man, I'm tired of being the little worm on a big hook."

Nick races to the outskirts of town, headed to his destination. He's lost sight of Sonny for the moment, but he's sure that she is headed to the junk yard a couple miles down the road. Before she was put on house arrest, Sonny flirted and seduced the security guard into allowing her to use the cars, and yard, as her own personal training ground. She called it her domain. The rain stings at his skin as he races down the wet road at breakneck speeds. He is able to ignore the sensation as his mind wanders through thoughts about his friend. Somehow he has to figure out how to deal with Sonny in her current state. He can't help but wonder if there is some kind of cure for her. For that answer, Nick would have to confront Masamoto with the question, but to do that; he will probably have to kill Sonny to get the opportunity. It seems like a vicious circle and that there is no way off this merry-go-round. To save Sonny, he would have to kill her, so that he could have the opportunity to find a cure? No matter what the solution, Nick can't sell Sonny short now. Even before this transformation, Sonny feared no one, and truly believed that she could kill anyone with her bare hands, and have no remorse for doing so. It is that lack of respect for life that makes her so dangerous. Now in her current condition, Nick will have to be at his very best if he is going to come out of this the victor.

Sonny drops down onto the stack of cars where Beth and JD are being displayed, with her appearance returned to human form. Her sudden arrival rekindles the fear in the reporter. Sonny pushes Beth over the edge of hysterics with a simple, "boo." It is more than enough to cause Beth to scream out with fear as Sonny starts to crawl down the side of the cars head first, like a spider moving in on its prey. Sonny stops when her face is next to Beth's, and says, "Oooooh, I know, isn't it all exhilarating? What's gonna happen next? Are you going to die? It's really like one of those cliffhanger episodes of an old TV show, isn't it?" Sonny leaps to the ground as her beastial followers come running at the sound of Beth's scream. JD watches as Sonny confronts her soldiers, awestruck at the way they all faced off against one another, like a pack of rabid wolves with Sonny claiming her rightful role as leader. With her followers under control, Sonny redirects her attention back to her captives. "Listen, I don't want you to be kept in suspense, so I'm going to give you a special update. Right now, your hero, or villain, depending on how your story and interviews translate, is on his way here just so that I can introduce you to the man of the hour, before I kill you, and feed you to my friends." Sonny pats the head of one of her beastly followers crouching on the ground in front of her. Beth finally breaks down and starts to sob uncontrollably giving Sonny reason to giggle. Then the madwoman lifts her head into the air, as if something had caught her attention. "Ooh, do you here that? That whine of a motorcycle engine in the distance is the sound of your savior rushing to his death. Don't go anywhere." Sonny extends her arms allowing her wings to spring forth. "I'll be right back, okay?" She roars at her followers sending them scattering out into the yard, and then Sonny leaps into the air and soars off into the night. This only adds to Beth's fear, causing her to scream out again at the sight of it all.

Nick slows down as he reaches the perimeter fence of Rusty's Junk Yard. This is where he should start expecting the unexpected. He quickly realizes that he should have started a little sooner, when Sonny swoops in and slashes the front tire of Nick's bike with her claws. Even though he had already started to slow down, the motorcycle was still moving thirty miles an hour when she made her attack. Immediately, all control of the vehicle is taken away from Nick. Combining his experience riding, with his martial arts training, he pulls his swords from the section of pipe and quickly maneuvers himself up as the bike lays down, so that Nick can stand on its side as the bike slides along the pavement. As its momentum is slowed, the rear tire catches one of the reflective lane dividers in the middle of the road, causing the bike to flip up into the air launching Nick away from the motorcycle, as it begins a disintegrating tumble down the asphalt. Nick hits the ground with a traditional tuck and roll away clear of the debris path. Unfazed by the sudden stop, Nick spins in a circle with his swords out to his sides, searching for Sonny's next assault. This is her style. Sonny's little ambush is just the first step in a long painful process of taking her opponent out one piece at a time.

"Yoo-hoo, Nickels, I'm over here." Sonny stands at the main gates of the junk yard some twenty yards away, daring Nick to make his move. She slashes the chains securing the gates with her claws, separating the metal links. A swift kick swings the gates open wide, before she turns back to face Nick. "Come on, Nickels, we're going to play a game," she declares, pointing her finger at him.

Nick stares at her trying to figure out what her next move will be. Facing off against his enemies in Japan was one thing, but Sonny's a whole different egg to crack. Ya never really know whether to expect a cold calculating attack, or an all or nothing, by the seat of her pants, out of control rampage to deal with. Sonny wiggles her index finger to tell Nick to come to her, and then runs off into the junk yard. The time has come for Nick to make a decision. He either walks into the yard to allow Sonny to seek her revenge, or he destroys what she's become. There is no other alternative. It's simply a matter of kill or be killed. "Okay, if this is how it is, then so be it." Nick takes off sprinting towards the main gates, accepting the fact that he is about to take Sonny's life. To do this, he must embrace a facet of his personality that has been dormant since he left the Navy. Nick must awaken this part of him that made Nickolas Landry a worthy leader for Sonya Richards to follow. He must become like her.

Stopping at the gate, Nick stares at Sonny standing in the middle of the main yard. "Here's how this is going to go, Nickels," she explains, standing proudly two hundred yards away. "You find me, or I'll find you. When we meet, it's a fight to the death. The rules are all or nothing, no holds barred. If you leave the fencing, your friends will be fed to my followers. If you run, I'll release my followers onto the streets of Miami. Those who don't die will become part of my new family." Sonny motions for her troops to reveal themselves before she runs off out of sight.

The innocent victims of her mad scheme leap from the stacks of cars and equipment around him, demonstrating to Nick that they were no longer human. Their form is still human, but their attributes are more reptilian in nature, complete with gnashing teeth and deadly claws. Somehow, Sonny has transformed them as well, but they're different appearing to be unable to revert back to human form. Now they are vicious predators out for blood. "Do you like them?" Sonny's voice echoes through the junk yard as her followers move to land the first blow against Nick. "I discovered that when I bit one, and didn't kill him, he turned into something like me. When he turned and attacked someone else, the bestiality was transferred, and so on, and so on,"

Nick weighs the situation in an instant. These attackers are no longer innocent people, but simply more casualties of this war. His blades rise up and meet Sonny's followers, eliminating the threat of two immediately, by skewering one, and removing the other's head. Each kick, each punch, each swing of his swords, lands lethal blows that fall two more before the rest back away. Nick takes the opening and runs after Sonny, yelling into the air, "It didn't have to be like this Sonny. We could have found a way to help you, together!"

His statement only fuels her rage. Sonny leaps from the top of a car and tackles Nick to the ground. Just to keep him there, she punches his ribs where she buried her claws. "I don't need your help, Nickels. I'm fine just the way I am!" Sonny draws back and punches at Nick's head, but hits the ground instead. With her weight off balance, Nick flips her off, sending her flying forward into a stack of cars. Sonny simply stands and dusts her self off, but the damage is already done. Before she realizes it the unbalanced tower of automobiles crashes down on top of her, sending Nick diving for safety, and buries her under tons of wreckage. The vehicles that were on top of the stack collide with other stacks across the makeshift corridor. Nick is sent leaping and bounding further down the path as demolished cars fall around him, until he is clear of the danger. Landing on his feet on the last car to move, Nick spins around and stares at the mountain of metal piled on top of Sonny, waiting to see what she brings next. He's certain that this didn't take her out. She's just waiting for the right time to make her move again.

So focused on her position, Nick doesn't see the next attack coming from his side. This just shows how much he is off his game. If he gets out of this, Nick's going to take a nice long vacation from life to regroup. If, he gets out of this. These attackers were just two homeless bums who had fallen prey to Sonny's scheme. The levels of their social status have no bearing on their present abilities. Nick is forced to fight again, knowing that these are innocent lives he is taking, as the two followers display their newfound talents slashing at Nick with their claws. One falls quickly as Nick thrusts his sword up in defense. The other of the two uses the demise of his partner to take the opening and attack Nick, raking his claws across Nick's shoulders as the attacker leaps onto his back. Forced to the ground by the added weight, Nick flips his sword around so that the blade is pointed backwards under his arm. As his hand makes contact with the ground, the Kashira, (or pommel,) embeds itself in the mud, driving the blade back up to slice the skin of Nick's ribs, before stabbing the attacker in his chest. Nick falls away allowing the body to slide down the blade, until the man's weight pulls him over onto his side. It wasn't quite the way Nick wanted it to work out, but the final result was still the same.

"What's wrong, Landry? You're not getting tired already, are you?" Sonny tosses, the car that laid on top of her over to the side, and displays that she is unscathed by the mountain of metal that fell on top of her. Exposing her wings again,

Sonny squawks out a call to her followers and takes to the night air. Three of her victims appear at the end of the drive way opposite of Sonny's direction. Another skirmish with her followers would only delay Nick more, putting JD's life in further jeopardy. Not knowing where Sonny was heading, and not wanting to lose her again, Nick takes chase. At the end of the corridor, he is forced to turn right and head down the next path of this maze of demolished cars. Appearing ahead of him at the end of the path are six more followers ready to join the chase. Nick charges forward right at them, until he reaches the next junction and takes a left staying just out of their reach. His new direction takes him right back into the main yard again, where he finally sees JD's situation. Nick also sees Sonny, twelve more of her minions, and a young woman who he doesn't know. Obviously, she is the one who Sonny referred to as JD's new friend, but Nick has no idea who she is, or how she is involved with all of this. It's time for him to take a new strategy; take out the biggest bad ass and hope that the rest fall back. Nick takes off again, just ahead of his pursuers, and flings one of his swords into the air as Sonny takes flight.

This is the one advantage that Sonny has that Nick can't duplicate. He halts his approach, sliding on the gravel strewn ground, as Sonny dives back in on him. Nick leaps into the air trying to meet her half way, striking at her with his sword before gravity pulls him back down to the ground. Sonny is able to defend the blow with her claws and rises back up into the air unharmed. Nick, however, hits the ground and loses his footing, sending him painfully to the rocky ground cover. Aggravated by the outcome, he scrambles to his feet, but the effort is too late in coming.

Sonny's followers pounce on Nick, tackling him down and pinning him to the ground. Instinct kicks in as the necessity to use the power of the talisman shows its face again. The followers clawing and ripping at his skin are obliterated by the discharge of power from the talisman. Nick tries to stand as more opponents rush in, but the best he can do is lean back against one of the cars. Again, he uses the talisman, rendering himself invisible. He clutches the talisman and raises his sword as one of the curious followers moves over to Nick's last position. Sniffing the air, the lost soul seems confused not understanding the situation. He could smell Nick's presence, but there is no sign of him anywhere, or is there. Nick quickly realizes that the power of the talisman was not cloaking the rain of blood falling at his feet. As soon as the follower steps forward to investigate, Nick runs the blade of his sword through the follower's chest. The bestial man howls out in pain, warning the others of Nick's location.

As hard as it is for Nick, he maintains his state of invisibility and charges at the oncoming followers, laying waste to the majority of them before they realize what was happening. Lofted in the air, Sonny is just as bewildered as she watches her minions fall. Her animalistic nature is having a hard time comprehending what she sees. Why can't she see Nick? Disgusted by the turn of events, Sonny flies back over to her guests and calls for some of her followers to gather below JD and Beth. "Nickolas, I have someone here who is just dying to meet you." Sonny looks into Beth's eyes as she hovers in front of the reporter's face. "Scream for him, my dear." Sonny's request is fulfilled as Beth gives her best impression of a B-movie scream queen. "Very nice," Sonny replies before facing the main yard again. "Show yourself, Nickels, or I'll feed her to my pets!" Sonny looks around expecting Nick to give himself up quickly. "Don't worry, sweet cheeks, he won' let you down. Sonny soars a little higher to see if she can spot Nick's movement. "Come on, Boy Scout, you've got to the count of three before I turn

Ms. Phelps into an oversized Happy Meal." Sonny starts the count out loud, at a very fast pace. "One, Two, Three!" She drops out of the sky and slices through the cable that held Bethany in place.

"NO!" Nick renders himself visible again, allowing Sonny to see that he is less than twenty feet away from her. His strength is waning. Nick knows that this is coming to an end soon, one way or another. To protect her self, Sonny sprays the ground with liquid fire to keep Nick at bay. His mind is becoming clouded and his reflexes are slowing, almost sending him face first into the wall of flames. Taking advantage of his awkward halt, five followers leap at Nick's position and tackle the Guardian to the ground. More blows are delivered, and more of Nick's blood stains the muddy ground. His fight against the followers is an uneven match, but Nick is able to drop a few of them before the growing numbers simply overwhelms him. Then, it all stops as quickly as it began, with Nick pinned to the ground to await Sonny's revenge.

The end is near, and Nick can feel the life draining out of him. He is at Sonny's mercy now, and this is what she wanted most of all. His mind screams out, "Help me!" But to no avail, the talisman doesn't respond. Why? Is his life force so weak that the talisman no longer recognizes his plea?

Sonny lands on the ground in front of Nick, seeing that he is now as vulnerable as she was, when he infected her with the egg. "Aw, poor Nicky, I wish you could see how pathetic you really look right now."

"Same ol' Sonny," Nick responds, choking on his own blood. "It really was easier for you to turn your back on everyone who cared about you, or tried to help you. Why put forth the effort, when it's easier to pout and cry, 'poor me'. Everybody, Charlie and Nicole, Jorge and Carla, and even me and Megan, were there for you, to pick you up every time you fell down. I guess you really weren't worth saving after all. Everything I did, for you, all of the help and support, was nothing but a waste of time, and this is how I am repaid. I loved you, Sonya." His statement gives Sonny reason to call off her troops. She sees that Nick is no longer a threat, and yet he surprises her by standing to face his friend once more.

You just don't get it, do ya, Nickels? Everything I've done, I did for you and me. I was the one who turned Charlie and Jorge away, so that I could have you all to myself. That bitch you were going to marry? I'm the one who ended her miserable life, because she wasn't good enough for you." Sonny smiles at the effect her statement has on Nick. A look of shock comes over his face as Nick staggers back a step, finding her statement hard to believe. "What?" Sonny follows Nick's movement stepping in closer to him. "Oh Nickels, you're gonna love this! When those ninja wackos attacked your rehearsal dinner, I was the one who switched the name tags for the place settings. Those assassins weren't aiming at her; you were just in the wrong seat. I saw the inside man spike the soup for you and your teacher, but I took the opportunity to right what was about to be wrong. After pulling one of the daggers from her chest, I simply laid its razor edge against her neck and looked her in the eyes. I really don't think you could know how easily that shuriken pressed into her throat. I barely had to apply any pressure at all. The fucking bitch, she didn't deserve you or your love! She proved that to you the first time she walked away from you." Sonny lashes out at Nick with her claws, this time shattering the blade of Nick's sword and ripping open his chest. Nick reels back in agony, unsure what to do. Unable to stand any more, he falls to one knee, and clutches his chest while gasping for air.

"Here's the part that set me off. After her funeral, when you needed someone more than ever, you rejected me and my companionship. After everything I did for you, for us, that was the thanks I got! I was so pissed at you for that, so I went out to vent my anger elsewhere. I was the one who provoked the incident at the night club. It took all of them to receive the punishment I wanted to give to you! Imagine if you will, the chances of you surviving everything I did to them." Sonny puts her hands on her hips and bends over, mocking Nick. "The cops and the Feds that died at the house; that was for you. They wanted to arrest you and take you away from me. Those people on the turnpike; I couldn't have that many witnesses for what happened between me and those agents either. They might have pointed their fingers at you for the blame. I couldn't have that. I wanted you all for myself!"

Nick can't believe what he is hearing. In Sonny's delusional state of mind, everything that has happened is Nick's fault. How could he have been so blind all of these years? Love is blind. "Sonny?"

Sonny reaches down and grabs Nick's face to force him to look into her reptilian eyes. "For the last time, Sonya Richards is dead!" She grabs Nick's arm with her free hand and slings him across the main yard to collide with the mast of a dilapidated old crane. He falls away to bounce off the body of the vehicle before hitting the hard ground below. It takes everything Nick has to roll himself over. His efforts are futile as Sonny descends upon him to sit on his chest in the sticky red life's blood leaving Nick's body. Why won't the talisman hear his plea? He rolls his eyes over to look at Sonny's captives and mumbles JD's name. "Oh I don't think you should be worried about yourself, instead of them, right now. Look at you! Aren't you supposed to be this great savior of the world? I can't believe the old man ever thought you had what it takes. You're too soft, Nickels. You care about everybody else, instead of your own problems!" Before Sonny can continue, her followers draw her attention away from

Nick, to see JD protecting Beth behind his force field. Nick had intentionally missed Sonny with his sword earlier, but he did place it within reach of JD, to free himself. "Cute trick, kid, you might be more fun to kill, than I thought."

Nick is dying, and he knows it. With panic setting in, he struggles to make a retreat, dragging himself across the ground. "Where in the hell do you think you're going?" Sonny stands and watches as Nick claws at the ground, trying to put some distance between him and Sonny. Before she has to make a move to stop him, Nick coughs from choking on his blood, and then collapses to the ground with his face in the mud. Sonny walks over to him and uses her foot to roll him over.

"I-I'm sorry, Sonny. I never meant to hurt you." His strength is dwindling and his eyesight is beginning to fade. Still, he can make out her silhouette as Sonny kneels down beside him. Using the last reserve of strength he has, Nick raises his arm in defense, only to have Sonny slap it down.

"Oh no, Nickels is dying." Her tone is soft and comforting as she leans over close to him. "Your heart is going to stop any minute, from the lack of blood in your body, Nickolas." She runs her fingers through his long hair, brushing it back away from his face. Sonny reaches back behind her back and produces the egg. It now resembles the dried out husk of a grapefruit, but his mind is unable to come up with any possible scenarios about what she's done. "You know, I tried to use this thing to upgrade some of my followers but it didn't do anything for them. So I decided that I would use this worthless thing to end your life the same way you ended mine. The only difference is that I will do the humane thing and put you out of your misery." Sonny brings the husk down onto Nick's face and crushes the remains trying to smother him.

To Nick, this is the end. He's too weak to try and stop

her, and can't avoid what is happening. Sonny had forced the egg onto Nick's face in such a way that the small bones of the embryo break, and puncture the flesh of the baby dragon inside the egg. A slimy fluid flows from the dead creature and washes over Nick's face and into his mouth. The last flash of panic takes over as his body starves for oxygen. His eyes, and nose, burn from the substance forced into his skull. His mouth suffers the same excruciating sensation as the black inky liquid coats the lining of his throat. He can feel the burning continue as it spreads throughout his body. Is this really how it ends? "I don't want to die!" His scream is only heard echoing through his mind as every nerve ending in his body seemed to be ablaze. Then, with a flash of light clearing his mind, Nickolas Landry gasps one more time before everything fades to black.

# Chapter XXV

J D watches the event unfold from a short distance away. He can't believe what he has just witnessed. Never would he have believed that Nick's life would come to this conclusion. JD truly believed that Nick couldn't be taken down this way. His friend is gone and there was nothing JD could do about it. For the first time in his life, JD feels a rage growing inside him that is about to take control of his actions. He and Beth just had to watch Nick die, and now JD has to be the one to pick up where Nick let off. He feels up to the challenge. In the past few days, he's fought ninjas, assassins, demonic spirits, and Sonny's followers. He stood toe to toe with Yukio Masamoto, and helped Nick save the world by defeating the Dark Lord, Doomsayer. It is these events that have awakened the hero inside of JD. He has the skills, ability, and knowledge to be successful. The only question is, can he? After all, Nick didn't fair too well against Sonny.

His head is aching from the continuous deployment of his force field to fend off Sonny's followers. The ones surrounding him and Beth have just about literally beat themselves unconscious slamming against the energy field. Now, Sonny and the rest of her followers are focused on him and Beth, slowly and methodically moving towards them. Sonny leads the charge with her followers close behind, picking up speed as they cross the main yard. JD pulls away from Beth's grip and leaves her side to run right at Sonny and the others. At the last second, he stops and braces himself to deploy his force field with all of his might.

The energy wave forms and spreads out away from JD like a concussion wave falling everything in its path with the force of a tsunami. On impact, Sonny and her followers are blown from their feet, as stacks of cars are toppled, and equipment is sent flying. The pain for him is excruciating, but JD fights through it to take chase after Sonny. Nick always told JD that the best time to take an opponent out is when you first get him down. At that brief moment, your adversary is vulnerable, and this opportunity only comes once. It is this opening that he needs to take full advantage of, facing off against Sonny. If JD had the time to stop and think about what he's doing, he would probably institutionalize himself, if he survives the night.

Sonny's still down, and appears to be slow to get up. First she ran head on into JD's force field, which did its fair share of damage. Then she was sent flying through the manager's shack and out the other side. Grabbing a section of pipe as a weapon, he knows that the time is now. What makes this seem easier for him than it was for Nick is, JD never really liked Sonny in the first place.

To his surprise, Sonny lifts her head and sniffs the air. Evidently, she wasn't as wounded as JD was lead to believe. Needless to say, he is quite disappointed, when she leaps into the air heading for the front gates, and right at JD. Sonny swoops down on his position and takes a swipe at him with her claws, slicing the pipe in half, just to prove that it was no threat to her. Then she continues on to the gates without any hesitation. She wasn't retreating or regrouping. Sonny had picked up the scent of Rawson's cheap aftershave and views him as an easier target. Sonny doesn't remember that he was one of the cops that kept a vigil at her bedside in the hospital. There is no way for her to know that the detective has no strong alliance to Nick, or not. All Sonny knows, is that Rawson is here uninvited and that makes him the enemy.

The truth be known, Detective Bill Rawson has no loyalties to anyone connected to this madness. All he wants is for all of this to be over. He hesitates before stepping over the first two casualties of this war, and enters the junk yard. Staring at the ghastly features of Nick's victims, Rawson is left wide open for Sonny's attack. He looks up just in time to see her descend out of the black sky before tackling him to the ground. With her hand held high, Sonny leans in over Rawson's terrified face and growls the word, "Kill!" She never gets the chance to land the death blow. JD leaps through the air and kicks Sonny off of the downed detective. She hits the ground hard, as JD lands on his feet to await her next move. "What you did to Nick was…" His statement is interrupted as two of her followers blindside JD when they rejoin the fight. So focused on Sonny, he had failed to see that some of the others were beginning to recover from the introduction to his force field. All is not lost, though. JD regains his focus quickly, and sends one of the followers into stacks of tires, where the lost soul is buried under the result of the collision. The other is drop kicked face first through a windshield, ending that threat permanently. JD's happily relieved that he has won this round, or so it would seem.

Sonny, however, refuses to see it that way. With his focus on her two followers, Sonny moves in for the kill. After scanning the area for any more potential threats, JD spins back around only to find Sonny standing right in front of him. Before he can react, Sonny grabs him by his throat and lifts him into the air. Her strength is incredible, as she squeezes his wind pipe shut. Unable to breathe, JD can't focus. Unable to focus, he can't deploy his force field. This means that JD is helpless to the situation as he grabs her arms to try to support his own weight. Again she growls, "kill," preparing to end the young man's life. Once again, Sonny is denied her opportunity for joy, stoking the fires of her rage, as a bullet from Rawson's pistol rips into her abdomen. Violently, Sonny is knocked from her stance, breaking her grip on JD's throat. He falls to the ground gasping for air as Sonny is sent rolling across the ground. Rawson hurries over to JD's side, before taking aim at a few more of Sonny's followers. Usually, a .45 caliber bullet would put a guy down for good. Rawson ordered these bullets special, after his encounter with Yukio, at Nick's dojo. Something told him that he would need stronger fire power before this case was closed. Even after all of the freaky shit he experienced with Landry, Rawson had no idea it would be like this. When Sonny simply stands up and brushes her self off, Rawson starts to wonder if he should have just gone with a bigger gun all together. Sonny looks over at JD as she walks by and says, "Don't go anywhere; I'll be right back to finish with you in a second."

At first, Detective Rawson was just a little curious with this case. After his first confrontation with Nick, Rawson became more intrigued by the mystique of it all. The attack at Nick's dojo legitimized the martial arts instructor enough, to intrigue the detective even more. He was hooked, and wanted to know it all. Somehow, in a very short span of time, Rawson's curiosity has turned into full blown fear. He squeezes the trigger again. This time Sonny recovers twice as fast and doesn't go down. Again he fires the weapon, and again it only slows her approach. Faster and faster he pulls the trigger, as his own dose of panic sets in. The bullets punch holes into her abdomen and chest, driving her back a step each time, but still she doesn't stop. Neither does Rawson, who keeps pulling the trigger long after the clip is empty. As a last ditch effort, he throws the pistol at her, before she slaps him to the ground. "So, you really want to go first, do ya?" Sonny stares at Rawson with a devious grin as she holds out her hands so that he can watch her claws grow to twelve inches in length.

"Sonny!!!" The sound of someone yelling her name comes from behind her, breaking her concentration on Rawson. She whips her head around like a predator that has heard the sound of its prey. To her surprise and shock, there stands Nick in all of his ragged glory, ready to go another round with his roommate. "You should have finished me off, just to be sure, you crazy bitch! Now, come here and take your medicine!"

Sonny grabs Rawson and leaps to her feet. This pathetic human is no longer a concern to her, so she simply tosses him over by JD, and turns to face Nick. How can he be standing there, taunting her like an old memory? She heard his heart stop. He's dead. Nickolas Landry is dead! "You're dead! You can't be alive!" Sonny breaks into a sprint running right at Nick expecting to drive him right through a wall of crushed cars. Instead, he grabs her and flings her into the wall of cars in question, and through the other side. With her unbalanced state of mind in control, Sonny jumps up and charges Nick again. Nick simply extends his arm and grabs her by the throat and stops her dead in her tracks. Her thoughts quickly become as unbalanced as her state of mind, with Sonny unable to rationalize the change of events taking place. How is he able to do this? Nick shouldn't be able to do this, if he's dead.

Nick tightens his grip as she swats at his arms trying to break free. When he lifts her into the air, the surprise of it causes Sonny to pause. "You always wanted to know if you could take me in a fair fight, Sonny. Well here's your chance to find out, kiddo."

Sonny lets out a roar of anger for his statement. She spreads her wings and lifts her legs to kick Nick in his chest to separate the two combatants. Nick rolls over backwards and stands to his feet, but doesn't wait for her next move. As she tries to stand, he charges her position and delivers a takedown of his own. When it comes to close quarters combat, Nick and Sonny were the best. Amidst the flurry of grappling, Nick is able to land devastating blows, but Sonny is still able to block two out of three. On the other hand, she finds it frustrating that she is unable to land any. She's injured now, and needs to regroup. Flipping her feet up into the air, she wraps her ankles around Nick's neck and flips him off to the side. Getting away from him now isn't going to be that easy. Nick latches onto her arm and pulls her over with him, unwilling to give her a chance to catch her breath. The two continue to roll around on the ground, holding onto one another with one hand, while beating each other to no end with the other.

Gaining the upper hand, Sonny back flips Nick onto the hood of a car, and then leaps into the air to deliver a crushing stomp to his head, that is hanging over the fender. Nick defends quickly by rolling his legs up to kick her in her chest as she drops into range. Before Sonny hits the ground, Nick is on her as fast as lightning, delivering a crushing blow to her head with his elbow, before rolling over to put an arm bar on her that delivers two compound fractures to Sonny's left forearm. He has now taken out her strength. Being left handed, Sonny was always deadliest with her left, but never took the time to better her right. This is a crippling move that he has delivered. Sonny howls out in pain, blinded to the true threat that Nick now poses. As a last resort, she sprays the ground around them, causing fires to erupt, sending Nick in a series of flips to avoid her assault.

Somehow, she needs to find a way to regroup. To make a better stand against her enemy, she needs a shield. The sound of gunfire catches her attention, reminding her of the other players in this morbid tragedy. While Sonny was focused on Nick, JD and Rawson have gone to the aid of Ms. Bethany Phelps. Sonny's followers were slowly moving in for the kill, making sure Beth has no way to escape. Had they attacked sooner, they might have gotten the chance to feed before falling, by one of Rawson's bullets. Needing to reach Beth before JD and the detective, Sonny breaks into a run of desperation heading right for the two heroes. Beth screams out again, this time warning them of Sonny's approach. Rawson turns and pulls the trigger to find that the clip is empty once more. He drops his arm and just stands there as Sonny charges right at him. He doesn't flinch or even bat an eye. Just as her fingertips are close enough to grab the detective, the point of a tire iron finds its mark on Sonny's back, before continuing through her to protrude out her chest. Rawson saw Nick make the throw, and sees the shock and surprise on Sonny's face for what just happened. She howls again because of the excruciating pain, before grabbing the detective and throwing him at Nick, to send both men to the ground.

Nick jumps up and shakes off the dazed feeling brought on by the collision. He scans the area for Sonny, and then looks over at Rawson and asks, "Are you alright?"

"Believe it or not, but I think I broke my wrist when we hit the ground." Rawson props his injured limb onto his belly and sits there not worrying about getting up. He looks around to see that there is no other movement coming from Sonny's followers, and he's glad to see that there is no sign her, either.

"Nick, are you alright?" JD leads Beth over to his friend after he convinced her that there was safety in numbers. Beth's hesitation with the act was that she watched Nick die as well, and was a little apprehensive about rushing over to meet a dead man. "Dude, even after all of that, she still flew out of here like a bat out of hell!" Still unable to convince himself that the danger has passed, JD scans the night sky for any sign of Sonny, wondering if she could be hiding in the low clouds. "What do we do, Nick? There's no telling where she is!"

Nick reaches out and offers Rawson a hand. "Are you going to be alright?" Rawson answers with a nod, and then takes Nick's offer to pull himself up off the ground. Turning to his friend, Nick looks at JD proudly. "JD, I want you to stay here with the detective until help arrives. Then I want you to get out of Florida, and on with your life in college, understand?" Nick looks back to Rawson. "I need your keys."

"They're in the car, out front." Rawson reaches out and grabs Nick's arm to question his motive. "I don't know what your next move is going to be, but you better do it fast before that bitch causes any more trouble for you, and me." Rawson catches himself looking up at the sky because of JD's paranoia.

Nick gives the detective a salute of acknowledgment, and then starts for the front gates, only to be stopped by JD. "Nick, what about Sonny? How do you know where she is?" JD looks to his sensei for more than just the answers to his questions. What he really wants to know if this is all over, and if he'll ever see Nick again.

"She's gone where every animal goes to die," Nick declares, never looking back.

"Where's that?" Rawson asks, favoring his arm.

"Home, Detective Rawson," Nick finally turns to face JD

one more time. "One day, I'll find you again, Jefferson. You did real good tonight, JD. I'm proud of you." Nick takes off running to the front gates and out to Rawson's car. He jumps in, starts the car, and then points it towards home. If he is right, home might be the only thing she would remember.

Nick pulls the car up into the driveway of his ill fated home and is reminded of the way he left it. Judging by the departing news vans leaving as he entered the neighborhood, the fire department must have left a few minutes before the news crews packed up their gear. "Lucky for them," he thinks before heading up onto the front porch. Slowly, cautiously, he makes his way into the condemned house. As he moves through the charred remains of his life, Nick constantly scans each room for any sign of Sonny. On the hallway wall, it looked like someone had drug four knife blades along the blackened drywall.

He walks into her room and finds Sonny lying on her water soaked mattress, sobbing in a pool of blood. The tire iron had torn the tendril free from Sonny's heart, eliminating her ability to heal, and trapping her in this gruesome form. Sonny will die, and people will see the true nature of the beast. Now it is her heart that is slowing, bringing the end nearer with each pulsating flow of blood from her chest. Even after all that has happened, Nick still feels compassion in his heart for her. "Oh Sonny, why did it have to end this way?"

The sound of his voice stirs the dying rage inside her. She throws herself at him in a feeble attempt to strike out at him, but her weight just carries her into his arms. Nick slowly lowers her down onto the bed and pulls the tire iron from her back. Sonny gasps at the sudden feeling of relief and reaches up to touch Nick's face. "You were the better man, Landry," she mumbles in a garbled voice. "I only wanted to love you completely." Then her eyes close for the last time as

Sonya Richards drifts off into oblivion. Nick begins to sob. He pulls Sonny close to him and holds her tight.

Nick looks at the carnage on display as his eyes well up with tears. His world is literally laid around him in ashes. Then, when he can take it no more, he screams, "Aaaaaah!!!" His cry is one of pain. It is a cry for the pain that he has suffered, a cry for the pain suffered by others, a cry for the pain of it all. Only now does he see how this so-called destiny could, would, and did, ruin his life. Nick thought that he could have prevented all of this from happening. Now he sees that there was no way for him to avoid any of this, because it is his destiny to follow this path without stray. Why? Why is it his destiny to suffer like this? Why couldn't he have been warned? He deserves to know, and someone is going to tell him.

He lays Sonny down on the bed and sits back clutching the talisman. Once he is in the right frame of mind, Nick closes his eyes and takes the journey to Masamoto's realm. When he opens his eyes again, Nick is standing in the middle of a great and dreadful battle field that is covered with decaying bodies, shrouded by an ominous sky looming overhead. Off in the distance, he can see the stone temple where Masamoto and the council reside. Between him and the decaying structure are the residents of this realm, picking through the carcasses, hoping to find an overlooked lost soul. There is no concern in him for the danger they present. Nick takes off running right at the demonic creatures, driving through their ranks and falling each one with a mere touch. Up the hill he continues until he runs right into the temple's main hall, out of breath and looking around the room, he asks, "Where are you, old man?" Nick kicks at the wall to vent his anger. The result dislodges several stones causing a hole to appear, letting in the gloomy ground fog from outside.

"This old place is falling down around me, isn't it? That

433

is the effect of the Devastator's reign." Masamoto appears behind Nick and walks up behind him, as Nick spins around. "Why have you come here? You were not summoned."

"This isn't a social call, Master!" Letting his anger guide his actions, Nick grabs Masamoto by the collar of his tunic and shoves the old man over against the wall. Masamoto is unfazed by Nick's actions. After a second, Nick just releases his grip and steps away from the old man. "Why me!?! You taught me everything I needed I needed to know, but you never told me why?"

Masamoto knows that Nick has passed his final test. "You know so much more than you realize, and yet you are a very ignorant and selfish man, Nickolas."

"That doesn't make sense, old man. How can you say that to me, any way?"

Masamoto waves his hand in the air "Dah, dah, dah, you came here, you will listen! I did not choose you for this destiny, my student. This destiny chose you for the role of Guardian, when the fabric of time was woven. Serving as the guardian was nothing more than a test for your true destiny to come. You know this to be true. When we first met, you confessed to me that you felt that you were meant for something more." Masamoto pauses and moves over to the window to check the grounds for movement. "That was the destiny calling to you. You answered the call, and now have embraced that decision. Nickolas, this is something that you cannot dismiss or discard. Did you not dispatch the beast of your creation?"

This is one of those questions that Nick wants answered, and was happy that Masamoto decided to change the topic of conversation. "If you knew it was going to happen, why didn't you tell me? So many people have died for nothing. If I knew then, what I know now; I wouldn't have intervened. She would have died, but all of those innocent lives would have been spared. The egg turned her into some kind of demonic creature, ultimately forcing me to destroy her any way. You could have prevented all of this in the very beginning, if you would have said something to me. Why, why didn't you tell me?"

Nickolas, the reason I gave you the egg is so that the event would take place. Now, explain to me what happened in the end."

Nick stares at the old man finding it hard to believe that the words just came out of Masamoto's mouth. "You bastards," He replies, turning away from his master. "In the end, I was dead, and then I wasn't. I opened my eyes with a newfound purpose, and was able to end Sonny's life." Nick thinks about it for a second, realizing that Sonny's actions against Nick forced the transformation within him to take place in him. If this is what Masamoto is talking about, there could have been a different way of handling it. No, there is no excuse for what happened. "So if it's you that I owe this debt of gratitude, fuck you very much, and have a nice life, or death, or whatever the hell you are!"

Masamoto ignores Nick's profanity as if it was never said. "So, you drank from the dragon's blood?"

Nick turns to face Masamoto, when a sharp pain begins to echo through his body. "Don't come looking for me any more, Master. Help like that, I don't need." The sharp pain hits him again, this time causing him to double over. He holds up his hands taking notice to how they are more translucent than the rest of his body, and fading fast. Again it hits him, causing Nick to double over again, and then fall to one knee, as the pain increases. "W-what's happening to me?"

"You must go! Someone has found your body and is trying to remove the talisman. If that happens before you return, you will be lost to your self forever, trapped in this realm. Go, my son! We will sort out your destiny another time."

Nick didn't quite understand the "lost to your self" bit, but the part about being trapped here is a bad thing for sure. He closes his eyes and concentrates to send him back home.

The rest of the council appears after Nick vanishes from sight. Masamoto turns to face them as if he knew they were there the whole time. "You heard what he said. The prophecy has been fulfilled. Should we not proceed with gathering his army so that all is ready for the end of times?"

"Master Masamoto, all that we see now, is that the Guardian is more powerful than ever, and has surpassed our control. At this darkest hour, we cannot gamble our efforts of eight hundred years, on the possibility of a prophecy coming true. You must remember that his true destiny is beyond the end of times. Our agents must remain diligent in their efforts in trying to prevent the end of times from happening. It has already been decided. The Crusaders will be brought in to dispatch Landry and remove the talisman from his possession once and for all. His purpose has been served."

"As you wish," Masamoto bows his head to the elders' council. "If I may, in the defense of my student; was it not you who guided me to Nickolas?"

"It was you who began the experiment, Masamoto. We simply monitored the results." With that, the council fades away.

Nick opens his eyes as a police detective finally snatches the talisman from Nick's hands. "Ah, Mr. Landry, it's good to see that you're still with us. Man. you sure had a death grip on this thing. I snatched on it three or four times before you finally gave it up. Detective Sean Borders turns away and barks at a nearby uniformed officer, "Hey, what's the word on Rawson?"

"He's already in route to the hospital with the other two victims, Sir."

Nick looks around, realizing he is in handcuffs and shackles again, and that Sonny's body is gone. "Where's Sonny?"

"Your roommate? She's headed down to the morgue and then upstate to Ripley's Believe it Or Not! I'll make a fortune!" Borders laughs at his comment, being the fifth time he's said it in the past fifteen minutes. He's quick to realize that Nick isn't laughing at all. In fact, Nick is looking pretty pissed off about what was said.

"That's not very funny, at all," Nick replies, giving the detective a menacing stare.

Unsure how to take that, Detective Borders grabs Nick's handcuffs to lead him out of the house. "Well, it looks like I'll be riding with you. Do us all a favor, pal, and don't get too uptight. I want you around for a little while to answer a shit load of questions. First, I need to talk to my partner.

# Chapter XXVI

"And I'm telling you, Rawson, I'm not buying it! I've read the reports, seen the photos, and know when to back up before I step on the wrong toes." Captain Russo slams his hand down onto the top of his desk, accidentally spilling his coffee, but emphasizing his point. Russo, like Rawson, only has a few more years before retirement, and would like for the time left to be as uneventful with catastrophes, like this. "Here's what I do know; Miami, LA, Japan, and even the service center up the road all have one thing in common. Nickolas Landry was there when a whole bunch of people died! Look at these reports, Rawson. Almost a hundred people in Japan, eighteen in LA, forty seven at the service center, and I'd bet my badge that we could find a way to pin the Biscayne Bay incident on him too!" Russo looks around the room and sees his graduation picture hanging on the wall, with him on one end of the lineup and Rawson on the other. It reminds him that at one time, the two men were close friends. If the Captain hadn't divorced Rawson's sister, they'd still be family. "Bill, I can't let you meet with the Federal boys and give them a story like this. The credibility of this department will be flushed down the toilet. If they want to see something different, then damn it let them!"

Rawson shoves the files back across the desk and turns to look out the window at his fellow detectives, standing outside the Captain's office, in the main bullpen of the fourth floor. He's known Charlie Russo for a long time. Instead of college, the two of them joined the Police Force together. Has Charlie's rank really polluted his reality to a point that he expects Rawson to buy this lip service? It's more than apparent that the Department's upstanding Captain has reached a point in his career, where a good clean image means more to him than finding the truth. "Ya know what? That right there is a damn shame, ol' buddy. I remember the day we signed up for the academy. Sure, over the years, we went our separate ways. You needed to fulfill your desire to grow, while I was content with being what I am, a good cop. The thing is, I always considered you to be a good cop, until now. Why do you refuse to see the truth that's right in front of your face?"

Captain Charlie Russo jumps out of his chair and walks over to the window, where he gestures at the rest of his detectives to get to work, before he closes the blinds on his window, to block out the audience on the other side. "Do you want to know what I see in front of me?" Russo asks, as he walks back over to his desk. He grabs Rawson's report to read portions out loud. "…She had wings like a bat that sprouted out of the middle of her back; between her shoulders…Johnston produced some kind of mental energy field that saved my life…" Russo gives Rawson a doubtful look. "Oh, and this is a good one, …Landry appeared to have died, but somehow revived himself and found a way to finally kill Ms. Richards, to save the hostages, and you." Russo looks up at his former brother-in-law, to see Rawson squirm in his seat a little.

Bill Rawson doesn't deny that his report sounds a little far fetched, but he saw every bit of what he recalled in his report, with his own eyes. "Charlie as hard as it all may be for you to believe, it was twice as hard for me to write that report, but it's all true. Go down to the morgue with me, and you can see the evidence first hand, for yourself. If you're so worried about the department's image, don't you want to be prepared when all of this goes public? You've got to know that as soon as the Feds get their hands on those bodies, all of this is going to leak out into the media." Rawson reaches in his pocket for a cigarette to calm his nerves, only to remember that his pack is still in his car. "God, I could kill for a cigarette, right about now."

Russo hangs his head, partly because he feels shame for what he is about to say. "That's not going to happen, Bill. The Feds are the ones calling the shots on this. They've got a sweeper team mopping up the junk yard, as we speak. The bodies should be loaded up to be transferred to a government crematory, where they will be disposed of in a few hours. Tomorrow morning, at seven o'clock, a bull dozer is going to scrape the lot where Landry's house sits. All the files have been gathered, and everything is wrapped up with a nice little bow for the Feds to pick up here shortly. You are the only loose end to this whole stinkin' madness, and I'm telling you right now to let it all go."

"My God, Charlie," Rawson can't believe what he's hearing. "You're not really going to cover all of this up, are you?" He stands up in protest of what his friend was saying. "Now, I'll admit that Landry isn't innocent, by no means, but he's certainly not guilty of what you're setting him up for!"

Trying to keep the peace; Russo motions for the detective to sit back down. He was hoping he wouldn't have to play this card, but it doesn't look like Rawson is going to give him any other choice. "Easy there, Bill, I have something else I want to read to you." Picking up another piece of paper, Russo clears his throat while looking for his starting place to read. "…It is my opinion that Detective Rawson is physically fit to return to light duty, but it is my medical opinion that he should undergo a psyche evaluation before returning to active duty. It is my belief that Detective Rawson is suffering from a form of psychological shock, from Post Traumatic Stress Disorder from this encounter." Charlie Russo looks up at the detective's face, and then spins the report around for Rawson to verify it. "Now can you see how this could screw up everyone's career, if this gets out? Even the doctor thought you had lost your mind, with some of the stuff you were babbling about. Do you really think the Feds are gonna let you throw egg on their faces?"

"Why not, Nick did." Rawson mumbles.

Russo just stares at his friend, not understanding the comment. "Here's what your lunatic ravings have earned you. Bill, I want you to take two weeks off, and let this blow over. Take the time to get your head right and come back to us. Prove to the doctor that you can pass the psyche evaluation, and you're reinstated." The Captain walks around the desk and sits on the edge, trying to ease the tension of the situation by acting like Rawson's friend. "This is how it has to be, Bill. It's really out of all of my hands now."

Rawson lowers his head in disgust, and then stands up to face his former friend. "Just remember one thing, Charles. You put that badge on for the same reason I did. You took the same oath to protect the innocent, find the truth, and arrest the guilty." Rawson pulls his badge off his belt and tosses it onto Russo's desk. "You can keep your lies, deceit, and dishonesty. I didn't sign up for this."

"Don't think that by walking away that it gives you carte blanche to tell the world! If you so much as breathe a word of this to anyone, you'll have every department of the law on top of you, to lock you up for the rest of your life!" Russo's face turns blood red with anger for the hand that Bill Rawson has just played.

"Ah, ah, ah, you should think about that a little more, for a minute, Charlie. If I did blab to the world, all of you 'cover up' conspirators might not have a job any more, that would allow you to arrest me." Rawson knows that whatever future he might have had, just went flying out the window, so to speak. There comes a time in every man's life, when he must stand up for what he believes in, no matter what the cost. Nick Landry taught Bill this. "Oh, and just so that we're clear about this, fuck you, Charlie! Now I know why my sister left your ass."

Russo ignores the remark and looks at Rawson, trying to figure him out. "What's with you, Bill? What made you go soft on this guy? If I'm not mistaken, Detective Bill Rawson was the one to first lead the crusade to bury this Nickolas Landry. What happened to that?"

"I found the truth." Rawson exits the Captain's office, sending a dozen or more faces back into their paperwork. He looks around, wondering how many of his fellow detectives had sided with Russo. Obviously, every one of them, because Bill was the only one called in to see Charlie. Before he could start for the exit, Rawson sees three large muscle bound men enter the main room, heading straight for Russo's office. Each of the men stand at six foot six or better, dressed in DSC attire. They walk with a presumptuous air passed the on looking detectives, heading straight for Captain Russo. Instead of leaving, Rawson sits down at an empty desk and picks up the phone. These guys aren't FBI, or even with the government for that matter. If they're here for Nick, the situation may be bleaker for the Guardian, than Rawson first believed.

"Captain Russo, My name is Lt. Colonel Carter Regal,

British liaison with Darkside Command. My team and I have been dispatched here to your fine city, to claim custody of Mr. Nickolas Landry." The leader of the trio stands at Captain Russo's doorway, as if he expected Charlie to jump up from his desk, to honor Regal's request. This proves Rawson's hunch right on the money. So focused on the Captain's office, the detective doesn't notice the young woman and another big man who accompanies her, walk in and stop right in front of cubicle where he sits. He looks up to see that she too is wearing the same DSC attire, but seems more out of place wearing it than her comrades. She is like a woman pulled from an earlier era to be thrust into the futuristic attire, and is now staring at him as if she knew he was eavesdropping. To try to throw her off, Rawson says goodbye into the receiver and hangs up the phone. He gives her a nod, which simply sends the lady on her way to join her colleagues, with her large companion following suit.

He probably shouldn't be surprised by the appearance of the unexpected guests. That doesn't mean that he likes it any. Where he comes from, you never talk out the side of your neck when dealing with your coconspirators. For this, Russo will throw in a monkey wrench, simply for personal satisfaction. "So, what happened to the Federal boys? I have to admit that I was expecting the FBI to walk in here, instead of the likes of you." Russo walks around his desk and takes a seat in his chair. "Judging by your accent, I would say that you're British, right? Well, I'm not sure how they do things in merry ol' England, but here in the States we have a thing called due process. So, I hate to break the bad news to you, Colonel, but you're not taking anyone, anywhere, until I check this all out."

Colonel Regal isn't accustomed to having his word questioned. In fact, the incident is down right aggravating to the DSC Official. Hoping to speed things up, he pulls a piece of paper from his coat and hands it to Captain Russo. "I believe that this should answer all of your questions, Captain." Regal motions for one of his men to close the door. "I really don't think you understand how dire this situation is."

This is Rawson's cue to get out of there. If he knows one thing, Charlie Russo doesn't like to be short stroked, and will probably delay this transfer as long as he can, just because he feels like his toes have been stepped on. Captain Russo may want to sweep all of this under the rug, but he doesn't care for the new carpet cleaning crew standing in front of him. Russo's delay tactics should give Rawson the time he needs to carry out his plan. It isn't that Rawson likes the decision that he's made, but he's a little more comfortable knowing that he might have a little extra time to carry it out. The time has come for Bill Rawson to take matters into his own hands, and prevent this serious injustice from taking place. Even the world's greatest pessimist knows when right is right. He may not know everything about Nick's destiny, but he's seen and heard enough to know that these DSC goons are bad news for Nick. If Captain Russo had seen what Rawson witnessed, ol' Charlie would understand a little better why his friend has chosen to throw his career away.

Picking up the phone again, Rawson quickly dials an inside extension, and waits for someone to pick up the line. "Yeah, this is Rawson in homicide, I want prisoner 101964 to be escorted to interrogation room three. No, I will be conducting the questioning myself." Rawson looks back at the captain's door to make sure it was still closed. "Nope, that'll do it." He hangs up the phone before heading off to carry out his plan. Unfortunately for one of his colleagues, Rawson turns the corner, not paying attention where he was going, and runs right into the detective, smashing the man's doughnut against his clean shirt. "Oh, wow, sorry about the doughnut, Sanchez. Hey, Gilbert, who's working down in lock up cage, tonight?"

"De Silva," Sanchez replies, trying to wipe the jelly filling off his shirt. "What were you doing at my desk, Rawson?" Sanchez sits his coffee down and tosses the remains of his pastry into the nearby trash can. He turns around to criticize Rawson for the condition of the shirt, but his fellow detective is already exiting the bullpen through the rows of modular furniture to take the back exit down the stairs to the evidence lock up. There inside the cage is Rawson's friend, De Silva, just like Sanchez had said.

"Sarge, ol' buddy, I hope you've got your running shoes on tonight, because I need you to hustle back there and pull six cases that I need verification of contents before tomorrow morning."

"Detective, ol' buddy, you can kiss my ass, if you think I'm gonna haul out a ton of shit, just so that you can tell me to put it back because it's all there! I'm too old for that kind of lifting, and they don't pay me enough to hustle anywhere." De Silva hits the button to unlock the security gate. "You get your butt in here, and do your own leg work for once. Just hurry up though, because I get off in thirty minutes. I don't want to explain why I left you in here alone."

"No sweat, Sarge, I'll be in and out of here before you know it." Rawson hurries into the cage and begins to meander through the rows of shelving, searching for the right case number. "Here we go." He pulls the plastic bag from the bin and drops it into the left sleeve of his coat. This is the point of no return. The decorated detective takes a deep breath and turns to leave. His moral compass is going haywire at the moment. What he is doing is wrong in so many ways, but he truly feels that it's the right thing to do. If his timing is right, Landry should be in the interrogation room by now.

"Hold on there a second, Detective!" De Silva waddles

over to stop his friend's hand from releasing the mag-lock on the cage door. "Rawson, you know I can't let you walk out of here without a scan down. The cameras can see you, and me." De Silva produces a metal detector wand from the clip on his belt and begins to scan the surface of Rawson's body. As expected, the wand sounds out as it passes over Rawson's left side. The tool is designed to detect any metal objects, or sensor tags on any nonmetallic items, to prevent the taking of evidence from lock up without authorization. Sergeant De Silva gives his friend a stern look. "What is that, Detective?" Rawson lets out a sigh of frustration, and then uses his wounded hand to open his coat, revealing his .45 automatic hanging in his shoulder holster. "Jesus Christ, Rawson, you know you're not supposed to bring your fire arm into lock up, no matter what! Now get outta here before we both get kicked off the force."

"Take it easy, Carl; remember, no harm, no foul." Rawson says his goodbyes and heads off to the stairway again. After climbing three flights as fast as he can, the nervous detective stops at the third floor landing to catch his breath. Standing in front of the third floor door, Bill Rawson says a silent prayer, asking that he be right about what he is about to do, before opening the door and calmly walking out of the stairwell and into the corridor.

He walks down the hall passing comrades and coworkers that he may never see again, after tonight. "Hey Kowalski," Rawson stops a fellow detective heading in the opposite direction. "Listen, here's that five I owe you." He reaches into his pocket and pulls out a five dollar bill he had put aside for a pack of smokes. "Don't let it be said that I didn't cover my debts," Rawson points out, hoping it might make a difference. Kowalski simply shrugs his shoulders and walks away with the money that he didn't expect to get back. Kowalski and the others may not know it, but Rawson is doing all of this for them, and for the entire world. This event has changed his outlook on mankind, and life in general, making him realize that no matter how bad it may seem in the world, it can always be a lot worse.

"Detective Rawson, the prisoner is waiting for you in the interrogation room." The ex-Marine, now Corrections Officer, stands at attention, causing Rawson to believe that the former drill instructor was going to salute him. The guard steps away from the door to allow Rawson to enter. "Do you want me to come in there with you?"

"No," Rawson's answer comes quick, almost too quick, raising the suspicion of the corrections officer, a little. This prompts Bill to offer an explanation just as fast. "There's no need for me to tie you up any longer. He's cuffed, right?" Rawson pauses for a second to look at the guard's nametag. "I'll give you a call when I'm all done is here, Meriwether." Rawson waits for a colleague to walk by. "Ya know; you could do me a small favor though. Stop in and shut off the cameras down the hall. I don't want anyone to see me lose my temper, if you know what I mean."

Meriwether gives the detective an understanding smile. Stan Meriwether was kicked out of the Marines for being too rough. After giving Rawson a wink and a pat to the shoulder for acknowledgment, the corrections officer walks away to carry out Rawson's request. With the hallway empty, Rawson enters the room as his anxiety levels begin to rise.

Nick sits at the table with his legs crossed in the chair, and his hands lying on his knees, palms up. He opens his eyes to see who had come to visit, and is surprisingly happy to see that it's Rawson. Nick jumps to his feet to face the detective, glad to see a familiar face. The detective waves him down for a minute while looking around the room. When he sees the little red lights on top of the cameras go out, then Rawson is willing to give an explanation for what's going on. "I'm willing to guess that without this thing; you have no idea what your up against, do ya?"

"Rawson, where's JD? And, what about the reporter, is she okay too?"

The detective gives Nick a chuckle as if he doesn't believe Nick's concern for the others' welfare. "Pal, you've got a whole lot more to worry about right now." Rawson reaches into his coat with his right hand, causing Nick to lean away a little. He pulls the plastic bag out and hands it to Nick. "You've got to get out of here as fast as you can." Rawson pauses one more time before releasing the bag to Nick. "Tell me one more time that this is all for real, right?" Nick nods his answer, surprised that the detective was willing to go to such extremes to help Nick. Rawson lets go. "Then you really need to get the hell out of here, if you can. There are some real heavy hitters upstairs that are here to take you out. I've done all that I can do. The rest is up to you. You better not make me look like a fool, Landry." Rawson walks over to the door, and turns to look at Nick one more time, before opening it. "I'm pretty sure I just threw my life away. You better make it count for something." Rawson is puzzled by the fact that Nick simply bows as a response, before the detective opens the door.

He's surprised to find the corrections officer standing outside, wearing a smile on his face. "Did it get carried away in there?" The guard's tone suggests that he hoped to hear some violent news. This disturbs Rawson causing the detective to give the guard a second look. "Do you want me to take him back down to holding?" He reaches for the door knob, only to be stopped by Rawson.

"Are you for real?" Rawson holds the door open wide for a second, until the corrections officer tries to look inside. He then steps out of the doorway in front of the guard as Rawson feels something brush against his shoulder. As the door closes, Rawson looks both ways up and down the hall before addressing the guard again. "Landry is fine. Leave him in there until the brass comes down to collect him. Stay here though, and don't open the door, and don't let anyone in. If I were you, I'd be expecting them any minute." Rawson turns away and heads straight for the elevator, believing he is about to leave the building for the last time. Oddly enough, it's something he wants to do as fast as he can.

"Yes sir, no, I understand completely. No sir, I agree with you one hundred percent. Landry should, and will, be handed over to them, immediately." Captain Russo hangs up the phone and calmly pushes his chair away from the desk, so that he can stand up to face the DSC operatives. "You'll be happy to know, that the Governor assures me that this is the right moves to make for all of us, and I am to offer you our full cooperation. Now, I don't completely understand all of the politics associated with my position, but one thing I do know is when I'm not getting the full story. I guess you can call it a policeman's intuition. Evidently, there are some very high profile people, all the way up in Washington DC, who wants Landry in your custody." Russo leans back against his desk and looks at the Colonel from Darkside Command. "Just between us, what's your stake in all of this?"

Colonel Regal gives Russo the complimentary smile that accompanies his next statement. "I'm sorry, Captain, but that is classified." His arrogant British tone gives Regal a pompous air.

Charlie Russo is quick to return the same gesture before replying, "yeah, and that's bullshit too." Russo snatches up the receiver of the phone and dials an inside extension. "Hello? Yeah, Russo here; I want prisoner 101964 readied for transportation." A look of shock and then anger crosses the Captain's face. "What do you mean he's not in his cell?"

Only one word has to be said to explain what is happening.
"Rawson!!!"

"This has gone on long enough," one of the big men says to the other. "Landry must be eliminated."

"We'll make a move like that when Carter feels it's necessary. He's still the one in charge, Michael." Sebastian replies.

"Actually, the council is the one who is in charge."

The leader of the DSC team doesn't need an explanation to know what is happening. Carter turns to face the young woman, as the rest of his team stands ready at attention. "Deidre, locate the Guardian! Find his location before he can get away." He faces the three huge men who await his orders, and waits for his wife to give them something to use.

The young woman closes her eyes and concentrates on the building's interior. When she opens them again, her eyes glow like two white hot flames shining in the dark. In front of her appears a translucent image of the police headquarters' lobby, and everyone moving through it. "He is on the ground level of this structure, heading for the main entrance," Deidre explains, as the detectives in the room stand frozen place, awestruck by what they are witnessing.

"I don't see him." One of the big men declares, staring at the image in front of him.

"He is using the power of the talisman to conceal his presence." Deidre closes her eyes and ends the vision. "Carter, we need to go!"

Colonel Regal motions for the twins, Sebastian and Benjamin to move, waving his hand towards the front wall of the building. Russo has his own way of handling a situation like this in his building. He picks up the phone again and presses a single button, to order the building locked down. Before he can hang up the phone, Russo hears the crashing of glass as the twins from DSC leap out the fourth floor windows with the third big man in pursuit. Carter and Deidre follow suit, joining Michael at the newly created opening, before all three leap out to the ground below. Everyone left in the bullpen are dumbfounded, frozen by what just happened, except Russo. He simply walks back into his office and opens the bottom drawer of the file cabinet to collect a twelve year old bottle of Scotch, and cracks the seal. Sitting down at his desk, Charlie tilts the bottle up into the air, before bringing it down to his mouth. This is a momentous occasion. Charlie Russo has now seen it all.

Rawson hurries across the street to his car, knowing that the cat is out of the proverbial bag. His first clue was the sound of the front doors locking down, just seconds after he exited the building. Once at his car, he climbs into the driver's seat, but before he can close the door, Rawson is shocked by the sound of the shattering glass from the police headquarters across the street. He is literally awestruck by the sight of the two big men crashing down on to the roofs of two parked cars. "Oh shit!" He exclaims, as he drops the keys into the floorboard.

Sebastian and Benjamin leap from the cars and begin to scan their surroundings for any sign of Nick. "Deidre, love, we need you to point him out to us." Benji suggests as he stares into the lobby. When the big man looks up to see his comrades floating down, he sees Nick's reflection in the glass in front of him. Before Benji could warn his brother that Nick was also on the outside looking in, their prey becomes the predator and charges them with the intention of cutting the odds in half.

As she descends, Deidre senses Nick's attack, finally seeing through his cloaked persona. "Sebastian, Benjamin, look out, he's behind you!" Her psychic warning is heard too late. Nick plows into the two behemoths, driving them face first into the concrete wall beside the glass doors of the lobby. With their faces embedded into the concrete, Nick turns to stare down the remaining trio of this group.

Nick looks to the young woman first. He too, heard Deidre's warning, and sees the potential threat that she poses. Ready for the conflict, he knows that she has to be the next to fall, especially if she can pinpoint his location. He leaps at Michael and grabs the goliath to swing him around, before sending Regal's First Knight colliding into his leader, but Nick doesn't let go after that. Unfortunately for them, Deidre's ability to "see" Nick is a second or two out of sync with reality. When dealing with a little bit of distance, it's not such a bad thing, but in these close quarters, her warnings are moot. By the time she recognizes his attack on Carter and Michael, Nick is already planning his attack on her. "Here, catch this guy," He suggests, as he spins around to release the big man, sending Michael flying at her. Deidre tries to offer some kind of defense, but the weight of Michael and the force of the throw, simply smashes her, and her mystical force field, into the front of an oncoming bus. The public service vehicle veers to the right and plows right into the unsuspecting Carter Regal, who was trying to recover from the collision with his teammate.

Those three are out for the count, but the first two catch Nick's attention again, as they pull themselves from the wall. Benjamin is stunned, but able to stand. Sebastian doesn't appear to be as lucky, needing a couple more minutes to recover. This makes Nick focus on Benji, being that the big man was the next thing closest to a threat. He knows that time is short and he needs to be moving on. For the moment, Nick's only opposition is basically down for the count. The damage done to the wall of the building has somehow jammed the door system, holding all of the cops inside at bay. Most of them didn't really appear to be in a big hurry to go outside any way, not understanding what was taking place. Still cloaked by the talisman, Nick steps up in front of the big man and delivers a crushing blow to the man's abdomen, evacuating all of the air out of Benjamin's lungs. "Tell your council that I said to back off, or next time you and your buddies won't be so lucky." To accentuate his point, Nick delivers an upper cut that sends the big man flying through the front glass façade of the police headquarters' lobby. Not quite what Nick had planned before he delivered the punch, but the cops inside still weren't in too big of a hurry to see what was outside.

Rawson just sits there with his mouth wide open. He, like everyone else, can't believe what they have just seen, and Rawson has witnessed some pretty incredible stuff as of late. To top it all off, Nick appears in the passenger's seat beside the detective, nearly giving Rawson a heart attack. Nick reaches down and picks up the keys to hand to the detective. "I suggest you start the car and get us out of here, before you are slapped with an aiding and abetting charge."

Rawson slams the car door and starts the engine. After wiping the sweat from his brow, he puts the car in gear and speeds off blowing through a red light wanting to put as much distance between him and the police force as possible. "If you ever pull that shit again, I swear to God that I will shoot you in the head, myself! Damn, you scared the piss outta me!" Rawson grabs the half empty pack of cigarettes from the dashboard to light one. He stares at the nine cancer sticks for a moment, and then throws the pack out the window. "I guess if I'm doing all of this so that you can save the world, I oughtta stick around long enough to see how it all turns out." He laughs to himself and looks down at his lap before turning to face Nick. "I'm serious, pal, you got me so good that I dribbled in my boxers."

"Whoa, too much information," Nick laughs to himself

at Rawson's discomfort. "I'm sorry Detective; I didn't mean to spook ya, like that. But, it was funny, to see the expression on your face." Nick cringes as Rawson barely misses the taillights of a car, as his sedan slides around the corner, headed for the southbound lanes of highway one. "Ya know, for whatever reason you may have, thanks for helping me back there. Nick looks out at Biscayne Bay and chuckles to himself a second time, remembering his little escapade with Billy.

Rawson looks over at Nick, impressed with what he saw on the street in front of the headquarters. "Ya know, me and your little buddy sure coulda' used your help at the junkyard. Ya know, after you and your girlfriend left the party, all of her invited guests wanted to keep things going. Okay, it's your turn, what's so funny?"

Nick looks over at Rawson. "It's just that this makes the second time a guy named Bill has helped reunite me with the talisman, that's all." Nick glances out the windshield to see a road sign announcing that they are entering the Florida Keys wildlife Preserve. "If you don't mind, would you care to tell me where we're going?"

Now it's Rawson's turn to chuckle. "We are going to the one place that no one but me, knows about." Rawson's smile fades as he makes eye contact Nick. "You my friend are going to open up to me about everything, exclusively to me. There is no other choice in the matter for you. I don't want to hear how that's not possible, or you're not allowed. If you need to, you can write it off as payment for services rendered."

Nick stares into Rawson's eyes, seeing that the detective is asking for more than just simple answers. Nick can see that his new friend is in need of justification. "Ya know what, Bill? I don't think that will be a problem at all. He looks back over his shoulder expecting to see a dozen or more police vehicles in a hot pursuit. Needless to say, Nick is happy to be pleasantly wrong for once.

# Chapter XXVII

"Ya know; the way you took out those goons at the station was something else! Tell me, how long have you known you can do that? I mean, you literally planted those guys right into the concrete wall! Man, I'm tellin' ya, that's the kind of stuff that you only see in the movies!" As his tension for the moment eases, Rawson starts to enjoy the adrenaline rush he's feeling. "I have to tell ya though; I did feel kinda bad for the little lady, when you sandwiched her between that bus and the big bastard you hit her with. Then, there was that guy, I think he was the leader of the group, when that poor guy stood up, just as the bus and his buddies plowed right into him. That had to be the best hat trick I've seen in a long time!" Rawson uses his hands to reenact the chain of events while he's driving, like a kid entertaining himself. "Slam, bam, crash, get out of the way!" He looks back over at Nick and sees a confused expression produced by Rawson's actions. Slightly embarrassed, the detective quickly changes the subject quickly, "As for where we're going; I've got a boat tucked away down in Key Largo. You know, like the Bertie Higgins song ...starring in our own late, late show, just like they did in Key Largo... Oh never mind. The first

455

thing we need to do is get you out of the States, and since we can't fly or drive out, the next best thing is by sea.

To say that Nick is shocked by Rawson's actions would be an understatement. Why would this man, a complete stranger to Nick's cause, be so willing to throw his life away to help Nick? The first guess would be personal gain, but Nick can't think of anything he has that Rawson could want, or benefit from, worth the risk he's taking. "Let me ask you something, Detective. Why are you so willing to help me? In doing this, you've tossed your career, and everything else, into the toilet, and for what? Most people, who make such a rash decision like this, do so because they're suicidal. You're not, are you?"

"Nick ol' boy, there comes a time in every man's life, when he has to sit down, look at himself in the mirror, and examine the worth of who he is. That time for me is long gone," Rawson stares out the windshield as if he was about to announce a great secret. "What I saw, when I looked in that mirror, was something I wasn't very proud of, one bit. What's even sadder is that I accepted what I was, and believed the time had passed to make a change. Call it stupid, but I feel like I've been given another chance to do the right thing, and give my life and time here on Earth merit." Rawson returns his focus to the road and sits quietly, humble and yet proud of himself.

Suddenly, Nick feels humbled a little as well. He remembers Master Masamoto's story about the supplemental soldiers who died for the possible salvation of mankind. It was a warning of sorts, about how many have died countless times, and countless ways, to keep the world from the reaches of darkness. Like the Viking, Ulmheir the Great, who gave his life to aid Lady Victorius and her man Lord Devare, Nick now sees Rawson in a whole new light. If nothing else, this gives Nick reason to reevaluate his standing in this matter. "You're alright, Rawson."

"Yeah, well since we're in this for the long haul how about you call me Bill from now on. Oh shit, here we go." Rawson pulls the car off the main road and drives slowly down the dirt driveway, trying to avoid as many potholes as possible. Hidden behind a wall of palm trees and mangroves sits an old fishing boat salvage yard. This exclusive yard consists of two relics that didn't look sea worthy sitting up on timbers, a stack of broken crab traps, and a two room shack at the water's edge. It's so exclusive that no one but Rawson, and the owner of the yard, go there. "I bought this old boat from a DEA auction a few years ago, and have been sinking my retirement savings into it ever since. Pardon the poor choice of words. That's her over there in the water," he declares, pointing at his pride and joy tied off at the dock. "Any way, she's not a luxury liner, by no means, but she'll get us anywhere in the Caribbean you'd want to go." Rawson suddenly slows the car down even more. "Oh shit, there's Manny, the owner of this dump. Quick; do that invisibility act of yours before he sees you." The detective glances over at the passenger seat, to find it already empty. "Are you still there?" He reaches over to touch the seat. Rawson thought he felt something bump him in the hallway outside the interrogation room. He suspected it to be Nick, leaving the room as well, cloaked by the talisman. If he was right, then he should be able to feel Nick, if he's still sitting in the seat.

"Rawson, what are you doing fondling your seat, and when are you going to get that wreck away from my dock?" Manny's broken English and high pitched voice makes him sound like the Taco Bell Chihuahua yelling at Rawson. "Just because you are a cop, doesn't mean you can take advantage of people's generosity."

The good detective reaches into his shirt pocket and

pulls out eight one hundred dollar bills, and hands them to Manny. "You did fix the fuel lines like you promised, right?" He hesitates letting go of the money, causing Manny to rip it from Rawson's fingers. There's an extra two hundred for your time, and another three for the rent on the dock." Rawson explains.

"Oh Detective Rawson, you are a generous man. Have I ever told you how much of a joy it is doing business with you?" Manny walks alongside Rawson's car, counting his money over and over, while his friend parks the car.

"Blow me, Manny," Rawson responds, as he gets out of the car. "Besides, I told you that I would have my baby out of here in two weeks. That was last weekend, so this makes me a week early."

"Amigo, where I come from, we would put down a baby like that."

"Whatever Manny; listen, I need you to fill up the tanks on the old girl. I've been given two weeks mandatory vacation, and I'm going fishing. Rawson walks over to his boat, with Manny and his dog close behind.

"Oh, I filled the tanks up for you, after I finished working on the fuel lines. You're already to go, amigo."

"Yeah right, you just did that so you could milk me outta more money for cheap fuel." Rawson climbs over the railing onto his boat, and looks back at his friend. "See ya, around, Manny."

"What, you're not bringing this ugly beast back here?"

"No Manny, I don't think I'll be back this way." He waves Manny off and walks down the starboard side of the boat to enter the main cabin. Rawson always dreamed of retiring on this boat. He never thought it would happen like this. After going through his check list for launch, he heads down below deck to check on the status of the boat below the water line. He opens the first cabin door, and then jumps back against the wall of the narrow corridor, spooked by the sight of Nick sitting on the small bunk.

"Hey, you keep that gun in its holster, pal. You're the one who opened the door. I didn't jump out at you, or nothing!" Nick drops the cat sitting in his lap and stands up.

"Yeah, well you still scared the shit out of me. I don't think I'll ever get use to that!" Aggravated by the sight of the feline, Rawson picks the cat up to escort it off the boat, preferably into the water.

"Amigo, are you talking to me?" Manny leans his head in over the side to look down the stairway.

"No Manny, I'm talking to your damned cat! Why can't he stay on dry land like normal cats? Walking to the end of the corridor, Rawson hands the cat up to Manny. "Now, will you both please get off my boat?"

"It's because your boat smells like fish, amigo. What else would you expect from the little gato? Do you want me to cast off the lines?"

"Yeah, Manny, cast off the lines while I start up the engines." He follows Manny up on deck, and enters the bridge of his magnificent ship. "So long, Manny, I hope you have a good life. Rawson starts up the engines, relieved that Manny had done what he was supposed to do. When Manny waves the all clear, Rawson puts the boat's drive into reverse, and slowly backs the fishing vessel away from the dock.

In minutes, the fishing boat is cutting out into the open waters of the Caribbean, destination unknown. Nick walks up to the doorway of the bridge, and stops out of maritime. "Permission to enter the bridge, Captain," Nick walks on in and up to the wheel where Rawson stares out at the evening sky. One thing is for sure, the detective was right; this is where he wanted to retire. Propped up on the instrument console, Nick gazes out at the rolling waves as well. "Ya know; this is the reason me, Charlie, and Sonny, joined the

Navy. There's something very serene about being out at sea. A funny story; we had this kid in our unit for a short time. His name was Johnny Watters, and he was one of the gutsiest guys I know. In fact this kid would take on an ass whipping while sparring with Sonny, just to feel her rubbing her body all over his. I remember Charlie and Jorge taking him down to the infirmary one time, after Sonny mopped the gymnasium with the guy. They said that they asked him if it was worth it, and Johnny replied, every painful, firm, minute. The only problem with Johnny was that he couldn't stand being out on the ocean. He'd jump out of a plane at thirty thousand feet, but he couldn't stand to be in, or on, water where he couldn't touch bottom."

Rawson laughs at the irony of Nick's short story. "And, this guy joined the Navy, with a name like Watters! That's a hoot!" The former detective turns around to see Nick wearing some familiar clothes. "Hey, those ol' duds don't look too bad on ya. All you need is a Detroit Tigers hat and a mustache to complete the look."

"Maybe, but it's really not my style." Nick feels like he should be going to a Hawaiian luau, in the tropical print shirt and Bermuda shorts. "That reminds me, I'm starving. Have you got anything on this tub to eat? All I've had in the past two days is a Snicker's candy bar."

Unable to keep from laughing, Rawson understands Nick's request. After all that has happened, Bill hasn't had a chance to eat, either. "I'll tell ya what. Down in the galley is a fresh stock of groceries, I brought on board last week. Why don't you go down and fish out a couple of those steaks out of the freezer. Once I get us across the shipping lanes, we can break out the grill and fire it up." He gives the engines a little gas as the waves start to grow more and more in the open water. "Hang on to something down there. This little crossing is gonna get rough."

Nick ignores Bill's warning and heads back downstairs with a strong desire to fill his belly. For the first time, in a long time, he feels like he can actually relax and breathe a little easier. Sure, he's on the run from every law enforcement agency in the country. Yes, by morning his image will be spread across the globe, creating a world wide man hunt. Not to mention, the fact that his life has been completely destroyed, but somehow he is able to find a small measure of peace, for the moment. For now, it is enough to keep him going. The more important necessity at the moment is sustenance. If his body runs out of gas, no measure of peace can keep him going anywhere. He opens the refrigerator, and is disappointed with the selection he finds. Two cans of sardines, a twelve pack of light beer, two sacks of cold cuts, a loaf of bread, and that's it. He opens the freezer door, to find it empty. "If you had to eat some of this, what would you choose?" Nick's question is to himself, but he knows that he doesn't have an answer. Opting for the least toxic, he grabs two slices of bread, and piles the entire amount of turkey on to make a sandwich. As Rawson walks in, he takes notice to the empty sack of turkey cold cuts. "Hey, what's wrong with grilling a couple of steaks?"

"There wasn't any, Nick replies, pointing to the freezer, and then takes another large bite.

Rawson hurries over to the fridge and snatches open the door. After staring into the empty box for a moment, all he can say is one word, "Manny!" He grabs two beers and closes the refrigerator door. "Oh well, I guess it's a good thing I prefer ham over turkey." He looks at Nick just as his guest shoves the remaining piece of the sandwich into his mouth. "Here, wash that dry bread down with this." Rawson opens up the ham and fixes a sandwich.

Nick savors the last bite of the sandwich, unable to remember when he had sliced turkey that tasted so good.

"No thanks on the beer. I don't drink. What I'd really like is some bottled water."

"Bud, this is the closest thing to bottled water within fifty miles, so unless you want to go dip a cup of sea water out of the ocean, I suggest you drink this." Rawson walks around the table and sits down on the bench seat across from Nick. "Do you believe that I paid seven hundred and fifty bucks for this fine sailing craft? Now, I know that she don't have sails, but who gives a shit, right? Ya know, your involvement in my life has really compromised my time schedule for having this ol' girl ready for our retirement voyage. Manny was going to pull her out of the water next week to scrape the hull and put a fresh coat of paint on her belly." Rawson twists off the bottle cap and takes a drink beer and then looks back at Nick. "So, where do we go from here, Mr. Landry?" He takes another sip from his beer. "You know that you'll be a wanted man wherever you go. How does a man serve as the savior of humanity, when he's hunted by the very people he's trying to save?"

Nick goes against his personal rule and pops the cap from his beer. He's never been a drinker, but when the choices are sea water and cheap light beer, he figures the beer had to be the better of the two. After a couple of swallows, he's almost ready to give the alternative the try. "To be honest with ya Rawson, I really don't know at the moment. I guess the smartest move would be to blend in to the background and disappear. People do it all the time, actually. At the moment, I'd be happy to take a couple of days and relax a little before I make that decision." Nick drinks down a couple of swallows trying to hurry through the unpleasant affair. "What are your plans, Bill? You do have some poles and tackle on this fishing boat, don't you?" Turning the bottle up, he gulps down the rest of the beer and tosses the bottle into the trash can on the other side of the room. "We can sail around the Caribbean, do a little fishing, and then whatever happens after that will take care of it self."

Trying to stay on the same level with Nick, Rawson tries the same move with his beer bottle, missing the trash can all together. "You're alright, Nick," Rawson pauses to let a burp fly. "To be quite honest, I think you're a hell of a man. I mean, damn, I've witnessed you losing everything, and here you sit planning tomorrow's activities as if nothing happened. How do you manage to maintain that persona of a cool cucumber?" Rawson stands up and walks over to get two more beers from the fridge.

Nick finds humor in Rawson's statement and laughs to himself. After a second of consideration, he simply replies, "My Master, Hiro Masamoto, once told me that for a man to exist in the future, he must first forget the past. To be focused on the future, he must exist in the present. There is no way to go back and change what has already happened. One must learn, adapt, and constantly move forward. That is the secret to evolution." Nick reaches out and catches the beer flying at him that Rawson tossed across the galley. When Nick finally turns his head, He sees Bill standing over by the refrigerator cringing.

"I am so glad you caught that," Bill admits, walking back over to join Nick at the table, as he cracks open his beer. "Ya know if you are ever in a financial bind, you could always do that kind of stuff in a sideshow carnival. How did you catch the bottle, without knowing it was coming?"

"After years of training, that kind of stuff becomes second nature." Nick twists the cap off the bottle, and is surprised, when he turns the bottle up to be so willing to drink another one. "Hey Bill, the engines just shut off. Do you know why that happened?"

Rawson finishes his second beer and chuckles. "Of course I do. Man, you really need to relax a little. I programmed the navigation equipment to take us to the western most island of the Bahama chain. Listen," Rawson puts his hand to his ear just in time to hear the anchor splash into the water. He listens for the chain to feed out, and then returns his attention back to Nick. "Oh don't go lookin' so surprised. She may not look like much, but she's top shelf under the hood." Still hungry, the retired cop goes for a can of sardines and two more beers. "Now that we're on our way with a cozy conversation, I'd like to toss around a few things." Rawson sits back down and opens his beer. "It'll be kinda like a fill in the blanks game." He offers Nick the third round before opening the can of sardines.

Normally, in a situation like this, Nick would turn his thoughts inward to bury the pain of the subject. The effects of the beer seem to let him be more open this time. He accepts the next beer and drops it into the cup holder, mounted to the table, and then takes another drink from the bottle that he's working on. "Okay, but since this might be one of those once in a lifetime events; I'm not holding anything back. I'll give you the truth as I know it; you believe what you want."

"Deal," Rawson replies as he sits up a little straighter. "Okay, now you and this guy, Masamoto, meet and he tells you that you have this destiny to take his place as the Guardian of the talisman. What made you say, okay, where do I sign up? I mean, the guy had to have given you some kind of warning how bad things could be, right?"

Nick finishes off his second beer, surprised to find that it doesn't taste so bad after you get the first two down. "To be honest, with ya Bill, I was more or less star struck with the guy. His philosophies on life, and how to approach living, were something that I had searched for a long time to learn. Of course, knowing stuff about me that no one alive could know had a certain way of calming my skepticism along the way. He taught me things that I could never have learned on my own. Masamoto gave me warnings about the risk, but he showed me the reason of his quest, and that compelled me to accept my duty. Do I regret it now? You're damned right I do, but in the same instance, if I had denied my destiny, and the talisman fell into the hands of darkness, would my life be in any less turmoil than what I'm experiencing now? There is no way for me to know that now. But, let's just go back a little and ask you a question." Nick opens the beer in the cup holder and takes a drink. "What if a man came to you, showed you the fate of the world, and asked you to choose. Do you embrace this destiny and forsake yourself, or throw in the towel and walk away with a chance to live out a normal life?"

"Well, that seems like an easy one to me," Rawson replies, interrupting Nick's hypothetical situation.

"Hold on a minute, there's a catch," Nick explains. "You may be able to live out your normal life without incident, but you have to live with the fact that in denying your destiny, you have condemned the future generations of mankind to a life of misery and suffering, forced to live in a state of hell on earth, for the rest of eternity. How do you live with yourself for the rest of your life, knowing this?"

"Wow, we really went off track with that one, didn't we?" Rawson takes a swig of his beer to wash the sardines down, and leans back against the galley wall. "To answer that question, I guess I'd have to be put into your shoes, to know what to do. Just for the record, I don't want your shoes anywhere near me, okay?" Rawson looks around as if he feels like something is missing. After taking another swig of beer, he realizes what it is and gets up to walk over to the stove. Down in the drawer beneath the oven, behind and underneath some pans, he finds a pack of cigarettes he had stashed for safe keeping. "Hey, Mr. Health nut, you don't mind if I have a cigarette, do ya?" Before receiving a reply, Rawson uses the stove burner to light one any way.

"I thought you were going to give those things up?"

He knew that was coming. "Yeah, but Damnit all to hell, they sure do go good with beer!" To point out his statement, Rawson holds up one hand holding a beer, and then the other holding the cigarette. Back at the table, he reaches above the light fixture and turns on the exhaust fan, and then opens the windows to give his guest fresh air. "In all honesty, I didn't know that the topic of conversation was gonna give me the jitters like this." He sits back down at the other end of the table away from Nick, and stars at him for a moment. "Ya know, if this is bothering you, we don't have to go on. Honestly, Nick, I had no idea what I was asking for."

Nick finishes off his beer before he takes the trip this time, to the fridge for two more. "No, it's okay. To be honest with you, Bill, it feels kinda good to let it all out like this. Believe it or not, I haven't run across too many people who would believe what I had to say."

"No!"

"Yeah, no, I'm serious! If I laid this on you at the hospital when we first met, would you have locked me up in jail, or an asylum?" Nick pops the top off one of the beers and hands it to Rawson before returning to his seat. "As for your smoking, it doesn't bother me a bit." He opens his beer and takes a drink before sitting back down. His look is confident, almost arrogant, as if daring Rawson to ask his worse. "So, where do we go with your topic from here?"

If there is one thing any detective has to know, its how to see what's right in front of you? What Rawson sees is a man who doesn't drink, succumbing to the effects of the alcohol. Then he realizes that the alcohol is merely letting the man show his true self. He leans back against the wall again and stares at Nick's chest, where the weight of the talisman lays against the inside of his shirt. "Okay," Bill points with his cigarette at Nick. "That medallion thingy of yours, what makes it so special? I mean, you're supposed to keep it away from these darkness guys, right? Why?"

Nick reaches into his shirt and pulls the talisman from inside, and lets it dangle in the air, at the ends of its chain. "Just remember, you asked for this, so no scoffing, or doubt." Nick hangs the talisman from the light fixture, and leans back against the wall behind him, to begin his tale. "Almost a thousand years ago, a dark force lead by an evil woman named Jezana, rose up across the lands, hell bent to rule the world in darkness. The first time…"

"You mean this happened more than once?"

Nick dismisses the question and continues with his explanation. The first time this happened, the forces of darkness were defeated by a member of the elf tribe of Ehbidday."

Once again Rawson interrupts with, "Really?" Nick replies this time with a look of distaste. "Okay, okay, I'll shut up."

"It was a girl, well, actually a woman, who prevented the opening of the portal. I never caught the specifics about what she did to accomplish the feat, but it had something to do with a powerful spell that sealed the portal shut for all times." Nick pauses for a second to take a drink of his beer, to wet his throat before continuing. "The next round involved that woman's daughter, named Lady Victorius. Just to let you in on a little secret, when I began my training with Masamoto, he would tell me these stories about the people who have already served the cause. I would lie awake at night and wonder what these people were like, how'd they look, and if I deserved to be included in their ranks." Nick sees the expression on Rawson's face questioning Nick's stability, based on what was just said, but the detective doesn't say a word. "Any way, she and a knight, named Lord Devare participated in an event called the witnessing. Evidently, they proved that humanity was worthy of life, and cast out the darkness from the lands. Jezana's plot was that if the witnessing was prevented, the spell sealing the portal would be broken." Nick looks around for a second. "Where's the latrine on this tub?"

Rawson stands up and motions for Nick to do the same. "She doesn't have one, or at least one that works, any way. If ya gotta go, it's either off the fan tail or into a bottle. Come on, I'll go with ya."

Nick smiles as the alcohol begins to take effect. "That's cool, bro. I don't need any help."

"Screw you, Landry. I've gotta go too. Not to mention the fact that you can keep going with your story, so I don't have to wait for you to get back." Rawson leads Nick out on deck and points him to a corner. "You take that side. I'm partial to the left." Rawson steps up onto the side rail and begins to relieve himself. "So, if this great event took place and erased the threat of darkness from the lands as you put it, how could there be a third time?"

"Ya see, Bill? That's what I like about you." Nick replies, as he finishes. "We both think alike. I said the exact same thing to Masamoto, or asked any way. His response was that even though the physical threat of darkness was dispatched from the earth, it could not be erased from the hearts of man. It is this darkness that manifested itself and brought about the third trial, and cast the talisman for this purpose." Nick stands around, awkwardly waiting for Rawson to wrap it up, before heading back inside. "After Victorius and Devare saved the world, a dark priest named Mandal Rayne set out to revive his queen and continue her quest to open the portal to the Devastator's dark realm."

"Have you noticed how many times you have used the word dark in this story?"

Nick scratches his nose with his middle finger, before continuing on. "One thing to note; gold retains the magic bestowed to it. Any way, this Mandal Rayne set out across the world stealing and pilfering any artifacts that were used in pagan or idol worship. Anything of gold dealing with the black arts was melted down to recreate the original scepter that could open the portal again. The gold was cast into six separate pieces, but when assembled, the dark magic would be channeled through the scepter and be used as a key to open the portal. It was Victorius' daughter Zoe who foiled the third attempt, with her army defeating the forces of darkness and destroying the temple that contains the sealed lock."

Rawson walks over to the fridge, desperately needing another beer and a cigarette after that little tale. He opens another beer and turns around to face Nick. "Okay, but if they were defeated a third time; how do you fit into the picture, so many years later?"

Nick motions for Rawson to get him another one too. "Well, here's where the story really gets out of hand."

"Is that possible?"

Nick blows off the comment and proceeds to carry on with his story. "When his queen and her agents were revived, their bodies had decayed away with time. That meant that their spirits had to possess the bodies of willing victims to carry out their plan. Due to whatever technical difficulties, their spirits are trapped here to wander earth and search for hosts, while waiting for the one chance to come, when a cosmic event would give them the chance once more to open the portal and become whole again. The prophecy calls this the end of times. The scepter is still the key component to their cause. A group called the council had it disassembled and the pieces scattered to the ends of the earth. This piece is said to be the most powerful, and can lead the possessor to the other pieces."

Rawson sits there in his inebriated state, staring at Nick like a kid listening to a Christmas tale. "So will you go after the other pieces?"

Nick gets up for another round of beers. Nope, I'm going to carry out my duty, and see to it that no one gets their hands on this again." Nick looks around, listening to the sounds of the night. "Did you feel something bump up against the boat?"

Rawson tosses a beer bottle at Nick. "Give me a break, Landry! We're in the middle of the Caribbean Ocean, and no one knows where we are! You really need to relax some more. Now, get back to your story and tell me why this council didn't just melt the pieces down and destroy them?" He stares at Nick some more, and then asks, "what have you seen Nick, to give you so much faith in this destiny of yours?"

"I've seen what you have seen, Bill." Nick pauses for a moment, studying the confused look on Rawson's face. "What did you see when you took the talisman from the police station's evidence lock up?"

"My life, flashing in front of my eyes, without pension and benefits," he answers. "Why do you ask?"

Nick takes the talisman and holds it up in front of Rawson. "Go ahead, touch it." Rawson leans away unsure of what Nick was suggesting. Nick shakes the chain to prompt Rawson again. "Go ahead, ya big puss. It ain't gonna hurt ya. Hell, JD did it."

Hesitant, Rawson obliges, not enjoying being called out like this. His fingers touch the talisman for only a moment, but in that time, he sees the carnage and suffering of countless lives. Snatching his hand back, Rawson loses his balance and falls over backwards off the bench. Scrambling to his feet, the detective notices a dark demeanor to Nick's laugh for the reaction. "Very funny, jerk." Rawson sits back down and gives Nick an angry stare.

"Sorry," Nick admits, having let the effects of the alcohol affect his judgment. "According to the prophecy, should darkness fail, there will be a rebirth for humanity. It's my duty to see that the prophecy comes true."

"Wow, if you think about it, it's kinda like the Book of Revelations stuff, ain't it? So, you think you'll be part of this end of times, don't you?"

Nick finishes his beer, and then raises the empty bottle to his friend." Actually, I think it's more like the Mayan prophecy, than the Book of Revelations. As for me, I guess you could say that I already am."

The two men continue their conversation for several more hours, trading stories of life and profession until both men begin to doze off from a combination of exhaustion and alcohol. During their discussion, Nick came to some conclusion about what he needs to do. Perhaps, it is this that allows him to get some needed rest. His mind doesn't dream. He isn't whisked away to some alternate realm. Nickolas Landry simply sleeps.

# Chapter XXVIII

Bill Rawson rolls over in his bunk, feeling every bit of the effects of the beer he drank last night. Like an undead corpse pulling itself from the grave, he climbs out of the narrow bunk to look for his drinking partner. Bill walks into the galley and finds it resembling a poor man's mad Scientist's laboratory. A tent of plastic is hung over two empty pots sitting on the burners, on the stove. Actually, he notices that the pots aren't empty, looking inside them to see a crusty white powder caked in the bottoms. On the counter are several paper towels that were layered with the same white crusty powder. On the floor are more empty pots and bowls with the corners of the plastic tent resting in them. "What in the hell did you do in here last night? Landry, wake up, so we can go catch some breakfast. Bill gives Nick a nudge, almost pushing him off the bench, and under the table.

Nick sits up quickly after catching himself, before rolling off onto the worn vinyl flooring. His first reaction is to yell at Sonny for the rude awakening. Then his mind clears, reminding him that she's not the culprit. Opening his eyes, Nick sees what Rawson was talking about, and offers an explanation. "I woke up last night, dying of thirst. So I took a couple of the beers, some sea water, combined the two, and then boiled and filtered it so that I could have something to drink."

"What was wrong with drinking the beer?" Disgusted by the alcohol abuse, Rawson exits the galley to head up on deck. "Come on, and let's go catch us some breakfast."

Nick grabs a bottle of his water, proudly ready to demonstrate his success. "It's a really good system to filter water. Ya see, you boil the water so that the steam rises up through the paper towels. This is the first filter. Then the steam collects on the plastic and runs down to the funnels at the end. There, I utilized some of that twine you had in the drawer over there, so that when the water vapor ran down to the ends of the plastic, the water would collect on the pieces of twine that were draped into the bowls and pots on the floor. The course twine actually served as another filter collecting more salt before depositing the water." Nick turns around to see that Rawson was long gone. "Hey that was a good explanation, pal." He sticks his head out the galley door, to see Rawson standing up on deck, gazing off towards the east. "What'cha staring at, Bill? You look like you've just seen a school of mermaids." Nick starts to go up on deck, and then turns around to retrieve the talisman hanging from the light fixture over the table. As soon as he drops the chain around his neck, Nick senses the danger present. With no hesitation, he runs up on deck, where he sees what Rawson sees.

"Nick, you do remember your buddies from the precinct yesterday, don't you. I think they're a little pissed about the way you treated them, and judging by their fancy outfits, I'd say that they want a rematch." Rawson slowly steps back a step or two, allowing Nick to take the lead.

Carter Regal and his team stands on the wing of their futuristic looking shuttle craft, floating on the waves just off the starboard bow. This time, Regal's men wear armored suits over their battle fatigues, suggesting that they are definitely here for one reason only. Still, Rawson can't help but marvel at the sight of the vehicle. It looks like a thick stingray with twin tails and exaggerated wings. Sleek, metallic, and built for speed, It's something that Rawson would love to give a test flight, or drive, or whatever you do to steer it. In a different situation, he would toy with the fancy of imagining himself in the pilot's seat. But, at the moment, his imagination has been temporarily shut off.

"I don't know what it is that makes you think this is open for discussion, Michael, but we are proceeding with this as planned. No one is allowed to use lethal force on Landry, unless there is no other option. I believe that we can keep this from escalating to that point, don't you?" Regal steps forward claiming his rank as leader. "Nickolas Landry, we represent Darkside Command, Her Majesty's Government, and most importantly, the Council. It has been deemed necessary for you to relinquish your charge, and surrender to us, for extradition back to the United Kingdom. The council will explain the rest." Sebastian and Benjamin step up beside Carter, staring at Nick with ill contempt. Obviously, they're still miffed about Nick's rough treatment, yesterday.

"Nick, from the looks of things, I don't think they expect you to lay down for them."

Nick smiles at Bill's statement. "Nah, he's just covering his bases for what's about to happen. Are we in international waters?"

Rawson gives Nick a confused look. "More or less, what does it matter?"

Nick clinches his fists and tenses up every muscle in his body, "Because they're dead men!" He leaps into the air rising twenty or more feet into the air. He's surprised at the feat, but in the same instance, it was like he knew he could do it all along. Rawson on the other hand, is launched into the air by his boat, when it rises back up out of the water. When Nick pushed off to leap into the air, the force to do so shoved the boat's stern deep into the water. Rawson is the only one suffering the effects of the action, as he lands on the deck with a loud thud. Now his suspicions about this group have been laid to rest. Nick is hanging in the air like a kite on the breeze.

Regal told Nick everything he needed to know about their purpose here, just by admitting to his affiliation with the Council. His new found determination to keep the talisman out of the hands of all others includes these clowns, Masamoto, and especially the Council. Gravity begins to pull him back to earth, with his angle of descent bringing him down on his enemies. He didn't want it to end up this way. He did his part, made his sacrifices, and accepted his role in this morbid game of life. Be careful what you wish for. Nick has no reason to hold back any more, now that he has nothing else to lose. With this frame of mind, he will finish what he started yesterday, holding nothing back. If a man opposes your place in the world, then he is the enemy. If these men and women are the enemy, then they will be treated as such.

Benjamin and his brother Sebastian leap into action, using their awesome strength to launch themselves at Nick, to meet him half way. Sebastian's assault is quickly cut short as Nick maneuvers himself around to land a devastating blow to the big man's gut, sending the big man flying back down to the water as Benjamin manages to wrap his arms around Nick's chest. Experience coupled with arrogance is the warrior's undoing, as the two find themselves plummeting back to earth together. Using his newly enhanced strength, Nick is able to break Benjamin's grip right before the two combatants hit the water. Immediately, Nick latches onto the big man as they disappear into the depths of the Caribbean Sea.

Benjamin's teammates rush to the edge of the shuttle's wing, separating themselves from Michael. Using the distraction to hide his agenda, Michael falls back to the shuttle's main hatch, as Deidre rushes over and uses her magic to help Sebastian out of the water. With her mind occupied on fishing Sebastian out of the water, she can't detect Michael's move. As for Sebastian, his ego may be bruised, but he's none the worse for wear.

"Deidre, take a position on the Detective's boat. Sebastian, Michael, get over here and locate Landry and Benjamin!" This has already gone farther than Carter wants, or expected. His information on Landry speaks of a more rational, reasonable, man of honor and duty. Deidre follows or leader's command and lifts herself psychically, and floats effortlessly over to Rawson's boat, watching Sebastian join Regal standing at the wing's edge. "Fair warning, girl, someone's coming up at the stern of the boat." Regal wants to be at her side to offer her the support a husband should, but he knows that logic dictates that he should not leave his command. It is his duty to monitor what takes place, and coordinate his team to act and react. His people are more than competent to handle this situation. Yesterday's encounter was perpetuated by a certain detective's interference. This won't happen again. "Natalya, get out here and give Deidre assistance in restraining Detective Rawson."

Hanging on the far side of Rawson's boat at the water line, Nick has the perfect vantage point to see his opponents. His movements and actions resemble that of a feral child, who had spent its childhood in the company of animals. Predatory urges begin to emerge, dictating his course of action as he calculates threat versus proximity. His first target has to be the young woman of yesterday, who could sense Nick's presence. At the moment, her focus appears to be on her teammate in the water, assuming that her comrades are watching her back. This is Nick's moment to attack. He knows the condition he left the big man in, and there is no way big Ben will be able to pull himself from the water, on his own. Nick forces down on the railing of the boat, propelling him across the deck, headed straight for the unsuspecting Deidre. The boat heaves from one side to the other throwing Deidre off balance as she lands on the deck of Rawson's boat. Nick slams into her back sending her into the water. As he helps to pull the big guy out of the water, Carter is almost sure he heard the loyal soldier mumble, "oh no," just before Nick hits him again. The crushing blow sends big Ben on a collision course with the fuselage of the shuttle.

Carter, Michael, and Sebastian are forced to dive clear of their incoming friend as Benjamin's massive form slams into the shuttle, ripping open a hole into the main cabin. Hitting the floor, Benjamin slides to a stop at the feet of his teammates, unconscious to the world. The pilot of the craft, Winston, surprised by the turn of events, looks to Natasha and overstates the obvious saying, "I don't think that was supposed to happen."

"Bohorodytsia Maty Bozha! (Mother of God!)" Natalya hurries over to the new opening just in time to see Nick following Benjamin inside the shuttle. To avoid the same fate, Natalya springs backwards into a series of back flips as Nick hits the floor of the cabin. Unfortunately for Winston, this puts him directly in Nick's path. Winston, caught completely off guard, is unable to avoid the Guardian's attack as Nick bounds up onto the command console and then back at Winston to drop kick him across the cabin. The muscle bound warrior's trajectory takes him right into some kind of secondary control panel that arcs and sparks from the impact. This causes Nick to take notice of how some of the shuttles systems begin to fail when Winston's body stops quivering. "Three down, plus the ship." Before Nick can continue the head count, the Russian female charges Nick's position. At first he thinks it's a noble gesture, but quickly realizes that she is more than capable of handling the task. Her martial arts expertise is unorthodox, but highly effective as her and Nick trade blows. Her ability is phenomenal as each move made appears to have been choreographed for this moment. It is obvious that she has trained for a lifetime, matching Nick move for move, but neither can land a solid attack. Her one attribute to be aware of is her awesome strength. If not for it, Nick probably could have bested her from the beginning, but with it coupled to her martial arts, Natalya is a formidable opponent for him.

When Regal and his teammates enter the cabin, Nick recognizes the fact that his time is up, and it's time for him to go. With the moment gone, Nick knows that he must return to his guerilla tactics outside the shuttle, before his advantage to flee is lost. When the opening occurs, Nick delivers a cheap shot to Natalya's throat, allowing him to break free from the conflict with her, and leave the confines of the vessel before anyone attempts to join in. Suddenly, he feels a sharp spike of pain rip through his mind. Shaking off the effects, Nick looks to the cabin hatch where he sees Deidre standing holding her fingers up to her temple, to deliver the psychic assault. The result only lasts a second, but it's long enough to give Carter and Sebastian the opportunity to take the offensive.

Michael, on the other hand, has different plans on how to end this. He reaches over and grabs an energy rifle from the nearby weapons' cabinet. It's obvious that Nick isn't going to give up freely. Michael can't understand why Carter believes that this can end any other way. The Council said to use whatever force necessary to obtain the talisman. The time has come for him to take charge of this mission, as he was ordered to do. He brings the barrel of the weapon up to bear on Nick, right between Carter and Sebastian, before they have a chance to act.

"Michael, what are you doing?" Carter raises his arm hitting the weapon, causing Michael to fire recklessly blowing the windshield out of the cockpit. Nick is distracted to say the least. He had never seen a weapon that offers such firepower. Sebastian takes the advantage, seeking a little retribution from yesterday's encounter. Nick makes a break for the hatch, but Sebastian is able to cut him off, and drive him to the ground. Before Nick, can offer any sort of defense, the big man is able to deliver a crushing elbow to Nick's chest, believing he had just ended the conflict. To his surprise, his attack on Nick had little effect, if any. His overconfidence causes Sebastian to relax enough to give Nick the opportunity he needed. Grabbing the warrior with unbelievable speed, Nick rolls his legs up under the large man's frame and catapults Sebastian at his teammates, before Michael can pull the trigger again. Angered by Carter's interference, Michael sends Natalya a psychic message, "Remember; if we claim the talisman, we can use it so that you can fulfill your vow."

It's not enough to distract her, but it does send her into action. On the move again, Natalya readies herself to resume her conflict with the Guardian once more. This is the worst mistake she could make, as she puts herself between Nick and his exit. The two collide and leave the shuttle through the hole created by Benjamin, and take their battle into the sea. Wanting to be ready when his chance presents itself, Michael pushes passed Carter to take chase after his prey. He's taking control of this situation, whether Carter likes it or not. Rushing out onto the wing of the shuttle, Michael points the rifle at the water's surface and waits for the first sign of Nick.

Rawson stands on the deck of his boat; amazed at the battle taking place in front of him. This is what he's here for.

Rawson believes this with his heart and soul. Everything that has happened has done so for this reason. Rawson is supposed to be here to help Nick in his duty. When he first heard Carter give the order for Rawson to be detained, Bill decided that he wasn't going down without a fight. His realization gives him the confidence needed to give it all he's got. "If ya gotta go out with a bang, make it a big one." He had already returned to the galley to collect his firearm. So, here he stands, pointing his gun at someone who has a much bigger gun, second guessing his previous plan. Now he is just waiting for his bravado to come up with something clever to say. "You need to drop that thing, right now, and keep this fight as fair as possible!" That wasn't it.

The thought of some mere mortal threatening Michael sends him over the edge. He has no reason to kill the man, but he does fire a warning shot that removes the top steering right off the cabin roof, sending Rawson diving for cover from the rain of debris. With this done, the threat Rawson posed is eliminated, allowing Michael to return his aim to the water.

"Michael, I order you to stand down at once!" Carter grabs Michael's arm, only to have his First Knight pull away from his grip. Carter turns to see that Sebastian had recovered and was standing beside him. "As soon as we have him located, I want you in to apprehend Landry, and restore order immediately. Deidre, can you locate Landry's position?" He asks, before turning back to confront Michael about his actions. Before Deidre can answer his question, Natalya's body hits the top of the shuttle, before landing at Carter's feet. "He's on the other side of the shuttle!"

Carter's statement is ignored as Rawson opens fire on Michael and the shuttle. At this moment in time, the former detective feels very threatened by Michael's assault on his boat, and has no problem letting his gun express that fact.

In events like this, Rawson has a tendency to take such aggression very personally. The .45 caliber bullets ricochet off of Michael's armor, offering no damage to him, but Sebastian takes a stray slug ricocheting into the back of his leg. It isn't a mortal wound, by no means, but it does take the big man down for the moment.

Michael simply looks at his fallen comrade, offering no assistance or compassion. In Michael's eyes, Sebastian should have been wearing his battle armor, especially after yesterday. Looking back at Rawson, this time Michael takes aim at the man, following Rawson's retreat down the side of the boat. He pulls the trigger, removing half the main cabin, and the detective, from the fishing boat. "You should have known your place, wretched mortal."

Carter is having a hard time understanding where he lost control of this situation and how it could have gone so terribly wrong. The council has assured him that there wouldn't be a conflict. What was Michael talking about inside the shuttle? Something has come over Michael to make him act so out of character. The question is, what is it? "Explain yourself to me, Major! What is the meaning of all of this?" Regal grabs the rifle and squeezes, demonstrating his vast strength to crush the barrel of the weapon, to end the threat once and for all. "Deidre, do you have a location on Landry, yet?"

Deidre kneels beside Natalya's side to check her status. She's alive, but she'll need a long time to recover fully. Waving her hand at Rawson's boat, she extinguishes the fires on board while moving over to examine Sebastian's leg. "I can't locate Landry, Carter. I can only presume that he is using the power of the talisman to block my vision." She applies pressure to Sebastian's wound while continuing to look around for Nick. "We'll need to get this bullet out of Sebastian's leg…Aagh!" Deidre falls back as Nick delivers a mental spike of his own, using the power of the talisman to duplicate her abilities.

As she falls back, writhing in pain, Michael and Carter scan their surroundings for their elusive opponent.

"Care to explain to me what you think you are doing?"

The tone of Carter's question prompts Michael to speak out against the team leader. "I was doing what I was told to do. The Council commanded that if there was any resistance on Landry's part, he should be destroyed. I am simply willing to do the job you can't bring yourself to do."

Hearing this only sends Nick further down a dark path. After placing Rawson's unconscious body back onboard his wounded vessel, the former Navy SEAL sets out to bring this to an end. Slipping back into the water, he plots a course deep under the boat, after memorizing the positions of each member of the Crusaders. Nick may not know the rest of the team's stand on the situation, but he is positive that Michael needs to be eliminated, if Nick is to have any chance at survival. Deeper he swims, until his senses tell him to change direction. Then, he turns and heads for the surface, faster and faster until he breaks free of the water's grasp, where he grabs Carter and carries him high into the air above the rest. "You can't kill me."

"We're not here to kill you, Nickolas. We're here to help."

"Find a way to stop this now, or your people won't survive!" Nick warns as the two men reach the zenith of their ascent. Before Carter has the opportunity to reply, he is hit full on by anther energy blast from Michael's rifle. Nick simply releases the target before the impact and falls freely back to the safety of the water again. Carter is completely incapacitated by the blast and falls helplessly back to the water as well, with his teammates watching in horror for what their comrade has done.

"Michael, have you lost your mind?" Deidre rushes to her husband's defense with Sebastian quick to offer her support, only to have Michael draw down on them. Reaching out psychically, Deidre plucks Carter's body from the sea, knowing that he was unconscious and helpless to drown in the water.

Nick surfaces right under the wing of the shuttle with Michael and the others standing right above him. Confused a little, he listens to what is taking place amongst his adversaries. "Move, damn you!" Michael's command is followed by the sound of footsteps on the metal surface of the wing, telling Nick that they are moving back inside.

"I don't have time for any more of this. I have taken command of this mission, by order of the Council. If you are not with me, then you are against me."

Sebastian quickly steps forward to be the voice of reason, knowing that at the moment, he is the only one capable of handling Michael. "Michael, this shuttle is damaged. The integrity of the fuselage has been compromised and she is taking on water. You are putting us all in a very dangerous situation. Landry is an ally. If the prophecy is true, you, we, cannot defeat him."

Deidre is unable to remain calm like her large friend. "How dare you do this to us, Michael? Carter has been your friend and mentor through all of this! How can you turn against us now when we need unity the most?"

Michael gives her a sarcastic chuckle, and then slaps her down. "The Council has made this choice, not I. My duty is to serve their command, not your husband's. If they feel he no longer has what it takes to do this, and I do, who am I to argue." Michael punches a couple of buttons on the small control panel attached to his gauntlet and adjusts his headset. The display tells him that his contingency plan has been compromised, losing one of its key components when the shuttle was damaged. Speaking into the microphone connected to his headset, he initiates his contingency.

"Sentry Knights One, Two and Four, react to my voice code only. Activate contingency plan Omega. The shuttle has been compromised and the Crusaders have been eliminated, save me." Michael watches as Carter tries to stand up. "I can't have you interfering, now can I?" Without warning, he hits Carter in the side of his head, sending his commander back to the floor of the shuttle beside his wife. With no desire for hesitation, Michael pulls a small box from the cabinet behind him and tosses it at the feet of his comrades. As soon as it hits the cabin floor, the box produces an energy containment field, trapping his friends in the doomed shuttle. "Sentry Knights, initiate orders, Michael Cross; code word authorization Excalibur Omega Three."

"Why Michael?" Regal wipes the blood from his temple and stands up to confront his friend. "Why have you chosen this path?"

"Because the Council has deemed it necessary!" Michael rushes to the energy field to confront his former leader, and removes his helmet. "Look at all of you! Benji, Winston and Natalya are down, you and Deidre can barely stand, and Sebastian doesn't have the stones to get his hands bloody!"

"Easy bub, you don't want to go getting personal."

Michael smiles at Sebastian's comment, before returning his focus back to Carter, knowing that Sebastian is in no position to make threats at the moment. "Face it, Carter, you have become blinded to the reality of the world around you, because you believe that our crusade can continue and remained concealed from the eyes of humanity. The events of this incursion alone should be evidence enough to prove you wrong! You believe that if our battle is brought to the streets of man, we would lose control. I say that the control you believed you possessed never existed in the first place. When you failed in your duties to recognize the necessity to evolve our procedures and protocols, the Council came to me to serve as their contingency plan." Michael steps over to the hatch to try and get a fix on Nick's position. "It is more than obvious that the prophecy will come true, old friend. All Landry had to do was follow one simple rule, and deny the prophecy. His actions now have set in motion a chain of events that can't be stopped. The end of times is coming, Carter. That is the one thing you refuse to accept. It is something that cannot be prevented, no matter how hard you try. Because of that, Landry must be stopped or destroyed, or mankind could be doomed forever. You will either accept your position in the coming war, or you will be replaced. I have accepted mine!" Michael raises his gauntlet and presses another button on the small console, "Execute." He grabs his helmet to complete his armor and heads for the hatch. The wing was beginning to dip down into the ocean, making him realize that he will have to accomplish his goal quickly to avoid his comrades dying because of his actions. He doesn't want them dead, just out of his way so that he can do his job.

Nick crouches on the bow of Rawson's boat, while checking on the status of his friend. Bill is still alive, even though he is unconscious and doesn't appear to be in any immediate danger. He plans to make sure it stays that way for Rawson; after all he's done for Nick. Just to be on the safe side, Nick ties Rawson to the forward crane, in a seated position, just to keep him from drowning. After hearing what's been said, now he has some kind of idea where he stands with these warriors. Now he knows where he stands with the Council and what they plan for him. As far as he can tell the rest of this team has been taken out of the picture by the black sheep of the group who is representing the Council solo. He doesn't know everything that is going on between his opponents, but he knows how Regal and his associates are feeling, right about now. He too was screwed over and mislead by the Council. For a split second, Nick entertains the idea of a possible alliance, but then returns his focus to Michael. If his teammates are shocked and surprised by Michael's actions, then there is really no telling what he has in store for Nick. Watching for the next attack, Nick sees three hatches open on the top of the shuttle, allowing three canisters, about three feet tall, to launch into the air. Once clear of the fuselage, panels open on the cylinders, revealing multidirectional propulsion systems, and a full armament of weapons. There they remain as their processors rewrite their protocols. Through what was left of the main cabin of Rawson's boat, Nick can see Michael climbing up on top of the shuttle for a better vantage point.

This is Nick's moment to strike. The thoughts and feelings of betrayal bring a wild anger alive inside him, fueled by animalistic tendencies that continue to take over his judgment. Nick takes off running as fast as he can across the deck of Rawson's boat. As he reaches the other side, he pushes off the railing, launching himself at Michael's position.

The robotic canisters, known as Michael's Sentry Knights, immediately come to life and take aim at Nick and fire, knocking him out of the sky. The weapons of the drones have little effect on him, other than bouncing him off the wing of the shuttle. A roll, and another leap sends Nick right back at the closest drone moving in on his position, plucking it out of the air like a piece of fruit. His mind rages with chaos, as he feels his hands ripping through the metal plating of the drone's outer shell. He fights past the rage, and focuses on his hands, quickly realizing what was taking place. Similar to Sonny, his anger is bringing about the full effects of the dragon's blood. His fingers are tipped with razor sharp claws and the skin color of his hands and arms is turning dark, dark, red, and almost black. Nick doesn't shun what he's become, or the changes taking place. Instead, he embraces the transformation, giving in to his anger fueled rage. No longer will anyone threaten or control his life again.

He slings the damaged drone back at the other two, as they change direction to pursue Nick's new trajectory. One is taken out by its damaged counterpart, as the other opens fire on Nick again. Suddenly, unknown how, Nick stops in mid-flight and closes his eyes. In that split second that he is suspended in time and space, the transformation is completed that will ultimately scar his life forever. His skin is deep red almost black, and shining with the reflection of the morning sun. For now, this will serve his needs. He doesn't know if this is the full extent of his abilities, but it is enough to serve his needs for now. He has no wings like Sonny, or the bony plating under his skin, and yet he is able to fly and the bullets from the drone just bounce off the surface of his body. He dives to meet the remaining Sentry Knight, wanting to eliminate the final nuisance, so that he can focus on the main threat. Michael just stands there on top of the shuttle as if he expects the robotic tin cans to be able to handle the situation. Nick has already downed two of the flying pests, making him wonder what this Crusader's true intentions really are. All the while, the little voice in the back of Nick's head keeps saying, "the shuttle is going down."

The drone suddenly changes tactics, and weapons, and launches a snaring net as it closes in on Nick. Before he can react, the netting hits him dead on, sending its weighted ends wrapping around Nick's body. Then on cue, the steel wire netting electrifies, hitting Nick with the full current. This is the opening Michael was waiting on. He takes aim with his energy rifle and hits Nick with a maximum charge. The impact with Nick creates such an overwhelming explosion, that it sends Nick flying across the water, and skipping off the surf a couple of times, before coming to a stop on the nearby shoreline.

"Sentry Knight Four, return to my signal and initiate program Omega II." Michael leaps from the shuttle and uses his awesome strength to propel himself over the breaking waves heading straight for his target's position. "Stand up, you dragon freak," Michael commands as he closes in on Nick. "Let me show them why you are not worthy of your destiny!"

Nick struggles to get to his feet, hindered by the result of Michael's assault. His injuries are minimal, but his dazed state makes it impossible to avoid Michael's next attack. As the Crusader drops in to tackle Nick, the fallen guardian can only brace for the impact of Michael driving Nick head first into the beach. Before Nick can empty both cheeks of sand, Michael grabs him, and slings Nick with all of his might at the tree line along the beach. Trees snap off deep into the jungle growth, until Nick comes to an abrupt stop. Michael takes flight again to seek out his prey. He is fortunate in that his search is brief, but unfortunate overall, when Nick flies out of the trees to meet him. "Tell me how you like these!" Nick drives his clawed hand through the armor plating on Michael's shoulder, burying his fingertips deep into the flesh underneath. Michael has no other choice but to drop his weapon, but this doesn't make him defenseless.

The drone designated Sentry knight Four flies over to Michael's position with Nick in his sights, but instead of bullets, this time the drone launches a salvo of titanium tipped darts, the size of a golf tee. Their honed tips ricochet off of Michael's armor, but their pronged points dig deep into Nick's bulletproof skin. This allows the explosives built into the shafts of the darts to explode at a very close range. For Nick, the barrage isn't life threatening, but it is enough to make Nick let go of his grip on Michael. For a moment, Nick falls away from his attacker, but a moment is all that the drone needs to execute its next attack. As it moves over

Nick's position, a small panel opens on the bottom of the drone's shell, and releases a dozen small explosives to rain down on Nick.

He is completely unaware of the approaching danger. Nick has barely had time to recover from the first volley delivered, and was trying to get a fix on Michael. As Michael crosses the sky above Nick, it is then that the Guardian sees the trap he has fallen into. Trying to intersect Michael's path of travel, Nick heads right into the cloud of explosives around him. Sensors on each device register his proximity, and detonate. Each one delivers the punch of a charging rhino to Nick's body, as the drone follows Nick down and snares him again with another net. He plummets helplessly to the water as the net delivers an electrical jolt to Nick's system.

The double shock of the electrocution, coupled with the slap against the water's surface awakens his rational side for a moment giving him an opportunity to rethink the scenarios. Once free of the net, he determines that the water is his only ally, even if it is for a short time. To end this, Nick realizes that he must use all of his abilities and attributes, so that he can see to Rawson. He doesn't think that Michael could pose much of a threat, one on one. The problem is that he knows that he'll never be able to land the knockout punch, as long as that irritating tin can keeps interfering. It's elementary, Watson, he has to get rid of the drone first.

Nick launches himself out of the water, rocketing skyward right past Michael, with the drone in hot pursuit. Higher and higher he climbs until he flies right through a low level cumulus cloud. As soon as he exits the water vapor, Nick uses the talisman to render himself invisible, and waits. When the drone breaks through the top of the cloud, it goes into sensory deprivation overload, unable to locate Landry anywhere. By the time the onboard computer finds a method to pick up Nick's presence, it's already too late. Nick clinches both hands together and swings them around like a big leaguer hitting a homerun. The drone is smashed beyond recognition and sent flying off towards the island.

"That was quite impressive, but I don't have a problem seeing you!" Michael taps his finger against the side of his helmet, as if saying the helmet is his advantage, and then delivers a similar blow to the middle of Nick's back, breaking his concentration and rendering him visible once more. The assault also sends Nick rocketing towards the doomed shuttle and its captive passengers. Michael's attack was obviously more than Nick bargained for, making it hard for him to recover before he plows into one of the tail sections of the shuttle. The impact rips the tail off the fuselage and lays it on the water's surface under Nick.

As the dislodged tail section drops below the surface, Michael drops in and picks Nick up out of the waves. "Do you not see that your end is near? Look at you; you're nothing more than an abomination who failed at his duty. All you had to do is stay away from Japan, and everything would have been alright. Your little friend should have been written off as a casualty of war, like it was meant to be."

"The shuttle is going down." The voice in his head confuses Nick, making him wonder why he should care about the event. As far as Michael's concerned, Nick has had enough. He's had enough of his pompous attitude and arrogant personality. He's had enough of the Council's fair weather interventions. Nick has had enough, period! "You want this so bad, then take it!" Nick's body convulses as a blast of energy is released from the talisman and hits Michael head on. The First Knight of the Crusaders is sent crashing into the fuselage, ending up firmly planted into the wreckage that was once the command chairs and console of the cockpit.

The shuttle is then hit by the energy wave, causing it to roll over some and take on even more water. It is done.

Nick struggles to fight through his pain and leaps over to the nose of the shuttle to verify the kill. Michael can barely move, but it really doesn't matter. His life is coming to an end quickly, but he isn't ready to go just yet. "Sentry Knight Four, initiate program Omega One, and target my signal." Michael closes his eyes for the last time, with a smile stretched across his face.

Nick's landing on the nose of the shuttle is sloppy, causing him to scramble with his waning strength to regain his footing and maintain his balance on the slick surface. There Michael lays, lifeless, just the way Nick wants it. Then, a needle stabs at his mind as Deidre reaches out psychically for help. "Landry, I sense the honor in you. Please, help us." Nick stares at the team trapped in the containment field, as they stare back at him. He can't help but wonder where they all would stand, if he was to give them aid. Who's to say they won't come back for him again?

Suddenly, Nick picks up the sound of a high pitch whistle closing in on their location. Distracted by Deidre's plea, Nick was unable to pick up on the sound until it's almost too late. As much as he would like to offer Carter's team some help, Nick is faced with a dilemma of save your self, or die with them. Regrettably, he dives to the safety of the water, seeking whatever refuge that's available. There is a flash of light, and then a brief moment of silence before the nose of the shuttle erupts from a massive explosion. Pulling himself up onto the deck of Rawson's boat, Nick is pelted with debris, as the water rises up freeing the anchor of Rawson's boat, setting the crippled fishing boat adrift. Nick rolls over just in time to see the shuttle slip into the deep blue waters of the Caribbean. Lying down on the deck, he screams out in pain, realizing that there was two pieces of shrapnel lodged in his back and shoulder. The first isn't very deep, but again he screams out as he pulls the jagged metal from his lower back. Unfortunately, the one in his shoulder isn't as easy to reach. Each time he grabs the blood soaked debris, it slips from between his fingers adding to the agony. Finally, after numerous tries, he is able to free the piece of metal from his flesh, giving Nick a much needed moment of relief. The sensation is actually overwhelming causing him to collapse back to the wooden planks of the deck. The physical transformation that had taken place has reverted, returning Nick to his former self, bleeding and unconscious to the world, while clutching the talisman in his hands.

# Chapter XXIX

Nick opens his eyes to find himself standing before Masamoto and the council. This is by his doing. He stares at the glowing translucent spirits stationed around him, seeing the surprised looks on their faces about his presence. "I just wanted to let you know that I'm through with all of this."

He stands defiantly as Masamoto moves forward to address his former student. "You have been through a most trying event. You have proven to the council that you are the chosen one to carry the mantle of the Guardian. We, the council, want to prepare you for what is to come."

"Oh, now you want to prepare me for what's to come? Let me get this straight. First you fill my head with half truths, keep vital information from me, let me kill my best friend, and then send your boys after me when things don't work out like you planned? Ya know what? You can take this talisman, the end of times, what's to come, and anything else connected to it, and shove it all up your spiritual asses! My life is destroyed because of this destiny! I have nowhere to go, no way to provide for myself, and no happy outlook on life! Oh, by the way, did I mention the fact that I just killed my best friend, to keep her from killing my other best friend?" Nick turns as if he was leaving, and then spins around to face the council once more. "Ya know, you told me once that this destiny of mine would change my life. I thought that was already covered when your son and daughter came calling the first time, the night you and Megan were killed. Now, there is nothing left. Why didn't you warn me about all of this? Why didn't you warn me about Sonny?"

"There are truths in one's life that can only be learned by experience alone. Outside information would only alter the chain of events to come, preventing the truth of the matter to be distorted." Mynan looks around at the other council members as if communicating psychically.

"Bullshit! I don't know who you are used to dealing with, but I don't need everyone around me to die, just to get an idea of how bad it could be! I'm done, Sensei. I feel like I've been used and abused, and discarded like a dirty rag. Next time, know your guardians a little better before you screw up their lives." Nick turns away, only to have Masamoto appear in front of him again.

Nickolas, this is not something you can walk away from. Do not believe you are the only one who has suffered losses. You are not alone in your efforts. Others have taken the call to serve a greater purpose, just as you have. Together you will all fight for the end of times." Masamoto's words are sincere, but they come across slightly hollow to Nick, offering him no comfort whatsoever.

"Yeah, well I guess it sucks to be them then, doesn't it? I think the best thing for me to do is ride off into the sunset and see what happens on a day to day basis. Yep, that's what I'm gonna do. See ya around, spooks. I won't come looking for you, so don't come looking for me, because you won't find me."

For the first time, the spirit of Mynan vanishes from his

station with the council and reappears in front of Nick. "You have never been alone, Nickolas Landry. My, our, agents have monitored your progress since the day you first encountered Masamoto. They are the same men and women you battled out on the ocean. Allow them to, and they will continue to aid you."

Nick laughs at the remark. Aid me? Where were they on the night Masamoto and Megan were were killed, huh? Where were they when Yukio abducted JD and took him to Japan?"

"Their intervention is solely based upon my determination of necessity."

"All I'm hearing is that you're the one who sent them after me, in the first place. Don't do it, again, or you'll be doing a lot of Guardian recruiting to refill your ranks."

Mynan's eyes begin to glow a little brighter, as his image grows darker. "If you try to walk away from us, I will be forced to send my agents against you again."

"Did you not hear what I was just saying? You don't really think you can use your scare tactics against me, do ya? You do what you feel is necessary, oh great council leader, but be warned. You need to think long and hard about sending your boys after me again. I once lived by the golden rule that if a man confronts you on the street, he is the enemy and should be treated as such. If you think they have what it takes, then come find me, if you can." With that said, Nick vanishes from within the council circle, returning to his own reality.

The spirit of Mynan moves across the main hall to face Masamoto. "He knows nothing of the true power that he possesses. The time is drawing near, Masamoto. If Nickolas Landry is no longer relevant to this cause, then we need to move forward with obtaining his part of the scepter."

"I do not dispute anything that is said." Masamoto moves across the dark chamber and takes his place in the circle, as Mynan appears at his station. "I am curious, however, as to why you sent your Crusaders to stand against the very Guardian that you had me recruit. Landry has proven that he is the chosen one. If it is his destiny to stand against the Devastator, then why try to change that? Would you not be jeopardizing all that we have tried to accomplish? You have failed in your efforts, once. Is it too costly to attempt again? I believe so. As you said, the end of times is drawing near. Do we dare decimate our own ranks trying to avoid the inevitable? I ask only that this council hold judgment for a time longer, until more signs are given to govern our judgment."

"Master Masamoto is correct." The spirit of Bonna Min brightens as she rises to speak. "However, you must not look at this attempt as a failure. Think of it as our participation to perpetuate this destiny along."

"M' Lady," The spirit of the majestic and wise Minotaur, Hyldegaarn, rises and takes the floor to offer his insight. "I say to you that I find agreement with both you, and Master Masamoto. However, I feel that we should not lose focus on the next event, involving Jezana's freedom. The players have been chosen, but much guidance will be needed for them to succeed."

"We will monitor what takes place, old friend. Master Masamoto has already selected our pawn for this next chapter." Bonna Min settles back into her station. "The betrayer of man will be an unlikely ally to our cause. He is the one who will require guidance, and guidance he shall receive."

Hyldegaarn faces Mynan with one last question, "and what of your Crusaders? They believe you have betrayed them with your deceit. Michael was one of them, and you exploited his weakness, ending in his death."

"Master Hyldegaarn is right," Bonna Min proclaims.

"Lord Regal will be summoned before this council to explain the actions that have transpired." Then she adds, "After he has returned to Britain."

"Very well, the council will weigh this and hold judgment until the next time we convene." Mynan crosses his arms and bows his head. "We must stay constant with our vigil. Our purpose for over eight hundred years is to prevent the Devastator from entering Earth's realm. Our efforts shall not be in vain." With that, the spirits of the council fade away into the darkness.

"Ahoy, this is the Coast Guard Cruiser, Depth Charge. Is there anyone there?" The voice calling out awakens Nick, sleeping on the deck of Rawson's swamped boat. He rolls over feeling less pain than expected. The voice calls out again, giving Nick a bearing on the approaching vessel. Rolling over to face the other direction, he is forced to use the talisman to render himself invisible as the Cruiser's spot light shines across the deck where Nick was laying. "Ahoy there, fishing boat, Golden Watch, is there anyone on board in need of medical attention?"

The sun is setting in the west, but Nick doesn't need daylight to recognize the condition of the boat. Rawson's pride and joy is barely able to stay afloat, and the larger waves of the shipping lanes are doing all they can to push the boat under. With his presence concealed, Nick makes his way over to his friend and kneels beside him. He checks Bill's pulse and breathing, happy to find that his friend is still alive. To let the Coast Guard know the Rawson was there, Nick lifts the detective's arm and waves his hand. He then unties the rope, just in case the boat decides to go under before the Coast Guard can get to him and fish him out.

"Captain," the crewman yells, "I have a survivor on the bow, Sir." The young crewman pinpoints Rawson's position using the spotlight, but no one notices the second shadow, or when it moves away from the survivor.

"Nick, are you there?" Rawson mumbles before blacking out again, as his rescuers begin their attempt to save him from the doomed vessel. Nick cringes as Rawson's body topples over face first into the shallow water on deck.

"Captain, we have a survivor in sight, on the bow. I'm making the jump to go in to retrieve him." Rodriguez has made plenty of these types of rescues in his career, every time, it seems that he's jumping into the waters at night. Why is it always at night?

The Captain responds through the headset, "Make it quick, son. That boat is ready to pitch under any minute."

"Roger that," Rodriguez replies. Removing his headset, he motions to his colleagues, "get that basket ready to go." Then, he leaps over the edge into the water between the Cruiser and the fishing boat. The Cruiser can't get any closer than this, simply due to the fact that an accidental collision could send the boat on its way, before the rescue could be made. Getting onto Rawson's boat is no problem for Rodriguez, with the bow starting to dip under the surface. He quickly makes his way over to the survivor and lifts his head from the water and begins to inspect his wounds.

As the water starts to drain from Bill's mouth and nose, he begins to choke and gag, bringing him back to life, in a very unpleasant manner. As the basket is lowered down, Rawson realizes that it isn't his friend that's helping him. "Where's Nick?" Rodriguez helps Rawson into the basket to be lifted away, as deck boards begin to splinter and pop from pockets of air trying to escape from the decks below. "Wait a minute, we can't leave without Nick!" Rawson tries to get up but the restraints hold him steadfast in place. "You have to find Nick. He's going to save us all by saving our world," he declares before passing out again.

The deck officer calls down to Rodriguez, "What was he saying?"

"He said something about a guy named Nick. I'm not sure if he's delirious, or if someone else was on board. I'm gonna look around real quick just to be sure."

"Negative, she's going under!" A rope is thrown down to Rodriguez as the bow of the boat dives under the waves. The crewman hooks the rope to his harness and leaps clear of the fishing boat as she follows her bow under the waves for the final time.

For Nick, this is over, for now. His friend maybe facing a ton of shit, when he recovers, but at least he's alive to do it. For the Guardian, this marks a new beginning in Nick's life. As the boat slips under the sea, he pushes himself away from the doomed vessel, holding on to an inflatable emergency life raft. Swimming away from the scene, he keeps a watchful eye on the Coast Guard Cruiser as it follows standard operating procedures, searching the waters south following the small debris field drifting on the currents of the shipping lanes. Minutes later, Nick inflates the life raft and climbs in to get some much needed rest. He looks south where he can barely see the lights of the Cruiser. After saying a silent goodbye to Detective Bill Rawson, Nick does his best to clear his mind of the recent events. This is the point of his new beginning. With the tides taking him eastward, Nickolas Landry is off on a new journey, destination unknown.

The morning sun is on the rise, casting its warmth on a beach of the western most island of the Bahama chain, revealing a group of local kids standing around the fallen members of the Crusaders. Sebastian is the first to open his eyes, scaring the children who didn't know if the men and women were dead or alive. Rolling over, the big man can't help but cough a couple of times, awakening the others. Sebastian can't help but see Michael's body lying beside him, taking notice to how someone had respectfully covered Michael's face. Slowly standing up, he turns to face the team's leader, desperately needing some kind of explanation. "What happened, Carter? What happened to us?"

Carter looks at his wife, happy to see that she has survived this encounter as well, and hoping that she can aid with the explanations. Reaching down, Carter offers a hand to his Russian teammate who was trying to get up. "Natalya, are you going to be alright?"

"Aye, I will survive. However, I don't know if I can say the same for Mr. Landry, the next time we meet. Thank the saints for the blue man who rescued us, yes?"

Slightly confused by her statement, Carter turns his

attention back to Deidre. "Love, can you sense Landry's location?" He doesn't mean to seem cold about his team's welfare, or the loss f his friend. Carter is simply trying to develop his next series of moves.

"Carter, I can't pick up Landry's location anywhere." She replies, worried about the outcome of the mission and team.

Sebastian and Benjamin move over to Natalya to question her statement. "Love, what did this blue man look like?" Benji is more than just curious, since he thinks that he saw the same thing, or person.

Before Natalya could answer the question, the children begin to dance around the warriors of light, singing, "you're talking about Charlie! You're talking about Charlie!"

Agitated by the children's' taunts and songs, Sebastian looks to his leader for the answer to his next question. "Where do we go from here, Colonel?"

Carter hangs his head and replies, "we take Michael home. Then, I need to go before the Council for the answers to my questions."

The encounter has ended in failure, or at least in her eyes, in more ways than one. Natalya Volkolov sits aboard the DSC transport discouraged and beaten down. Her comrades all share her feelings of disappointment and shame over this encounter. But for her, it is more than that. She didn't sign on to fight in this crusade. Her goal was simply to avenge the deaths of her loved ones. Her confrontation with the Guardian has changed her outlook about her affiliation with this group known as the Crusaders. She feels that Michael mislead her, and her abilities used and abused, to serve his purpose instead of her own. She once believed that in serving their needs, her actions involved would serve her own in the long run. Her problem now is that so much time has passed that it would be impossible for her to pick up the trail of her target that has been cold for over thirty years. To completely understand Natalya's story, you must go back to the beginning. But, her story doesn't begin with her alliance with the Crusaders. It doesn't begin with the vow that she made decades ago. To know and understand Natasha Volkolov, you must go all the way back to the genesis of her life.

It all started many years ago, near the end of the Soviet regime. The place of this beginning was a formal banquet hall in the middle of Moscow Russia, near the end of the Cold War. The air was frigid and the ground was covered with a fresh blanket of snow. The people attending this event were heads of state, and military advisors, honoring the scientific community. The guest of honor was Natalya's father, Dr. Sergei Volkolov, the Soviet Union's top mind in genetic research. It was a night that the scientist would never forget…

You can now go on line and get a taste the next book in the End of Times series, North & South part II: Lines Drawn, due to release later on this summer/fall. You can also find Natalya's story later on this year in the End of Times series, Part 3 titled; The Crimson Tempest, with the first chapter teaser of the book being released later this summer on my website.

Welcome to the frontline!
Stacy A. Wright
www.frontlinefiction.com